A BOMBAY AFFAIR

Recent Titles by Elisabeth McNeill from Severn House

A BOMBAY AFFAIR
DUSTY LETTERS
MONEY TROUBLES
TURN BACK TIME

A BOMBAY AFFAIR

Elisabeth McNeill

This first world edition published in Great Britain 2000 by
SEVERN HOUSE PUBLISHERS LTD of
9–15 High Street, Sutton, Surrey SM1 1DF.
This first world edition published in the U.S.A. 2000 by
SEVERN HOUSE PUBLISHERS INC of
595 Madison Avenue, New York, N.Y. 10022.

British Library Cataloguing in Publication Data

McNeill, Elisabeth
          A Bombay affair
          1.Bombay (India) – Fiction
          2.Love stories
          I. Title
          823.9'14 [F]

          ISBN 0-7278-5514-X

Typeset by Palimpsest Book Production Ltd.,
Polmont, Stirlingshire, Scotland.
Printed and bound in Great Britain by
MPG Books Ltd, Bodmin, Cornwall.

'LOVE, The folly of thinking much of another before one knows anything of oneself.' Ambrose Bierce, *The Devil's Dictionary*

"Guess what. Baby Maling-Smith's getting married!"
"What? I don't believe it. Who to?"
"I've no idea."
"When is it to be?"
"It's not fixed yet but soon she said . . . before the monsoon at least."
"Is she pregnant?"
"I shouldn't think so . . . She just wants to get married."
"Oh, poor Baby!"

One

Bombay, January 1959

The moment he stepped off the P&O liner *Canton* at Bombay's
Ballard Quay, the squalor of the city repelled Dennis Gillies.
He stood on the bottom of the gangway, tall, fair-haired and
handsome in his crisp, new tropical whites, and felt his heart sink
as he watched the teeming, filthy throng jostling and pushing on the
cobbles in front of him. A strong smell hit him like a blow in the
face – the smell of sun-baked tar, of curry, of garlic, of urine and
human sweat. It turned his stomach.

He was twenty-seven years old, six foot in height and spec-
tacularly muscled. The frank, slightly puzzled expression that was
habitually his was a good clue to his innocent and trusting nature.
When he accepted the offer of a passport officer's job in the
Australian High Commission in Bombay he hadn't expected anything as dreadful as this. Somebody, he thought, should have warned
him, but the only person he knew who'd ever been out of Australia
was his Uncle Joe, a red-faced Sydney policeman, who'd been sent
to North Africa during the war and had called in at Bombay once
on a troopship.

"A great place for a young lad," Joe had cried, throwing an arm
over Dennis's shoulder, "Go to 149 Grant Road, boy, and say Aussie
Joe sent you!"

Dennis's parents, Denzil and Maud, had not shared Uncle Joe's
enthusiasm and demurred a little at the idea of their cherished only
child going so far away. And the thought of him patronising any
dubious establishment recommended by Joe terrified them. They
said perhaps it would be better for Denny to find a job nearer
home – they would even stretch a point and agree to him going
to Brisbane.

"Let him go to India. It'll be the making of him," cried Joe, who
privately thought his nephew too law-abiding and not hell-raising
enough to qualify for the title of a real man. "He'll see the world
and get paid for it, not like those no-gooders that take off for London

1

with knapsacks on their backs and never come back. If our Den goes out with the government at least he'll get a return ticket."

There had been plenty of the knapsack lot on the P&O liner sailing out of Sydney. They propped up the third class bar all day, vomited over the side, chased each other with carnal intent, played cards and generally horrified the repressed Dennis whose idea of rebellion till then had been reeling home slightly tipsy after imbibing one beer more than normal. The fact that he was still a virgin was something he would have vehemently denied if asked an outright question about it. He longed to get laid but didn't know how to go about it.

His problem was swiftly solved however and he wasn't to be a virgin much longer after boarding the *Canton* because a big breasted blonde girl called Janette got her eye on him and pretty soon – on the third day out in fact – made her intentions obvious.

"Boy, I'd like to lay you," she told him on a blazing noon as they lay on the deck steaming towards Singapore.

To cover his shock, he grinned and said, "Not many places to go though, are there?"

She looked sideways at him with her pale blue eyes and said, "'Course there are – plenty of places. There's my cabin for a start. The girls are taking turns. I get it tomorrow afternoon. It's deck nine, cabin three six five. Be there at half past two."

"Um, I don't know . . ." said Dennis.

"Aw gee," cried Janette sitting bolt upright like a jack-in-the-box, "You're not one of them, are you? You're not a poofter! Not with that lovely body, surely not, what a bloody waste." She had a loud voice that made the other sun worshippers on the lower deck turn their heads and stare. Denny went scarlet. "'Course I'm not," he said.

"Half-past two tomorrow then," said Janette, patting him fondly on the crotch.

So he had to go. Not that he was reluctant, only scared, but it was a wonderful experience, at least for him, though Janette looked a little disappointed when she sat up in the bunk a few moments later and started pulling on her clothes. "You've not been around much, have you?" she asked him.

"'Course I have," lied Dennis, "You're not my first."

"Second maybe," said Janette pushing him out of the way as she struggled out of the bunk to the floor for she was a big girl and it was a very narrow bunk. "Never mind, you'll probably get better with practice."

The practice wasn't going to be with her though because later that night he saw her disappearing into a lifeboat with one of the ship's junior officers and she never crossed his path again.

The trouble was she'd opened Pandora's box for Denny and he landed in Bombay ten days later burning with frustrated desire – he needed a woman and as soon as possible. Every female he'd seen since his spurt of passion with Janette now aroused his long slumbering libido, even three most prim and proper missionary spinsters who came aboard at Singapore and sat in a regimented row on the sun deck, doing their tapestries or reading paperback romances, stirred him in a way that was disturbingly new.

In his fantasy life he swept among them, ravishing as he went, turning them out of their deck chairs and mounting them, one after the other, in a frenzy of priapic passion. While all this was going on in his head, he limped tumescently past with his head down and his eyes averted, hoping that none of them were mind readers. As a result of his frustration he spent a great deal of time in the shower to the annoyance of his cabin mate, another young clerk bound for the High Commission in Delhi.

"Christ Den, you're gonna wash it away if you don't watch out," he bellowed through the bathroom door several times a day. Then he'd laugh like a hyena and Dennis, gritting his teeth, seriously wanted to kill him.

The immediate effect of India was to quieten him down, however. He stared out of the window of a yellow and black taxi as it carried him from the quay to the Australian High Commission and couldn't believe that people lived like that. Camping out beneath the trees that lined the main streets were entire families, babies, dogs, wrinkled half-naked grandmothers crouched round little smoking fires.

"Refugees, are they?" he asked Bob Bates, the affable senior passport officer who'd been sent down to the harbour to get him off the ship.

"Naw, they're always here. They're born on the street and they'll die on the street. You'll get used to it, lad."

But he didn't and his horror at the fetid city increased so much that even a week later he was reluctant to go outside because it seemed that squads of beggars were lying in ambush especially for him. The moment he showed his face from the boarding house where he'd been allocated a room, they appeared, whining like chainsaws, the fortunate among them extending cupped hands under his nose. The unfortunate didn't have hands to extend, only sawn off stumps that they waggled in his direction. They pressed themselves against him, laying their deformed limbs against his shirt front and rubbing their bellies to show how hungry they were.

"Baksheesh, baksheesh, sahib, you are my mother and my father," they moaned and he had to run to get away from them.

Even when he made it into the sanctuary of the air-conditioned office in the middle of the business section of the city, he wasn't free because a glance out of the window was always enough to freeze him to the spot. Down there on the street he'd see a woman falling dead into the gutter or a sweating man hauling a barrow piled to the heavens with goods. One afternoon he watched a taxi run down an old beggar man who only that morning had been making a nuisance of himself to Dennis. The driver hopped out, kicked the body to the side of the road, got back into the driving seat and accelerated away. People standing by did nothing.

At the end of his second week, he turned back from staring out of the window and said to Bob, into whose job and whose flat he was going to move when Bob went home for good in two weeks' time, "I can't stand this place, Bob, I'm going to ask to go home."

"You can't mate. You've got to stick it out for six months at least or they'll charge you for your passage. You've only been here two weeks. That's not long enough to know if you're going to settle or not."

"Oh yes it is. I hate it. I hate the city, I hate the climate. I hate the food. I hate the beer . . . I hate all the snobby bastards in the clubs and I hate the natives. I hate those lizard things that walk about on the rafters of my bedroom roof all the time. I hate everything."

The older man laughed. "The lizards won't hurt you. They're called geckoes and the locals think it's lucky to have one in your house. But I know what you mean. It's all a bit of a shock at first and I hated the place too till I met Monica. Get yourself a bit of skirt, Den, and then you'll be fine."

Denny groaned like a man in torment. "I never meet any women except other guys' wives."

"There's plenty of them rarin' to go, believe me, but that can lead to trouble. One of the blokes who went home last year tried to top himself because his wife was having it off with some Brit she met in the Gym. I leave my old lady at home in Perth looking after the kids. That suits both of us. Stay off the white women, that's my advice."

"Who's Monica then?"

"Monica's my bit on the side. She's local, chi-chi, and as pretty as one of those little china dolls old ladies keep in their china cabinets.

Get yourself a Monica, lad, and your troubles are over. These girls know how to look after a man – in every way, believe me. You say you want to go home, but if you've got a Monica, you'll be happy to live here forever – it's paradise, mate, paradise."

Dennis sat down on the edge of his colleague's desk and asked, "How, tell me how."

"Colaba Causeway. Take a walk down there about eleven o'clock at night and you'll be tripping over them. Girls that look like film stars, only kids too most of them. Not a day over eighteen. And not black either. As white as you or me."

From the amazed look on Dennis's face he could see he had a captive audience and went on, "Anglo-Indians, you see. White blood way back someplace. Washed up here after the British left. Indians look down on them and so do the Brits. Poor little cows. All they want is to get their claws into some white guy to take them away from all this . . ." he waved his hand towards the window, beyond which the mad city raved, shouted, whistled and screamed.

"Tell you what. I'll ask Monica to fit you up with one of her friends. How does that grab you?"

It grabbed Dennis so violently he almost doubled up with the pain at the thought of it but at the back of his mind he remembered his father putting an arm over his shoulder before he left Sydney and saying, "Remember and look after yourself, Den. Enjoy yourself but don't catch anything if you know what I mean . . ."

"But what about – what about the clap?" he asked his friend.

Bob was outraged. "Come on. These girls aren't cheap tarts. If that's what you want there's plenty of them walking around in front of the hotels. You must have seen them. Girls like Monica are husband hunting and they're nice clean girls. You buy them a few drinks, take them out and they start to think it's going to work out for them so they come up with the goods to make sure of you. The only thing you've got to remember is to keep your head. Don't marry one. They're lovely when they're young but by the time they hit thirty they run to fat and lose the white look. It's amazing! Anyway the boss wouldn't let you marry one. He'd ship you home if you even suggested it. He's a real racist that guy. But I happen to know he's got a neat little chi-chi girl himself . . . That's another story though."

Two

When the *Canton* was three days out of Bombay, it sailed past its sister ship, the *Chusan*, that was heading east. Passengers lined the decks to watch the white liners salute each other, the crossing of lives and roads in the middle of an infinite ocean where the marks of passing disappeared with disquieting speed. Few of the people on either of these magnificent ships realised that they were already out of date, and soon would be as forgotten as their ruffling wakes, for they were relics of another time, the last of a glorious era.

Baby Maling-Smith – whose real first name was Roberta but who was always called Baby by everyone except her father after whom she'd been named – did not bother to leave her stateroom to watch the other liner pass by. She'd seen the *Canton* often enough – and had sailed on it too, for she was a seasoned traveller. Over the fourteen years since the war ended, Baby had been back and forward to England ten times, and she always travelled first class.

Even the luxury of her state room failed to make her happy on this voyage for she was sunk in bottomless misery which was made all the worse by the necessity to hide it from her friends on board. None of them must know how she was feeling, none of them must extend sympathy towards her. She was a proud, self-protective and rather unimaginative young woman who preferred to suffer alone.

One of the friends whose pity she was anxious to avoid was Winks Willoughby, a buck-toothed debutante with eager, ingratiating ways. Baby and Winks often travelled to and fro to Europe at the same time for they had once gone to school together at a rarefied ladies' college near Eastbourne where the curriculum studiously avoided anything 'heavy' like Latin, Greek, the sciences or advanced mathematics but instructed the girls in how to talk amusingly to men, how to pretend to knowledge of opera or the arts, how to arrange flowers Constance Spry style, and how to conduct themselves at cocktail parties.

Winks tracked Baby down however. "Do come out, darling. We've just passed the *Canton*. There's a lovely breeze and they're having the shuffle-board final," she carolled, pushing her blonde head round the corner of the door.

"I didn't enter the shuffle-board tournament," said Baby glancing up from her book, *Doctor in the House*, which she'd borrowed from the ship's library.

Looking concerned Winks stepped inside and sat down on the end of the bed – Baby's state room, she noticed, had beds, not bunks like the cabin she shared with her younger sister Mags two decks below. She put a hand on her friend's outstretched bare foot with its brightly painted toenails and said solicitously, "I do hope you're going to cheer up soon. We're all worried about you. What are you going to wear to the fancy dress tomorrow night? Have you brought something special?"

"No. I couldn't be bothered. They're always the same, those things. Somebody goes as Napoleon with his hand in his jacket front and his hat on sideways and there's always at least five women who go as tarts."

"Mags and I are going as tarts . . . We went specially to a shop in Shaftesbury Avenue and bought two pairs of those fish-net stockings that chorus girls wear," said Winks in a deflated voice.

Baby laughed, "Sorry Winks. You and Mags at least have great legs. You should win the first prize."

"I hope you're going to come too. There's all those lovely young bachelors raring to go. There's a smashing chap on board that works for Lloyds Bank and is being transferred from Calcutta to Bombay – he's the one with the little moustache, you must have seen him. He says he knows our aunt in Hindhead and I think he's quite keen on Mags."

P&O liners on their way east were happy hunting grounds for the daughters of burra sahibs working in India. These girls were the modern equivalents of the eighteenth- and nineteenth-century 'fishing fleets' who came east to catch husbands and thought if they landed at their port of destination without at least one proposal of marriage they were complete failures. Winks (real name Winifred), at twenty-six, was two years older than Baby, and four more than her sister Mags, a scheming, sexy little thing who always got the men while her nicer, more earnest sister ended up the wallflower. Winks, a veteran of ten P&O trips, had begun to reconcile herself to the role of the maiden aunt.

"I bet he only knows *of* your aunt," said Baby. "He probably cashed her cheques in the Hindhead bank once." The aunt had married a title, and was much boasted about by the girls and their parents.

Winks was not to be diverted, because she was worried about her friend. Baby's elaborate act of brittle cynicism during the voyage had not deceived her. "Do come to the fancy dress dance, Baby. You can't hide away from the world forever you know – or hanker after him for ever either. He's married now. You'll just have to accept it," she said, boldly taking the bull by the horns.

Baby laid her book face down on the bedcover and said, "What *do* you mean?"

"I mean you'll have to get over Charlie sooner or later. That's what this is all about, isn't it? I do sympathise, I really do. I know what it's like to be terribly hurt . . ."

Baby sat up and looked directly at her friend. Winks was totally genuine and her concern was real. She also knew what it was like to long for a man who belonged to someone else, for a couple of years before her only serious suitor had been stolen off her by the unscrupulous Mags, who then dropped him.

"I don't think I'll ever get over him, Winks," Baby told her friend, relieved to be able to talk about her agony at last. "I really loved him and I thought he loved me . . . Oh, I know, it's my fault. He never told me any lies. From the beginning he said he was going home to get married at the end of his tour and that was what he did. I just thought I could change his mind. Right up till the last minute I didn't think he'd go through with it . . ."

"Did you know that Mags and I went to his wedding with Guy?" asked Winks, "We hired a car and took Guy out of hospital for the day."

Baby shook her head, "I didn't know." On the day of Charlie's wedding, she'd gone to the National Portrait Gallery in Trafalgar Square and sat on a plush bench beneath dark oil paintings of long dead kings and queens weeping her heart out.

"The wedding was in Sussex, near Horsham. Isobel, the bride, her father's a vicar there. Charlie came up and asked me about you."

The breath caught in Baby's throat as she asked, "What did he say?"

"He said he hoped you were all right and that I was to tell you he'd asked about you. He said he hoped you'd be happy . . . It wasn't easy for him either, Baby. You wouldn't have thought so much of him if he was the sort who'd back out of an engagement," Winks solemnly told her. "If he'd said he was going back to marry a girl in England, he would. He kept his word."

"Just my luck to fall in love with the only honourable man I've ever met," said Baby bitterly.

She didn't go to the fancy dress dance – and Winks and Mags didn't win the first prize. That went to a banker's wife with precisely plucked sickle moon eyebrows who had brought a Cleopatra costume, complete with asp, out in her luggage expressly for the purpose of winning the shipboard contest.

When their ship was nudged by two dark green painted Port Authority tugs into the P&O berth at Bombay however, a cheerfully smiling Baby was on deck with her friends. She was hatless and wearing pink cotton trousers with a loose white blouse tied in a knot at her waist. Beside her she led a toy crocodile on wheels, its body made of articulated bits of wood that clicked and curved in an unnerving, almost lifelike way as she pulled it along.

Mags, a spoiled-looking, pouting girl who'd been told by an admirer that she looked like Brigitte Bardot and modelled herself on the star ever since, even going so far as adopting French phrases and, when she remembered, the accent, recoiled at the sight of Baby's crocodile.

"Where on earth did you get that?" she asked.

"In Hamley's. I just fell for him. I call him my man eater."

"I think he's horrible, but at least he won't last long. I expect someone'll stand on him at one of the rugby club parties. *Quelle dommage!*" said Mags.

Winks was leaning over the rail staring down at the knots of welcoming people standing in the shade of long sheds that lined the quay. Suddenly she waved, "There's Papa! There's Mums. Oh, there's your mother and father too, Baby. Hello darlings, hello . . ." And she fluttered her hands, throwing down a rain of kisses to the waiting parents.

"She's always like this, every time we come out," muttered Mags who wasn't waving or throwing kisses. This trip, she was determined, she was going to find a suitable man to marry. She was getting on in age and would soon be on the shelf like Winks if she didn't hurry up for she was tired of being shuttled to and fro like a piece of merchandise in search of a spouse.

Baby's parents, Sir Robert Maling-Smith and his wife, Lady Barbara, were always moved to tears which they strove to conceal, with success on his part but not on hers, by the sight of their only child after an absence, and this time Baby had been away from them for three months, not as long as periods they'd spent apart.

9

in the past but long enough to miss her desperately. The one who not only missed her but worried about her too was Baby's mother who knew without having been told that her silent, reserved daughter had been in the toils of a terrible sadness when she left Bombay. Now she was anxiously craning her neck for the first glimpse of the dear girl, sure that she'd be able to tell from one glance if the corroding sorrow had left her.

The Maling-Smiths made an odd-looking couple, for he was bulldoggishly short and squat with a sullen looking purple face and his wife very tall and thin, the archetypical aristocratic English woman, with an equable but equine expression and sparse hair that had once been blonde but was now a streaky mixture of white and yellow. The bones of her legs and arms were extremely long and her hands knobbled by arthritis, but the unmanicured fingers were weighed down with beautiful rings – rubies, diamonds and a huge, dirty solitaire emerald worth thousands of pounds.

When she married her husband she had been thirty-nine years old and, like Winks, reconciled to spinsterhood. Her father was a Colonel in the Frontier Guides but even the advantages of marrying the Colonel's daughter had not been enough for any of his subalterns to take on Barbara Maling, who was considered extremely odd and unfeminine.

She scorned social graces, had no ladylike hobbies, and was happiest on a horse for she was a superb rider who looked far better up on a saddle than she did on the ground. But it was her height, six foot one inches in stocking feet, and her conversation that drove away the young officers. They were unnerved by having to stare up at her and by her inability to call a spade anything other than a bloody shovel, as well as her unfailing ability to pinpoint other people's sensitivities and comment on them, not through malice but through pure interest and an unfortunate ability to pick up other people's thoughts – almost like the second sight.

She'd never have met plain Bob Smith if they hadn't been involved in a road accident because, being a box wallah and in trade, he could never have infiltrated her military circles, for their encounter took place in 1934 when the snobbery of the Raj was in full flower.

They were riding in separate taxis one steamy Bombay evening, unaware that the drivers were bitter enemies. The driver of Barbara's taxi spotted Robert's, and deliberately rammed it, throwing the passengers onto the floor. Barbara was knocked out cold.

When she came round she was lying on the pavement with a crowd of interested, chattering spectators around her and a white man on his knees beside her wiping blood off her face with his handkerchief.

She stared up at the sky, tried to wave a hand at the crowd to tell them to go away, and managed to articulate the first words that came into her mind which were, in order of precedence, "Shove off!" – but in more impolite Hindi terms than that – to the onlookers and "What the hell happened?" to Robert.

"D'ye want me to fetch a doctor?" asked the stranger. He had a strange accent, she noticed, very Scottish.

"God no. I'm all right. I've had worse falls than this. Let's see. I can move my legs . . . and my arms. Help me up. Go away . . ." The last two words were again spoken in colloquial phraseology to the chattering, giggling crowd who, of course, didn't do anything but exclaim at the white woman's ability to swear in Hindi, and pressed closer.

Her saviour hailed another taxi and escorted her to the huge bungalow in the Colaba cantonment where she was staying with a colonel friend of her father's before embarking for home on a liner that was due to sail in three days' time.

She didn't board it but instead stayed on in Bombay and six weeks later married Robert Kitchener Smith in the little Anglican church on the top of Malabar Hill.

Her father and his military cronies were horrified. "Poor Barbara. He's an absolute prole," they commiserated with the bride's father in the mess.

"But a rich prole," said her father's Colaba-based friend who had the advantage of local knowledge and knew that Robert Smith was managing director of a huge cotton weaving company and had already amassed the equivalent of a million pounds in rupees.

On the day he married, he was three years older, as well as eight inches shorter, than his bride, and had been in India since he was seventeen, coming out as chauffeur and motor repairer to another cotton magnate who'd been impressed by the young lad's skill with machinery when his monumental, snorting Armstrong Siddeley broke down one day in the middle of Glasgow and Bob stepped off the pavement to get it going again.

Bob didn't stay a chauffeur long because his employer, who was childless, more or less adopted him and found him a position in the company he managed. From that the only way for Bob was up – and up – and up. Not only was he ambitious but he was adroit, brave and slightly unscrupulous too.

When he'd been in India for a few years, he saved his employer's life when a howling, enraged mob of striking mill workers seemed to be on the verge of lynching him. Bob faced them down and amazingly they turned back. From that day he became aware of his power to dominate other people, quickly learned who to contact to sabotage the plans of anyone who crossed him, and by the time he was thirty-five, when his original patron died, he had become one of the three most important businessmen in Bombay, controlling and part owning a company that employed twenty-five thousand men and ran five enormous cotton mills that never closed but throbbed and thudded and steamed and roared round the clock seven days a week, fifty-two weeks a year.

He settled the giddying income of a thousand pounds per annum on his new wife and she, on her part, accepted this bounty with grace, making only one stipulation. "I can't go through life being called Mrs Smith, Roh-bert darling. We'll have to stick a hyphen in – Maling-Smith'll do very well."

As it turned out she wouldn't have been called Mrs Smith for long because, during the second world war, in recognition of his generosity towards the war effort at home, as well as his diligence in keeping his mills working overtime with military orders and his ability to raise funds from less generously inclined tycoons in India, Robert Smith was knighted by a grateful government. Lady Maling-Smith sounded very well even to Colonel Maling, who by that time was dying of liver failure in Kashmir, his last days made more comfortable by money provided by his son-in-law.

Barbara and Robert stood side by side on Ballard Quay, she swaying slightly like a tall poplar tree assailed by a persistent wind, as their daughter approached them dragging a clockwork crocodile behind her. Her mother was pleased to see that Baby was beaming, happiness apparently radiating from her. She was a very good actress.

They were not a demonstrative family, so the greetings they exchanged were mere pecks on the cheeks, unlike the tearful huggings that Mags and Winks were being subjected to by their parents. Baby noticed with an upsurge of irritated love that her mother smelt of carnation soap and gin – it had always been the same, Roger and Gallet's soap and Parry's gin, with the gin predominating. Her father, also as usual, smelt of Indian cigarettes, the kind called bidis that the servants smoked.

"What's that?" said Sir Robert pointing at the crocodile.

"My new friend," said Baby lightly.

"Is it smiling?" asked her mother, bending down to peer at the toy.

"I don't think so," said Baby, bending down too.

"Good thing!" said Lady Maling-Smith standing up again. "Remember that poem about the person with the smile that rode off on the back of a crocodile and when it came back, the smile was on the face of the crocodile."

Baby laughed, "The poem's about a tiger, mother," she said.

"Does it matter?" asked her mother and laughed again but Sir Robert didn't. "Pick the thing up," he told his daughter, "The coolies are staring at it."

"They probably think we do puja to it," said Baby's mother, folding her hands and making a genuflection to the crocodile like a Hindu supplicant. Baby laughed again and took her mother's arm as she walked towards their car, dragging the crocodile defiantly behind her.

Lady Maling-Smith looked fondly down at her daughter for Baby was short like her father, only five foot two. "Did you have a lovely time at home, darling? Did you go to that wedding that everyone's been talking about? Lots of champers I hope. I love champers but you can't get any here now – not a bottle to be had for love or money. You didn't bring a bottle off the ship, did you?"

Baby's "No" was drowned by her father snapping, "Lots of gin to be had here though."

"Gin, gin, wonderful gin," carolled his wife, "What would life be like without a little drop of gin!" She had long ago given up trying to hide the extent of her toping.

Three

M en squashed into the seats of the train going to Chembur
stared openly and lasciviously at Monica Fernandes as she
sat pretending to be engrossed in the pages of a women's magazine
called *Eve's Weekly* during the short trip out of the city into the
suburbs.

Only months before Monica had been a pretty girl with a strong
resemblance to the Hollywood star Myrna Loy, but now, though
still eye-catching, she was developing into a full blown woman
with a network of tiny lines marking the skin beneath her eyes and
round her prettily curving mouth. Every night she rubbed handfuls
of Pond's Cold Cream into those lines but it wasn't helping, age
was catching up on her.

In fact, she was thirty-one and the veteran of several amorous cam-
paigns, two illegal abortions and three doses of venereal infection but
she regarded those vicissitudes almost with pride, as a soldier would
look on the scars of battle, and still hope for victory in the end.

Victory for Monica would be capturing a white man in marriage.
Her present quarry was Bob Bates of the Australian High Commission and it was on his behalf that she was going to Chembur.

"I'm worried about young Denny, Mon," Bob had said to her a few
evenings before as they sat side by side drinking iced coffee in one
of the air-conditioned cafes along Church Parade, "He's not settling
down. I told him to get himself a girl but he's a slow starter, I guess.
D'you know any young bit of fluff you could fix him up with?"

Monica knew lots of bits of fluff of varying ages but most of
them she wouldn't let within a mile of Bob because she couldn't
trust them not to try to take him off her. A diplomatic man
was a great catch because he could get his hands on duty-free
alcohol, imported make-up and exotic food – and what Monica
and her friends considered exotic were delicacies like tinned button
mushrooms and Chivers jellies, Bovril and Edam cheese in a wax
covering that made it look like a big red football. None of those
things were available on the local market, even for enormous prices,

14

and Monica's mother was especially fond of Edam cheese, which she claimed to have enjoyed 'at home' in England although in fact she had never been out of Bombay.

"I've a cousin who's very sweet," she told Bob after a moment's thought during which she fetchingly pursed her lips but took care not to wrinkle her brow.

"Is she pretty?" he asked.

"Oh very! Prettier than I am."

"Not possible, girlie. Nobody's prettier than you." He squeezed her leg above the knee as he spoke and she slipped her foot out of her high-heeled white shoe to rub it against his ankle. Nobody played the game better than Monica.

"Have you written to your wife about me yet, Bob?" she whispered.

"Yes," he lied. "She's thinking about whether she wants a divorce or not. I reckon she'll make it difficult for me. She's an RC and she's going to consult her priest."

In fact the absent Mrs Bates was doing nothing of the sort and was superbly indifferent to anything her husband got up to in Bombay providing he continued to send her enough money every month to maintain her house and swimming pool in Perth and pay for the kids' surfing lessons. Neither he nor she had any wish for a divorce so long as they didn't have to spend too much time together.

"What's your cousin called?" asked Bob.

"Carole."

"Carole Fernandes?"

"No, Carole MacLeod. Her mother's my mother's younger sister and her father was called Tom MacLeod. His father was in the army here . . ."

Bob got to the nitty gritty. "Is she white then?"

Monica bristled. Her own skin was what she described as 'wheat coloured' and was kept that way by strict avoidance of the sun and liberal application of cold cream, but she knew she looked and sounded Eurasian and was sensitive about it. "She's very pale skinned," she said stiffly.

"What colour?" persisted Bob insensitively.

"Magnolia," said Monica.

"Fix her up with Denny, then," said Bob who wanted to see his young assistant settled soon. If Dennis carried out his threat of resigning from the High Commission, it might mean Bob would have to stay on for a few more months till they shipped out another passport office clerk and he didn't want that at all. In fact he hadn't

15

told Monica how soon his planned departure date would be. He didn't want her making a fuss either.

At Chembur station Monica fought her way out of the train, elbowing aside men who deliberately tried to rub their bodies against her, and at last found herself on the long empty platform. The sun was blazing down with unmitigated ferocity because it was two o'clock in the afternoon and most sensible people were enjoying an afternoon sleep.

She started walking up a rutted, dusty road towards the golf course, fixing her eyes on the tops of mango trees that formed its hazards and were visible above a slight rise to her right. Carole lived with her mother and sister in a bungalow on the far side of the eighth green, a privilege accorded to them because Auntie Fifi, Carole's mother, was conducting a long-standing affair with the golf club secretary Major Motiwala.

When Monica eventually reached the door of the bungalow, the family dog, a huge Alsatian, rose from the shade where it had been lying and loped towards her, lifting black lips from its teeth, snarling silently.

"It's Monica," she told the dog but stopped in her tracks and raised her voice to shout, "Carole, Auntie. Let me in."

Fortunately Aunt Fifi heard her and popped her head out of an open ground floor window. "Sabre. Lie down," she yelled and when the dog sank onto its haunches, she told Monica, "Come on in. What's brought you out here today?"

Aunt Fifi always looked regal, like a well-tanned English duchess. She had run to fat recently but it was well distributed, most of it having settled on her breasts and buttocks while her waist, legs and ankles remained trim. Her hair was piled up on top of her head in a sort of crown and it was tinged with streaks of grey in a most fetching way. She had been a great beauty and was still a very sexy-looking woman.

When Monica was settled on a plastic-covered settee in their sitting room with a glass of lime soda in her hand, she got straight to the point, "Where's Carole?"

"In bed. She spends most of her time there. You couldn't get her a job could you? Amy's got a job as a stenographer in a shipping office and she's doing very well."

Aunt Fifi had two daughters by different fathers. Amy, the eldest, was twenty-four and had been born when her mother was sixteen. The father had also been sixteen and a Goan, son of Fifi's next-door neighbour in Bandra, and he had been fairly dark skinned so poor Amy was never going to make it in the world of the pretty chi-chi girl, for colour was of paramount importance both to the girls and the men who displayed them on their arms. She had turned out to be a proud, sarcastic girl possessed of considerable intelligence, who would certainly make an excellent stenographer for some thick-skinned employer who was able to ignore her sharp wit.

The younger sister Carole was nearly eighteen and a carbon copy of what her mother had looked like at the same age. Her father had also been Anglo Indian, and a singer with a dance band, who claimed direct, one generation ago, descent from a Scottish regular soldier who'd been killed in the Burma campaign. The singer was the only man Fifi ever loved – out of more than thirty who'd thought she loved them – and of course he treated her badly, beating her up, stealing her money, and eventually running away with her best friend when Carole was nine years old. Though he turned up asking for money from time to time, the last his family heard of him he'd been singing with a band in Calcutta under the name of Tony California.

The only memento they had of him was his real surname because Fifi married him. Since his defection, she'd maintained herself and her children by granting her favours to a succession of men who were prepared to pay for the privilege of sleeping with her and enjoying her familiarity with the *ars amati*. Major Motiwala, provider of the bungalow, was only one of several.

"Carole, Carole," she called up the narrow stairs, "Come down baby, cousin Monica is here."

The first sight of Carole was a long pair of naked, shapely legs coming down the stairs. Then the elegant figure came into sight, clad in very small, very tight black shorts and a pink sleeveless blouse. Her luxuriant and curly black hair was tousled, her eyes heavy with sleep and she had her left thumb stuck firmly in her mouth. The sexy beauty she exuded was breathtaking.

It had been more than a year since Monica last saw her and now her first thought was disquiet. Would it be safe to present such a beautiful girl to a friend of Bob's? What if Bob took a fancy to her?

For in her heart Monica knew that Bob had no real intention of marrying her. She was deceiving him by pretending to believe his promises as much as he was deceiving her by pretending to want a divorce. Realistically it was best to accept the good things he had to offer for as long as he was prepared to give them and not worry about the future. If she kept him happy in bed, he wasn't likely to take off with anyone else, especially someone as inexperienced as Carole. He might even leave her a bit of money when he went.

She put her proposition to her aunt rather than to Carole. "I have this friend who works in the Australian High Commission, and in his office there's a young man who's just come out and is very lonely. My friend Bob wants to cheer him up and he'd like him to find a nice girl . . ."

Aunt Fifi knew the score exactly. "Is he married?" she asked, looking at the sleepy eyed Carole.

"My friend is but the other man isn't. He's quite young, only twenty-six or twenty-seven, and very green Bob says. He's a decent young man too, doesn't drink too much or take drugs or sleep with boys . . ."

Aunt Fifi sniffed as if she found the existence of such a paragon difficult to credit, "You want him to meet my Carole?" she asked.

"Yes. I think it would be a good thing for both of them. He might marry her and take her back to Australia with him."

They both looked at Carole, speculating about her chances of bringing off this magnificent coup. She lounged on the sofa, legs tucked under her and thumb still in mouth, sex personified. If she couldn't do it, nobody could. They could almost see the tickets to Australia dangling before their eyes.

Four

The first time Baby Maling-Smith noticed Dennis Gillies was the day the news came through that Buddy Holly had been killed in an air crash. She and her friends, who never bothered to read political news items but kept up with the latest developments of pop music and always brought the newest records back with them after a trip home, were mourning this death as they sat at the side of Breach Candy's outdoor swimming pool where Dennis occasionally went in the late afternoon to work off his frustrations by ploughing across the vast expanse of aquamarine water with his magnificent crawl.

It was impossible not to pick him out as he powered to and fro, head down and legs flailing, kicking up a massive white wake behind him. The other swimmers, cutting through the water with laboured breast strokes, their heads well up to avoid swallowing any of the germ-laden water, looked like wallowing canoes compared to his ocean liner.

It was Mags, always on the lookout for new men, who first approached him.

"*Who* is that?" she asked, lifting her dark glasses off her eyes and sticking them on the top of her head as she pointed over at Dennis who was just then heaving himself out in preparation to sitting on the stone edge of the pool with his legs dangling down into the water. The muscles of his tanned back glistened as they flexed and his head was wet and sleek as a seal's with the hair plastered down on his shapely skull.

"Just look at him!" said Mags again, "What a lovely body!"

"I've never seen him before," said Winks who found it unseemly to comment on men's bodies, "Don't stare Mags. He'll see you."

"Good," said Mags, standing up and positioning the straps of her bikini top on the points of her shoulders in the hope that this would make her rather meagre breasts stick out a bit more, "I'm going to speak to him." And with that she dived into the pool, creating hardly a splash, and struck out underwater, not surfacing till she was almost halfway across.

19

The next Baby and Winks saw of her was when she swam slowly past Dennis's dangling feet. Then she materialised sitting on the pool edge by his side. About ten minutes later her head bobbed out of the water beside where her sister and Baby lay stretched out on towels beneath two of the swimming club's striped umbrellas.

"Meet Dennis," she said, gesturing behind her to where the power-swimmer was treading water, "He's Australian and he's only been out a couple of weeks. Doesn't know a soul, poor fellow."

Then she climbed out and sat down beside Winks. "Do join us," she invited him, patting the grass at her side.

Awkwardly he sat down, worried about his baggy swimming pants, and hugged his knees, saying, "Pleased to meet you," when introduced first to Winks and then to Baby.

"We're just about to have something to drink," said Mags, "Will you join us?" As she spoke she was gesturing towards the bow-legged little waiter who sat in the shade watching their section of grass. He came running, holding his tin tray out at the ready.

"Three Coca Colas – and what for you Dennis?" said Mags.

"How about a beer?" he ventured.

The girls laughed. "It's obvious you've only just come out. You can't get beer here. This is a prohibition area. Haven't you heard about permits?"

Dennis had a permit. He'd thought it was a joke at first, having to apply for an official government permit in order to be able to buy a beer, but so far he'd had no opportunity to use his. Any drinking he'd done was in private in his boarding house room and he had a good stock of duty free alcohol to finish up before he got round to buying any outside.

"You mean you can't even buy a beer here?" he asked.

"Not as much as a sip," said Winks brightly, "and if you were Indian you wouldn't be able to get in at all. This is for Europeans only, hadn't you noticed?"

He looked around. Every swimmer, every sunbather was white. "Is that allowed, keeping people out because of their colour I mean?" he asked in disbelief. The still-prevailing atmosphere of the Raj seemed totally illogical to him and he couldn't understand why the Indians put up with it now they were independent.

"It's lasted so far. It's a private club you see. They've let you in because you're obviously white but you'll have to join eventually. This is the last relic of the Raj, this place, like the hospital next door. It used to be the *British* hospital but it lets Indians in now and even some of the doctors are locals too . . . The swimming pool'll have to give in eventually as well, I expect."

Mags sounded mournful at the prospect but Baby shrugged. "About time," she said.

"Oh Baby," said Mags, "you just say things like that to be provocative. You know as well as we do how this place would simply go to pot if they let the natives use it. The hospital's not what it was either already. Ralph's the only British doctor left!"

Baby turned on her face like a grilling chop to allow the last rays of the afternoon sun to tan her already golden-coloured back. "The Willingdon hasn't gone to pot and Indians have been members there for ages," she said.

"Their committee is very fussy who they let in and it's very expensive," Winks reminded her.

"And this is Bombay where rich Indians are even more snobbish than rich Brits," said Baby into her folded arms.

"*You* should talk," snapped envious Mags.

The arrival of the Coca Colas in fluted bottles, fresh from the ice box with droplets of cold water glistening on their sides, stopped the argument. When they'd drunk their fill, Mags suddenly said, "I'm starving. Let's have something to eat."

"Tell me what you want and I'll get it," said Dennis standing up but Baby stopped him, saying, "You can't. I'm a member here and you're not. I'll sign for it . . ."

The waiter was told to bring club sandwiches which soon appeared under a white cloth on his tray. "Take care when you're eating," Winks told Dennis, pointing up to birds that looked like eagles soaring lazily in the air above their heads, "Get under the brolly before you take your sandwich out of its wrapping or one of the kites'll snatch it out of your hand. They've got frightful talons, can tear the flesh off your fingers or slash a gash across your head. Nasty!"

Laughing, but nervously, he huddled companionably with the girls under their umbrellas while they ate and after a while the sun went down in an explosion of light over the sea on their right. When that happened a shudder of cold went through each one of them and they stood up, grasping their arms round their chests, eager to get out of their damp suits and into dry clothes.

"Hope to see you again," said Mags to Dennis before they left, "We're here almost every afternoon, always in this corner. Don't forget . . ."

When he rode back to his room in the boarding house that catered

21

for young bachelors, he felt happier than he'd been since he came ashore off the *Canton*. He lay on his bed with his hands clasped behind his head and thought of the afternoon – of the swimming, the sun, the crowds of people beneath the striped umbrellas – and the three girls. They were nice girls and pretty too, especially the one they called that ridiculous name – Baby. Perhaps life was not going to be so terrible after all. He hadn't realised how lonely he'd been till he met those girls.

In fact his luck had definitely turned and things did get better because after dinner that evening Bob Bates turned up and invited him to go for a drive.

"There's someone I'd like you to meet," said Bob, taking Dennis's arm and guiding him down the boarding house front door steps to a waiting car where Monica sat in the back seat looking like a starlet from a Hollywood movie.

She was excessively cordial to Dennis and patted the seat at her side, inviting him to climb in beside her. Bob got in the front beside the driver.

"I thought we'd go for a little drive," said Bob, "Monica's cousin lives in a village called Chembur about fifteen miles away. Thought we'd take a run out and see the place. D'ye play golf Den? There's a good golf course there apparently."

Dennis played golf. In fact he was quite good at it, as he was at most sports. "Great," he said, settling back beside Monica and inhaling her spicy perfume that made his head swim.

They drove north, first going through close-packed roads that ran between the high walls of thudding mills – which, had Dennis but known it, were under the rule of Baby's father. Then came suburbs of more prosperous-looking houses where the roads were wider and less squalid . . . after that they drove into open country where little stalls selling fruit or bales of cloth, and lit by paraffin lamps, clustered on the corners. Now and again they saw tiny temples built round the trunk of massive banyan trees and Dennis leaned forward to stare into the lighted squares of the doors. The darkness by this time was thick and velvety, sliced through by the twin beam of the car's headlights, and broken sometimes by a spectral walking figure of a man dressed in white or a wandering cow with its ribs sticking out of its coat like a collection of coat hangers.

Their journey ended half an hour later when the car drew up outside a small, white painted house with lights blazing in every window. As soon as the driver opened the door to let Monica out, the house door opened too and a full-busted woman emerged with her hands outspread, exclaiming, "What a surprise cousin Monica, so good of you to come and see us. Come in, come in . . . bring your friends."

The room where they sat was lit only by one central light in a pink glass shade round which a skein of moths fluttered and swooped. Dennis, who hated the burgeoning insects of India almost as much as he hated the house lizards, eyed them anxiously, not sure that he wouldn't be stung if one landed on him and dreading the thought of getting them caught in his hair.

Their hostess pulled out chairs from around a plain wooden table covered with an oil cloth and urged them to sit down. Bob had brought a bottle of Gordon's gin, which he plonked down on the middle of the table, from which it was immediately snatched and carried through a door shrouded by coloured strips of hanging plastic into what was presumably a kitchen by a bent and toothless old woman in a white sari. A few minutes later she returned with a tin tray decorated with large red and yellow roses on which stood six thick glass tumblers containing a couple of fingers of gin in each. This was put on the table and later accompanied by six open bottles of soda water.

"Drink!" said the old woman and disappeared.

"Girls!" shouted their hostess, who, Dennis was told, was Monica's aunt Fifi. As if on cue there was a clattering of heels from upstairs and a vision of pure loveliness emerged down the stairs.

Carole was looking so spectacular that even Bob, who had been warned by Monica what to expect, paused and stared with his glass of gin and soda half way to his lips. "Jeez!" he said half under his breath.

She was wearing white – full-skirted and V-necked. Her hair was tied back from her face with a wide white ribbon and her lips were discreetly carmined but that was all the make-up she wore. The effect was girlish and virginal. One foot in front of the other she paused at the bottom of the step, hand on the newel post, and smiled.

"Hello cousin Monica," she whispered as if she hadn't seen her relative for months.

"This," said her mother to the men, "is my youngest daughter Carole." Her manner was that of a well-to-do madame. She couldn't help it.

"Carole darling, Mr Bob has brought us some real gin. Do you want one?"

Carole wrinkled her adorable nose. "I don't like gin mumsy, you know that. I'll just have soda."

"Wise girl," said Bob taking a huge swig from his glass and avoiding Monica's eye. Dennis also drank his gin but almost without noticing what he was doing. Carole, he thought, was the most beautiful girl he'd ever seen in his life – a dead ringer for his favourite film star Natalie Wood. He was in heaven.

When Amy came in from the kitchen only Dennis noticed her because they were all laughing at Bob's stream of jokes. The other girl stood with one hand on the door jamb and a judgemental look on her face as she surveyed the gathering. She was darker skinned than her sister and not so tall; and different too in that her dress was skimpier, a checked button-through shirt-waister that looked as if it had shrunk in the wash. Her hair was cut short in a Joan of Arc style and she had a pert, snub-nosed face with wide-spaced dark eyes beneath curving brows.

"Has Sabre been fed?" she asked her mother who looked up in the act of pouring another generous slug of gin into her glass.

"Not yet . . . he can wait," she said.

"No, he can't. I'll feed him," said the girl and turned to go back into the kitchen but her mother stopped her. "Haven't you said hello to Monica and her friends – Mr Bates and Mr . . ."

"Gillies," said Dennis standing up for he had been very well brought up by his loving mother.

"This is my other daughter, Amy," said Carole's mother, "Have a gin Amy, it'll sweeten your temper."

"No thanks," said Amy, "I'd rather feed the dog." And she disappeared not to be seen again that night.

By eleven o'clock they were all – except Carole – fairly drunk and very hungry so the old woman was summoned to fry them eggs which they devoured enthusiastically and after the plates were cleared away Dennis found himself sitting beside Carole. Somehow, he wasn't quite sure how, they made an appointment to go to the cinema together two days later and after a short time he, Monica and Bob piled back into the car and were driven back into the city. Dennis fell asleep before they reached the racecourse and had to be wakened out of a wonderful dream when they drew up in front of his boarding house. The trouble was he couldn't remember which of all the girls he'd seen that day was the one he'd been dreaming about.

Five

"I love this country, I just love it . . ." sitting in the back of one of her father's fleet of cars, one of the first air-conditioned black Cadillacs with tail fins and long strips of chrome along its sides, Baby Maling-Smith felt an aching pull at her heart as she watched the world of India through the tinted glass windows. The dusty road was lined on one side by scrappy-looking palm trees, and skirted on the other a stone-walled tank covered with a carpet of purple water hyacinths, their deceitful beauty making the surface of the water look firm enough to walk on, deep and enticing like a lusciously piled carpet.

Walking away from the tank were two pedlars bearing trays loaded with pots of the flowers on their heads. She knew they'd sell them to gullible English women in the fashionable flats of Malabar Hill. Beguiled by the beauty of the flowers and by their memories of scented hyacinths and spring at home, the women would pay two or three rupees for each pot and then exclaim with irritation a few hours later when they visibly wilted and died.

When her car slowed up to pass them, Baby smiled at the pedlars as if she and they were conspiring together. One of the men hopefully held out a pot of flowers to her and she made an expressive Indian gesture signifying she was aware of his chicanery. He looked surprised to find a white women not ripe for deceiving.

But she was almost as much part of the country as he was. She had been born in Bombay, spent more of her childhood with the native servants than she did with either of her parents, spoke Hindi and Gujerati before she spoke English, stayed there through the war years and was then sent away, violently protesting, to school in England at the age of twelve. She had been a disruptive pupil, expelled from two prim boarding schools for girls because of her cavalier attitude towards regulations. At seventeen her formal education, such as it was, ceased and she came home again – for Bombay was home to Baby. Since then she'd shuttled to and fro between India and Europe with or without her parents . . . staying in the best hotels, visiting

25

the most important sights, spending her father's money . . . but that way of passing the time was beginning to bore her and she felt panic when she contemplated her future.

Basically Baby was of a melancholic turn of mind and anything or anyone that lightened her mood was precious to her. For most of the past year she had been in a deep depression which was all the harder to bear because of her determination to hide her true feelings. She loved her parents and she loved India but she was beginning to realise that to stay on, meeting the same people, doing the same things was a recipe for disaster. She would have to make a break, change her life – but how?

"What am I going to do? Where am I going to go?" The questions plagued her day and night, especially since her disappointment over Charlie. She'd travelled and seen lovely places but none of them had enticed her away from her first love – India. In other places – even in England – she felt foreign. She was only at home and at ease in this mysterious, frustrating country.

She was being driven along the road that led out of the main city onto Trombay island situated in the straits between the island of Bombay and the mainland. The driver of the car knew where she was going for he had taken her there many times before, though not for a long time now. The place where they had to turn off the main road was not easy to spot because it was hidden behind a thicket of huge, fiercely speared cactus plants and a clump of palm trees, but the driver changed down well before he reached it and swung the big car round so that its wheels would find the ruts of the lane without jolting his passenger.

On the other side of the main road lay Chembur golf course and the bungalow lived in by Carole, her mother and her sister, people Baby knew nothing about and had never seen.

In spite of the driver's care the roughness of the lane made her rock about in her seat. "Bad road, Missy Baby," said the man behind the wheel who had worked for her family since she was a child.

"It's always bad," she agreed but she liked it that way. Because it was so difficult to negotiate, cars never tackled this road unless they had good reason and knew where they were going. She hoped no improver would ever lay a good surface on the red dust and build blocks of luxury flats in this secluded and beautiful little corner of Trombay island.

Ahead of her rose a jungle-covered hill topped by a tiny temple, from which a single flag fluttered on a long, whip-like pole. A holy man lived there and had never come down for thirty years though his acolytes carried food up for him, fighting their way through dense undergrowth to reach him.

On her right was a fruit farm, rank after rank of eight-foot-tall pomelo trees, each topped with a globe of closely pruned branches of glossy green leaves that sweetened the air with a sharp citrus smell, especially in misty early mornings when the sun started to rise.

The car crawled past the gate to the farm and she sat forward to stare out at a stone-walled well where a cluster of women, with scarlet or orange cotton saris looped up between their legs, were gossiping as they filled old Dalda cooking oil tins with water. One or two of the women caught sight of her in the back seat and gave almost imperceptible little nods. They'd seen her before and recognised her.

"They probably know all about me, and my broken heart," she thought because she knew that secrets could not be kept from the servants in India and no details of their employers' lives was too trivial to be discussed and analysed by them, their friends and their neighbours.

The Gulmohurs, the house she was visiting, was named after a tall tree covered with long flourishes of orange flowers which grew at the gate. The bungalow lay hidden behind a thicket of other trees and huge sprouting bougainvillaea plants with purple, pink and white flowers on the lower slopes of the hill. It had a white five-barred gate like the sort of gates that gave entry to English paddocks and, behind its hedge, was a vast expanse of emerald-green lawn bordered by curving flower beds packed with mother-in-law's tongues, canna lilies, poinsettias, zinnias and marigolds.

Charlie had laid out this garden and she helped him, tracing the plan of flower beds onto huge sheets of drawing paper and translating his orders to the bright-eyed gardener Birbal. The result had been exactly what he wanted, a very beautiful English-style garden stocked with Indian plants, an essay in nostalgia by a man stranded far from home. Her first glimpse of Charlie's garden again made her heart contract with pain when the car turned in at the gate and drew to a halt opposite the crouching bungalow's front door.

Mohammed, the house bearer, came down the steps in typical stately fashion to open the car door and welcome her. She could tell from the glint in his eye that he was wondering why she'd come back, for he too knew everything about her affair with Charlie and probably did not expect to see her now that her lover had gone away.

"I am happy to see you again, Missy sahib," he said in his oily, obsequious way. Though she smiled brightly at him she neither liked nor trusted the man – he was too smooth, too perfect, a villain she was sure, and she'd often told Charlie that, but he and his two friends, Ben and Guy, who established their riotous bachelor household out here in the country, were bedazzled by Mohammed and boasted he was the best bearer in Bombay.

Charlie had gone, of course, back to England to marry his childhood sweetheart Isobel. Guy was away too, sent home on sick leave for treatment at the London Hospital for Tropical Diseases because he was suffering from virulent amoebic dysentry. Only wild Ben, who fought off all disease by a liberal intake of whisky, was still in residence with a new wife called Dee, an odd girl who didn't fit into Bombay society. Ben had brought Dee out from home a year ago and Baby wondered how she got on with Mohammed because it was rare for bachelors' bearers to adapt well to new wives. They usually left within a few months, unable to cope with serving a woman, but Mohammed had a lot to lose and he would want to stay. If Charlie and his friends thought they had the best bearer in the city, Mohammed would certainly know he had the best job. The boys had let him do exactly as he liked.

I bet it's a contest of wills between Ben's bearer and his wife to see who quits first, thought Baby as she stepped out of her car and asked Mohammed, "Is your memsahib at home today M'med?"

"Memsahib is in the garden," he said. "I will take you to her."

"Don't bother. I'll find her. I know this garden very well," said Baby.

Ben's wife Dee – real name Deborah, but, like Baby, only ever addressed by the name her family and friends had christened her with – was lying in a homemade hammock constructed out of a threadbare old rug and strung perilously between two neem trees by lengths of fraying rope. All Baby could see of her were bare brown legs propped up above her head and long-fingered, elegant hands holding up a thick, hardbacked book. Another book was lying on the grass beneath the hammock.

Baby walked soundlessly across the spongy grass – so they were still watering Charlie's garden morning and evening she was glad to see – and coughed to alert the girl to her approach.

Dee dropped the book and almost fell out of the hammock. Alarmed she stared at the approaching figure before she recognised the visitor. "Baby!" she cried, "When did you get back? You're looking great. You've had your hair cut, haven't you?"

"Yes. I went to Harrods."

A yearning look crossed Dee's face. Unlike Baby she was not

good at hiding her feelings. "Harrods! London! What's it like these days?" In fact Dee had never set foot in Harrods but, like so many other things and places which she had read about in her constant devouring of books, she felt she knew it well.

"Very busy. Lots of people. London's full of dozens of new shops. There's lovely things to buy . . ."

"God, what fun!" said Dee enviously. Any mention of home started her on a train of melancholy thoughts which she had to strictly control.

"How's life with you?" asked Baby cautiously. When Ben came back from leave with a wife he'd only known for six weeks before they married, his co-tenants in the bungalow had been variously amazed, apprehensive and disapproving. Guy, the third tenant, a small, rotund sybarite whose only aim in life was to enjoy himself round the clock and do as little work as possible, had been particularly enraged. His world of male matiness was threatened.

"Bloody fool," he said when Ben's telegram announcing his marriage arrived. "Bloody fool! If he'd stayed single we could have afforded to build a swimming pool in the garden!"

Charlie's doubts about the marriage were more measured, especially after he met Dee.

"I don't see it lasting," he told Baby when they talked about it, "She's very different to Ben, quite academic really – got a university degree apparently. Do you know any other woman in our set with a university degree?"

Baby shook her head. She couldn't boast a female degree holder in her whole acquaintance in India or Europe. "What did she want to marry Ben for?" she asked in amazement.

"Well he's a good-looking bloke isn't he, very sexy, women tell me. And he's good fun, but wild. Maybe she likes living dangerously."

"And he's broke," said Baby who had enough of her father in her to have more than a mild respect for money. "I've heard he's on his last chance with his company. If he doesn't pull in some business soon, he'll be out on his ear. He works for Marwaris and you know how tough they can be – and they always pay the smallest salaries."

So when she asked Dee how things were going now after a year of marriage and living in the Gulmohurs, her tone was deliberately neutral.

"*Comme ci, comme ça,*" said Dee, "Sometimes more *ci* than *ça,* though. We're so bloody hard up we can hardly afford to eat. Last week Mohammed lent us five rupees to go to the cinema because he wanted us out of the house so's that he could entertain his friends in peace."

Baby laughed. She'd forgotten Dee's way of sprinkling her conversation with swear words, a habit of which she seemed totally unconscious but which Baby found strangely endearing because it reminded her of her mother. "Mohammed can afford to give you five chips. He's been bleeding the boys for years," she said.

"I know. I'm watching the bugger and he knows it. We're fighting a secret war," Dee told her, "But sometimes I feel as if I'm in jail with an ever attentive jailer. There's no phone here and most of the time I've no car . . . and I've read all the books in the place that Charlie left behind. I'm reduced to Shakespeare and the Bible now but I'd prefer a few good novels."

"My father has quite a big library. You must come into town and take your pick," said Baby whose stomach had lurched in the old familiar way when Dee mentioned Charlie's name.

"Oh God, could I really? When?"

"Now if you like."

Dee, who was wearing white shorts and a faded red halterneck top, looked down at her bare brown legs and feet. "I can't come now. I'd have to tidy myself up for Bombay. And anyway I haven't the car so it would be difficult to get back. Ben's taken it up to Deolali to look at some factory site he's hoping to build on soon. I might be able to come tomorrow or the next day though . . ."

"Come to lunch then," said Baby, "and we'll pack up the back seat of your car with books. Father's got a complete set of Dickens and another of Scott. I don't think he's ever opened one of them . . . He's got lots of poetry too."

Dee clasped her hands, eyes shining, almost looking like the bright and pretty girl she'd been when she first got off the plane at Santa Cruz airport twelve months before. When they'd met each other by the hammock, Baby hadn't been able to say that her friend too looked well, because she didn't. She'd lost weight and seemed jaded, her hair was long and straggling and the bright brown sheen it used to have was gone.

"Oooh lovely – Dickens and poetry. I'm not so keen on Scott though I'm Scottish. I think he's an old windbag. Your father hasn't any Jane Austen, has he? I always like to read her if I'm feeling ill," she said, taking Baby's arm.

"Are you ill?"

"No, no, of course not. But Jane would be like a mental first-aid kit for me in case I *get* ill . . . I'm just damned bored and lonely, I suppose. I've been trying to write a book myself but I can't get it right somehow. I'm sublimating my disappointment by reading other people's. It's so bloody frustrating. There's no one here except the servants all day long. I'm pleased to see you Baby. You must stay for lunch. Don't go away too soon. I don't think we've any gin – but I can offer you one of Mohammed's famous lime waters. The best in Bombay, according to Guy. I sometimes think lots of Ben and Guy's friends come out here to kowtow to Mohammed rather than see them." She didn't say 'us' Baby noticed.

"Guy's away right now – for how much longer?" asked Baby.

"They told him at the hospital about three months . . . three whole months without Guy." Dee didn't sound sorry. Then she added in a different tone of voice, "Did you go to the wedding, Baby? Guy was determined to attend it even if he had to go on a stretcher."

Baby was staring ahead at the bungalow verandah where Mohammed stood with a tray in his hand, the absolute model of a perfect bearer, "Yes, I heard he went. Winks and Mags hired a car and took him. I wasn't there though . . ." she said quietly.

"Of course you didn't go. How could I be so crass! I'm sorry, Baby."

"Don't be. I've put the whole thing out of my mind. There's no point hankering after what you can't have. I'm planning to have a great summer, Dee, and when the rains come I might take a trip to Australia because it'll be their winter then. I've never been there and my father says I should go. He's got some business interests in Canberra and I might drop in on them for him."

"That's a good idea," said Dee, "Have a glass of Mohammed's special. At least it's nice and cold even if it isn't alcoholic."

They ate mince and spaghetti, one portion stretched out to serve two, and a fruit salad of bananas and papayas from the trees in the bungalow garden. Then they climbed the narrow twisting stair to the first floor verandah and the long room that had been Charlie's and was now a sitting room.

Baby paused in the doorway, remembering the many days and nights she'd spent there, especially remembering the agony of longing for Charlie to take her in his arms as they sat together on the long settee that took up most of the floor and on which he used to sleep. He was the only person she knew who was unaffected by mosquito bites, who kept all his windows wide open to the mysterious night and slept without a net, sometimes even pulling his bed out into the open on the verandah so that he could watch the spangled heavens above his head.

They'd shared such wonderful, velvet-black nights when the sky was studded with stars like diamonds, with Nat King Cole singing on the record player and the air heavy with the smell of jasmine. Baby had been absolutely, completely, insanely in love – the first time in her life that she'd felt entirely free and light-hearted – and it hurt like a stab in the guts to remember the joy of it.

Her only consolation was that he'd loved her too – at least for a while – she was sure of it.

Sick with longing for him, she walked over the marble tiled floor and lay down on his settee with her face against the high back.

"Careful," said Dee, standing beside it, "There's a nest of rats in that now. I heard the buggers scrabbling away the other day when I was up here reading."

"I'm not afraid of rats," said Baby, lying down with her cheek still against the prickly red material that covered the settee, "At least not little furry ones."

Dee laughed. "Neither am I, but I'm scared of big ones like Mohammed – and Guy."

"Have they been giving you a lot of trouble?" asked Baby from her prone position.

"A bit. Mohammed's working on me, trying to get me on his side. The other day he confided to me that he was ordered by Guy to tell me that a taxi had arrived for me the first morning after I arrived here . . . that's what he used to do when Ben and Guy brought tarts back here with them, called a taxi to take them home in the morning. I didn't understand what he was getting at at first . . ."

Baby sat up abruptly. "That's awful!"

"He made it sound as if he was confiding in me, making it look as if he was on my side but he was really spreading poison, you see. He's as bad as Guy. The pair of them want me to quit and go home – or die – or disappear – in any way it can be arranged."

"Charlie always thought Guy's a bit infatuated with Ben," said Baby carefully.

Dee nodded, "I know. I think the same. He's like a jealous woman really, but Ben just sails on impervious. When I say anything about it to him he's horrified. Really, Baby, I sometimes think it would be best for everyone if I did go home. I don't think even Ben would miss me all that much . . ." The words she didn't mean to utter poured out of her. She'd been welling them up for so long.

"Don't give Guy and Mohammed the satisfaction," said Baby

sharply, recognising the other girl's misery, but Dee recovered and laughed, making light of everything again. "That's one of the things that's keeping me here. Bloody-mindedness! No, really, I'm only joking. Ben and I'll be all right now that we are on our own with time to get to know each other. We were really strangers when we got married, you see, we'd only known each other for a few weeks. We rushed into it. It takes time to settle down. And everything's so strange for me . . . sorry to bend your ear with this. I'm only having a moan and it's not at all serious! *We're in love with each other.* We'll be OK." The words were vehement.

"If you love him, stick it out," said Baby. To her, at that moment, love was the most important thing in the world.

Dee got up from the other end of the settee and walked across the room to a range of wooden bookcases that stood below a big arched window that overlooked the green sea of the pomelo trees and a dry river bed that divided the Gulmohurs garden from the farm boundary.

She stared out in silence for a few moments and then she said, "When I was looking through Charlie's books, I found something belonging to you Baby. I wouldn't have opened it if I'd known it was private . . . I'm sorry. But I didn't show it to Ben and I've kept it for you."

"That's what I came out to collect," said Baby bleakly, "Charlie sent me a note saying he'd left it here. He didn't want to take it home with him, in case his wife found it, I expect. He wrote to tell me where it was and said I was to come and get it."

"And he didn't want to burn it either," said Dee gently. "Don't worry Baby, I haven't read it but I could see that it was treasured."

She was pulling paperback books out of the shelf. "I only found it because I've read my way through the books one after the other. It would have been perfectly safe if Ben and Guy were living here on their own – neither of them ever read anything except *Time* magazine. He stuck it behind *King's Row* and *Peyton Place*. I don't expect he thought I'd read them but when you're desperate you'll read anything. I quite enjoyed them actually."

She came back across the floor with a cardboard box file in her hands and laid it on the sofa top beside Baby, who touched it gently with her finger tips.

"What's in it?" she asked.

"His memories, I think," said Dee. "Look, I'm going downstairs to have a sleep and a shower. You stay up here and look through the box. Leave whenever you like, and don't let me know you're going if you don't want to."

"All right. But I meant it about lending you some of my father's books. It'll be nice for them to have someone reading their pages after all those years. Come to lunch on Friday and meet my parents."

She wept heart-brokenly when she opened the box. Charlie had kept a collection of photographs, dance cards, show programmes, road maps, pages out of guide books, newspaper and magazine cuttings, all relating to her or to places they'd visited or events they had attended together. But most important of all, he'd also kept her letters, the outpourings of love she'd sent him when she was trying to stop him leaving her and going home.

'I love you, love you, adore you. I'd go anywhere with you,' she'd written in the middle of one miserable night when she couldn't sleep. 'We don't ever have to go back to England if you don't want to. Let's go to Australia or Japan or America – we could go anywhere and be happy, just the two of us.'

It was true. They could have been happy together in Antarctica or Timbuktu. They liked the same things, laughed at the same things, had the same reactions to other people. They were never tired of each other, never at a loss for something to say, and sometimes one would even start talking about a subject that the other had been silently mulling over in their mind – like telepathy, Charlie said.

He'd loved her. She knew that when she saw the care he'd taken to preserve the fragments of their time together – two years all told before he went away for good six months ago. He'd inscribed the back of each photograph with her name, the place, the date and the occasion. 'Baby in her blue dress at the Boat Club party, 1958' . . . 'Baby at Guy's birthday on Marvi Beach, October 1958' . . . 'My pretty Baby in a big straw hat, December 1956' . . . That was when their affair began really, on the day he and she found this bungalow when they'd gone exploring the country outwith the city one cool winter Sunday.

They'd wandered around the overgrown garden, watching out for snakes; walked through dusty rooms and had then gone over the road to the neighbours to find out who owned it and whether it was for rent. Miraculously it was and the owner was an old Englishman and his Indian wife who had retired to Madras and were only too delighted to get English tenants. A month later Charlie and his two friends were installed and set about transforming the place.

She wept even more when she found the last letter she'd sent him. As she always was with Charlie, she'd been totally frank and open, not afraid of revealing herself.

'You can't leave me now. Not after last night. You can't go away and marry someone else when we have been so much to each other . . . My whole body aches for you and I know you are aching for me too. You are really my lover now and every time I see a sky full of stars I will remember you.'

They'd made love the previous night, after wanting to for so long. She kissed him and held his head to her bare breasts, smoothing his hair and telling him how much she loved him. She'd lain on the settee and pulled him down beside her . . . Baby's hand stroked the red cushions as she remembered . . .

"I can't," he said, "I can't, darling. I've got to go home and marry Isobel."

"I don't care," she lied. "Just lie down here and let me lie beside you. Look at the stars. Isn't the sky black tonight? I wonder how many people are lying like this all over the world under these stars, loving each other . . ."

In spite of his scruples, he made love to her then and it was the most wonderful, most longed for thing that had ever happened to her. Their bodies had fitted together so beautifully, as if they were designed for each other. When she went home in the cool dawn she was triumphant, sure that now he was hers forever. But that was not to be. A week later he went home to marry his fiancée.

When he told her, said he must go, she'd retreated into her self-protective mode and pretended to be far more sophisticated than she actually was, "Of course you must go. I understand. Of course I don't hate you. Why should I? What happened was as much my fault as yours. I'll put it down to experience. I had to lose it sometime. You did me a favour."

But in the box he'd kept a brittle brown sprig of white jasmine that he'd pulled from a bush in the garden and stuck in her hair that only night they made love. He'd pressed it carefully in the middle of a notebook and written beneath it . . . 'Memories'.

Six

When she heard Baby's car driving away from the bungalow Dee Carmichael was sitting in front of her bedroom mirror chopping off her long hair with a pair of blunt nail scissors. She was always extremely sensitive to other people's reactions and, though Baby's surprise when meeting her again had only been momentary, she instantaneously realised that the way she looked had caused it. Leaving Baby upstairs weeping over her box of memories, she'd gone down to the bedroom she shared with her husband Ben and, in misery, stared at herself in the mirror for a long time.

"Poor bloody women, we have a hard time, don't we? And you're a mess. You look completely wrecked," she said aloud to her reflection.

A year in Bombay had wrecked her.

No, that wasn't fair, a year of marriage had wrecked her. In fact she loved Bombay, what she'd seen of it, though she didn't exactly love the European society there. She couldn't understand how it was that so many of the white people she'd met hadn't yet realised – twelve years after Independence – that the British no longer ruled the subcontinent. Some of the Indians were almost as bad. She hated it when Indians tried to ingratiate themselves with her by saying they wished British rule, the Raj, was back, and it always embarrassed her when a queue opened up and people insisted on her going to the head of it – just because she was white.

She liked Baby and she'd liked Charlie, however, but she'd never felt comfortable with most of Ben's friends. Nearly all of the men he knew were hearty but brainless rugby players; and the women were their enthusiastic supporters who stood round the piano at the parties that took place every weekend, singing chauvinistic songs. These songs revolted her because they were full of not very subtle innuendoes about 'arseholes', 'cats on the rooftops' and 'jolly old monks called Roger' or mill wheels that 'went in and out, in and out'. Women were only seen as sex objects, slabs of meat to be serviced. She infuriated Ben by telling him she thought rugby was a homosexual game.

Dee had not endeared herself to his friends either by asking some of the other wives, 'How can you join in with those horrible songs? Don't you realise they're demeaning to women, utterly demeaning!'

So she rapidly acquired the reputation of being odd, disapproving, po-faced and puritanical. 'Poor Ben,' said her husband's friends, 'he's landed himself with trouble there. And Ben's a good bloke, a real piss-artist too.'

Unknown to Dee there were a few other women in the crowd who shared her opinions, among them Joan, an American college girl with unfashionably long and straight blonde hair held back from her face with tortoiseshell grips. This girl sat alone in the Gym every morning reading English magazines and speaking to no one – like Dee, dismissing all the other wives as being of the same male-conniving kidney. Ben, who in a way admired her, pointed her out to Dee and said, 'She's pissed off because her husband is the randiest man in the club. He'd fuck a hole in the wall.'

Dee tried to speak to the American girl but was rebuffed. However she felt a deep affinity with her. They were the odd women out. On the surface Dee was not so obviously disaffected as Joan. Through Ben she had lots of acquaintances – but she was really happiest alone, lying in her home-made hammock in the Gulmohurs' garden and reading, devouring words on paper like someone suffering from acute starvation. Frustrated in her efforts to write her own novel, and miserable because of it, she lived in the pages of other people's writings, existing in imaginery worlds, buttressed by them from reality. Books and the characters she met in them were more real to her than the actual world in which she moved and she could understand them far better.

In a way she'd always lived like that, for books were her most precious possessions and had always been so. She'd started losing herself in them as soon as she was able to work out what letters meant for she'd had an unhappy childhood, used as a weapon by fiercely fighting, mismatched parents, each of whom tried to enlist her on their side.

They would never separate or divorce, but stay together relentlessly eating each other away. She almost preferred it when they were at war because when they were in a truce situation, they turned their ferocious attention to their children, particularly her mother who concentrated her venom on her daughter, the father's favourite.

The only people she felt safe with, the only people she could trust to be consistent, were the ones she met in fiction. From them she learned how people could behave in ideal situations – or at least in consistent situations.

That was why Baby's promise to lend her books was the most cheering thing that had happened to her for months. While she read she'd be able to put off thinking about her situation.

When she wasn't reading, she wrote letters to her friends at home, mostly to people she'd worked with on a big newspaper in Edinburgh where she had been a very happy news reporter. Unconsciously she must have been communicating some of her unacknowledged misery in the letters, although her intention was always to be bright and cheerful, to tell about the funny and strange things that happened to her in India, but recently Andrew, one of her correspondents, had written back saying, 'You sound very unhappy. Why don't you come home? You'd easily get your old job back again here . . .'

When she'd read his letter she was genuinely shocked at the inference he'd taken from what she'd written to him. What could she have said to make him think like that? Then she asked herself, Maybe he's right. Why don't I go home?

So she sat down and made a list of the reasons why she had to stay.

First of all, though she didn't look it, she was actually very combative and didn't want to give Guy and Mohammed the satisfaction of having driven her out. They were not to be allowed to win against her.

Secondly, she loved Ben and took the vows of marriage very seriously. At least she thought she did, though sometimes she wondered why she'd married him on such a short acquaintance. They were having to get to know each other now they were legally tied together but what she'd told Baby was true on the whole – she was liking what she found out and hoped he was doing the same. They were slowly finding out about each other, little bit by little bit, through midnight conversations as they lay side by side in bed, sweaty after sex.

If she was honest however, she had to admit that the bond that tied them together was sex. They were both highly charged sexually and making love twice or three times every day was, like her obsessive reading of books, a way of preventing either reflecting too much on other aspects of their marriage, it helped them ignore how very different they were. She also had to ignore her misgivings that the man she'd married had an incredible roving eye. At parties she suffered agonies of concealed jealousy at Ben's flirting.

Things can only get better, she told herself. She really loved Ben, who was trying to work harder for his company and get himself into a position where he could ask for a salary raise, because one of the big problems they had, a problem that she was unable to talk about to him for he dodged away from it every time she brought it up, was their total lack of money.

Most companies increased an employee's salary when he married but his did not because, they said, he had married without their consent, and he had been walking a very thin line between acceptance and being fired anyway.

So Dee and Ben were scraping by on what was called 'a bachelor's salary' which did not meet their fixed outgoings every month. To add to this anxiety, soon after she arrived in Bombay she discovered that she had married a man with a burden of debt round his neck – Ben owed money to his tailor, to the petrol station that filled up his car with petrol, and to the big grocery store in Crawford Market that supplied his food – thousands of rupees in all when his salary was only two thousand a month.

Worse than that, now that he shared the Gulmohurs with only Guy, since Charlie had gone home for good, Ben's expenses had doubled. All the furniture in the bungalow, and half of the car, belonged to Guy whose company provided far more generously for him. When he married, Ben literally owned nothing except what he stood up in and they were unable to look for another place to live because they would not be able to furnish it even if they could afford the rent.

It also seemed ludicrous to Dee that they, totally penniless, were maintaining a staff of five people – a cook, a bearer, an under bearer and a gardener, plus a man who did nothing except wash out the lavatories twice a day. He at least was shared with the other two bungalows that clung to the side of the jungle-covered hill. Though she'd never done any cooking in her life, she offered to take the place of Pasco, the cook, but Ben and Guy were horrified at the very idea.

Guy, a very upper-crust English ex-public-schoolboy, had said, 'My God, we'd never get a decent servant to work for us if you set foot in the kitchen. Talk to her, Ben, for God's sake!' When he went home to London on sick leave he told Ben that he would continue sharing the bungalow and its costs in future, providing everything remained the same when he came back. Especially the staff.

Dee had made enquiries about getting a job but the only employment possibility for a white woman in Bombay was as a clerk in the offices of the British Deputy High Commission, and even if she did get taken on there, which was unlikely, for, like many reporters, her typing was strictly of the two-finger variety and her shorthand of her own invention, she needed a car for they lived too far away to travel by bus or train. The wages were too minuscule to cover the cost of transport. To bridge the gap between their outgoings and their income, she had begun selling her possessions, her gold watch, her camera, and next to go would have to be her typewriter, the journalist's most valued asset.

This catalogue of troubles had to be kept to herself. Though Dee came from well-off parents, there was no possibility of asking them for help because her father had warned her that she was making a mistake by marrying Ben – "He's a waster," he'd warned. "You'll be back here penniless, with your tail between your legs, within a year."

So she couldn't go home and admit that he was right and she was wrong. In a way, she had been forced into the marriage by the violence of her family's reaction to Ben who they disliked on sight. There had been a tremendous family row when she told her parents she was going to marry him.

"What about the doctor?" asked her father incredulously when she introduced him to this new boyfriend. At university Dee had met a medical student who was devoted to her and who her parents thought she ought to marry because doctors held great social status in Scottish middle-class families. But Dee hadn't loved him, though she liked and admired him. Most of all, she didn't want to go to bed with him. When she met Ben she wanted nothing else.

When she persisted with the idea of marrying Ben and going to India, her father pulled out all stops to prevent the marriage, even putting private detectives onto Ben in the hope of finding something damaging about him. The worst they could come up with was that he was penniless, but Dee knew that already and so she was deaf to her father's charge that Ben was marrying her for her money.

"I haven't got any money," she said.

"But I have. He's after my money. But you can tell him I've cut you out of my will and you won't get a penny."

"I don't care. I don't want your money and neither does he." She really meant that too, but now, looking back, she realised it was easy to be cavalier about money when you've always had it.

She was twenty-four years old when she married, so her father couldn't forbid it, but he and her mother subjected Dee to such a vicious campaign of harrassment and accusation that it almost broke her nerve and she was unable to talk about it, even to Ben, without breaking down in tears. It had ended with her being thrown out of her parents' home in the middle of the night, for, though she longed to be free, it was not done for young girls at that time, even girls earning good salaries, to live away from the family home until they married.

When she moved out, she took a room in a small private hotel in the middle of Edinburgh and a week later married Ben, without any of her family attending the ceremony. On the night before her wedding, she lay sleepless on the hotel bed, with a book of course – Surtees' *Mr Sponge's Sporting Tour*, chosen because in her youth she'd been an enthusiastic follower of hounds – and a half bottle of whisky, a drink she loathed, to bring on unconsciousness. It worked.

She was thinking about fox hunting and Surtees while she cut off her hair, chopping away at the long strands which fell in thick, dark-brown heaps onto the top of the dressing table – a dressing table that belonged to Guy, she reflected bitterly. She remembered past winters when her hair was long and she used to coil it up and tuck it into a thick-meshed snood when she went hunting.

Tears came into her eyes at the memory. Would she ever ride a horse again? As she savagely chopped at the long strands it seemed like she was looking back on someone else's life.

By the time she'd reduced the hair to the level of a respectable bob, a strange sort of madness seized her and, like a criminal carried away by the adrenalin of stealing, she went on cutting, turning her head to and fro to look at the back of her head, staring at her profile as if at a stranger. She was slightly Jewish-looking, although her eyes were large and blue, but she had high, give-away Slavic cheekbones, a prominent straight nose, a very determined chin and full, sensuous lips – a peasant face, as a drunken woman at a Bombay party had recently told her.

'That's because I am a peasant, from solid peasant stock,' retorted Dee, a confirmed Socialist, another thing that made her unusual in Bombay's European society.

By the time the peasant stood up from the dressing table and shook the last strands of hair off her shoulders onto the floor, she'd been transformed into a skinny schoolboy. Cutting her hair was a very significant gesture of independence though she didn't really know why she'd done it.

She'd been born with poker-straight brown hair and when she was small her mother tortured her every night by screwing her tresses up in long strips of cloth in an effort to make her look like Shirley Temple. The Temple effect only ever lasted for a couple of hours however and she was such a grave disappointment in the tonsorial department that by the time she was nine or ten her mother had given up trying to beautify her ugly duckling daughter.

For her fifteenth birthday her father paid for her first perm and she'd worn her hair the same way ever since – cut just below the ears, swept back from the face and crimped in what were meant to be winsome curls, Hollywood style. Photographs of girls with identical hair styles beamed out from the pages of the *Women's Home Companion*, an American magazine that Dee's mother devoured whenever she could get her hands on a copy.

Longing to please, anxious to conform, agonised by her own shortcomings, Dee wanted to be like those models with the same hair style, same penny loafer shoes, same gleaming teeth and virginal-looking frilly dresses. They were all so clean, so good, so wholesome, like the girl in the popular song, 'The girl that I marry will have to be as pure and as sweet as a nurser-ee, the girl I'll call my own, will wear satins and laces and smell of cologne!'

In spite of the perm however Dee could never reach their unattainable limits because she preferred wearing jodhpurs or khaki ex-army trousers and suspected that she smelt more of straw and saddle soap than 'cologne'.

She knew she was a disappointment to her parents, for every nine months or so, her father would look at her in despair, reach into his pocket, pull out a five pound note and say, 'Go and have another perm!'

She always did as she was told, intimidated by her remotely beautiful mother whose hair was regularly permed and never allowed to grow into any shape that looked remotely natural.

So perms, and the suffering entailed in having one, became associated in Dee's mind with a woman's duty – like childbirth perhaps. Only girls with perms would ever catch a boy's eye.

But that winter when she was seventeen she thought she'd try growing her hair. She liked it long, straight and glittering; she liked coiling it into a bun and sticking it into the black net snood when she went hunting. It felt good nestling soft against the back of her neck, not prickling and curly like wire wool.

But one day, riding back from the meet, her illusions were

shattered by Hughie, the groom who practically brought up Dee and her brother because they spent more time in the stables at the back of their father's hotel than they ever did with their parents and hung on Hughie's every word as if it was Holy Gospel.

"It's the Hunt Ball next month," said Hughie turning in his saddle to look sorrowfully at her. "Has anybody asked you?"

She shook her head. She knew it was Hughie's ambition for her to mix with 'the nobs' but, like in so many things, she was a woeful failure in that department. Few 'nobs' even addressed a 'Good morning' to her, the daughter of a man who kept a pub, and she was certain none of them would ever ask her to the ball even if she looked like Doris Day, Hughie's latest heroine who had taken him by storm in her film *Calamity Jane*.

Hughie sighed. "Somebody'd ask you to the Ball if you got a perm!" said he. So once again, for his sake, she submitted herself to ordeal by curlers and chemicals but nobody asked her to the Hunt Ball, that year or any other. What a failure she felt.

She remembered all this as she stood under the shower for half an hour, soaping herself and her shorn head. It was nearly six o'clock when she stepped onto the verandah to stare down Mohammed's astonished expression and watch the sun slowly sink behind the palm trees at the end of the garden. Two huge, bald-headed vultures roosted in those trees and when she'd first arrived she'd been afraid to sunbathe on the open grass because of them for she was sure they'd think she was dead and try to peck the flesh off her bones if she lay down. Now she knew that vultures had other ways of discerning death than mere stillness.

So she dragged a chair out onto the middle of the lawn and sat in it, defying them. Just try it, she thought, staring at their hunched outlines. In a way they represented all the problems that haunted her.

She was still sitting there when Ben arrived home and came bouncing across the grass with his hen-toed walk. As he bent down to kiss her, he stopped.

"Hey! What've you done?" he asked.

She glared up at him. "I cut my hair."

He stood up straight and tried to smile. "It's – nice. It'll be much cooler anyway."

She didn't ask if he liked the new hair cut. "I like it," she said defiantly, consigning Hughie, her parents and all those bloody perms to the past. She didn't care if nobody except her liked the new crop; she didn't care if the gossiping women at the rugby club parties did double takes – as she knew they would. She'd brazen it out.

43

Seven

"How's things these days?" asked Bob while he bustled about the office, putting his papers in boxes and throwing other bits and pieces out in preparation for his departure.

"Good, much better, thanks Bob," said Dennis who was poring over a pink covered file at his desk beneath the window.

"You're looking fit," said Bob, chucking a framed photograph of his family into an open cardboard box.

"I go swimming almost every afternoon at Breach Candy. It's a great pool."

"Lots of good-looking women too," said Bob. "And talking of good-looking women, how's Carole?"

"Great, great. We went to the cinema again last night. Saw *One Hundred and One Dalmatians*. She loved it."

"Bedded her yet?"

Dennis looked up, slightly shocked. "She's just a kid, Bob. And I'm not serious about her."

"For God's sake Den, what's serious? She'll think there's something wrong with you. She'll expect it. Do her a favour, and yourself as well."

Dennis changed the subject. "When are you off, Bob?"

"Day after tomorrow. You can move into the flat that night. I've told Govind, the bearer, to stay. He's a decent old stick and fairly honest, you should keep him on."

"Are you sorry to be going?"

Bob straightened up and laughed, "You must be joking. I can't wait. I've done two and a half years and that's approximately twenty-nine months too long." This was not what Bob had previously told Dennis but the discrepancy didn't seem to bother him.

"What about Monica?" asked the junior man.

"What about her?"

"Will you miss her?"

"Yeah, suppose I will. She's a good lay, better than the wife anyway, but I won't have to stay at home long. I've put in for

44

another posting. I'm hoping to get sent to London and there's lots of pretty girls there."

"Does Monica know you're going?"

"She knows I'm not here forever but she doesn't know exactly when I'm off."

"Don't you think you ought to tell her?"

"Come on, Den, she's a tart. It's a job for her. I'll leave her a bit of cash and she'll move on to somebody else. Sharpen up. That's the way things work out here."

When Bob went bustling about, Dennis folded his arms behind his head and leaned back in his chair, staring out of the window at a segment of unnervingly blue sky that showed above the rooftops in front of him. Work seemed unimportant when that sky beckoned.

I'll go to Breach Candy at half past four and see if the girls are there. Then, tonight, I'll drive out to Chembur and pick up Carole, he thought.

From feeling totally isolated in a strange city, as alone as a man on the moon, Dennis's life had undergone a transformation, almost too much of one in fact. The girls he'd met at Breach Candy had proved very friendly, always beckoning him over to join their party if they were swimming at the same time as him but he was too much in awe of them to ever suggest that they meet away from the pool. Their talk was of parties they attended but none of them ever suggested that he might be included in this social circle. Being so carelessly excluded would have made him feel even more lonely if he hadn't met Carole but she was almost as much as he could cope with at one time. Sometimes he was afraid that she was going to take him over, she was so possessive, hanging onto his arm when they went to the cinema, sitting with her head on his shoulder in the flickering darkness and talking continually about marriage, his parents and what life was like in Australia. She was distinctly unsubtle and that was the real reason he'd fought off going to bed with her though he was acutely conscious of her physical charms.

He had a car now, a little Fiat that nipped in and out of the traffic with satisfying niftiness and on the stroke of four thirty, he ran down the High Commission stairs and into the car which was parked close by, round the corner. The air inside it was stifling when he opened the door and the steering wheel was so hot that he couldn't hold it in his bare hands so he wrapped handkerchiefs round it and steered tentatively into the traffic.

Breach Candy pool was packed with people because it had been a very hot day. He paused at the entrance and stared across at the girls' corner. The three of them were there – Winks, Mags and Baby.

Mags was a sexy little piece but spoiled; Winks was friendly and pleasant but plain; Baby was cool, distant and alluring. Brown-haired Baby was the one he really lusted after but she, most of all, terrified and intimidated him and he was sure she'd never look twice at him.

They were watching for his arrival and Winks sat up waving her thin arms in his direction. Mags and Baby only stared expressionlessly at him through the black lenses of their sunglasses. He waved back and walked in their direction with his towel carelessly draped over his broad brown shoulders and his new tight black swimming trunks emphasising his maleness. He didn't know that all three were watching him with breathless admiration.

They swam, they chatted, they drank Cokes and ate sandwiches and Dennis told them that he was on the verge of moving into his new flat. "Day after tomorrow in fact," he said carelessly though he was feeling intense excitement at the very idea.

"You'll have to throw a moving-in party," said Mags.

This had never occurred to him but now he said, "Of course I will. Would you come?"

"Of course," they chorused.

He became very bold. "Then you're all invited. Next Friday at seven o'clock. Bring anybody you like because I don't know a soul to ask. I'll give you the address before I go."

Baby smiled at him and said, "What a dangerous thing to say, bring anybody . . . you don't know who you're going to end up with."

"I don't care," said Dennis boldly. "It's a big flat. I've loads of beer and the more the merrier."

Mags patted his arm, "We'll make sure you meet the crowd, Dennis. They never have enough beer, believe me."

When they parted he didn't go back to his boarding house but drove on to Chembur to find Carole.

At the top of the side road that led down to the bungalow, he saw a girl walking alone in front of him. She was striding along in the middle of the road and he would have had to toot his horn to warn her to step aside if he was to pass. As he drew nearer he realised the girl was Carole's awkward sister Amy. He gave the horn a little push making it erupt with a strangulated cough and then he leaned over, opening the passenger door to offer her a lift. He was holding the door wide when she stalked over to it, bent down and stared in at him, her sharp eyes hostile.

"What do you want?" she asked. She looked tired and dusty, as unlike the bandbox-trim Carole as it was possible to be.

"I'm offering you a lift home," he said.

"I don't want it," she said straightening up. "I'm almost there anyway and I'm not for picking up, not like my sister or my mother."

"I wasn't trying to pick you up. I just thought you looked tired . . ."

"I am tired. And fed up. You'd be the same if you had to fight your way home from the Fort in that packed train every night. On you go, my sister'll be waiting for you. She'll have been sweating over a hot dressing table all day!"

He stared at her slightly puzzled. Had she been making a joke? But her expression was fierce and her brows drawn down like someone who wanted a fight so he took the line of least resistance, sat back, switched on the ignition again, for the engine had conked out when he braked, and drove away, warily watching her out of his driving mirror as he went.

Carole and her mother had obviously been watching for him though he'd made no definite appointment to visit that night. As soon as his car stopped in the middle of the sun-baked square of red earth opposite their verandah, they appeared, neat as new pins and smiling ecstatically. In seconds the old servant woman also came out with a cold bottle of beer and he was seated in a cane chair enjoying it with Carole by his side.

She stroked his hand lovingly, "Where are we going tonight, darling?" she asked. He wished she wouldn't call him that, especially in front of her gimlet-eyed mother.

"I don't know. Where would you like to go?"

"I'd like to see that film again, the one about those dogs. They're so *cute!*"

His heart sank. Two doses of dalmatians in one week was almost too much for him, but she obviously wanted to see it again and he could always sleep through it. The swim at Breach Candy had tired him. "All right," he said, just as Amy appeared in the doorway.

"Humph," she snorted, looking at him.

Carole gave her a glare, "We're going to see the film about the dogs again," she told her sister triumphantly.

"About your level," said Amy sharply and withdrew into the kitchen, from which she did not re-emerge that evening.

They went to the late show and so it was one o'clock in the morning before he dropped her at her home again. They lingered in the car, kissing and petting, with her squeezing her beautiful body against him in a tantalising way. He remembered what Bob had said and wondered how far he dared go but something cautious in his make-up stopped him, though on the long drive back to the city he knew he would castigate himself for being a fool.

After a last long and lingering kiss, she drew back a little and asked him, "When does Bob go?"

She's asking on Monica's behalf, he thought. "I'm not sure," he lied.

"Monica says it's in two days' time. She says you'll move into his flat when he goes."

So Monica knew after all. "Yes, I will. I'll be glad to get out of that boarding house," he said.

"Then I'll be able to come and stay with you," Carole whispered, resting her head on his chest, "We'll be able to go to bed together then."

"I won't be moving into the flat till next week," stammered Dennis, who was utterly confused and afraid that he was being rushed into something he couldn't control.

"Then next week I'll be able to move in with you," said Carole.

How do I get out of this? he thought.

His new flat was in a curving, cream-painted 1930s block on Marine Parade, overlooking the bay. He'd been in the flat once when Bob was living there but had not paid much attention to it. Now that it was his however he was filled with pride of possession and stood on the long third-floor verandah overlooking the sea, watching the gloriously technicoloured Indian sunset with his heart full of expectation of happy days to come.

There were some slightly unravelled cane chairs on the verandah, and behind him was a large, well-furnished sitting room; two bedrooms with their own bathrooms; a kitchen; a servant's room and a back entrance as well as a polished teak front door with his card inserted into a brass card holder on it – his personal domain. He planned to invite his parents to fly out on a visit. His mother would be impressed by his new home though he wasn't too sure how she'd take to surrendering management of the establishment to a servant, the bearer Govind that Bob had bequeathed to him.

Govind, a thin old chap with a faint grey stubble on his brown cheeks, was now advancing solemnly on Dennis and offering him a tumbler of whisky and soda.

"Thanks," said Dennis, not knowing you weren't meant to thank your bearer for doing his job. "I've – er – I've invited a few people over for drinks tomorrow night." He sounded apologetic for making trouble and work for Govind.

"How many people? Will they be staying for dinner?" asked Govind calmly.

"I'm not sure how many . . . ten, fifteen . . . sandwiches perhaps?" suggested Dennis.

"I'll tell the cook," said Govind. Till then Dennis didn't even know he had a cook.

At least there wasn't any worry about booze. He had plenty of that and on the morning of the party he was told by Govind that he was going to pile four dozen bottles of beer in the spare room bathtub and put blocks of ice in beside it to keep it cool.

"Good idea," said Dennis. His only worry now was whether the girls would remember to come to his party.

Eight

A t seven o'clock on Friday morning Dee and Ben Carmichael drove out of the Gulmohurs and bumped down the lane to the main road into Bombay.

Their car, which Ben co-owned with Guy, was a 1948 grey Studebaker, solid as a tank, and dull of paint now but sturdy and threatening on the road. It would be a brave taxi driver that dared to bump it with his wing for he'd be sure to come off worst. Because it was so old it had begun to develop some peculiar traits, rather like a grumpy pensioner.

The one Dee found most distressing was when the horn suddenly decided to go off and could not be stopped. This usually happened when she was driving on her own in the middle of a thick traffic jam; she had to get out, open the heavy bonnet and pull out the electric wires that ran to the horn mechanism.

Its other peculiarity was suddenly to lose all headlight power, which could be even more unnerving on unlit roads.

The car had originally belonged to Guy but when his company upgraded him to a new Ambassador, which was technically meant to be used only for business purposes and not for pleasure outings, he sold half of the Studebaker to Ben whose company would not provide him with any transport. Ben was paying it off at so much a month – another drain on their resources that Dee had only recently found out about.

She loved the characterful old car though. Sitting up on the leather bench-seat behind its ivory-coloured steering wheel, she felt as if she was in charge of a bus. It had a very distinctive number plate – BMZ420X – and the first time she ventured with the car into the crowded back streets near Crawford Market, she was surprised by the excitement it caused. Little boys jumped up and down, giggling and pointing. "Char so bis wallah, char so bis wallah," they shouted at her.

"What's char so bis?" she asked Ben when she met him in the

Gymkhana club that night. She already knew that 'wallah' meant 'fellow' or 'person'.

"Oh, Hindi for four twenty – the number of the car. I forgot to tell you about that. Have people been shouting at you? You shouldn't mind. They do it all the time."

"Why?"

"Well there was a film a couple of years ago, a big hit made by our next door neighbour, Bombay's biggest star, Raj Kapoor. Its title was *The Four Twenty Man – Char So Bis Wallah*. You see 420's the number of the article of the local criminal code that petty thieves are charged under."

She laughed, pleased to have a car that proclaimed itself to be a petty thief.

On the morning she was going to have lunch with Baby, Ben was driving, and he was the one that was doing the shouting of insults, every now and again sticking his blond head out of the open window and yelling at other drivers or people wandering aimlessly in the middle of the road. "Bloody fool. Half wit! Ulloo! . . ." he yelled.

She was used to his peculiarly aggressive driving habits by now, only saying occasionally, "Do calm down, Ben. You'll give yourself a heart attack." He didn't calm down of course and she didn't really expect him to. It was just how Ben behaved.

"It's because they don't get enough to eat – just rice – and their brains don't work properly," he told her swerving past a tall thin man in white who didn't seem to be aware how he was risking his life by stepping off the pavement into the path of the Studebaker.

She looked back at the man who had so narrowly escaped death and he seemed to be praying. "Maybe their minds are on other things," she suggested. "They're very civilised, very spiritual. Think of their culture, their art, their fascinating religion."

But Ben only snorted for he wasn't interested in things like that. "Meet you tonight in the Gym at half five," he told her when they drew up outside his office building at the end of Hornby Road. "Have we any units left?"

"I've got six but we haven't any money," she told him. The units he referred to were units of alcohol left on her drinking permit which had to be passed over and marked off every time they bought a bottle of beer or a glass of gin in one of the few government licensed bars of the city. They were grim places, those bars, with an armed guard at every door, usually a shambolical-looking soldier in crumpled khaki with a loaded rifle sloped against the wall by his side.

"Good," he said, "we'll go to the Ritz before we go home."

"We can't go to the Ritz, Ben. Didn't you hear what I said? We haven't any money."

"I'll sign a chit. Mario won't mind." Mario was the Italian proprietor of the Ritz hotel, a saturnine individual who'd seen many heavy-spending young men come and go.

"Mario will mind and we have to pay him sometime," said Dee firmly. She had no intention of going anywhere near the Ritz.

When she dropped him off at the office she drove to Crawford Market and left the car in the circular car park opposite the main gate. A squad of small boys who carried baskets for patrons of the stalls inside the market came rushing up the moment she opened the car door, but she always chose the same one, a tousled-headed, squint-eyed little chap of about eight whose ugliness endeared him to her.

He recognised the car. "I'm your boy, I'm your boy," he shouted as he ran towards her.

"Poor little bugger," she thought, "I wonder where his mother is and if she knows he's living on the streets like a lost dog."

For the first six months of her marriage she had not wanted to become pregnant. One of her mother's accusations against her was that she was marrying Ben because she was pregnant – 'You're a whore,' she'd shouted at her. 'We know why you're marrying him. It's because you're pregnant. You're nothing but a loose woman, an easy lay.' In fact she'd been a virgin on the day she married, chastity imposed on her not by virtue but by fear of conceiving and proving her mother right.

It had been important not to have a baby immediately so she could disprove the charge of licentiousness and babies had never appealed to her much anyway, but recently she'd been surprising herself by strange, unexplained longings. Catching sight of plump, spoiled Indian babies with black lines of kohl painted round their huge eyes, she'd felt a funny tugging at her heart and it struck her that if she had a child she would not be so lonely. Month after month however her period arrived with precise regularity and when she woke up to find herself bloodied between the legs, her heart sank. Perhaps she was never going to have a child at all. Maybe they should adopt one. What would Ben say if she decided to adopt the squint-eyed little beggar?

She was only going into the market to look around because she delighted in its lines of stalls piled high with fruit, vegetables and pulses. She loved watching the sellers weighing out purchases on brass weighing machines that they held high in the air with one hand, surreptitiously laying a finger on the loaded scoop if they thought the customer was too green to notice.

"What you want?" asked her eager escort, his eyes dancing. "Tell me and I get it for you cheap."

What he meant of course was that he would guide her to a stall holder who would give him something for directing a customer that way. She didn't mind.

"Oranges," she said.

"Only oranges?" he was disappointed.

"And some bananas maybe . . . and a couple of cans of Coke."

It wasn't much of an order but it was all she could afford. "Good, good," he said dancing along. "I get that for you cheap."

She passed a happy hour in the market, walking up and down the aisles, admiring the high-piled fruit and inhaling the scent of cleverly arranged flowers, especially the tightly packed pink rosebuds that had so beguiled her that she once bought a bunch of them and was disappointed to find that each rose head had been picked off its stem and stuck onto a little cane. Like the purple water hyacinths that she had also bought – only once – they were dead by nightfall.

When they finally returned to her car and the boy loaded her meagre purchases into the huge boot, she slammed the lid down and then asked him, "What's your name?"

He pointed at his chest and said proudly, "Jai."

"That's a nice name. Where is your home?"

His face seemed to close down. "Here, my home is here."

She didn't persist.

There was still some time to pass before her twelve-thirty invitation to Baby's, so she drove into the teeming area of narrow streets around a huge mosque at the back of the market. This was the Thieves' Bazaar, an area Mohammed had been horrified to hear she was in the habit of visiting.

"That is a bad place, memsahib," he warned her. "Men there steal white women. You should not go there alone."

But Dee was not afraid. She felt strangely invulnerable, almost invisible sometimes, and that gave her a defence against the outside world. Mohammed's warning made the Thieves' Bazaar even more attractive to her and she pushed the stubby bonnet of her car through close-packed crowds in its narrow alleyways, occasionally sounding the horn for them to make way for her. It did not matter if her progress was slow because that gave her time to watch the world outside, to look up at the tilting wooden houses with ramshackle balconies where women stood in heavy black burnouses with gold mesh squares over where their faces must be. She could not imagine what the lives of those women were like any more than they could imagine hers.

Her favourite part of the bazaar was where furniture was sold, line after line of open-fronted stalls packed full of broken chairs and tables, chipped china, oil lamps, chandeliers, primitive paintings, verdigrised bits of brass and copper. Once she saw a military trumpet hanging from the front of a stall and another time a magnificent red and cream uniform that must once have graced the body of an officer in the army of the East India Company.

Now and again she'd stop the car and get out to bargain for a bit of china or glass in one of the stalls but she rarely bought anything. The touts had ceased to bother her because they recognised her and her car now and knew she was a poor spender.

At a quarter past twelve, she headed for the way out. As usual, for a moment, she felt a spasm of fear grip her heart because every road, every alley in the bazaar looked the same and, though she had a good sense of direction, the maze of honeycombed streets she passed through had been disorienting.

How do I get out of this? I don't know! she thought. Then she calmed down a bit and looked over the rooftops to find the tall minaret of the mosque . . . it was her compass point, and she headed for it knowing that it stood at the end of one of the main streets of the area. Turn right opposite the mosque and head for Crawford Market and she'd be back in the world where European women were safe.

She thought it was necessary to be about ten minutes late for her lunch appointment with Baby and her parents, that was only politeness, so she drove sedately along Marine Drive, past Kemp's Corner and down the hill to Nepean Sea Road where Sir Robert Maling-Smith's bungalow occupied a large site on a leafy corner, well-positioned to catch breezes coming in different directions at various times of the day and during the changing seasons of the year.

It was surrounded by a high wall, erected by a nervous occupant the year after the Mutiny, but that was the only big change made to it since it was first built about 1830. The main walls were constructed out of blocks of roughly hewn stone with wooden verandahs all round the ground and first floors. The kitchens and the servants' quarters were in a separate house at the back. This was designed to prevent the main house being burned down if there was a conflagration over the cooking stoves.

The walls were white and the doors and wooden verandahs painted dark green. There were slatted shutters on every window and slatted strips set in the middle of every door, of which there were many because there were four large ones opening into the ground floor and many more lined along the upper verandah. The only change that time had brought to the internal arrangements of the house in nearly a hundred and thirty years was the provision of baths, lavatories and washbasins in the bathrooms that opened off the back of each bedroom. That improvement had only been brought about within the last ten years and up till then the family had bathed in hip baths filled every morning and evening with hot water, boiled up in the kitchen and lugged upstairs in buckets by the servants. Instead of flush lavatories, they had 'thunderboxes', polished mahogany seats over white earthenware pots. When they finished whatever was necessary, they shouted for a servant to carry it away through a little trapdoor behind the thunderbox.

Lady Maling-Smith had not wanted to update the bathrooms. She thought flushes insanitary and preferred her hip bath to the vast white cast-iron monster that was shipped out from home.

"It takes too much water to fill and it's not nearly so comfortable to sit in," she complained and sometimes, as a treat, asked the servants to bring her hip bath back and she'd sit in it happily pouring alternate libations of warm and cold water over herself from a small brass receptacle that she'd had since she was a little girl.

When Dee saw the number of servants who looked after the three people in this bungalow, she realised that the Gulmohurs was not over-staffed at all.

First to greet her was the watchman, a Pathan in a straw beehive hat wound round by a pale blue scarf, a black waistcoat over a white shirt and baggy white trousers. He bent down and stared at her through the open window of her car when she stopped at the gate. His eyes were very pale green and his beard dyed red to show he'd made the pilgrimage to Mecca.

"I've come to see Miss Baby," she told him and he nodded for he'd been told to expect her. Then he swung a huge wooden gate open and admitted her to the garden where three gardeners were toiling up and down the paths dragging yards and yards of green hosepipe after them.

The car door was opened for Dee by a solemn young man in a white suit and a black pork-pie hat, who escorted her to the foot of the steps up to the lower verandah where the head bearer was waiting. He was an impressive old fellow in a long white coat and a white turban with a scarlet flash across the front of it. Pinned in the middle of the flash was a brass brooch bearing the insignia of Sir Robert's company.

Without speaking he gestured to show that she ought to follow him quickly. "I'm late," thought Dee. "I should have arrived precisely on time."

Baby was sitting with her parents in a long room with windows on both sides and three fans circulating slowly in the ceiling. White muslin curtains fluttered slowly in the moving air and the waiting people all had glasses in their hands.

When Dee was introduced to Sir Robert and Lady Barbara, he announced, "Let's go through and eat then."

The visitor's stuttered apologies were ignored and they filed through a door at the end of the room into another as large, but dominated by an enormous, gleaming table bearing heavy silver cutlery, tall-stemmed glasses and linen napkins artistically folded so that they looked like miniature castles. On the spaces between the windows, gilt-framed paintings were hanging – seascapes mostly, but one or two lighter ones of hunting scenes in the style of Lionel Edwards, Dee thought, not realising they were actually the work of the artist. Everything was very grand and expensive-looking.

The food was borne in by two male servants while the chief bearer stood by supervising. First arrived soup in a silver tureen that was poured into their plates from a silver ladle. It was a pale consommé and fairly tasteless. Then came a vast tray covered with a silver dome. This was set down in front of Sir Robert and the top taken off with much ceremony. Nestling beneath it was one plate of mashed potatoes with three sausages and fried onions in the middle of them.

Seeing Dee staring at this, Baby explained, "Father is always served first because he likes his sausages to be hot and he never eats anything else. We're having fish."

The fish was fried pomfret, a local flat fish, with slices of lemons and chips. This was followed by glass dishes of custard and sliced bananas. Water was served but no wine, for this was prohibition Bombay and wine was almost impossible to find, even by millionaires.

During the meal Lady Barbara, who seemed to be drinking vast amounts of water because she was always passing her glass to the head bearer for re-filling, did her best to put the visitor at her ease and leaned forward eagerly in her chair to question Dee.

"How long have you been out, my dear?" she asked.

"Just over a year. Fourteen months actually."

"Do you like Ind-yah?"

"Yes, what I've seen of it, which isn't a lot. I keep staring at those mountains on the mainland and wishing I could cross them. They tantalise me."

Sir Robert joined in now, "You'd just find the same sort of things on the other side of the creek as you find here," he said.

His wife disagreed, "Not at all. It's amazingly different, everywhere's different. It's a wonderful country and even if you lived to be a hundred, you'd never really know its secrets."

"Balderdash," said her husband. Their exchanges seemed more like verbal fencing than conversation but Dee soon realised that neither of them paid any attention to what the other said and certainly never felt aggrieved by it.

"What sort of car do you drive?" Lady Barbara asked, after rapidly downing yet another glass of water.

"A Studebaker but it's rather old – 1948."

"One of those big ones that look like porkers? I love those cars. I had one during the war, didn't I Robert? I used to call it my Sturdybugger, didn't I? *Sturdybugger*, get it?"

Dee got it and laughed, whereupon Lady Barbara repeated her joke again and it struck Dee that Baby's mother was actually drunk and getting drunker. There was more than water being poured into her glass. Nobody else seemed to either notice or care.

The lunch lurched to a finish when Sir Robert rose from his chair and announced he was returning to the office. His wife then rose too and staggered to the door, waving a kindly hand at Dee as she went and saying she sincerely hoped to meet her again some time. Then she disappeared and Baby stared across the table at her friend who didn't know whether to say something or keep quiet.

Baby broke the silence. "My mother likes you," she said.

"And I like her," said Dee. It was true, for Lady Barbara was immensely appealing even when telling her Studebaker joke.

"I'm glad," said Baby, "because I adore her."

That, thought Dee, was that.

The promise of books was more than kept by Baby, who took her visitor into a room at the end of the house where there were lines of heavy bookcases, all of them packed full with books.

Dee paused on the threshold and gave a sigh of admiration. It was like being given a glimpse of paradise. The problem was what to choose.

"There's a lot of rubbish among them," warned her friend, "and the silverfish have been at others. Just look around and pull out what you want."

"What will your father say?" asked Dee who had been totally intimidated by Sir Robert.

"He knows. I asked him about them. He said to tell you to take anything you want but be sure to bring them back again."

"Oh I will. I promise I will."

They pulled books from the shelves, scattering insects and throwing up dust. coughing and laughing and reading each other extracts. During the picking of the books they grew easier with each other and at the end of an hour, Dee had collected together Dickens' *Bleak House*, the complete works of Tennyson, Thackeray's *Vanity Fair* and Mrs Gaskell's *Cranford*, which she had read before but wanted to read again. These books represented hours and hours of happy forgetfulness in another world for her.

While one of the junior servants carried this bounty to the car, she hugged Baby in delight and said, "You're an angel. You've saved my life. I'm going to be so happy reading them."

Baby, amazed that anyone could get excited about dusty old books like those, so out of date and boring, laughed and said, "You should get out more, Dee. Why don't you and Ben come back to town tonight? There's going to be a party in an Australian's flat. Mags and Winks and I met him at Breach Candy. There'll be oodles of booze because he's in their High Commission and you know what that means – gin by the diplomatic bagful."

"I'm not great at parties," said Dee.

"You'll be all right at this one. It's not just the rugby crowd. Come with me. I could do with the support. Everybody keeps asking me about Charlie, did I go to the wedding and stuff like that. Come and keep me company. You can tell me what I ought to be reading. I feel quite guilty having all those books in the house and never even opening them."

Dee laughed. "All right. We'll come. Where is it and when?" She knew there would be no trouble persuading Ben to go to a party for he was the most sociable man in the world.

"He gave us his address. It's in one of those nice flats in Marine Drive. I'll get you the number out of my notebook. Come about half past ten. It should have got going by then."

At the door of her car, Dee paused. "Is it a BYOB, Baby? If it is, we can't come. We haven't a bloody drop of gin left this month." BYOB was Bombay shorthand for Bring Your Own Booze and most of the parties operated on that basis.

In fact they did have some units left. It was money to buy the drink that they hadn't got.

Baby waved a hand. "It's not a BYOB. At least he didn't say it was. Don't worry about the gin. I'll rifle my mother's cellar and get enough for the three of us. Just come."

Nine

W hen no one had arrived at his flat by ten o'clock, Dennis was sure that the girls had been playing a trick on him or that they had forgotten his invitation entirely. Why should they want to come to see me anyway? he asked himself, leaning over his verandah rail and watching cars swish past below.

Trying to ignore the hovering Govind, to whom he was sure he was a bitter disappointment, he stared out over the curving lights of the road that looped round the bay. According to Bob these lights were knows as 'The Queen's Necklace' because they looked like a string of pearls, curving sinuously as jewels round a beautiful neck. On his right, a huge blue and white circular sign advertising Mercedes Benz turned slowly on a high rooftop. This was a relic of pre-Independence times because no amount of money could have bought a new Merc in the whole of India at the moment – luxury imports were banned.

Typical, thought Dennis bitterly staring at the enticing sign: India was all promise and no performance. It would not surprise him if Mags enjoyed playing cruel practical jokes on people for she had a hard little face, but he had not expected to be strung along by Baby and Winks.

It's my own fault. Who in their right mind would get involved with girls who had names like that? he asked himself. They inhabited a world that was totally alien to him, a world of privilege that had no contact with hard reality. He remembered the casual way they signed their pool bills, and went over their conversation in his mind – gossip, chatter about travelling on liners to England, but never about money. They had plenty of it, so it wasn't important.

His broad shoulders drooped when he turned away from the view and walked back into the room where all the chairs had been pushed back and a record player, with a pile of records he'd bought that day from the shop in the Gym, lay with its lid up waiting to pour out music.

Consulting his watch he saw that it was twenty-five past ten. "I'm going to bed," he told Govind. "You'd better turn in too."

The bearer said nothing but in fact he was sorry for the lad who had obviously been anticipating having this party. "It is not too late, sahib," he said tentatively for he was more familiar with European party habits than his employer.

"Nobody's coming now," replied Dennis and went into his bedroom banging the door.

At seven minutes to eleven he was having a shower when there was a hooting of horns and a banging of car doors from the roadway in front of his block of flats. He didn't hear this however because he was standing with water pouring down over his head. Govind had to hammer on the bedroom door to alert him to the fact that something had happened.

Not knowing what to expect, he stepped into the living room, wearing a white towelling bathrobe tied loosely round his waist and another towel over his shoulders, to find the place full of people. A young man, seeing him in the doorway, gave a whoop and yelled, "It's one of those parties!" before starting to tear off his clothes. Soon some of the other men had stripped down to their underpants – at least they kept them on for the meantime though several ended up stark naked before the night was out. The girls were more circumspect but most of them were very lightly clad anyway.

Someone had switched on the record player and Buddy Holly's 'That'll Be The Day' blared out. It was not a disc that Dennis had bought. Already couples were dancing, throwing each other to and fro in the middle of the floor. People kept coming in, handing bottles to a gratified Govind at the doorway, and Dennis stood gaping like someone who was witnessing a miracle.

Suddenly a hand gently touched his arm and Baby was there, dressed in a pink sack dress with a toy crocodile on a string beside her. She looked very pretty, her smooth tanned skin glowing with health and her hair glittering like silk in the lamplight.

"What a lovely flat this is," she said. "It's so kind of you to let us come to your flat. I hope they don't wreck it."

He stared dazedly at her. "I'm glad you came. I didn't think you were going to – and I've got all this beer!"

She laughed, "Didn't you realise that we're night owls? At weekends people here party all night and sleep all day."

Dennis clutched at his robe. "I'll have to go and get dressed," he said.

"Oh don't bother. You've set the tone. It's going to be wild. Come and dance with me."

"This thing won't stay closed if I start dancing," said Dennis.

"It will if you pin it tightly. Hold on, I'll use my brooch. Turn round and I'll pin it up for you."

She took a brooch in the shape of a big daisy off her shoulder and, laughing, pinned it in at his waist. When he felt her hands brush the bare skin of his chest, a thrill like an electric shock went through him. She felt it too and it surprised her because she didn't think she would feel that magic, sensual thrill ever again after Charlie.

By the time Dennis had downed a couple of big bottles of beer he'd stopped worrying about losing his dignity or his bathrobe, which, fortunately, stayed in place. As he gazed around his gambolling guests, it struck him that the only Indians present were the three servants. Everyone else was white – and nearly all English except himself and a couple of Americans.

He danced with Baby, he danced with Winks, he even danced with Mags, but only once. He danced with other people too and was propositioned by a wrinkled-looking blonde woman called Diana who was wearing dozens of golden bracelets on both of her arms and five gold chains round her neck.

"You've just come out, haven't you?" she said. "I must take you in hand. Teach you about life in Bombay . . . Come round to my flat tomorrow afternoon. My husband'll be out visiting his mistress then."

Then she slid both of her hands down his chest and murmured, "Mmmmmm, lovely."

The woman who danced with him next had slanting green eyes like a cat and a face like a wicked pixie that grew even more wicked when she told him, "Saw you being given the treatment by old Diana. Watch out, she always likes to get the new meat before anyone else has a chance. She breaks in all the bachelors!"

At that point Diana's face appeared at Dennis's elbow and she hissed at the pixie, "Hands off. I saw him first."

"Darling," said the other woman putting her arms round Dennis's waist under the robe. "It's amazing you have the stamina at your age."

Unnerved by this, Dennis retreated to his bedroom to dress himself properly, and there found a couple making love in his bed but they paid no attention to him while he searched in the drawers for a shirt and a pair of shorts but he couldn't find his shoes which Govind had taken away for cleaning. When he returned to the party, he was

A Bombay Affair

buttonholed by a languid young man who was leaning against the wall with a foaming glass of beer in his hand. He was naked except for dark glasses.

"Great party, what?" he said. "All that Aussie beer, incredible! Who's giving it? D'ye know him?"

"He's over there I think," said Dennis gesturing towards the balcony. He escaped and went looking for Baby.

He found her kneeling on the floor by the record player with fragments of her toy crocodile in her hands. When she saw his bare feet beside her, she looked up sadly and shook her head. "I shouldn't have brought him. Mags said someone'd stand on him and that's just what happened. Poor old man eater, he didn't last long."

He bent down too and picked up fragmented bits of balsa wood off the tiles. "Too many people for him, too crowded," he said sadly.

She gave a forlorn smile. "He was probably a loner. I should think crocodiles are, don't you? Couldn't stand crowds and maybe committed suicide, threw himself under the nearest pair of dancing feet."

"We should give him a decent burial," said Dennis. "Where would you like to do it?"

"Let's float him out to sea like one of the Hindu gods. Let's go to Chowpatti beach and do it now. Come on." She stood up with the fragments of her toy in her cupped hands and grinned at him. He hadn't a clue where Chowpatti beach was but nodded his head, "All right. Let's go. My car's outside."

"We don't need a car," she said, "The beach is just at the far end of the Parade. Come on, none of this lot'll miss us."

Pausing only to put on a pair of gym shoes that stood beside the front door – they weren't his but they fitted – he followed Baby down the stairs to the roadway. There she handed him half of her broken crocodile bits and said, "You carry half of him and I'll take the rest. Come on. What a lovely night for a funeral."

Baby and Dennis had already left the flat when Dee and Ben arrived, having been held up by an argument about money and a subsequent making-up which involved falling into bed and making violent love. Ben was in an excessively good post-coital mood that became even more expansive when he saw the array of bottles of real Australian beer and the gathering of all his friends, jiving about in the middle of the cleared floor and hanging over the verandah shouting to people on the road below.

As was his habit, he left his wife to her own devices and dived into the melee, glass in hand and whooping. Dee watched him go with resignation for she knew better than to expect him to stay by her side. At parties like this, he always reverted to his bachelor self and would have been genuinely surprised and put out if she'd complained about his abandonment of her.

'For God's sake,' he'd exclaim, 'you can't expect to hang onto me all the time!'

She didn't, and so she headed into the crowd looking for people she knew and especially hoping to find Baby who she'd tell about her enjoyment of the books – she'd already started on the Thackeray. She stopped to talk to a woman called Anne, a beautiful, statuesque blonde married to an excessively jealous and possessive man whose paranoid suspicions made her life a misery.

Unlike Ben, Anne's husband Bill never left her side at parties, standing silently glowering even while she chatted with her female friends. Comparing him with her absent husband, Dee decided she preferred being married to a man who wanted his own space and was prepared to give her hers.

Then she talked with Ralph, the English doctor from Breach Candy, who was weaving about among the dancers, very drunk to all appearances, but she'd seen him like that before when a fellow party-goer cut his hand on a shard of glass and blood spouted out in a terrifying cascade. Then Ralph had sobered up in an instant, and all signs of drunkenness disappeared. It was a magical transformation that made Dee wonder how much of the doctor's apparent dissoluteness was assumed and how much real.

Standing with Ralph was one of Dee's favourites among the rugby club crowd, a craggy faced bachelor called Bruce who came down to Bombay with his pet bull terrier from a distant posting in Maharashtra about once every six weeks and proceeded to spend his whole weekend's leave in an alcoholic stupor, sleeping on the sofas of his friends. Tonight however Bruce looked relatively sober and was making sense. "I met the most wonderful girl in the Ambassador bar. She's a Qantas air hostess," he was telling Ralph.

Bruce was very susceptible to women and was always falling in love but never with any success. He was a bit like the male version of Winks.

"You should have brought her with you," said Ralph, who was equally susceptible to female charms but ten times more predatory than Bruce.

"I did. She's out on the verandah. She's lovely . . ."

There was a crowd on the verandah but Bruce pointed out an extremely tall, dark-haired girl in white who was the centre of an interested circle of men. Ralph took one look and headed in her direction too, ignoring the malevolent stare of his wife who was on the other side of the dance floor.

Sensing that Bruce was about to lose this girl just as he'd lost so many others in the past, Dee stayed with him making conversation but wishing she could give him some advice like, "Don't give in. Fight for her if you really want her . . . You're so much nicer than any of the others and if she's got any sense she'll see that." But Bruce was pretending not to notice how his girl had forgotten all about him and it would have been tactless to point it out.

The party roared on, and Dee began to feel the consciousness-softening effect of alcohol that made time immaterial and blurred perception. She was talking to Anne again when Bruce went rushing past with his dog at his heels, heading for the front door. She watched the door bang behind him and wondered why he was leaving so precipitately. Looking for his girlfriend, she turned and stared at the revellers – dancing, drinking, sprawling on the floor. Then her eye was drawn to a corner of the verandah, shadowed and secret behind a dropped chick-blind. Standing half-hidden was the Australian air hostess in the arms of a man who was kissing her passionately and running his hands down her breasts – I thought so. That's why Bruce left, said Dee to herself. But suddenly, with a sickening thud in her guts, she realised that the man who'd taken over the girl was her husband, Ben.

Anne saw them at the same time and put a hand on Dee's arm as she said, "Pretend you don't notice, darling."

Dee turned furiously on her, "Don't be bloody stupid Anne. I'm not going to turn into one of those women who look the other way while their husbands carry on and then take their revenge by having tawdry little affairs themselves."

Seething with anger, she shook off Anne's well-intentioned hand, stormed across the floor and onto the verandah. The amorous couple were still locked together in an embrace when she took hold of her husband's shoulder, pulled him back and shouted, "You bastard. What do you think you're playing at?" Before he had time to realise what was happening, she swung back her arm and let Ben have her balled fist in his right eye. The blow brought him to his knees.

The air hostess didn't hang around long enough for anything similar to happen to her but sprinted off the verandah and out of the flat. She didn't even wait long enough to find out if her original escort was still there.

To do him justice Ben did not hit Dee back or protest his

innocence. Chastened, he followed her furious little figure out of the flat and managed to jump into the passenger seat of the Studebaker as she was starting it up downstairs on the road.

A huge silver moon had risen and was casting an unearthly silver avenue of light over the surface of the sea as Dee turned the car and set off at a roaring pace towards Kemp's Corner. Ben managed to summon up the courage to say, "Sorry, Dee . . . I don't know what I was thinking about . . ."

Seething with jealousy, she turned her face towards him, making the car swerve alarmingly as she took her concentration off the road. "Shut up, just shut up. If you say one damned word, I'll stop and put you out." He knew she was quite capable of it so he sat silent, with one hand cupped over his aching eye, during the long drive home.

The moon that lit up the road to Chembur and made headlights unnecessary for Dee enchanted Dennis and Baby as they stood staring over the spread of unmarked silver water that stretched towards the distant horizon. It was all Dennis could do not to step off the promenade and try to walk out on it.

"It's a full moon," he said staring up entranced at the huge silver saucer in the sky.

"Don't look into it. It'll drive you mad," she cautioned.

"I don't care. If this is what it's like to be mad, I don't want ever to be sensible again," he told her.

"In that case, perhaps I'd better look at the moon too then," she said and turned to stare into its beneficent face as well.

It had taken them more than an hour to slowly wander along the sea front to a small sandy beach tucked into the corner of Walkeshwar Road where it began to rise up to Malabar Hill. As always in India, though it was well after midnight, there were still lots of people about – it seemed impossible ever to go any place that was absolutely deserted – and a few of them trailed after Baby and Dennis as they waded into the sea and floated the bits of the crocodile on the water of the ocean. There were no waves and the temperature of the sea was like a tepid bath. It washed round their ankles with the caress of silk.

"This is a sacred beach, you know," said Baby. "We should have brought some flowers and sent my poor man eater off in style." She watched the soft ebb taking her toy away, and whispered, "There he goes. I wonder where he'll end up."

"Australia maybe," said Dennis.

They didn't go straight back to the flat after launching the broken crocodile but sat on a stone wall that fringed the road and the sea, watching the mystery of the moon on the water and mysterious phosphorent flashes that sparked here and there in the vast blackness in front of them. It was so awesome that they only spoke in whispers, like the acolytes of some esoteric cult.

He told her how pleased he was that she'd brought her friends to his party and said that he'd been very lonely and isolated since arriving in India. "I was considering quitting and going home but now I think I'll stay," he said. He didn't tell her about Carole.

She told him that she was also undecided what to do with her life. The aimless round of partying that went on in Bombay was beginning to bore her and she was contemplating a trip abroad, perhaps to Australia. She didn't tell him about Charlie.

Before they turned to go back however they agreed to meet again on Sunday and drive to Juhu beach for a swim. "You'll like it. It's lovely there," said Baby.

By the time they got to Dennis's flat again it was dawn and only a handful of revellers were left, still dancing. Empty beer bottles were piled in the corners and an exhausted looking Govind was on his knees wiping slops off the middle of the floor.

Baby looked round. "Winks has gone. Mags is still here with that new man she met on the boat coming out so I won't interfere. I'm exhausted. I'd better go."

"You're not driving yourself are you? I'll take you back," said Dennis but she laughed.

"I'll be all right. My driver brought me. He'll be asleep in the car. I've only got to wake him up."

"Poor sod!" exclaimed Dennis; he couldn't help himself.

"It's his job," said Baby, surprised.

Ten

M ost of the guests at the Marine Drive party, except a few unfortunate men employed by old-fashioned companies that still opened their offices on Saturday mornings, spent the next day in bed.

Ben Carmichael, who had to go to work, groaned as he sat upright and pressed his fingers to his aching temples, trying to remember the events of the night before.

His wife was lying beside him, curled up like a kitten, but she'd wrapped a sheet around herself like an Egyptian mummy and when he saw her so tightly cocooned, he suddenly remembered his transgression of the previous evening.

The bird with the black hair and the legs! The goer. He groaned and rubbed both hands down over his face, which made him wince. His left eye was throbbing with a deep, painful pulse. He rose naked from their sagging bed and padded across the marble floor to the looking glass which showed that he had the most beautiful purple shiner, the sort that cannot be camouflaged. As he tentatively touched it, he silently congratulated Dee on the accuracy of her aim and the strength of her swing.

Over his shoulder in the glass he could tell from the clenched look of her body that she was not asleep but only pretending. He'd better act contrite though he wasn't really. What did she expect? He'd been a bachelor so long that it was sometimes difficult to remember that he couldn't go hunting any more.

"Sorry about last night," he said to Dee's reflection.

She said nothing.

"I got drunk and forgot . . . she was asking for it really."

That was the wrong thing to say for he saw his wife's shoulders tighten.

"I'm a stupid bugger, Dee. I really am. It's you I love. She was just there . . ."

Dee still said nothing. It wasn't like her not to rise to his bait.

He walked back to the bed. If he could get her to sit up, have a weep and then make up, he might have a bit before he went to work. "I'm really sorry," he said again.

She still said nothing and a feeling of uncertainty took hold of him. He was never very sure of how Dee's mind worked. Sitting down on her side of the bed, he began putting on his clothes. She lay like a frozen effigy, not moving a muscle.

"It's you I love, I really do," he said again and turned intending to put his hand on her shoulder but before his hand made contact with her body, he heard her voice. "Do not touch me. Don't even try."

He drew the hand back as if it had been scalded. Her head with the cropped-off hair was sunk deep in the pillow so he couldn't see her face. Why had she cut off her hair like that? He'd liked it long.

"You're over-reacting," he said.

That should have got her going, but it didn't. She was still silent. God, she was starting to worry him.

"I was drunk," he said feebly. "I wouldn't be able to recognise her if I saw her today. I don't even know her name. She was just an easy lay."

"Get out," said his wife into her pillow.

As he drove into the city he debated with himself. He probably shouldn't have made such a massive move on the Australian bird but she was more than co-operative . . . a really first-class-looking woman, skinny, haughty but willing – the kind he liked. If he'd had time he'd have fixed something up with her . . . but Dee had put a stop to that. You'll have to be more careful, lad, he told his reflection in the driving mirror, but not to worry, Dee couldn't go anywhere. She'd still be there when he got back to the Gulmohurs.

She was terribly touchy but what did she expect? He wasn't the sort of man who could make do with only one woman and anyway he'd more or less been rushed into marriage . . . sometimes the weight of his new responsibilities irked him and he longed for the old days when he and Guy had shared the bungalow and the birds without a thought for money, or careers or any of those boring things that so obsessed his wife.

He was completely unaware that Dee too was suffering from similar feelings of regret but the mistake that both the Carmichaels made was not to talk to each other about the circumstances of their marriage although they discussed everything else very freely and openly. They kept their anger and confusion hidden from each other.

They both felt they'd been railroaded into getting married. And now that he was trying to excuse himself for his lapse of the night

69

before, Ben consoled himself with the thought that one moment he'd been a carefree bachelor, home on leave in Edinburgh after three and a half years in Bombay, when one night at a dance he met this girl and everything ran right out of control. They went on holiday to France and Italy with a group of friends. He got drunk and proposed to her in a town called Avalon, which sounded romantic. She didn't accept at first but three days later, when he asked her again in Venice, she said, 'Well, OK. Maybe.'

If she'd said to him that she wanted time to think about it; if she'd said 'Why don't you go back to Bombay on your own and I'll come out later?' he'd have left and the affair would probably have fizzled out, but her terrible parents drove her into a corner and he couldn't let her down. That would have been a real shit's trick and he wasn't a shit.

So they got married, both of them rather glum. Dee had worn a fur coat, a red dress and a black beret made of amoeba-shaped sequins. She'd bought the dress because the saleswoman said it flattered her figure and she didn't say she was going to get married in it or she might have been steered towards another colour because, as she discovered later, marrying in red was thought to bring very bad luck indeed.

As he took his vows Ben didn't know if he loved her really, for it certainly wasn't a grand passion. Not the sort that made blokes want to kill themselves or put them off their food, but the sex between them was magnificent and she was funny, when she was in a good mood. He'd never known a woman who was better company or who interested him more. It was impossible for him to feel bored with her around. What also bound him to her was that he was never sure of what she was thinking. He couldn't guess how she was going to react to anything that happened and she continually surprised him. Just like she did this morning when he expected her to be ready to row but instead she just lay there brooding, plotting – what?

I hope to God she's in a better mood when I get back this afternoon, he said to himself. He was too hung over to put a lot of effort into the reconciliation.

In fact Dee *was* very much awake when her husband got up – she'd been awake for hours, thinking and internally fuming, but she lay still, stopping herself from recoiling when he tried to touch her and keeping her eyes closed till she heard the car swishing down the road on the other side of their hedge. Then she turned over, stretched and looked at her toes sticking up like two little hills under the sheet which was the only covering she could bear now that the weather was heating up. The fan above her head was slowly turning and she could hear Birbal, the gardener, giving the grass its morning libation outside the bedroom window.

It was half-past seven and she was furiously angry, even angrier than she'd been the night before. The memory of her husband and the air hostess in that deep embrace was engraved on her memory and the extent of her fury surprised her. Why? Was it because she loved Ben so deeply that the thought of him with another woman was like a stab in the heart? Or was it for some other reason? Was it anger at herself for landing in this hopeless situation with a man who didn't care for her? Who blatantly shamed her in front of other people. Or, was she using his transgression as a focus for other dissatisfactions in her new life?

"I've got to think about things. I've got to work out what to do," she told herself aloud. "I've got to think really hard. I'll go for a walk . . . I always think better when I'm walking."

The water in the shower was cold and refreshing and she stood beneath the large, round, metal rose, letting it cascade down over her head, ripple over her shoulders and breasts, down her legs to her feet. Then, gasping, she emerged to towel herself and put on her cotton shorts and a shirt. When she drew back the bedroom curtains, as always the glory of the sun blazing down outside astonished her.

When she'd first arrived at the Gulmohurs, she used to cry out in delight every morning, "It's going to be another lovely day!" till Ben stopped this by laughing and saying, "You'll get used to it in time. It's a lovely day every day here until the rains come . . ."

Ben, the bastard! She hated to think he'd demeaned her before other people.

When she emerged from the bedroom, Mohammed was waiting, his Uriah Heep look on his face, with a cup of black coffee on the tray in his hand. She was sure he'd heard Ben trying to make it up with her. "Breakfast memsahib?" he asked.

She drank the coffee standing up. "I don't want any breakfast. I'm going for a walk," she said.

On the verandah she paused, unsure of which direction to take. If she walked down the lane she would end up on the main road. By going left she'd pass the film studios where Raj Kapoor's company made epics about warriors and lovely maidens thwarted in love. Sometimes when she passed the lot she saw actors tearing around a dried-up bit of open ground on skeletal horses, waving cardboard swords and screeching fiercely.

If she went to the right, she would pass the police station and

71

the post office. She might see her favourite postman, the one she called the 'BA with the bike', because he'd told her he had a BA in chemistry but being a postman was the only job he could get. They'd become friendly and he used to ring his bell very loudly and wave his hand as he approached the bungalow if he had any mail for her. The arrival of mail was big event in her life these days.

No, she didn't want to go down the lane. She'd go somewhere different for a change.

Across the river bed was the fruit farm where she occasionally went to make a telephone call because the only telephone for miles brooded like a black frog on a table in the farm office. Making a call had to be arranged however, booked in advance if it was to Britain, and cleared with the farm manager. It also had to be paid for at the time and, once again, she had no money – and no one to phone come to that.

She had phoned her family at Christmas, for she missed her father. In spite of their terrible row about Ben they had been very close and she remained fond of him, as he did of her. She understood what had driven him on – he hadn't wanted her to leave him, he didn't want to lose his daughter to a man he disliked and distrusted – perhaps with good reason – but the only way he could express his love for her was by hectoring. She thought if she'd wanted to marry a saint out of heaven, her father would have raised some objection or other. It was her mother, who had always resented Dee, who'd urged her father on till it ended with the family being irrevocably broken up.

When she thought of her father she felt sympathy and pity for him. We're two of a kind. I'm as bad as he is. I'm emotionally crippled too, she thought for she could never have told him that she loved him and she couldn't really tell Ben either, but could only express her feelings by making physical love. It was hard for her to talk about how she felt, or to express her affection by the tender pats and caresses she saw other women giving to their men. It always embarrassed her when Ben, who was more open and demonstrative than she was, patted her bottom or cupped her breasts in public.

Coffee finished, she walked into the garden and stood staring around, trying to decide where her walk should take her. No, she decided, she didn't want to go to the fruit farm. She'd rather go up the hill to the little temple that lured her like a beacon from the top of the hill. Perhaps she'd meet the old holy man who lived there.

She'd never been up to it because it was quite far away, a stiff climb, and would take at least a couple of hours to reach, a gruelling ordeal in hot sunshine. She'd have to follow the nullah, the bed of a dried-up river which ran between high banks along their boundary. Its course was clearly traceable down the flank of the hill but there hadn't been a drop of water in it for months, though, during the monsoon that lasted from June till September, it had filled up almost overnight as soon as the rains broke and tumbled down like a Scottish mountain burn, foaming and splashing from rock to rock and pool to pool. There had even been fish in it then. Where had the fish gone now that the pools were only open stretches of sun-baked, cracked mud? That was another Indian mystery. Life was full of them.

Birbal, the gardener, his skin so black that it looked purple, the colour of an overripe blackcurrant, was watching when she slid down the bank from the high garden to the river bed, scattering little stones under the soles of her sandals. There were both cobras and krites, the bite of which was an instant killer, in the nullah, so she carried a stick of Guy's because she'd been told that when walking in the jungle you should thud a staff on the ground to warn snakes of your approach. When they heard you they ran away. She hoped that was true.

As she walked up the dry river bed, hopping from rock to rock, she was delighted to find that bamboo thickets closed in around her, almost obscuring the sky with their tall, feathery pennants that floated above her head like the flags at a mediaeval pageant. Eventually, after half an hour of toiling uphill in the ever-growing heat, she found a flat shelf of rock like a table top in the middle of the stream and sat down on it, hugging her knees. She didn't think she could walk much farther because the muscles of her calves ached – she was not taking enough exercise those days, but the pain was not unpleasant or disabling so she sat in the deep silence, mulling over her confusions. There was not a sound, not a rustle, not a soul to be seen. She liked that. Being alone suited her, especially when she was troubled.

What do I do now? she wondered. Do I cut my losses and go home? Do I walk out on my marriage?

There were so many problems – Guy's hostility, Ben's flirting, Dee's failure to find a place for herself among his friends, her feeling of displacement and isolation and, worst of all, money.

If the Carmichaels could have been translated into an Indian couple, it would have been obvious that the major problem they faced was that they had married out of their caste. Ben, a clever and ambitious boy, came from the working class and had grown up with an insouciant attitude towards paying bills. If you didn't have much money, you kept one jump ahead of people intent on taking it off you. His was the world of the rent collector and the insurance man and when, by a stroke of luck, he found himself among the minor public schoolboys of Bombay, he adopted their attitudes easily. They believed if you owed money to someone, hard luck. You'd pay them – or not – when it suited you. It was damned cheek of them to ask for it.

Dee was a typical product of the petit bourgeoisie. Her family, for generations, had been self-employed, property-owning shopkeepers who scorned non-payers. To owe money was to them a bigger sin than adultery or blasphemy. They relied on people paying their bills and were profoundly money conscious, driving big cars and wrapping their wives in fur coats to reflect their prosperity. Dee's father drove a Jaguar and her mother wore a mink.

It was torture to her when she found out the extent of Ben's indebtedness – for the car, to his tailor, to the Gym, to the grocery store in Crawford Market. She spent hours of her solitude working out sums on the flyleafs of Charlie's old paperbacks – and it always ended up with the certainty that paying off what he owed was next to impossible. She cringed when he negligently drove into the petrol station where he hadn't paid his bill for a year and expected the man to fill up the tank. If she spoke to him about it, he only laughed. 'They know they'll get paid eventually,' he said.

But how did they know that? She, his wife, wasn't sure.

She sat on the flat grey rock, warmed by the slanting rays of the sun on her back and pondered her situation. Why should she stay with Ben?

For love? She'd thought she was in love when she married him but now it seemed to her that romantic love was a lot of nonsense. Had she ever really believed in it? Certainly she hadn't till she met Ben and was swept off her feet. An agnostic verging on atheist, she used to put *love* in the same category as the church's doctrine of life after death. Logically it wasn't possible and she only respected logic.

Love, as written about in novels and praised in poetry, she regarded with tolerance as a writer's conceit. She had believed people only fell in love for biological reasons – men and women were programmed to breed and to find suitable mates with whom they could produce good-quality children. That was why good-looking people married other good-looking people and the plain were left to do the best they could with the rest.

That was it: biology was to blame. She was a pretty, healthy-looking girl, she knew, and she'd picked Ben for his looks – for he was tall, straight, broad-shouldered, blond-haired like a Viking with a strong, prominent nose and bright hazel eyes. The sort of man that girls turned and looked at in the street – and kissed at parties.

But if it was a biological urge that had pushed her into marriage, something had gone wrong. She couldn't get pregnant. Not for want of trying either. Huh, so much for love. Perhaps she was dissatisfied now because her mind was telling her something her body had chosen to ignore. Maybe she should get out while the going was good, before any children were born. It would be quite easy to break up if there was only herself and Ben to consider.

She had a secret that she'd never told her husband and the secret was that she had an escape route and could go home at any time she wanted because before she left Britain, her father had told her that he would leave a voucher for a first-class one-way ticket back to London with B.O.A.C. in her name. All she had to do was claim it. It couldn't be converted into money, of course, only into a flight.

That was the secret she'd kept from Ben. Sitting on the rock in the middle of the stream, she thought about the ticket. It would be very easy to go really. She could go today. Ben was at work; she could send Mohammed for a taxi to take her to Santa Cruz airport. The taxi man would be told to go back and get his money for the fare from Ben later. The B.O.A.C. plane left at one p.m. every day. She consulted her wristwatch and found it was not yet nine. If she went back to the bungalow now, and threw a few things into a bag, she could catch it.

But then she thought of her father's glee; she imagined him saying, "I told you so!" For the rest of her life she'd never be allowed to take another decision without being reminded of her disastrous marriage. She'd be rendered impotent for all time – the prodigal daughter who would have to pay with meekness for being received back into the family. Was it worth going back to put up with that? Was she strong enough to admit she'd made a mistake? Divorcees were rare among her parents' acquaintance. She'd be regarded as fallen, unfortunate and fast.

Don't be a fool, she then told herself. You don't have to go back to Edinburgh. Get off the plane in London and find a job there. She had friends working in Fleet Street who'd still remember her for she hadn't been away all that long. Getting a job wouldn't be all that difficult for she had been a very good reporter – and part of her misery in Bombay was because she badly missed the journalistic life. She especially missed her raffish friends who, though wild and often drunken, were moral and respectable compared to some of the people in the circles she moved among now. And her old friends had brains and ideas, they liked talking about subjects other than gossip and tittle tattle. They read books, kept up with the news and had informed opinions. Oh God, how she missed them!

The decision was made. Yes, she'd go. She'd leave a letter for Ben explaining that it had all been a terrible mistake. I don't suppose he'll be too worried, she thought. He'll be back chasing air hostesses without anyone telling him off at the next big party. And won't Guy and Mohammed be pleased!

When she was standing up to climb down from the rock, and already composing her farewell letter in her mind, she was suddenly frozen to the spot by an ominous crashing noise coming from the bamboo thicket on her left.

She slowly stooped and picked up the walking stick, staring wide-eyed in the direction of the noise, waiting for the emergence of some dangerous wild animal – there were panthers, hyenas, jackals and wild pigs with huge tusks roaming the jungle-covered hill, she'd been told. God, it might even be a tiger!

That was how he first saw her – a wide-eyed, comically crop-headed white girl in black shorts and cheap sandals, brandishing a puny-looking stick at him when he came out of the jungle.

They stared at each other, both amazed. Dee felt her heart give a funny kind of jump in her chest when she saw what looked like one of the handsome gods that were illustrated in a book of Indian legends she'd had as a child – her favourite had been Krishna sporting with the milkmaids. Only this one was alone and he was twentieth-century gorgeous.

His skin was the colour of milky coffee; his hair was dark and waving, slightly long on his neck; he had wide, sexy shoulders and long, well-muscled legs which she could see because he had on a minuscule pair of white shorts – and his long-lashed eyes were bright green like the eyes of the fierce doorman at Baby's bungalow. He was the most beautiful man she'd ever seen.

In one hand he was carrying a double-barrelled sporting gun, the gleaming, silken-looking barrels pointing down at the earth. It never struck her for one moment that he might turn the gun on her.

"I thought you were a tiger," she said, sitting weakly down again on the flat rock. It was as if the power had left her legs and they couldn't hold her up any longer.

He shook his head and said in carefully modulated Indian-upper-class English, "Don't worry. There aren't any tigers here. To bag one of them, you've got to go a long way, beyond Nagpur – I do hunt them sometimes, when I can."

He sounded exactly as Krishna would if he ventured into English, she thought. Then she stood up again and smiled, sticking out her hand. "My name's Dee Carmichael. I live in the Gulmohurs down the hill there."

He laid the shotgun on the river bank and scrambled into the nullah to stand beside her and take her hand. "I live in the house at the fruit farm. My name's Shadiv Kanji."

She remembered being told that a film actor lived in the flat above the fruit farm office.

"You're a film actor," she said, still holding his hand, and he nodded.

"Not a very famous one though I'm afraid." And then he smiled at her again, a rueful smile of such infinite sweetness that it made her head swim.

"My God," she thought, "I'm being enchanted."

"I thought you were a tiger," said the wide-eyed girl in the striped cotton shirt. He smiled as if she'd made a joke – he had as much chance of finding a tiger on Chembur hill as he would have of finding an ice-field – he'd be lucky to get a shot at a wild boar. But in fact he was as surprised at meeting her as she had been to see him. Every day when he was not working, he roamed the hill with his gun, thinking about his next part, going over his lines, worrying about when he'd get his big break, and he'd never stumbled across anyone up there before, especially not anyone like her.

His eyes when he looked at the girl were reassuring and friendly, for he didn't want to frighten her. He was a very courteous man with a gentle reverence towards women. Then he realised that the girl sitting staring at him was pretty, which was a surprise because he knew few Europeans and, like many Indian people, did not consider the shrill-voiced, pale-faced women he had viewed from a distance particularly attractive, preferring luscious-limbed, sleek-skinned Indian girls.

What struck him first about this girl however was how her enormous blue eyes seemed to dominate her sun-tanned face. Why did these European women lie out in the sun till they turned brown, he thought? His wife would never allow her skin to go that colour for she was proud of her pale ivory complexion. The eyes that looked levelly at him however were as blue as a cloudless sky and the whites startlingly white, which gave her gaze great intensity and candour. When she smiled, the smile showed in her eyes too. She was not at all inscrutable, or coy like Indian girls, and he really liked that.

77

It was a pity though that her brown hair looked as if she'd cut it with a knife and a fork. He gestured at her head. "Did you fall out with your barber?" he asked, without thinking. Then he began to apologise for he was very good-mannered and if he'd made such a personal remark to his wife, she would have been horrified and probably burst into tears.

To his relief the girl laughed. "I'm afraid I did. I went mad with a pair of scissors. But it'll grow again, I hope. If it doesn't I'll have to buy a wig."

He laughed too. "It's unusual. I think it suits you."

She thought about this for a moment. "Do you? But you've never seen me before. How do you know it suits me. I think I look a fright but I'm not going to admit it to anyone – except you!"

And they both laughed together at that. "I won't give away your secret," said Shadiv who was enjoying this strange conversation that had sprung up between them as if they were old friends. He'd heard that one of the wild men in the bungalow across the nullah had brought a wife back from England with him not long ago. This must be her.

"You live in the Englishman's house, don't you?" he asked.

"Yes, I'm married to Ben Carmichael. Have you ever met him or his friend Guy who lives there too? Except he's on sick leave now."

"No, we haven't met but my wife and I've not been living on the fruit farm long and we're away a lot. We hear the music you play at night sometimes though."

When Ben and Guy were together they often blasted out their favourite records till long after midnight, raucous ones like 'Won't You Come Home Bill Bailey' and 'Twelfth Street Rag'. Although the houses were quite far apart in this jungle, the din reached the fruit farm in the stillness of the night. It was probably heard by the hermit in the hilltop temple too, Shadiv thought.

"Don't you mind the noise?" the girl asked.

His wife hated the Englishmen's music. When it blasted out she lay in bed with her hands over her ears complaining, "How can they listen to such horrible noises?" However he told the blue-eyed girl, "I quite like that sort of jazz music but my wife complains sometimes. She's an actress and has to get up very early when she's making films."

"Gosh, that's interesting. So you're both in films. Is she making a film now?"

"She's making three." His wife Leila was much more famous

than he was. Acclaimed as a dancer and a singer and seven years older than her husband, she was a plump-faced beauty with an air of sensuality that appealed to her many fans. When he married her eight years ago, she'd been twenty-six and he'd been nineteen and his father, a professor at Allahabad University, was appalled. To him, all actresses were loose women, and in fact many of them had fought their way off the street, but not Leila, who came from a famous family of female entertainers.

The girl was suitably impressed. "Three films at once! She must work very hard."

"She does. She goes to one studio in the early morning, then to another at midday and finishes up at the third by afternoon. She comes home exhausted."

She also came home petulant and snappy, given to reminding him that she was the one bringing in the money. She was right of course, and he felt bad about that. One day, he told her, his break would come; one day a director would call him up on the fruit farm phone and offer him the part that would make his name, a part that would put his smiling face on the enormous film posters that were plastered all over Bombay. Leila was on the posters already, mouth pouting like a pink rosebud, and alluring cleavage well displayed – the epitome of sex.

The girl asked, "How many films are you making?"

He shrugged, "I've just finished one. That's why I've got time to go out shooting." She seemed to pick up his desperate desire for success, his disappointment at his own slow progress, and sympathy flooded into her wonderful eyes. "You're going to be very famous one day, I can tell," she said. Somehow he believed her, somehow he knew that this girl was not just feeding him polite untruths. She really thought he'd be famous.

He picked up his rifle and they walked down the river bed together, talking animatedly. She asked him what he was hunting for and he told her he'd taken a few pot shots at jackals but had really hoped to shoot a wild pig.

"Will you eat it if you do get one?" she asked.

"I will but Leila won't. She's very strict about her religion. Do you like roast wild pig?"

"I've never tasted it."

"If I get one I'll send half of it over to you. And I go out looking for guinea fowl sometimes too. The next time I get one I'll send it to your bungalow. They're wonderful to eat."

"I didn't realise there was so much game around us. I've never shot anything but when I was younger I used to go fox hunting . . .," she said and sighed as if she was made sad by her memories.

He nodded, "I've read about fox hunting – Mr Jorrocks. R.S. Surtees, isn't it? They talked about it at my school. I really like tiger hunting but there's not much chance to do that. It's very expensive. Sometimes I think I've been born too late. I'd like to have been an Englishman in the last century, one of the kind who hunted or a District Officer who went out shooting tigers from an elephant."

She looked at him in frank amazement. "You know about Surtees! And you'd like to have been an Englishman! How amazing. You're much better the way you are, believe me."

He laughed, "Do you really think so?"

"Oh, I do, I really do. I think your country is the most marvellous place. I only wish I knew more about it."

"Isn't that funny, I'm Indian and you're English and both of us are hankering after each other's country," he said.

"I'm not English," she told him proudly, "I'm Scots and that's very different."

The only thing he'd ever heard about the Scots was that they were fierce fighters and the soldiers wore kilts when they went into battle. He looked down at the girl by his side and felt strangely impressed by her, so small and slight but so definite in everything she said.

"Tell me about the Scots," he said.

She laughed. "God, even the Scots don't know about the Scots. We're the most disputatious, argumentative people in the world. It would take me a lifetime to describe us."

A lifetime, he thought, this girl is like Scheherazade, she could keep me listening for a lifetime though I've no idea why.

They walked down the river bed, and when they reached the place where the path to Dee's garden led up to the higher level, they lingered as if reluctant to part. He found it difficult to drag himself away from the Nordic blue of her eyes and though she'd spent more than a year in India, it was the first time she had ever had a long conversation with any Indian. She'd once been introduced to Ben's gimlet-eyed employer, Ratanlal, and his plump wife, whose English was only good enough for the most stilted exchanges, and otherwise her only other encounters had only been with servants or people serving in shops, the bearers at the Gym or at Breach Candy swimming pool.

Apart from the people they worked with, Ben and Guy didn't know many Indians either and only had one close Indian male friend, a slightly effete Parsee called Dadi who had been the only

non European so far allowed to join the Bombay Gymkhana Club
– they'd lobbied to get him in because he wanted to play rugby and
had the build for a half back, a position which was not satisfactorily
filled in the current team. As it turned out he never made the team
but he was in the club and that was what mattered to him.

Anyway Ben's friend wasn't very Indian in his aspirations or
mannerisms, modelling himself on the Englishmen he so admired,
miming their behaviour, their ways of speaking and their clothes.
The only thing that wasn't true blue English gentleman about his
assumed persona was his fondness for scented soap. Like Baby
Maling-Smith's mother he always smelt of Roger and Gallet's
'Carnation' which he bought at vast expense from the chemist's
shop on Kemp's Corner. Because it had to be imported – smuggled
in fact – in its rupee equivalent it worked out at about seven pounds
ten shillings a cake.

The talk she had with her new friend Shadiv however made Dee
feel as if a window had opened in her life, showing her an entirely
new vista. A land of constant surprises and discoveries lay before
her. When she eventually had to turn away to climb up into her
own garden she waved back at him and said, "If you like Ben's
jazz records, come over one evening and we'll play more of them
for you. Come tonight if you're not doing anything else. Bring
your wife."

He gave her another smile that turned her bones to water. "If I
can't come tonight I'll try to come tomorrow," he said, "and I'll ask
Leila but she's often too tired to go out in the evening . . ." He knew
however that he was not going to pass the invitation on to her.

It was after eleven o'clock when Dee sat down on the verandah
and picked up that morning's *Times of India*. Her fury at Ben had not
abated but become less dominating, and in a way she was looking
forward to the magnificent row she knew she'd have with him when
he came home from work. It was only after a while when she checked
her watch and found it to be one fifteen that she remembered she'd
planned to be on the plane that had left Santa Cruz fifteen minutes
before. So she wasn't going home after all. Not this time.

Eleven

It was rare for Madame Mae, manageress of the Juhu Hotel on a golden stretch of beach ten miles north of the centre of Bombay city, to be cordial to any of her customers but she had known Baby Maling-Smith since she was a toddler and when the girl and Dennis walked through the main door of her thatch-roofed bar – which, because of prohibition, could not serve alcoholic drinks any more – she deigned to emerge from the shadows of her sitting room with her white Pekinese at her heels.

"How are your parents?" asked the stately old lady. In spite of having spent over forty years in Bombay, she spoke with a strong accent which she had never lost. She was aggressively French, and on the breast of her plain black dress she sported the red ribbon of the Legion D'Honneur, awarded to her by a grateful French army in recognition of the excellent management she'd exercised over her Grant Road brothel.

"They're very well, Madame, thank you," said Baby.

"I haven't seen either of them for years, not since they used to bring you here to swim on Sundays, but I know your father's business is thriving. I have shares in one of his companies and they always do well."

Baby beamed. "He'll be glad to hear that," she said.

Madame Mae clapped her hands to summon a young man who came running up. "Everything Miss Maling-Smith wants will be on the house, John," she told him. And to Baby she said, "Have a pleasant time, my dear. Use one of the cabins. The water is very calm today and it will be pleasant to swim – or so they tell me. I don't swim myself." Then she stalked off, supporting herself on a silver-topped cane. The dog followed her like a shadow.

Her duchess-like mien intimidated Dennis who walked behind Baby through the bar to a table beneath a huge red and white umbrella on the edge of a grassy garden. In front of them creamy waves softly curled like frills of lace on unmarked yellow sand. In the surf a few couples of westernised Indians, the girls in tiny bikinis

82

and the men in boxer shorts, were feeling very bold and splashing each other, shrieking and laughing.

As soon as they sat down, a waiter in pristine white with a red cummerbund put two glasses of ice-chinking cola on the table beside them.

"What an amazing woman," said Dennis when the waiter was out of earshot.

"Madame Mae? She's one of the characters of Bombay. She's been here for years, almost as long as my father, and she has a very colourful history though no one's very sure what's legend and what's true."

"Tell me your version of it," he said leaning forward.

"Well, as you heard she's very Frrrrrench, and they say that during the war she was madame of the best brothel in Bombay – number 149 Grant Road. It was famous."

Dennis kept his face straight as he remembered Uncle Joe recommending Number 149 to him.

"Is it still there?" he asked innocently.

Baby shrugged. "It isn't what it was in Madame's day. She retired in 1947 and married an Englishman but he ran off with all her money, so she had to start again – then she bought this place and went straight. But when she retired the first time, the French government gave her an award for keeping the best brothel in the East. Trust the French, don't you think? Practical above all else. She wears the ribbon of her medal in her dress. Did you see it? She was very strict with her girls and her clients apparently – and she'd only entertain officers – no lower ranks were allowed into her house."

So either Joe had been lying about his adventures in the East or Madame Mae let her standards slip sometimes, because Joe had never risen above the rank of lance corporal. Dennis permitted himself a smile. "What a wonderful story," he said, turning to look back into the shadowed interior of the old bar but there was no one to be seen.

When he turned back to Baby another thought struck him. "What was that she said about your father's company? What does he do?"

"He runs some cotton mills," said Baby lightly. She was glad that the old lady had not referred to her parent by his title. Probably to Madame Mae he was still plain Bob Smith.

Madame had said they could use one of the cabins and after they'd drunk their Cokes, Baby stood up and said, "I'm going to change into my swimming things. The cabins are at the back of the bar

– you usually have to pay to use them but Madame said we could have one for nothing. They're very nice. I'll go first and when I come back I'll show you where to go, then we can have a swim. The sea's lovely here, and very safe."

When she returned, walking confidently across the grass, Dennis felt his heart start thudding at the sight of her because she was wearing a tiny yellow bikini that left nothing to the imagination as far as her figure was concerned. At Breach Candy she had always worn a modest, all-in-one black suit and he hadn't really noticed how lovely she was, but now he could see that she was a pocket Venus with rounded breasts and pert buttocks. Since landing in Bombay, Dennis's troublesome libido had subsided, but the sight of Baby in her bikini put him back into almost the same state of excitement as he had been in during the last days of his trip on the ocean liner.

She put a hand on his arm and said, "I left the cabin door open so's you'll know which one it is. Give your wallet and your watch, anything valuable, to Madame's young man for safe keeping and join me in the water." Then she ran lightly across the sand and plunged into the sea. He watched her go and then limped to the cabin. When he came out again he was calmer.

They stayed in the water for three hours. Dennis was a good swimmer, striking out towards the aquamarine line of the horizon with a great feeling of freedom and release, though he missed the challenge of the Australian breakers. Ploughing back and forward across the pool at Breach Candy was not his idea of swimming for it was far too tame. Baby however preferred to stay in shallower water, floating on her back with her eyes closed and her breasts pointing at the sky. The sight of her drove Dennis to even greater athletic efforts.

Eventually she said, "I'm starving. I'm going in to have one of Madame's four-tier club sandwiches, they're famous. They have fried eggs and raw onions in them!"

She ordered one for him as well and had it waiting when he came dripping out of the water. As she watched him approaching her table, her thoughts ran, He's very handsome. Better looking than Charlie even . . . What would people say if I married him? But her next thought was: Don't be stupid. You don't know anything about him.

They were eating their sandwiches and drinking coffee when they heard someone shouting, "Yoo hoo, Baby!"

She stared in the direction of the voice and Dennis saw a look of irritation cross her face but it was too late to escape because Mags,

with the moustached young banker and another couple in tow, was
advancing on them.

"You sly thing," cried Mags, slipping into a chair at Baby's side,
"What are you doing here?"

"Swimming," said Baby shortly, "I brought Dennis out to show
him Juhu."

Mags gave a shrill laugh, "I bet you've a cabin."

"As a matter of fact Madame Mae said we could use one free of
charge."

"Lucky you. People say she still lets them out by the hour, if you
know what I mean."

The other man, who had not been introduced, said, "You can
take the woman out of the brothel but not the brothel out of the
woman."

Mags shouted with laughter again. It was obvious she'd been
drinking. "You're a dark horse," she said to Dennis. "Curing Baby's
broken heart, are you?"

Baby stood up abruptly, almost upsetting her chair, "I'm going
to have my last swim. Coming?" she said to Dennis who followed her into the sea. When he joined her in the water she was
flailing her arms and legs furiously, throwing up plumes and sprays
of water.

"Mags is such a bitch," she said angrily. "You'd never guess she
and Winks are sisters. Let's stay here till they go away."

The sun was beginning to sink by the time she agreed to emerge
from the water, and goose pimples were prickling on Dennis's back
when he sat down again at their table.

"Brrr," said Baby, "let's get dressed. Come on, the cabin's big
enough for two of us."

They were both very modest, shrouding themselves with their
bath towels as they took off their wet suits and put on their ordinary
clothes again. When she returned the cabin key to Madame Mae,
who was now sitting in solitary state on the verandah with a tall glass
in front of her, Baby kissed the old woman's powdered cheek and
said, "Thank you very much, Madame, you've given us a wonderful
afternoon."

Sharp black eyes scrutinised her face. "I heard you had a disappointment my dear. Is that over?"

"Yes, it is," said Baby brightly.

"I like the look of that young fellow," said Madame in a low
voice, nodding at Dennis who was waiting at the door. "He doesn't
look like a heart breaker. Perhaps you should marry him. The dashing

ones only bring trouble to women. Always try to be the one that's loved and not the one who does the loving."

Baby's face was forlorn. "I'll try," she said.

Dennis was driving Baby's car when they headed back to the city in the dusk. Within minutes, it seemed, it was dark. There was no evening, no slow fading of the light in Bombay.

For a while they drove in silence, neither of them knowing what to say. Dennis was thinking about Mags' remark about Baby's broken heart but not daring to mention it, and she was thinking about the idea she'd had of marrying him. Would marrying cure her broken heart? Would another man drive Charlie out of her heart? She didn't love Dennis, but she was sure she'd never love anyone again, certainly not as she loved Charlie . . . but she liked Dennis because he seemed to be a good, rather equable sort of person, and most of all she longed for safety, for an escape from the turmoil of passion.

The silence of their private thoughts was broken when Baby, who was sitting curled up in the passenger seat, turned to stare out of the window and suddenly said in a dreamy voice, "I love Bombay at night, I simply adore it."

He was genuinely amazed at this. "What about the smell?" he asked, for just at that moment they were going through an area that smelled so strongly of raw sewage that you could almost cut the air in blocks.

"What smell?" said Baby surprised, "Oh that! It always smells like that here. Smells don't matter. It's the magic of the place that I love – the lights and the people, the hustle and bustle, there's always something happening. Look out at that little bazaar . . . look at the stalls and the paraffin lamps, look at the women with flowers in their hair and the lovely children all in their best clothes! Isn't it wonderful?"

He looked and could not imagine what she meant for, try as hard as he could, it was impossible for him to come to terms with the smells, the deformed beggars and the jostling, vacant looking crowds that impeded the passage of their car, with the scabby pye-dogs and hideously skinny cows that ambled aimlessly along. "I don't think wonderful's exactly the word I'd use," he said cautiously.

"You'll see it in time," Baby told him. "The skin'll fall off your eyes and you'll see the wonder of India. At least for your sake I hope you do."

She insisted on dropping him opposite the doorway of his block of flats, and before she slipped across the front bench seat of her car, she leaned across and kissed him on the cheek. "Thank you very much for a lovely day," she said sweetly.

He smelled her soapy scent, he felt the softness of her skin and every nerve in his body was activated. Never in his life had he wanted a woman so much, but he knew that if he grabbed Baby and kissed her as he wanted to kiss her, he'd probably never see her again. So he just stammered something about enjoying himself too, and jumped out into the middle of the traffic, almost getting himself killed by a passing car as he did so. She laughed, waved her hand, threw the car into gear with the short stick on the steering wheel and drove away.

The table lamps in his sitting room were burning, making welcoming pools of light, when he let himself into the flat and threw his rolled towel and damp shorts onto the sofa. Govind was hovering in the doorway of the kitchen.

"Get me a beer," said Dennis and headed for his bedroom.

"Sahib—" said Govind but his employer did not wait to hear what he had to say. He was intent on having a shower and then lying in bed thinking about his afternoon with Baby.

The bedside lights were on as well and there was someone in his bed. He paused on the threshold and stared at the tumble of black hair on the pillow, at the curve of the girl's back and the outline of her bent legs beneath the sheet. She was lying with her thumb in her mouth like a delinquent child and she was sound asleep.

"Christ!" said Dennis loudly.

Govind was behind him with the glass of beer on a tray. "She had a key, sahib. She said you'd given it to her . . ."

Carole sat up, pushing her hair out of her eyes and smiled at Dennis. She was so beautiful, and his need was so intense, that he felt himself stagger. Taking the beer off the tray, he closed the door on Govind and walked across the marble tiled floor to the bed.

She was sitting up now, the sheet held modestly around her for she had nothing on. "I fell asleep waiting for you," she whispered.

He sat down heavily on the edge of the mattress and said, "Did Monica give you her key?"

"Yes. I wanted to surprise you." She leaned towards him and he caught a whiff of patchouli from her. It wasn't a scent he liked but that suddenly didn't matter because she stretched out one thin arm and pulled his head towards her.

With a groan like a man being led to execution, he fell into the bed.

Twelve

E ver since she married, Barbara Maling-Smith had been looked after by an ayah called Parvati and they had grown old together.

Twice a year, as part of her salary, Parvati was given a new white sari with a narrow coloured border, and, twice a year, she sent last season's sari to her sister in a tiny village in the Western ghats near Mahableshwar.

She had been a monkey-faced, dark-haired young woman, a widow already although she was only twenty, when she first went to work for 'My Lady' as she called Barbara. Now, though there was almost twenty years between them, they looked the same age, for Parvati had gradually dried up like a brown nut, her comical little face had crinkled all over, and there were white streaks in her glossy hair.

What was unchanged however was her ribald sense of humour and her devotion to her employer. She would have died for *My Lady*.

Often, when Sir Robert had retired for the night to his room next door to his wife's, and when Baby was away from home, the ayah and her mistress would settle down for a good gossip, the ayah squatting on the floor and Barbara lying stretched out on her bed with her long arms crossed behind her head. They talked in a mixture of Hindi and English, often breaking out in cackling giggles because they shared an earthy sense of the comic, and especially enjoyed slightly dirty jokes. There was nothing that happened in the household that Parvati did not tell Barbara, and these confidences often caused ructions between her and the rest of the staff, for there was always someone operating one scam or another – but Barbara had been in India long enough to know that, and also to accept that a certain amount of speculation must be allowed if good relations between employers and employees were to be maintained. She only began to act the strict memsahib when things looked like getting out of hand.

It was Parvati who told Baby's mother what the bearer Mohammed from the Gulmohurs had told the Maling-Smiths' driver – that Baby had spent a night with Charlie Grey, that she was desperately in love with him, and broken-hearted when he went back to England to marry another girl.

Baby herself had confided none of this to her mother, but Barbara was too loving and too observant not to sense her daughter's deep unhappiness. She wasn't shocked, she wasn't disapproving of Baby or angry at Charlie – she was only sad that her beloved daughter couldn't have the man she wanted. She knew what it was to have a happy marriage because, in spite of their apparent gruffness with each other, in spite of the way Robert seemed to disapprove of things she said or did, they loved each other and when she looked at him across their vast dining table, she was always vastly grateful that fate had literally thrown them at each other.

If only I could arrange something like that for Baby, she thought, if only. When she tried to bring the subject up however, her daughter fended it off like a tennis player taking a wild swipe at a whizzing ball. She didn't want to talk about it.

But the time was coming when Barbara knew that she and Baby would have to have a real talk – and she had been putting it off too.

She was still in bed on the morning after Baby's trip to Juhu when Parvati came into the bedroom with a glass of orange juice in her hand. She screwed up her face at the sight of it.

"Ugh. I don't want that. Bring me a gin, Parvati."

The little woman laid the juice down on the marble topped side table with a defiant thump and said, "Too early for gin, madam. Drink the juice. It's good for you."

"It gives me belly ache. You know that."

"You are hurting?"

"Yes, I am."

"I'll send a boy for sugar-cane juice then. It's good for hurting bellies."

Barbara sighed. "I think I'm past sugar-cane juice too. Just bring me a gin. That's the only thing that helps now."

"Ay-eee," sighed the servant softly but she took away the juice and a few moments later was back with a clinking glass of gin – a double.

When Barbara drank it she felt better and sat up, reaching towards the side table for her array of rings which she slipped onto her fingers, one after the other. When she finished she held up her right hand and waved it in the air, making the rings rattle. "They're loose," she told Parvati who shook her head.

"You should go to the hills soon – Kandala or Mahableshwar – you are always better up there in the hot weather. You'll get fat again," she said.

Barbara laughed, "You mean *you* don't like the hot weather down on the plains. I'll probably go up soon. I was planning to phone the Mahableshwar Club to book our usual rooms. Do you think Baby will come?"

"Our Baby has found a new man. She went to Juhu with him yesterday."

Barbara looked up sharply, "Who is he?"

Parvati shrugged to signify she did not know.

"Has your secret service let you down?" asked Barbara incredulously.

"I will find out in time. I know he lives in Marine Drive and is handsome, healthy-looking, will make good children I think."

"Well, that's comforting," said Barbara. When she put her bare feet on the floor and stood up, however, she could not stop herself grimacing in pain.

Immediately Parvati was at her side, taking her arm. "You must go to the doctor, madam," she said solemnly.

Dumbly Barbara nodded. "I know," she replied, "but before I do, fetch me another gin."

Dr Green had a consulting room in his flat above a pork butcher's shop in a side street between the Fort and the Taj Mahal Hotel. The butcher was famous for his salami sausages, which were particularly popular with Parsis, and on the days when he boiled up the ingredients for these famous delicacies, the doctor's flat stank. Fortunately the sausage making only happened one day a week – every Monday. It took the other six days however for the smell to clear away completely.

The doctor's late wife Hannah used to complain about the location of their dwelling. "We must move," she would cry, throwing open the door of his consulting room when she knew there was no patient with him. "We must move at once. That stink is turning my stomach. I am a Jew, you are a Jew – how can we live with the smell of pork in our nostrils all the time?"

"Very well, we will move. Look out for another place," he always said but, though she looked, she never found another flat that suited them as well. In spite of the smell, their home, on the first floor of an old building, was rambling and cool with windows looking out across the city on one side and to the Gateway of India and the sea on the other. The rooms were high-ceilinged and spacious, and very reminiscent of the flat they had occupied in Vienna when they were first married.

Both of them got used to the smell in time, and now that Hannah was dead, he had ceased to notice it at all.

They had landed in Bombay, 'washed up' he used to say, in 1937, when he had realised the direction life was taking for Jews in Vienna. Because they were young, with little to lose, and without children or parents for both of them were orphans, they closed the door of their flat one night and simply vanished. He had always been fascinated by India and so that was where they went.

When he set up his practice, Barbara Maling-Smith was one of his first patients. Hearing how clever he was, for his reputation spread swiftly among the European society of the city, she took her daughter to him when Baby was suffering from a bad dose of measles.

He was always good with children and children's ailments, and it seemed to Barbara that from the moment he laid a hand on her child, Baby began to get better. The next time she consulted him it was on her own behalf – she had a miscarriage, and was not only severely debilitated but also bitterly disappointed at losing the child – a boy. Dr Green treated her mind as well as her body, counselling her with gentle wisdom so that she was able to come to terms with her loss and accept the fact that her child-bearing years were over.

Since then, from time to time, he had treated her or Baby, rarely Robert however who claimed never to be ill anyway and on the rare occasions that he was – when he got hepatitis for example – liked to go back to England, to Harley Street, for he was sure that the size of a doctor's bill was a sign of his expertise. Dr Green's charges were always modest for he was not a greedy man. In Vienna he had seen too many members of his community revelling in their wealth – and he'd seen what happened to them. Sometimes he wondered about the fate of cousins of his or Hannah's, and shuddered. It was hard for him to accept that such evil abounded as gripped the people he had known and liked when he was young but who turned against him and his people. He tried not to think about it.

He had not seen Barbara Maling-Smith for some time on the morning when his secretary Mrs Gomez, who had worked for him ever since he first arrived in India and who had a mind like a calculating machine, never forgetting the most minor detail about any patient, knocked on his door and said, "Lady Maling-Smith has arrived to see you, doctor. She hasn't an appointment but I think you ought to fit her in."

He was working at his desk, gold-rimmed spectacles perched on the lower part of his nose and his wiry grey hair all sticking out like a saint's halo. "Is she in trouble?" he asked anxiously for he was fond of Barbara.

"I think she is," said Mrs Gomez, who liked her too.

Dr Green – though Green was not his real name but only an Anglicised one he had adopted when he came to Bombay – had the magical gift of diagnosing through his eyes. He did not have to take tests, or even touch a patient, to know what ailed them and he often found this ability of his to be a disadvantage, especially when he was fond of the person who was consulting him.

When Barbara came breezing through his door his heart sank. She was as scattily eccentric-looking as ever, as smiling and friendly, but he could see that she was ill, perhaps very ill. Always thin, she was now almost skeletal and there was a haunted look around her eyes that he had seen many times in others and which always upset him. Her charm was unaffected however.

"Darling Doctor," she cried, and took both his hands in hers, "Aren't you looking well!" It was as if he was consulting her and not the other way about.

"I am well," he agreed, "but what about you?"

She sat down in the chair he pulled out for her beside his desk and said, "As a matter of fact I'm not brilliant. I've got this bloody awful pain in my gut. And I can't eat. I'm living on gin, in fact, and Robert's very fed up with me."

"On gin?"

"Yes, bloody awful Indian gin too, usually Parry's, not even decent Gordon's."

"How much gin?"

"About six or seven doubles a day – well, maybe ten or eleven."

He gave a little gasp. "How do you get your hands on it?"

She waggled the beringed fingers around, "Oh that's easy. We've our own bootlegger. He brings it to the house. God knows where he gets it; sometimes I think from the taste of it that he makes it himself."

He took her bony right wrist between his finger and thumb and silently counted the pulse beats as he told her, "You shouldn't be drinking as much as that. I've told you so before."

"I know, you've always saying so, but you see, there's days I simply can't get through without it. It's the pain . . ."

"Where?"

She laid her other hand, palm-down on her abdomen. "Here." Then she put the hand on her back, "And here."

Feeling very sad, he stood up and told her, "Well, we'd better have an X-ray first, don't you think? I'll ring Breach Candy and they'll do the X-ray and send it back here to me. Can you go there now?"

She nodded. "You're so good to me," she said, and then she looked up at his face and asked, "Tell me, what's your name?"

"Green of course, you know that."

"I know that. I mean your real name. Your real first name. What did your mother and father call you?"

"Moshe Grenfeld . . ."

"Moshe. Is that like Moses?"

"Yes."

She laughed. "That's something to live up to, isn't it?"

He laughed as well, relieved to be doing so. He dropped her hand and told her, "Go and have the X-ray now and come back in three days' time. Then we'll work out how to treat the pain without quite so much gin."

Her eyes were suddenly unguarded and infinitely sad as she looked at him, the first time he'd ever seen her like that. "You mustn't worry," he said softly.

Fortunately she did not ask anything else. It was as if she knew too.

Thirteen

The glory of dawn streaking the sea and throwing a miraculous light through his uncurtained bedroom windows had woken Dennis early that morning.

It took him a few moments to gather his wits, and it was not till he saw Carole curled up beside him that the full force of realisation struck him.

"Oh my God," he said aloud, sitting bolt upright and staring at her.

She rolled over, opened her almond eyes and smiled at him. "Good morning," she whispered.

He leapt out of bed as if she'd jabbed him with a needle. "It's late," he jabbered, "You'd better get up and I'll take you home."

She looked surprised. "Home? To Chembur?"

"Yes."

"Can't I stay here? Monica stayed here with Bob. She looked after him. I'll look after you."

He didn't want looking after but was too polite to tell her that. "It's not that. It's because your mother will be worried about you, Carole. I think I'd better take you home."

"Oh my mother won't worry . . . and what about last night?" she whispered, kneeling up in the bed and slipping her hands across his bare chest. He recoiled, feeling guilty.

"It was very nice . . ." I sound like a child saying, 'Thank you for a nice party,' he thought. But panic was stronger in him now than libido.

She smiled, "Wasn't it? You were *wonderful* . . ." She bent forward and kissed him on the lips.

That didn't cut much ice with him though. He was still determined to take her home. "Get dressed, Carole," he said firmly. "I'll take you home before I go to the office and I've got to be at my desk by nine o'clock."

She huddled in the front seat of his car, like a child, sucking her thumb, a habit that was beginning to irritate him intensely, as

94

he drove like a maniac along half-empty roads. Occasionally she removed the thumb for long enough to give a little gulping sob but he ignored her and they didn't speak till the bungalow with the Alsatian prowling to and fro on the end of its long rope in front of it came into sight. Then she perked up, brushed her tumbling hair back from her face and asked, "Will you come back for me tonight?"

"Not tonight. I've got to go to the Gym tonight."

In fact he had no plans to go anywhere but he didn't want to be hooked in by Carole, even though he felt a complete rat by refusing her – she'd slept with him after all, hadn't she? She'd given herself to him. How was he ever going to get rid of her?

She didn't take his refusal amiss though. "Come tomorrow then," she said equably, "We can go to the cinema. To the Metro. Marilyn Monroe is on."

He couldn't refuse her again so he said, "OK," as he pulled the brake on in front of her house and when she invited him inside, he refused saying, "I have to go to the office, Carole. I'll be late if I don't go now."

"All right," she said with a smile, and turned to walk up the steps to the door, swinging her hips in a passable imitation of the famous Marilyn. He watched her with fascination, excited in spite of his warning conscience.

He was about to turn the car onto the main road again when he saw Carole's surly sister Amy standing at a bus stop on the other side of the pot-holed tarmac beneath a ragged-looking palm tree. Her head was down and she was reading a book held up to her face in her left hand. From her right dangled a black fake-leather briefcase. She looked tired and dejected already though the day hadn't yet begun.

He tooted the horn and drew up in front of her, leaning over and rolling down the window.

"Are you going into the city?" he asked.

Although she was alone at the bus stop she looked around her in an exaggerated way and then said, "Are you speaking to me?"

"Yes, you're Carole's sister, aren't you?" For a moment he thought he might have confused her with someone else.

"I have a sister who calls herself Carole."

"Calls herself?" His neck was beginning to hurt from straining across at her. Either she got into the car or she didn't. He wished he hadn't stopped.

"Her real name's Minnie."

"Minnie!" Why did he keep repeating what the woman said? She was staring at him expressionlessly, her eyes cold. They were golden brown like sugar syrup, he noticed.

"Do you want a lift to the city?" he asked again. "I'm going into the Fort and you work in the Fort, don't you?"

"Yes. I work in the Fort. I missed my train. That's why I'm waiting for a bus."

"Get in," he said and opened the door wider. Amazingly she did as she was told but it soon transpired that she'd only accepted the lift in order to torment him.

She started off by sitting as far away from him as possible and not saying a word although he tried making innocuous conversation about the places they were passing.

They'd been driving for about twenty minutes and were passing a large junction with a petrol station on one corner when he asked in an effort to force conversation from her, "What do you call this place?"

"Worli."

"That's an odd name. Sounds Australian."

"Austreyleyen . . ." she repeated, mimicking his accent. He flushed and said, "I mean it sounds as if it might be a place in Australia." He knew he was digging himself in deeper.

"You've only just arrived in India, haven't you? You've never been away from home before," she said, and it was a statement, not a question.

"That's right," he agreed, deliberatedly and forcedly cheerful.

"Are you planning to take my sister Minnie back to Austreyleya?"

He glared at her and saw she was smiling sweetly at him, so sweetly she almost looked pretty. When she smiled there was a trace of Carole's pertness about her face.

"I hadn't thought about it," he told her.

"She has. My mother has and our cousin Monica has. You'd better watch out. They're formidable women when they get together."

He could well believe it but loyalty to the girl who had so recently shared his bed made him change the subject. "You don't seem to like your family much," he said.

She stared ahead out of the dusty, smeared windscreen. "They're not very likeable," she said bitterly and there was something desolate in her attitude that made him soften slightly towards her.

"What's your name?" he asked. "Is Amy your real name or do you have a pseudonym too? Like Carole for Minnie . . ."

"A pseudonym isn't a real name, it's an alternative false name.

Carole is Minnie's middle name. Our mother called her after Carole Lombard."

He didn't want to get tied up in shades of meaning, or dispute the nuances of words with her. "Is Amy your real name?" he asked again.

"Amy's what I call myself. I picked it out of a book called *Little Women*. Have you ever read it?"

Dennis didn't read much so he shook his head. "You mean you weren't christened Amy?"

"That's right. I was christened Philomena. I think it's a horrible name so I changed it. What's your full name?"

"Dennis Joseph Gillies but my family call me Denny or Den."

"Den – like a hole in the ground," she said and smiled like a satisfied cat. He regretted unbending towards her and couldn't think what to say next.

They were at Kemp's Corner and hitting the really heavy traffic into the city when she next spoke. "If you want to keep my sister out of your flat you ought to change the lock. Monica gave her a key and she'll be dropping in on you all the time if you don't."

"There's not much sisterly affection between you, is there?" he said.

From the corner of his eye he saw her shrug. "Not a lot. She's always been my mother's pet because they look so like each other. I take after my father. But our mother's very bright and Carole's lazy and rather stupid. She's a tart because it's easier than working."

He gritted his teeth and drove on. "You work?" he asked.

"Yes."

"Do you like your job?"

She turned her head and looked at him, "Not a lot but I wouldn't stop working and start sleeping with men for money if that's what you mean."

"Has anyone ever asked you?"

She was bending down and picking her briefcase off the floor. "Just stop here and let me off. I'll catch a bus now," she said.

He pulled up right beside another bus stop and watched as she got out. Normally he would have run round the car and opened the door for a girl as his mother had taught him, or at least reached over and released the handle but he did neither for her. She was looking angry as she stumbled out onto the pavement. She didn't thank him for the lift but her parting shot was, "Don't say you weren't warned."

"Thank you Miss Amy," he said and drove away.

When he went home at lunchtime however he gave Govind orders to change the door lock. Then on his return to the office, he found a Bombay telephone book and looked up Maling-Smith. Not many private houses in the city had a telephone but Baby's family did and he was genuinely surprised when he saw that her father was listed as Sir Robert.

"Oh God," he thought as he closed the book without calling her, "I haven't a chance with her. What would she see in me?"

As it turned out however it was Baby who contacted him. She rang the High Commission that evening at about five o'clock when he was thinking about going home. The two Indian clerks who worked with him were eagerly eavesdropping as he took the call, because one of them had got to the phone first and said to him, "It's a girl and she wants you."

At first he thought it might be Carole and considered getting his clerk to say he had gone home but decided to brave it out and accepted the proffered receiver. He was glad he did because the voice that spoke was not Carole's sleepy sing song. It was Baby's well-bred English drawl and he was surprised at how pleased he felt when he heard it.

"Hi," she said brightly, "I just called to say how much I enjoyed myself yesterday and to ask you if you'd thought about going to the boat club dance next Saturday."

"I'm not in any boat club," he said confusedly. For a moment he had trouble remembering what bit of yesterday she was talking about. So much had happened to him.

"Don't worry about that. I'm a member. They have a dance every year on an island in the creek. It's always a great do. You'd enjoy it and you'd meet lots of new people."

"You didn't tell me your father has a title," he said in a rush.

There was a slight pause and then she said, "No, I don't usually talk about that. Does it matter?"

"No, of course not. I just thought . . ."

"Don't be silly, Dennis," she said quite sharply, "Would you like to come to the boat club dance or not?"

"Yes, I would," he said.

Fourteen

"Old Guy's coming back," said Ben when he tore open and read the airletter that the BA on the bike had brought to the bungalow on Wednesday morning. It had brooded on the dining table all day but though Dee knew who'd sent it – Guy's handwriting was unmistakeable – she resolutely forbade herself to open it because it was addressed to Ben alone and she would have taken it very amiss if he opened one of her letters when she wasn't there.

They had been studiously polite and considerate with each other since the Marine Drive party. Ben had apologised and promised to mend his ways but though she pretended she did, she hadn't really believed him.

"When's he coming back?" she asked, sounding abrupt in spite of herself.

"In ten days . . . The Hospital for Tropical Diseases have signed him off and he wants to get back as soon as possible, silly bugger."

She looked down into her glass of lime soda, acutely conscious of Mohammed hovering, ears twitching, at the verandah door. "That's good. You'll be pleased," she said.

Ben was watching her cautiously, not sure of what she was feeling, and she knew he always found her hard to read.

"Money'll be easier when he gets back. We won't have to carry the expense of this place on our own . . . We couldn't have gone on doing that much longer," he said, knowing how much this concerned her.

"Yes," she agreed and smiled but still sounded despondent for she did not relish the prospect of having to endure Guy's ill-concealed hostility again.

Ben suddenly grinned at her, his eyebrows peaking in the devilish way they did when he was particularly pleased about something. "Cheer up, duck face," he said. "I've just heard that the company's getting that contract to build the nylon factory at Deolali. The boss is over the moon and I'm the blue-eyed boy at the moment. It's the biggest thing we've ever done and the work starts before the rains come. Aren't you pleased? They're going to give me a car and travelling expenses."

Her smile and delight this time was genuine. "Why didn't you tell me immediately you came home? That's absolutely wonderful. You've done terribly well. They'd never have got that contract if it hadn't been for you!"

Ben, who'd studied mechanical engineering at college but dropped out to take up the offer of a job in Bombay before he graduated, had really put his back into securing that contract, making frequent trips to Deolali, negotiating with the company that wanted to build the plant, undercutting the prices of other contractors, and spending hour after hour planning the intricate piping layout, even building a miniature model of the factory to show the clients. His industry and interest in this job had impressed Dee who'd never seen him give much attention to any professional concern before. Unknown to her, however, her constant concern and growing disillusion about their prospects was beginning to influence her husband.

She rose from her chair and went over to hug him. "Well done, you deserve it," she said.

"I've only got to build it now," he said. "It means that I'll have to spend a bit of time away from home when it's going on. I'm glad Guy'll be here and you won't be alone. I've a feeling that our luck's turning. In fact I might even be able to talk old Ratanlal into giving me a raise." Ratanlal, the Indian owner of the company Ben worked for, was notorious with them for his reluctance to part with money and for his previous disenchantment with his youngest European employee.

"That would be wonderful," she said, delight brimming out of her, "And they're giving you a car! Does that mean we'll be able to sell the Studebaker?" BMZ420X was not paid for by Ben's employers and was an immense drain on their slender resources but impossible to exist without till now because Ratanlal said that if Ben chose to live out in the jungle, that was his problem and no reason for the company to provide him with a car or travelling expenses.

Ben shook his head. "No, let's hope not. You'll need it here because I'll take the company one to Deolali . . . and anyway it's not a car I'm getting, it's a Willy's jeep. Those roads off the island are very rough."

Dee laughed. "Trust Ratanlal not to indulge you." But the idea of driving around India in an open-topped jeep enthralled her, especially when Ben said, "We'll take a trip in it. We might be able to go to Poona and Deolali next weekend."

"Great!" she cried clasping her hands together, for it was always difficult to persuade Ben to venture off the island at weekends because he preferred going to the perpetual Saturday night parties that the rugby set organised. The misty amethyst outline of the hills on the eastern horizon beyond Bombay island lured her with an almost unbearable pain. She longed to go there, to see what it was like on the other side of the stretch of water, on the other side of the flat plain that fringed the Indian subcontinent, to climb the road up the Western ghats and find herself in village India.

As they talked, darkness crept up their garden like a silent thief; the heady scent of the jasmine called Queen of the Night floated sleepily into the house; in the bushes small animals and snakes rustled; the smell of cooking fires burning cow dung and wood came down the hill from the buffalo camp where the gossiping women who visited the well lived. As they waited for Mohammed to announce that dinner was ready, Ben smoked his Camel cigarettes and talked about his nylon plant. Dee listened, curled up on the cane sofa, watching him, taking pleasure from his new optimism. Somehow it was easier to live with him now that a certain distance had opened up between them.

From the kitchen at the back of the house came the sounds of rattling pots and hissing voices. How ridiculous it is, she thought, that we are sitting here waiting to be served by a household of servants when we haven't two cents to our names. She needed a new pair of sandals but hadn't the money to buy them and had mended the broken strap of her old ones with sellotape. Yet when Mohammed went off for his half day a week, he was always resplendent in a white duck suit and black and white 'co-respondent' shoes. She'd seen him the other day climbing into a taxi at the gate and been impressed by his prosperous-looking finery.

But things were surely going to get better. Ben would make a success of his factory and their situation would improve. She was sure of it. She looked across at her husband's face, alight with enthusiasm, and felt a surge of new affection for him.

They had finished dinner and were back on the verandah, childishly playing noughts and crosses together, when there was a rustling from the shrubbery along the edge of the nullah and a figure stepped out into the middle of the lawn. It was Shadiv and when she saw him Dee's heart did what felt like a double somersault in her chest and she dropped her pencil. Bending down to pick it up, she thought she was going to faint and was genuinely shocked and surprised by the effect he had on her.

He was grinning broadly as he came leaping up the verandah steps with his hand extended towards Ben.

"Hi," he said, "I'm your neighbour, from over there . . ." gesturing across the dark ridge of the fruit trees. "I met your wife the other day and she said to come over and meet you."

Ben was always good with new people and he greeted Shadiv like an old friend, inviting him to sit down and clapping his hands to summon Mohammed who was instructed to bring out one of their last bottles of beer. Mohammed, too, was excessively cordial, bending like an acolyte over the visitor as he poured the liquid out of the bottle into Shadiv's glass. He obviously knew who this handsome Indian was and Dee's standing had gone up with him because of her ability to lure this film star into the house.

Because of the prohibition laws it was illegal to serve alcohol to an Indian guest who, like Shadiv, had no drinking permit but they had no prying neighbours and an impressed Mohammed would keep their secret.

Dee sat watching them and felt as if her bones had turned to water. My God, what's happening to me? she wondered and was glad that there was little light on the verandah so that her confusion would not be noticed. She recovered her composure by the time Ben started to play their favourite records. Music poured out, jazz riffs of Dave Brubeck and Louis Armstrong's trumpet filling the velvet night while they swayed in their chairs, chattered, laughed and started to get to know each other.

Watching Shadiv sitting back in his chair and thrusting out his long legs, it struck Dee that he and Ben were actually very much the same type, not in appearance of course because Ben was Viking blond, but in character for both were essentially male, sporty, sociable, sentimental, men of action – and sexy of course. All the 'S's. That must be the type of man I go for, she thought.

It was nearly two o'clock in the morning when their visitor left. That night, their differences forgotten, Ben and Dee made love and fell asleep entwined together in the tangled sheets of their bed. When she woke, Dee lay still beside her sleeping husband and resolved to do nothing to fuel the feelings she was surprised to find she had for Shadiv. It was possible, she told herself, to nip those sort of things in the bud, to stop them before they started. They were married people, who had made promises that should not be broken. She remembered how angry she'd been when Ben had made a pass at that air hostess. She couldn't justify that sort of anger, expect him to understand her need for him not to flirt, and engage in a dalliance herself.

Besides wasn't it presumptuous of her to imagine that Shadiv could ever feel the same way about her as she did about him – why should he? His wife, who she had never seen in person but who smiled down from movie posters all over the city, was beautiful, pneumatic breasted and sultry. It was like pitching oneself against Helen of Troy.

"Pull yourself together," she told herself, as she pulled on her dressing gown and went through to the shower to prepare for another sweaty day. Though it was early, not yet seven o'clock, it was already hot and day by day the temperature was climbing steadily. Soon it would be almost unbearably hot round the clock in the run-up to Dee's second monsoon. Somewhere she'd read that in the old days when young women were shipped out to India, their average life expectancy was only three monsoons . . . would she last longer than that?

Not that she expected to succumb to some tropical disease, but she might decide to bale out after all before her third monsoon was over. Especially now that Guy was coming back.

That thought too she routed, soaping her cropped head and letting the jet of cold water pour over her as she told herself, Think about the trip up-country, don't think about Guy. Think about how this hasty marriage of yours is going to work out . . .

Fifteen

The X-rays from Breach Candy were hanging up on the illuminated viewing stand and Dr Green was staring at them with a stricken look on his face when Mrs Gomez walked into his consulting room to tell him that Lady Maling-Smith had arrived.

"Damnation!" he snapped and he was a man who very rarely swore.

"Will I ask her to wait?" asked Mrs Gomez anxiously. She could see that there were long worry lines running down each side of her employer's mouth and he looked desperately tired. The coming of the hot weather always exhausted him.

"No, I'll see her. Just give me time to take these down." And he wrenched the horrible-looking pictures from their grips. Though she'd worked for the doctor for so long, Mrs Gomez always thought X-rays looked frightening. She didn't want to know what was going on inside her. Those awful films were the ultimate invasion of privacy as far as she was concerned.

"Will I bring in some coffee?" she asked, backing out of the office.

He was back behind his desk, putting the films into a blue cardboard folder. "Yes, bring coffee and some of those little biscuits with the sugar on them," he said. Mrs Gomez knew that if he was giving Lady Maling-Smith sugared biscuits he was also going to have to give her bad news.

Barbara was feeling better that morning. She'd woken up without pain for once and almost persuaded herself that it had gone for good, so she was smiling when she swept in to see her friend the doctor.

"Isn't it a beautiful morning, Moses? The sea is absolutely turquoise. I love this season, you know."

He came round from the back of his desk and pulled out a chair for her. "How long have you lived here?" he asked.

"Guess!"

He spread his hands in a very Jewish-looking gesture, "How can I? Tell me."

"I was born in India, in Darjeeling as a matter of fact . . . how long ago? I never remember my age. Sixty-five years. I've never been away from it for more than six months at a time. This is my country. My great great great grandfather came out as an officer in the East India Company's army at the time of Clive and we've been here ever since. The cathedral's full of plates and tablets commemorating my relatives."

"Living history," said Dr Green.

Barbara laughed. "I'm a bit of a relic, I suppose. You're right."

When she settled herself in the chair and pushed out her long legs, Mrs Gomez came in with the coffee. "How lovely!" cried Barbara to her, "You always make the most delicious coffee, and I love those little biscuits. Where do you get them?"

"In Colaba Causeway, the big grocery store half-way along on the left . . ." said Mrs Gomez and would have lingered if the doctor had not given an impatient cough telling her to go away. Barbara noticed the cough too and her expression changed when she looked across the desk at him.

"You've got my X-rays?" she said quietly when they were alone.

"Yes, drink your coffee, my dear and we'll talk about them." It was not his policy to tell patients lies about their condition unless he felt they would not be able to face up to the truth. His respect for Barbara Maling-Smith was immense and he was certainly not going to lie to her.

She sipped the coffee and laid down the cup with a hand that showed not a tremor. Then she smiled at him and said, "Right. Let me have it. What have I got?"

When he told her she did not blink and he was reminded of all those soldier ancestors who had faced up to horrible dangers in the past.

"I have cancer," she said. Few people could bring themself to say the word but she uttered it without flinching.

"Yes, I'm afraid so." He felt sick as he said the words.

"How bad is it?"

"Very bad. You must have suffered considerable pain."

She shrugged, dismissing pain. "Gin helps," she told him, "I hope you're not going to tell me to stop taking it because I won't."

"I won't tell you any such thing. If it helps, take it."

"How long have I got?" was her next question.

He put his frizzled grey head in his hands and groaned, "Not more than about three months."

"Are you sure?"

"Yes."

"So there's no point trying to go back to England, is there?"

"Well you might want another medical opinion . . . I know Sir Robert likes Harley Street. I could tell you who to go to there."

She snorted. "My husband likes Harley Street but I don't. I much prefer you. What you say is good enough for me. And three months is quite a long time, isn't it? A lot can happen in three months."

He hoped she wasn't holding out false hope for herself. "It won't change," he said cautiously.

"Of course not. I don't mean that. I mean I might get eaten by a tiger or something . . ." And she laughed her peculiar braying laugh that his wife used to say reminded her of a donkey. Hannah had been jealous of Barbara Maling-Smith.

He stood up behind his desk, sticking his trembling hands into the side pockets of his linen jacket as he did so. "Do you want to see the X-rays?" he asked her.

"Oh yes, I was hoping you'd show them to me and explain what they mean," she said earnestly.

So he brought out the negatives again and pinned them up once more, averting his eyes from the virulent patch in the centre that he knew to be cancerous. She spotted it at once. "That's it. That's my trouble, isn't it? Horrible stuff," she said, shaking her bejewelled fist at it.

He nodded silently. He was finding this even harder than he'd imagined. If there was anything he could have done to reverse the diagnosis he would have done it. She saw his distress and told him, "You mustn't upset yourself. I've had the most wonderful life. There's not many people who have been as blessed as me."

Dr Green wiped his eyes with a huge white handkerchief and said, "Do you want me to tell your husband for you?"

"Oh no. I'm not going to tell him yet. He'll just get into a terrible state and there's no point making him suffer before he has to."

"But you'll have to tell him eventually. Do you want me to do it for you then?"

She shook her head, "Thank you but no. I'll do it myself. We've been through a lot together, my Bobby and I, and we'll get through this too."

"What about your daughter? What about Roberta?" It didn't seem right to refer to her as Baby at this time, so he used her proper name.

Her mother's face clouded. "I've been wondering about her too.

My Baby has had a bad time recently, Dr Green. She's been very sad but it looks as if she might be coming out of it. I'm not going to make her sad again so I won't tell her yet."

He knew it wasn't the professional way to behave but he walked round his desk and gave her an enormous hug, squeezing her thin body in his short arms and wishing with all his heart that he could perform a miracle and make her well again. That was why he'd become a doctor in the first place, to make people well, and when it wasn't possible, he truly suffered, though he'd never suffered as badly as he was doing now, not even when his Hannah died. It suddenly struck him that he'd been in love with Barbara Maling-Smith for years and years.

"You mustn't worry – about the pain I mean. I'll help you," he promised her.

She patted his cheek. "Thank you," she said.

Picking up her capacious crocodile handbag from the floor beside her chair, she strode out of the office, pausing to congratulate Mrs Gomez on her coffee on the way out. To look at her no one could have guessed that she'd just listened to her own sentence of death.

Her car and driver were waiting at the entrance to the doctor's flat and when the driver saw her emerge, he leaped out and held the passenger door open but she shook her head. "I'm going along to the Taj for a coffee," she said. "Pick me up there in an hour."

She entered the Taj Mahal hotel by a side door that took her along a colonnaded arcade lined on both sides by little shops that used to sell the most luxurious items of perfumery, leatherwork and clothing from Europe but were now reduced to empty windows or pathetic little displays of Indian soaps. One of the shops was a photography studio with the window full of pictures of chubby babies and radiant brides in white crinolines. Barbara stopped in front of this display and stared at the brides, suddenly feeling her heart ache in her breast.

The one thing she wanted most in the world before she died was to see her daughter happy; to see her beloved Baby married to a good man who would look after her as dear Bob had looked after her mother. There was nothing modern about Barbara's way of thinking. For her a woman's destiny was to be married and have children.

There were tears trickling down her cheeks when she climbed the curving stairs to the lounge overlooking the sea and ordered coffee. There she sat for more than an hour, staring out at the Gateway of

India and the sparkling sea beyond it. She was praying, not to a Christian god but to all the pagan deities that had figured in her bedtime stories as a child.

'Please let me see Baby happy,' she pleaded with them.

Sixteen

When Baby slowed down her car on a bend of the road going to the airport and pulled over onto a muddy-looking track, Dennis's heart sank for it was all he could do to stop himself gagging. This was the place where the smell of raw sewage was the worst he'd ever experienced – and in Bombay that was, he reckoned, really saying something.

"Is the party *here*?" he asked in disbelief when he saw lines of other cars drawn up on the edge of a stretch of evil-looking water, the surface of which glittered green, yellow and purple in the car's headlights as if it was covered with a sheet of oil.

"It's Kurla Creek. The party's on an island out there," said Baby pointing across the horrible water.

The stench was all pervasive now, throat-catching and sickening, and he couldn't believe she was serious.

"But what about the smell?" he wanted to call it a stink but censored his words.

She stared at him wide-eyed. "What smell?" she asked.

"Oh come on, Baby, you're kidding," he said, trying to laugh and wishing he could call her by some other name. She couldn't have been christened that. Baby sounded so pretentious and silly, he thought.

"I'm not," she said.

"But it's a swamp, it's a sewer. I've never smelt anything like it."

She laughed, giving him the slight hope that she had been leading him on. "Well actually it is a sewer I suppose but you do get used to it. Old hands don't smell it after a bit," she said.

"You mean you can't smell that?" he asked waving his hand at the front windscreen of the car where he imagined the smell hung like a visible miasma.

"Compared to some Indian smells it's not too bad," said Baby, opening the car door and stepping out into the night. Immediately two ragged-looking men came running up shouting something and she called back to them. Then she turned to Dennis and told him, "One of the boats is just about to go across. They'll take us too if we hurry up." And clutching her bottle of gin she began running towards a rickety wooden jetty that stuck out into the fetid water. Dennis, also carrying gin, had no alternative but run after her.

There were six people already in a leaky-looking little rowing boat that floated so far down in the water that there was only about two inches of wood showing all the way round.

Baby climbed aboard, greeting the people already there. Two of them were Dee and Ben, both looking glum because Dee was in a very bad mood at Ben for wriggling out of his promise to take her exploring on the mainland in order to attend the boat club party.

"I don't want to go to that party," she'd said when it dawned on her what he was trying to do, for if they went to the party they would certainly not wake till Sunday afternoon – too late to go exploring, "It'll just be like all the other Bombay parties – same people, same jokes, same fights, same scandals . . ."

"Oh no, this one's different. The boat club party is always special. Different people go and they hold it on an island in Kurla Creek, there's bonfires and a barbecue. Goody Servai's band plays and they're always great. It's the best party of the season and we couldn't go last year because you were sick, remember?"

She remembered very well being felled by violent sickness, the peculiar disease called 'Bombay lurgi' that gripped every European after they'd been a few weeks in the city. Ben said you had to get it over with and afterwards you were fine providing you drank enough whisky to sterilise your gut. She remembered how bereft he'd been at having to miss the boat club party but at least he'd stayed at home with her while Guy went and next morning regaled them with stories about the magnificent event. She supposed Ben was trying to make her feel guilty about forcing him to miss two boat club parties on the trot.

"You promised to take me up-country, remember," she told him.

"We can go up-country any weekend. What I'll do is ask old Dadi if we can go to Kandala and spend the night in his family bungalow up there."

"When?"

"I'll ask him if we can go next weekend. I promise. I'll ask him at the party – he's going. Everybody's going."

It was hopeless. She groaned and agreed to the inevitable. When she saw Baby climbing into the rowing boat, however, she cheered up a bit. Baby at least was interested in things other than who was sleeping with who this week.

A stranger climbed in after Baby and was introduced around to the others as Dennis. Though Dee and Ben had been at his party in Marine Drive, they did not know him because he'd left the flat with Baby before they arrived.

"Who're you with Dennis?" asked Ben in his friendly way.

"I'm in the Australian High Commission."

"Lucky bugger. Lots of duty-free booze," said Ben.

That's all this lot seem to think about, Dennis said to himself, but he had more on his mind at the moment than duty-free booze because, as he settled down on the narrow plank seat and watched the two ragged fellows take the oars, he was disquieted to see how much water was sluicing around at his feet.

"Are you sure this is safe? How far do we have to go?" he asked the other passengers. On the other side of the thin cockleshell frame of the boat, the water lapped menacingly and the most evil smell came off it like a wraith.

"Not far – about five hundred yards or a little bit more," said Ben reassuringly.

Five hundred yards! Dennis wouldn't have been happy if it had been fifty. He tried not to let his feet settle into the bilge water for fear that the evil germs it contained would infiltrate his skin. No one else seemed very bothered but most of them were wearing thong sandals and no socks. Dennis had on shorts, proper shoes and knee-length white socks his mother had bought for him before he left home, thinking they'd be suitable wear for a young man in India.

"I think this boat's overloaded," he told Baby. "Maybe we should get out and wait till it comes back again."

She laughed. "It's all right. We can all swim anyway, can't we? Besides they've never lost a European in the creek yet and they've been holding this party since about 1890."

An older man, sitting in the prow turned his head and said, "But five years ago they lost the bearers. Were any of you there that year?"

Dee Carmichael sat up straight with surprise. This was news to her because Ben had never mentioned it. "What? They lost some servants? How many?" she exclaimed.

"Three drowned. The rest got ashore. There was ten in the boat apparently and it was swamped."

"My God, that's awful. What did they do?"

"What did *who* do?"

"The club I mean. What did they do for the men's families?"

"They must have paid them something. I never heard," said the older man, looking disapproving because he didn't like people like her who kept banging on about the way servants were treated. They were the sort who were spoiling the old, established way of British life in India – paying too high wages, giving servants holidays and getting matey with them. Bloody ridiculous. Then he put in his cruellest stab as he said with a laugh, "At least they were all natives. No white people were drowned, thank God."

That crack reduced Dee and Dennis to silence and stayed with them both for the rest of the night, ruining any enjoyment they might have got out of the boat club party.

The island, when they landed on it safely, was already crowded with people. A huge fire was burning in one corner, well away from low-branched trees where some men were already perched on the branches like monkeys. A wooden dance floor had been laid and on a dais behind it a smart-looking, ten-piece band, led by a chubby, cheerful chap in a white dinner jacket, was playing. As soon as Ben appeared the band leader raised his baton, signalled to the band and they launched into *Blue Moon* – Ben's favourite tune. Goody Servai always did that when he turned up at any party where the band was playing.

Ben rushed over to speak to the band, abandoning Dee as usual, and she drifted from group to group of the party-goers, where she heard some people discussing Baby's new man. "He's a bit of a drag, isn't he? Not much to say for himself," was the general opinion and Dennis was dismissed. She felt sympathy for him, knowing they said much the same about her. Sitting on a blanket at the edge of the dance floor, she eventually located Anne and her husband Bill and sat down beside them.

"Where you here when the bearers were drowned at the boat club party?" she asked Bill.

"Yes, we came that year but we left before it happened. They were drowned at the end when they were taking stuff back to the mainland after the party was over."

"Did you know any of them?"

"I suppose we did. They were club bearers – I don't remember their numbers though."

The Gymkhana club servants had no names, only numbers. One of Dee's acquaintances had a bearer who was hired because his father was Number Five in the club. Number Five and his family were more proud of that title than of any family name they bore.

Dee sat with her chin on her fists and stared through the trees at the glittering water that looked cruel and menacing now. How terrible to drown in it, to be dragged down to its depths by strangling weed. How terrible to be dismissed as only a bearer because your skin was a different colour to the people who snapped their fingers at you and demanded your attendance.

Shadiv was Indian and there were people, both here and at home, who would look down on him because of that even though they were infinitely inferior to him in every way. She couldn't shake off her misery and was far from festive when Ralph the doctor, who knew about her growing anxiety because she couldn't conceive, but was too tactful to mention it, sat down beside her and said, "What's up with you Dee? You look like the ghost of Hamlet's father."

"It's just a touch of angst," she told him and he clapped his hands with delight. "Angst! How do you define angst?"

She stared at him, "Anxiety, I suppose, a feeling of not being in control of events . . . a kind of sadness . . ."

Ralph nodded, "My God, how did a woman who knows about angst end up here?"

How indeed? thought Dee just as Ben threw himself down beside her and took her hand, asking her to dance with him. He'd taken her outburst after the Marine Drive party to heart, she suddenly realised, especially when he said, "I've asked Dadi about his bungalow. He says we can have it for the whole of next weekend."

On the other side of the dance floor Dennis was no happier though he tried to keep up a facade for Baby's sake as one after another of her friends pounced on them, crying out things like, "Where did you find him, darling?" as if he was a piece of stock from a cattle market, and asking her if she'd heard anything from Charlie in tones that he guessed were malicious.

Eventually when they were dancing he asked her, "Who's Charlie?"

She stiffened in his arms and said, "An old friend of mine, someone I used to know."

"Were you a couple?"

"Not really. He was engaged to a girl at home and always said he was going home to marry her. We were only friends. But people here read more into it." Her tone was light but he was not deceived and knew she'd been hurt.

"They'll forget in time," he said gently.

"Of course," said Baby brightly but silently she was wondering, Will I though?

Then she looked up into Dennis's face and saw quite clearly that he was not enjoying himself. "This isn't really quite your sort of thing, is it?" she asked.

"I like parties well enough but I can't get those drowned bearers out of my mind."

"I saw that upset you. It was a genuine accident. They overloaded the boat. They had trestle tables and soda water crates and all sorts of stuff in it as well as people. They're much more careful now," she reassured him.

He shook his head, "It's not that. It's just that it's such a horrible place to drown, I don't think I've ever been anywhere more sinister . . . It gives me the creeps."

They walked back to the fallen tree where they'd been sitting and she held his hand, "You're serious, aren't you? It's really got to you. I'm sorry. Let's leave. We can cross back in the next boat that arrives."

"I don't want you to miss your party," he said but she shook her head.

"Don't worry about that. I've been to dozens of parties like this. In fact, as I mentioned to you once before, I think I'm maybe getting a bit tired of them too. Let's go for a drive. We could go to Bassein. There's an old fort there that looks wonderful at night."

He stood up and held out one hand, "All right. Let's go. But tell me one thing. Do you have any other name except Baby?"

The old Portuguese fort at Bassein jutted out into a very different sea from the sluggish waters of Kurla Creek. The view from its tumbling stone ramparts was across the black and silver waters of the Indian Ocean, the sea across which Vasco da Gama had first come in his flimsy, rat-infested wooden boat.

As they sat side by side on moss-covered walls and stared out across the never ending lines of white-crested waves that rolled in from the mysterious depths beyond, Dennis and Baby – who he now called Roberta – were silenced and awed by the majesty of the scene.

"How old is this place d'ye think?" asked Dennis gesturing around the ruined battlements behind him.

"Gosh, I don't know, but the Portuguese were here before the British came and we got Bombay in Charles II's wedding contract in the 1660s, I think, so it's probably nearly four hundred years old," she said in a soft voice, rubbing the palms of her hands on the worn stone.

"For four hundred years people have sat here like us staring out at the same water. When they first built this nobody even knew Australia existed," said Dennis awe-struck.

"That's not old by Indian standards," Baby told him. "There's temples in the south that were built long before Christ was born."

"Have you seen them?" he asked.

"I've seen some of them – there's too many to see them all. My mother likes that sort of place. She used to take me travelling when I was small."

"Your father didn't go?"

"No, he's always been too busy working to travel much but my mother's family have been all over India, from the north to the south. It's in her blood. I sometimes think she's more Indian than English. I can't imagine her living at home."

"It must be in your blood too then," said Dennis.

"I suppose I have some of it from her side. Her ancestors were all soldiers; one of them joined Clive's army in Madras about two hundred years ago. He's buried in St Mary's Church there, and there's others buried in various places from Bombay to Darjeeling."

"So not many of them went back home."

"Not many, hardly any, in fact. That's why I worry about Mummy."

"Will she have to go back?"

"Yes, she will. My father's talking of retiring because he's been out here since before the First World War and he wants to go back to Scotland."

"One of my mother's ancestors came from Scotland," Dennis told her. "His name was McNab." In fact Ewan McNab had been transported for sheep stealing in 1845 but Mrs Gillies never admitted that. She preferred to think of him as the carter he became when his sentence was served.

"McNab sounds as if he came from the Highlands," said Baby.

"My father's from Glasgow. He's told me that he was brought up with four brothers and two sisters in two rooms in a tenement in a place called Govan. He doesn't want to go back there, of course, but he does want to return to Scotland. He's got agents looking out for suitable property in a seaside place called Helensburgh. His church's Sunday School used to take the children there for an outing once a year when he was small and he thought it was like paradise."

"How will Helensburgh suit you?" asked Dennis.

"Not very well. I've only been to Scotland three or four times and on every visit it rained. But I don't have to go if I don't want to. They're not demanding parents. They'll let me do whatever I want – the trouble is I don't know what that is."

Her face looked downcast and he took her hand. Then to his surprise she leaned her head on his shoulder and said, "I'm in such confusion . . . will you listen to me and give me your advice?"

Thrown by her closeness, by the sweet smell that came off her and the soft touch of her hair on his face, Dennis could only stutter, "I'm maybe not a very suitable person to give anybody advice. I'm in a bit of confusion myself to tell you the truth." He was thinking of Carole, who was proving difficult to shake off.

"I think you'd be a very good adviser," said Baby, who sat up straight and told him about how much she loved Charlie and how she'd suffered when he left. She didn't say she'd slept with him though, but he guessed that she had.

Dennis listened in silence, watching her face all the time she talked and admiring the brave way she could tell the story without breaking down in tears. When she finished by saying, "So what should I do? I don't want to go back to England and I'm tired of people asking me about Charlie here. Where should I go?"

Poor little girl, was his first thought as he listened to her and when it was his turn to speak, all he could say was, "The bastard."

This reaction shocked her. "No, no, he's not. He never told me one lie. It was all my doing. I think he was as sad as me about it ending," she protested and then she told him about the collection of mementoes Charlie had left behind in the Gulmohurs.

"I think it's very sad," he said at last, "but there's nothing you can do to change it. You've got everything going for you. You just have to go on living."

"Have I got everything going for me?" she asked sadly and he hurried to reassure her.

"Sure you do. You're a stunning-looking girl . . . you're lovely."

She turned her face towards him and looked genuinely astonished. "Do you really think so? That's very nice of you. I tell myself I can do anything I want and go anywhere I please but I don't know where . . . I'm sort of paralysed in a way. I know I'm almost finished with Bombay though I love it. I'll never be free of it, I know – it's all those dead soldiers inside me. I could go anywhere in the world I wanted but I can't make up my mind where."

She looked up at him so longingly that the one thing he wanted to say was 'I love you' but he was too shy and too in awe of her to get the words out. She put a hand on his cheek and whispered, "I shouldn't be bothering you with this."

His heart was hammering and his brain buzzing with all the wonderful things he wanted to say to her. If only she wasn't a Sir's daughter, if only she wasn't rich. Then he would tell her how he loved her face, her hair, the way she wore her clothes, the way she spoke, her gentleness . . . Her hand stroked his chin and he groaned. "Christ, Roberta," he whispered.

Very slowly she leaned towards him and kissed him on the lips very tentatively at first but the kiss lasted, deepened and was prolonged into an intense embrace that surprised them both by the passion that it aroused in them.

When at last they drew apart Dennis said, "I've just had an idea. Why don't you come to Australia – with me?"

Her eyes were enormous and the black pupils seemed huge as she stared at him. "What do you mean?" she whispered.

He surprised himself with his own eloquence. Taking her hands in his, he said, "I mean I'm in love with you. It started when we went to float that toy crocodile at Chowpatti and it got worse on the day we spent at the beach. I'm mad about you. I think about you all the time. When I go home after being with you I think over and over again about everything we've done and everything you've said. I play it back in my mind like a movie. Please don't say anything, because I know you don't love me. Why should you? I'm not nearly good enough for you."

Then he shook himself like a big dog. "I'm sorry. I shouldn't have said all that."

She was staring at him, the whites of her eyes glittering like silver in the moonlight, "Why shouldn't you have said it? Is it not true?"

"Of course it's true. I just don't want to embarrass you. I don't want to lose your friendship. It's made such a difference to me. I wanted to quit my job and go back to Australia before I met you."

He'd completely forgotten about Carole. She wasn't important compared to this.

"I'm very flattered," said Baby slowly and Dennis cringed inside because he thought this was only the preamble for her adding, "But I'm afraid . . ." However she didn't say that. Instead she took his hand and held it very softly as she went on, "It's a tremendous surprise. I need time to think about it. I know that sounds a bit old-fashioned but I'm not the sort that rushes into things."

"I'm not either usually," he told her, "but this has taken me by surprise. Please don't think I'm rushing you. I'm just telling you how I feel, telling you what's happened to me. I don't expect you to love me back."

She laughed, "Why not? You're terribly handsome you know. All the girls think so. Mags would drop her banker in a second if you looked twice at her."

"*Mags!*" he said with scorn. There was never any chance of him falling for her.

They sat hand in hand, staring over the sea in silence for a bit till Baby suddenly said, "Can I take a bit of time to think about what you've said? I want to be sure I'm not rushing into something because of Charlie, you see. That wouldn't be fair to you."

"Take as long as you want," said Dennis gallantly, "I'll wait. But I want to marry you."

She leaned across and kissed his cheek. "Thank you. I'll think about it. You're one of the nicest people I've ever met," she told him. The kiss was chaste, like an embrace exchanged by friends, and he was surprised that he didn't want to grab her and become passionate again. It was as if their relationship had entered a different, more formal footing. She'd think about his offer. He was prepared to wait for her decision though he wished the proposal hadn't slipped out the way it did, and had been made in a more exciting way.

Seventeen

T he BA postman delivered telegrams as well as letters to the Gulmohurs and it was growing dark when Dee heard him ringing his bell in the lane to let her know he was on his way. Anxious in case the yellow envelope contained bad news, she opened it though it was addressed to Ben who had not yet returned from Deolali and read, 'SORRY OLD BOY DEPARTURE DELAYED ARRIVING NEXT WEDNESDAY GUY.'

"Thank God," she said aloud, for Guy was meant to arrive on Friday night and she knew Ben would have used that as an excuse for not going up-country – or worse, he would have insisted on taking his friend with them. Dee was looking forward to their expedition for two reasons – to get a taste at last of mysterious India away from the city, and secondly to try to get back on really loving terms with Ben because she was afraid of her growing fascination with Shadiv. Every evening she waited, hopes high that he would pay them a visit. If he came she was ecstatic; if he didn't she was in deep gloom. No matter how much she lectured herself, she could not get common sense to prevail. She felt as she had done when she was fifteen and in love for the first time.

Ben realised from her constant references to their expedition that it was very important to his wife, quite why he was unsure, and he knew better than to make any objections this time. It was half-past four on Saturday morning when they drove out of the Gulmohurs' gate. Because they were taking enough food for two days, two books for Dee – she never went anywhere without something to read – and their bedding, they didn't take the jeep but loaded up the capacious boot of the Studebaker instead.

There were only a few pale streaks of light in the eastern sky as they drove to Thana where they heard bugles announcing the new day to the policemen living in a huge barrack block at the tip of the island. Crossing a crumbling concrete causeway fringed by a huge water pipe bringing Bombay's water supply from lakes on the mainland, Dee reacted with horror when Ben told her a dead body had been found in the pipes last week.

But that was forgotten when, all of a sudden, they were engulfed in a glorious dawn. Even over the throb of the old car's engine they heard the dawn chorus and it seemed that every bird in the world was singing its heart out. Ahead of them the sky was a riot of colour like a painter's palette, reds running into oranges, pinks and purples, yellows and palest amethysts. The glory of the Indian dawn filled Dee with the certainty that she was experiencing a once-in-a-lifetime event that she would cherish in her memory forever.

The first part of the road led off the island straight as an arrow over a flat plain of rice paddies, dotted here and there with little thatched houses clustering together beneath guardian trees for shade and protection. As the light was growing stronger they passed a lacy-looking tree with tiny oil lamps glittering in its branches, like a pagan Christmas tree, said Dee, but Ben, who was suddenly proving to be a wonderful source of information about India, said it meant that someone in the village had died and the little lamps were lit to help their soul escape.

For long parts of the journey she sat silent, the breeze from the open window blowing in her face, drinking in the new world outside with something like hungry desperation. She saw people – men, women and children – labouring with hoes as they tilled the black earth of small fields where they would plant rice as soon as the rains came, and occasionally their car passed high-loaded, perilously swaying wooden-wheeled carts pulled by white Brahmin bulls with swinging dewlaps and brightly coloured ribbons twisted around their curving horns.

They reached a small town centred round a very English village green and dominated by a Christian church with a tall steeple, where they overtook a smartly trotting pony pulling a little gig in which at least eight people were crammed though there only seemed to be sufficient room for two. She waved to the people in the gig and they all waved back.

It was almost noon when Ben pointed ahead and said, "There's the ghats. That's the difficult bit. I hope this old car makes it."

Dee stared at the threatening stone face in front of them. The Western ghats towered to the sky and as far as she could see there was no way up them. "Where's the road?" she asked.

"Wait and see, you're in for an experience," laughed Ben. "It's like a corkscrew, not a straight stretch in it for miles. Dozens of lorries plunge off it every year. Most people who go to Kandala or

Poona make the journey by train. Dadi thought I was mad when I said we were going to drive."

She was too fascinated to be scared though, and hung out of the window, watching as the narrow road climbed up, up, up, till she was able to look down into the hearts of trees clinging to the rock face. Beneath her, cotton trees were clustered thickly, with swirls of white fluff falling out of splitting seedcases and some scarlet flowers still blooming on the ends of the twigs. There were no pony gigs or bullock carts now, for the gradient was too steep but they met several brightly decorated lorries, painted all over in viridian green and pink with friezes of lotus blossoms, always driven by Sikhs, either toiling up or careering downhill with terrified-looking men and women standing up and clinging together in the back.

After about an hour of climbing, when the Studebaker's engine was steaming, they stopped beside a little shrine in which a shaven-headed priest crouched with his hand stuck out. Dee was surprised when her husband, who always remonstrated with her because of her liberality to beggars, walked up to the priest, made the *namaste*, the folded hand gesture of respect, and handed him a few coins.

"That's not like you," she said when he came back.

He grinned his wolfish grin that she always found so attractive as he said, "It's insurance money. If you give him something he says prayers to make sure you get back down again safely. By the time people get this far they're usually so terrified, they empty their pockets for him."

They reached Kandala, a little village perched on the top of the ghats and peering timidly down into the abyss and the plains far below, at about half-past three when the sun was beating mercilessly down on the roof of the car. Dadi had given precise directions about how to find his bungalow and they were both thirsty, dirty and exhausted when they turned down a red-dust track towards it.

The long, low house, once painted white but now grey, teetered like a would-be suicide on the very edge of the rock face. It was surrounded by a dried-up garden fringed by a hedge of cactus plants and entered through a wooden gate set between a high pair of stone pillars, on the top of one of which brooded what Dee thought was the carved statue of a crouching man resting his head on his fist.

It was only when they drew level with the gatepost that the statue jumped down and loped away. It was not a statue but a huge male rhesus monkey with a long furry russet-coloured coat.

The verandah of the house was very dusty and unlived in, with drifts of dried straw and withered leaves heaped in corners.

Obviously no one had been there for a very long time but there was a caretaker who had to be roused from his afternoon sleep to let them into the locked main rooms which were equally unkempt, but that didn't matter to Dee, who wandered from room to room with her eyes shining, imagining the place inhabited by some English officer and his family at the time of the Mutiny for it looked as if nothing had been changed since then.

Ignoring the caretaker's warning against panthers and snakes, they hauled two beds onto the verandah and spread their bedrolls out on them. Then they lay down and slept the sleep of exhaustion till the sun set and a little breeze came in from the garden to gently wake them.

The two days they spent at Kandala were the happiest they'd experienced since they married and put them back on the happy footing they had enjoyed before Dee's parental troubles engulfed them and drove them to the altar. They laughed and joked, they made love and talked more freely than they had ever done. It was as if they'd become different people up here in the clouds and left their other roles, their old resentments down on the plains.

The caretaker cooked their food over an open bonfire behind the bungalow and they bathed in a tin bath in the red tiled 'thunderbox' bathroom, pouring hot water out of a tin bucket over each other. The evening was made wonderful by the smell of burning wood and hissing oil lamps which were the only illuminations available. Then they fell asleep in the same narrow bed, clinging tightly together in each other's arms, with a myriad of stars spangling the sky in front of them and panthers coughing in the shrubbery.

When the time came to leave the next afternoon, Dee walked through the rooms again, looking at the antiquated furniture and wondering who had brought it all up the steep ghats to this precipitous site. At the end of the verandah there was a high umbrella stand with a few rotting brollies stuck in it and she stopped in front of it surprised to see that while one of its legs was intricately carved, the other was not.

"Look at this," she called to Ben. "Why would they carve one leg and not the other?"

He came across and grabbed her hand as she was about to stroke the carved leg. "Christ, it's a snake! Don't touch it," he cried. The carving turned out to be a boa constrictor, not a very big one but big enough to cause trouble if disturbed. They retreated laughing and as they drove away Ben said, "Well the local wildlife have certainly put on a good show for you at least."

"Everything's put on a good show for me," she said, turning in her seat to get a last look at the old house, "I don't think I've had such a good time for months and months. Thank you for bringing me here, Ben. I promise I'll never be nasty about Dadi again."

Going back down the ghats was a quicker journey than going up, and it was late afternoon when they were on the last stretch of plain before the sea. On their right was a small range of jagged hills, the largest of which, according to Ben, was called Wellington's Nose because it had the same outline as the Iron Duke's dominating facial feature.

"I bet he'd be flattered to know an Indian hill is still named after him when he's been dead for a hundred years," said Dee. "Oh, Ben, I love this country. I simply love it."

"I do too," he said and they finished their journey singing a selection of old music hall songs in very loud voices, not caring if they were out of tune. Their special favourites were 'Lily of Laguna' and 'I'm 'Enery the Eighth I am'.

Guy came back three days later. Ben took the day off to meet the plane and Dee had ordered a special dinner from Pasco, the cook, to celebrate his return.

Guy always reminded Dee of Winnie the Pooh and he came bustling down the steps of the plane bearing a Fortnum and Mason carrier bag (that turned out to be full of cans of pâté de foie gras) which he waved cheerfully to Ben who was waiting with Dee behind the fenced-off section on the tarmac. As Guy walked past, Ben reached out and clapped his friend on the back. "Welcome home," he cried. Dee stood behind him saying nothing, just hoping that absence had softened Guy's hostility towards her.

She soon found out it hadn't.

He resumed his campaign at dinner that night, after having gone through the house and fastidiously undone any changes she'd made since he left, including complaining that she'd replaced a line of ornaments in the bookcase with books – the ones she'd borrowed from Baby as it happened.

When they were drinking their coffee, he suddenly disappeared into his room and came back with a photograph album which he opened and held out to Ben saying, "Look what I found in my room. Remember that girl? She's the one you met at the Ambassador Hotel. You must remember *her*."

Then he flipped the page over and pointed at another photograph,

"What was that girl's name again? She stayed a week with us, didn't she?"

Then, brandishing a snapshot of a smiling dark-haired girl in a boat, he assumed a solemn face and said, "Sorry about this one. I know how upset you were when she married that other fellow."

The last photograph was not in the album but was a separate studio picture of a beautiful Indian girl in a shimmering sari and when Ben saw it he pushed it back to Guy saying, "Aw no, not that one Guy."

He was obviously ill at ease but didn't want to alert Dee to his discomfort too much for he was not sure what Guy was going to say.

"Not Grace? Haven't you told Dee about her?"

Smiling like Judas he reached across the table and turned over the disc of the gold identity bracelet that Ben wore on his right wrist. Dee had never seen him without it.

"You must have noticed this, Dee?" said Guy sweetly, holding her husband's wrist towards her though Ben, thunder-faced, tried to wrench it away. On the back of the bracelet label was engraved. 'With all my love forever, Grace' and a date which Dee realised, with a shock that hit her like electricity, was only a few months before she and Ben were married.

Without saying anything, she rose from the table, folded her napkin and laid it down, before walking calmly to her bedroom. The two men watched her and Ben stood up in an effort to stop her going but she pushed him off. "Leave me alone," she said.

She was still awake when Ben came to bed about half an hour later.

"Sorry. I didn't know he was going to do that," he said sitting heavily down on the edge of the bed.

"Who was she?" Dee felt as if their wonderful weekend had never happened.

"She was an Indian Jewess. I did fall in love with her and she with me, but her family wouldn't allow her to marry me. They sent her off to America where she married a distant cousin."

"When?"

"Just before I went home on leave . . ."

"And married me."

"Yes."

"You should have told me." Her tone was flat and level because she was bitterly angry and disappointed that he had not shared this important thing with her.

"It never struck me. It wasn't important."

"That's a lie. It must have been *very* important – or were you only fooling around with her too?"

"Well, maybe I didn't want to talk about it. You had other people in your life before me, didn't you."

"And I've told you about them. You should have done the same and then it wouldn't have been such a shock to me out there. He couldn't have done that to me if you'd been honest."

"It's just Guy—"

"It's not *just Guy*. He's trying to break us up. He's queer and I'm amazed you can't see it. He's been trying to make me leave since the day I arrived here and you shouldn't let him do it."

"Oh come on, Dee, you're being paranoid. He's not queer. He's a great one for the girls. He's just angry because we can't live the same way we used to do now I'm married."

She was angry now. "He's queer I tell you – or at least he's bisexual. You just don't want to accept that because you're afraid it would make you queer too. You should stop him baiting me. You should speak to him. If it was somebody baiting you, I'd stop it. But you just sit there and pretend it isn't happening. He's a shit, an utter shit and he's trying to break up your marriage."

Ben stared at her stricken, "You don't think I'm queer, do you? He's my friend, that's all, and he was only joking, Dee."

"I know you're not queer but the way you lived out here suited you as much as it suited him. If we hadn't got married, you would have jollied along together, getting drunk, picking up women and staying bachelors till you drank yourselves to death. Perhaps I should cut my losses and leave you to it."

Ben stood up and went over to stare out of the window and look out into the garden. The air of false reassurance had left him. "You're right. It's not on. I'll speak to him and I'll never wear the bracelet again. I realise it must be hard for you but I don't think you understand old Guy. Things would be better if he got himself a girlfriend. He's jealous. It's just we used to be such mates and he misses that."

She snorted, "He's jealous right enough but I'm not sure that finding a girlfriend would cure him."

"It would. I'm sure it would. He's a randy little bugger really and I was always the one who pulled the birds so he went along with me because he's not good at making the first move."

"You're not suggesting that you go out and find a woman for him, are you?"

"No, no, I'll just tell him that's what he ought to do . . ."

125

"That and lots of other things like letting me alone. If he knows you're serious, he'll stop trying to break us up – providing you are serious of course. If you're not, we might as well stop this now."

He came back to the bed and put his arms around her, hugging her tight. "Of course I'm serious. Aw, Dee, don't leave me. I like being married to you. I didn't realise how he was getting at you. You seem to take everything in your stride. I'll speak to him and sort things out – and I'll sell the bracelet. It's quite valuable."

"Good. We can use the money to pay our petrol bill," said Dee bitterly.

Eighteen

Parvati was padding around Baby's room, her bare feet making a soft shuffling noise on the tiled floor, while the girl lay in bed with the mosquito nets looped back, staring at the slowly circulating electric fan in the ceiling. It was having a hypnotic effect on her, helping her to concentrate on the matter in hand, which was whether or not she should marry Dennis Gillies.

She wasn't a snob, so the difference in their backgrounds, which she worked out from things he had said, didn't worry her. Her father, after all, had been a working-class boy and, thanks to him, she would always have sufficient money to secure herself and anyone she married a place in society and a comfortable life.

She was a realist who had come to accept that no amount of yearning would bring Charlie back to her; for it was most unlikely that he would leave Isobel. She would have been deceiving herself if she thought he'd gone home to be married under a sense of obligation alone. Charlie loved Isobel. Baby knew in her heart that what happened between them was at her instigation more than his. He'd liked her, he'd loved her in his way – but he loved Isobel more. She knew that now, after her first agony of loss had subsided.

Pride dictated that she do something to stop her friends and acquaintances feeling sorry for her, because, unfortunately, they had all known about the Charlie business. Baby found it impossible to hide her love for him. Marrying Dennis, the handsome Australian about whom there was not a whisper of gossip, who had no track record of old affairs behind him, would restore her pride. For Dennis, she knew, was a good man, a steady man, the sort who made good fathers and husbands. He'd never run after other women, he'd never become jealous and abusive like Anne's husband Bill; he didn't look cheap and caddish like the man Mags had snared. Dennis was a catch.

But did she love him? Love, what's love except heartache, she said to herself. It was better to settle for safety and companionship, and she was sure she'd get all those things from Dennis. She herself wasn't a very exciting person really, she knew. She was deeply conservative in fact and didn't long for the unattainable – except for Charlie, of course. She didn't want to go big-game hunting in Kenya or living in New York's Sutton Place, though she could do either of those things if she wanted. Her idea of the ideal existence would be settling down with someone kind and having children in an idyllic house – she wasn't sure where but she had a vision of it, like the picture on the top of a jigsaw-puzzle box, in her mind. Mummy and Daddy would come to stay and there would be ponies for the children, fair-haired, handsome children that looked like – like Dennis. He must have been a very handsome small boy.

"You want tea, Miss Baby?" asked the ayah interrupting her reverie.

"No thank you Parvati."

"You want orange juice?"

"No." Spoken more shortly this time.

"You want some coconut milk?"

"No. No. I don't want anything." What she really wanted was to be left alone to look up at the fan and think, but it was obvious that Parvati had something on her mind and wouldn't go away till she'd relieved herself of it.

Baby sat up against her pillows and stared angrily at the old servant. "What is it Parvati? What do you want?"

"I am not wanting anything," said the ayah with dignity. "I am tidying your clothes. You always throw them on the floor and I am picking them up."

"Thank you, but when you've done that please go away."

"Are you not getting up? It's nearly ten o'clock and your mother has been up for two hours."

"Mother is always up early. Does she want to see me? Is that what this is about?"

"No. She has not asked but it would be nice if she saw you."

So they were approaching the purpose of Parvati's hanging about. "I saw Mother yesterday," said Baby.

"But not to talk, not just the two of you," said the ayah.

Baby sighed and swung her legs out of bed. "All right. You want me to go to make conversation with Mother before she has drunk too much gin to make sense, is that it?"

Parvati prickled visibly, her nostrils flaring out like a little horse. "My lady has had no gin today," she snapped.

Ashamed at her own irritation, Baby became conciliatory. "All right, I'll get up. I'll have coffee with Mother on the verandah.

Don't let her go off anywhere before I get there though because I want to shower first."

The shower was a wonderful place to dally in the hot weather but she couldn't waste time today, so she was washed, dressed and downstairs within ten minutes to find her mother sitting on the verandah staring into the garden, a smoking cigarette in her fingers and a half-empty cup of coffee on the cane table in front of her. Her long legs were stuck out as usual and when she almost tripped over them Baby realised with a shock that they were very thin. Surely she hadn't always been as thin as that?

"Hello darling, it's lovely to see you. Parvati said you wanted to have coffee with me today," Barbara carolled in cheerful tones when her daughter sat down beside her, pecking her lovingly on the cheek as she did so.

"Did she?" said Baby wondering what Parvati was playing at, contriving to get the two of them together by telling the one that the other wanted to see her.

"Yes, she said I wasn't to go off to the club till you came down. Is there something you want to tell me?"

Baby thought about Dennis Gillies' offer of marriage but decided against telling anyone, especially not her mother, until she made up her mind whether to accept it or not. How on earth could Parvati know that there was something quite big she might have to tell her mother though? The woman was psychic.

"Not really darling, it's just nice for us to be together on our own," she said.

Barbara's hand was shaking slightly as she lit another cigarette but she sounded very bright and breezy as she agreed, "Yes, it's lovely. Do you remember how we used to sit here together when you were small? The pony man used to bring a little bay mare and you rode it round the garden every morning and I would sit here and watch."

Baby laughed, "I hated that pony. I was such a disappointment to you. You wanted me to grow up a horsewoman like you but ponies made me sneeze and Dr Green said I wasn't to go near them any more."

"Yes, Dr Green realised that horses made you sneeze and cough . . . He's very clever," Barbara's voice trailed off as she drew deeply on the cigarette and then coughed while her daughter re-filled their coffee cups from a fresh pot the bearer brought.

"Mummy," said Baby, "I think you smoke too many cigarettes. They make *you* cough."

129

"Oh darling, I've been smoking for years and it's too late to stop now." There was a note in her mother's voice that made Baby look sharply at her, "Are you all right Mummy?" she asked, remembering the skeletal legs.

"Of course I'm all right, never better. I'm thinking of taking rooms again at Mahableshwar for May and June. Do you want to come?"

That was another thing they'd done together every year when Baby was small, repair to the hills for nearly two months while the people on the plains, including Baby's father, sweated in the fierce unremitting heat.

"I'll come for some of the time perhaps but not for it all . . ."

"Any special reason you want to stay here?" asked her mother lightly as if this was not the question that the whole charade had been set up for.

"Not really but there's quite a lot going on – parties and everything."

"Good. How are the gels?" By 'the gels' Lady Maling-Smith meant Winks and Mags whose parents, Elisa and Tony, were old friends of hers and whose children had been Baby's closest friends all her life.

"They're very well."

"Their mother was telling me that Mags has got a new man, someone who works in a bank apparently. It could lead to a wedding, she thinks. What's he like?"

Baby laughed and leaned over to hug her mother, "You crafty old thing. You and Elisa have been gossiping about us haven't you? And you're trying to get the low-down from me to pass on to her . . ." But she also guessed that her own mother had been told that she had been seen around with a new man and was trying to find out about him even more than she was about Mags' man.

"Well, let me put you out of your misery. Mags' new man looks like an advertisement for men's suiting. He's very, very dapper with a neat little moustache that's always very carefully trimmed and I've never seen him with a hair out of place, not even on the beach. He's got one of those very pukka voices that aren't quite right somehow but he's trying like mad and I'm sure one day he'll make it. He'll probably end up a very burra sahib indeed."

"Oh dear," sighed Barbara, "that's what her mother thinks too. N.Q.O.S. . . ."

"Very much Not Quite Our Sort, I'm afraid, but that's not always a bad thing, as you and Daddy proved, is it?"

"Your father isn't anybody's sort – he's quite unique," said

Barbara with a laugh. "But I agree that the young man shouldn't be condemned out of hand because of where he comes from – Surbiton, I think Elisa said."

"Really? I didn't know that. I thought it was Hindhead."

"That would be a bit better, but it's Surbiton. He says his father works for the Post Office and Elisa's afraid it means he's a postman."

Baby laughed. "Oh Mummy, would it really matter?" I wonder what Dennis's father does, she thought.

"It wouldn't matter a jot providing he's a nice fellow. Is he?"

"I don't know. He's a bit older than her and I think he's probably rather boring and narrow-minded . . . and I'm afraid he might be mean. He always hangs back when it's time to pay for anything. I've never seen him put his hand in his pocket actually." But Mags wasn't exactly a fireball of fun or a fount of generosity either, she thought but again didn't say it.

Her mother said it for her though. "That won't worry Mags too much, his being boring, I mean, for she's rather a boring girl herself. What'll matter to her is if he can give her the status she wants."

"I think he might in time. I can see them in a few years being the pillars of society, going to church and sitting on charity committees, that sort of thing. Two problem children and a flat in Putney to go back to when their time abroad is over . . ."

Lady Maling-Smith laughed. "So you don't like him," she said.

"Not much. He's very, very uninspiring but Mags just wants to get married and almost anybody will do. I could see she'd marked him out as a possible when we were on the boat coming out. He hadn't a chance, really," said Baby.

Her mother suddenly stubbed out the cigarette and took her daughter's hand, "I wish it was you getting married, darling," she whispered.

Baby stared at her, surprised, and saw there were tears in her eyes. "Oh, dearest, why? I haven't thought about it," she lied for she hadn't made up her mind about Dennis yet.

"I just wish it was. I'd like to see you settled with someone kind. I'd like to be a grandmother!"

Baby hugged her again. "Sweetest, you will be one day, I promise. You'll make a marvellous grandmother, telling all your stories about being up-country with your father's regiment in the old days. My children'll love you!"

"It's not just that though," said Barbara, suddenly very solemn. "It's just so important that you find a good man. I know how unhappy

131

you've been and I don't want that to happen to you again. Oh, I know what you're going to say, that Charlie Grey was a good man and, I agree, he was, but he was pledged to marry someone else and it was a pity that both of you allowed it to go so far between you. It could have been stopped early on."

Still holding on to her mother, Baby said, "I'm over it, Mummy. I really am. But it's given me a yardstick. I know the sort of man I want to marry now because of knowing Charlie. It was what they call a learning experience."

"Don't look for the same man again, keep an open mind," said her mother solemnly. Then she briskly shook off her daughter and jumped to her feet. "I must go darling. I'm playing bridge with Elisa this morning and I'm late already."

Baby stood up too. "At least you've got something to tell them," she laughed.

When her mother's car drove out of the garden, Baby still sat on the verandah sunk in thought. What should she say to Dennis? Should she accept him or not? He didn't thrill her to the marrow, the way Charlie had but Charlie could never be replaced, never, ever. As her mother said, she must look for someone different.

She rose from her seat and went into her mother's sitting room looking for a pen and some paper to write down the Pluses and Minuses of marrying Dennis. She always made lists like that when she had a difficult problem. There were no pencils lying about so she let down the flap lid of the little escritoire that stood slantwise against one corner of the room and as she did so a sheet of paper fluttered to the floor and lay there quivering in the down draught of the overhead fan.

When she lifted it up she could not avoid seeing that it was covered with her mother's large, open scrawl and the words at the head of the paper were 'My Extra Bequests'.

Top of the column beneath the heading was the name Parvati and against it the sum of 70,000 rupees.

Baby reeled. Her mother was leaving the ayah about £4,500 – a fortune even by European standards.

Beneath Parvati's name were listed their other servants, including Lady Maling-Smith's durzi who'd made her dresses for years, and the woman who came every Wednesday afternoon to give her a massage. Their bequests ranged from 500 rupees to about 5,000 but no one got as much as Parvati.

The last name on the list was 'Moses'. He was to receive the two very valuable paintings by Sir Alfred Munnings that were her mother's greatest treasures.

Who's Moses? Baby wondered. She couldn't think of any old retainer with that name, and certainly no one who deserved the Munningses. Then, feeling guilty and extremely disturbed, she put the paper back in the desk where she'd found it and left the room. Why is Mummy making a new will? she asked herself and went in search of Parvati who knew most of her mistress's secrets.

The ayah was in Lady Barbara's dressing room, slowly ironing beneath the fan. With one hand she sprinkled water over the clothes from a little earthenware pot on the end of the ironing board and with the other she pressed the steaming iron onto her employer's cotton dresses, many of them faded now but still kept because Lady Maling-Smith loved them. Barbara was not fashion conscious and had never changed her dress style since the 1930s.

"Parvati," said Baby from the dressing room door, "why were you so anxious that I have coffee with my mother this morning?"

"Because my lady was lonely and needed to speak with you." The ayah spoke without turning round.

"Was it because someone told her that I have been going out with a new man and she wanted to find out about him?"

"No. She knows about your new man. She is just waiting to see what will happen."

"Is my mother quite well, Parvati? She has got very thin recently, I think."

The iron was carefully laid down and switched off. Then Parvati turned round and Baby saw with consternation that she was crying.

"My lady has been going to Doctor Green but she has not told me what he says. When I ask, all she tells me is that she is quite well but I don't think that is the truth. She has much pain sometimes, especially at night. Then I run and get her a glass of gin. It puts her to sleep."

"I think you give her too much gin," said Baby sharply.

Parvati was just as sharp in her reply. "Not too much. It stops her hurting. I would give her anything to stop her hurting."

The midday traffic in the middle of the city was solid when Baby was trying to reach the Gateway of India but eventually she managed to get free of the jams and parked her car outside Dr Green's consulting rooms. Mrs Gomez, who was eating at her desk, picking food out of a series of tin dishes with great fastidiousness, was surprised to see her.

"The doctor is having his tiffin now and then he has his sleep. He doesn't come back to work again till three fifteen," she said to Baby.

"It's only a quarter to one. He won't be asleep yet and I won't take up much time because I don't want to consult him medically. I just want to speak to him about my mother," pleaded Baby.

Mrs Gomez shook her head, torn between pity for the girl and protectiveness towards her employer. "I don't know. He'll be eating. It's not good to disturb an old man at his meals."

"I won't disturb him. I promise I won't. It's just that this is very important, Mrs Gomez. I'm worried about my mother and I know she's been consulting him recently, hasn't she?"

"She has been here." Mrs Gomez knew the diagnosis that had been given to Lady Maling-Smith but all the torturers of the Inquisition wouldn't wrest it from her.

Baby folded her hands in supplication. "Please Mrs Gomez, please, just pop next door and ask the doctor to give me five minutes, only five minutes. You can time me . . ." What made the secretary do as she asked was the fact that there were tears in Baby's eyes when she made her request.

Dr Green himself came to the door between the office and the consulting room to beckon her inside. He was still wearing his white coat but there was a large, stained napkin tucked into his shirt collar and flopping down onto his chest. His hair, as usual, was springing up all round his head like wire wool.

She slipped in beside him and looked at him beseechingly. "I won't take up your time. I can see you're eating, but I've come about my mother."

He gestured to her to sit down and pulled the napkin out of his collar at the same time. "Is your mother sick? Have you come to fetch me?" he asked.

"No, no, I came because I'm worried about her. She's got very thin recently and today I discovered that she's been making a new will . . . I know she's been to see you once or twice in the past couple of weeks and I wondered if there's something she's hiding from us."

His sharp eyes scrutinised her keenly and he asked, "Has she said anything about being ill?" he asked.

"No, she's very cheerful and bright in fact, more so than she's been for some time, but she's drinking too much. You know she drinks a lot of gin . . ."

"Your mother is not an alcoholic," said the doctor sharply.

"I know. I just think sometimes that the ayah lets her have more than is good for her. I've spoken to Parvati about it but she doesn't listen."

"I wouldn't worry about the amount of gin your mother drinks," said Dr Green.

"All right," said Baby who was more than a little in awe of him and always had been. "But is she all right, doctor? I mean, what did she come to see you about?"

He looked hard at her again and seemed to make up his mind about something. "Your mother consulted me because she's been suffering from stomach pain. I was able to examine her and – reassure her. We talked about it and when she left she seemed much less worried."

Baby nodded, "Yes, she's been quite skittish for the past few weeks, I've noticed. So it was nothing." This was what she wanted to hear.

"I didn't say that exactly but it will resolve itself in time. Your mother just needs a lot of love and attention, Roberta, and I know how fond she is of you and your father. You're her entire world, you know. Look after her."

There was a cold feeling in Baby's heart when she heard his words but fear warned her to probe no farther. She didn't want to hear the worst so she drove away the opportunity of pressing on. From the closed look on Dr Green's face she knew she'd been told as much as he was prepared to divulge and it was up to her to go home and work out the inferences of the words he'd used with such care. She stood up to leave, saying, "I'm sorry to intrude on you like this. Please finish your meal."

In the outside office, Mrs Gomez had tidied away her dishes and was preparing to doze at her desk for an hour or so. She looked at Baby with eyes full of sympathy and, sensing this, the girl stopped on her way out to ask, "There's something I've always wondered, Mrs Gomez. I know the doctor's initial is M, but I don't know what it stands for."

"It stands for Moshe," said Mrs Gomez.

He's Mama's Moses, thought Baby.

Nineteen

"**P**eople get randier when the temperature goes up," said Ben happily one brilliant morning after he and Dee had made more enthusiastic love than they had enjoyed for quite a while. He was feeling relieved because his wife seemed less tense these days, not harping on about that air hostess any more and getting on better with Guy who seemed to be making more of an effort to be civil to her, perhaps because Ben had had a word with his friend.

"Lay off Dee, old boy," he'd said.

"What on earth do you mean?" Guy replied, falsely innocent.

"Just lay off her, that's all," Ben told him. That was about the extent of any discussion that took place between them. They dealt in facts, not theories.

"Yes, the hot weather makes people randy," Ben repeated, hopping naked across the floor in search of his clothes.

"Does it? Is that possible?" asked Dee, thinking of the people she knew who were already rampantly randy and had been that way for months.

"Just wait and see. There'll be dozens of new affairs before the rains come."

After her husband and Guy drove off to the city, Dee sat in the garden wondering if what was wrong with her was just a climatic thing. Could it only be a rise in the temperature that was making her feel so peculiar? For peculiar she was, very peculiar indeed.

In fact she was beginning to wonder if she was physically ill because every time Shadiv appeared, and these days he came almost every night, she felt strangely lightheaded and a wave of heat seemed to sweep through her body from her head to her toes, making the tips of her ears burn. She was so affected that she could hardly speak.

"It's high blood pressure, that's what it is," she told herself. "I'll have to go to Breach Candy and get Ralph to take my blood pressure."

The garden of the Gulmohurs was a good place to dream away a day. Her hammock was still strung up between the trees and she climbed into it carrying the last of Baby's father's books, the works of Alfred Lord Tennyson. 'The Lady of Shallot' entranced her and she read it over and over again, relishing the imagery but also feeling disquieted by the message it contained:

> His broad clear brow in sunlight glow'd;
> On burnished hooves his war horse trode;
> From underneath his helmet flow'd
> His coal black curls as on he rode,
> As he rode down to Camelot.

That was Shadiv, 'some bearded meteor trailing light', and she was the lady who said 'I am half sick of shadows'. But was this infatuation doomed to disaster like the one Tennyson summoned up? Would her mirror 'crack from side to side' if she allowed herself to look out into the real world, to examine all her confusions, admit to all her forbidden longings?

By the time evening came round and the people from the buffalo camp went back up the hill, driving their animals before them for milking, Dee, bourgeoise to the backbone, had almost convinced herself that strength of will would cure her of this unseemly longing for another man – and an Indian at that! A boy of about eight, who reminded her of Jai, the boy at Crawford Market, stopped by the hedge and played her a little tune on his flute. She got out of the hammock and walked over to try to speak to him but when he saw her coming, he ran away.

She had changed into her favourite full-skirted white dress with wide-spaced black spots, and they'd finished dinner, when the familiar whistle came from the garden – Shadiv was there. In an instant, all Dee's good resolutions vanished. To hell with the cracking mirror! It was all she could do not to run out and meet him.

He was grinning as he walked into the sitting room and on the glass-topped coffee table he laid two books and said to Dee, "I know how much you love books so I brought you something to read. I thought you'd enjoy them."

Books! She looked at them with shining eyes and then at the man who'd brought them to her. If he'd brought her diamonds she couldn't have been more grateful.

"What are they?" she asked, putting a hand reverently on the red and white cover of the one on top. It was a paperback Penguin. The other was a big hardback bound in blue.

"This one's about Oscar Wilde," said Shadiv putting his hand on the top book too, though they were careful not to touch each other. Contact might have been more than either of them could withstand. "And the one beneath is a collection of letters between Vincent Van Gogh and his brother Theo."

"How wonderful," said Dee, lifting the smaller book, which turned out to be *Son of Oscar Wilde* by Vyvyan Holland. She'd heard about it and could hardly wait to start reading. The Van Gogh letters were equally enticing. How could he have known to pick such wonderful books for her when all that was available in the shops around Breach Candy was a sea of American pulp fiction?

Ben laughed as he lit a cigarette. "Sounds pretty heavy going to me," he said, "but it was good of you to bring them. I'm sure Dee'll enjoy them. They sound just her sort of thing."

Dee smiled at Shadiv. A lock of dark hair had fallen over his right eye and he was looking eagerly at her. "Are they? Just your sort of thing, I mean?"

"Oh absolutely. Where on earth did you find them? I've never seen any books like that in the Bombay shops."

He laughed, beautiful teeth flashing. "I just found them and thought of you. I'll read them after you've finished and we can talk about them."

She lifted the book about Wilde, lightly riffled the pages and told him, "I'll enjoy every word, I know. Thank you very much." Though she sounded quite cool, she was really feeling as if he'd reached up and pulled down a rainbow for her.

She dreamed of him that night, a wonderful erotic dream that made her feel ecstatic when she woke. As a sort of apology she took the initiative – something she usually left to Ben – and woke him with kisses and an urgent handling of his penis. It was the least she could do to clear herself of the guilt of adultery in the mind.

"I told you the hot weather made people randy," he said when they'd finished.

"Can I come into the city with you today?" she asked as they ate breakfast. "I want to go to the hospital and speak to Ralph."

Ben looked anxiously at her. He knew how much she longed for a child and what misery the arrival of her period always caused. "Are you OK?" he asked.

"Yes, I'm fine but I want him to check my blood pressure. I think it may be up."

"This weather's enough to put anyone's blood pressure up," moaned Guy who did not enjoy the hot weather.

*   *   *

138

The hospital was crowded as usual and Ralph looked sceptical when he took the reading. "There's nothing wrong with you," he said, "Don't start being one of those hysterical women who come rushing in here all the time thinking they've got a mortal disease. Are you still worried about not conceiving?"

She shook her head. "I'm not so bad now," she said. She wondered what he'd have said if she told him why.

"Relax and everything'll work out," he said in a kindly tone for he liked this girl who observed their social scene like a spectator at a tennis match. What does she think of us all? he wondered.

She left the hospital only partly reassured. Would everything be all right? But she doubted it for she had farther to fall than most people do when they plunge into love. When sceptics and cynics lose their senses, they suffer badly and Dee had a very severe case.

She went home in the Studebaker – Ben would come back in Guy's Ambassador – and started to read the books Shadiv had given her, weeping passionately over the Van Gogh letters which seemed so hopelessly doomed and tragic. There was nothing either of the brothers could do to escape cruel fate.

She finished the book on the second day and gave it to Shadiv that night. When he finished it he felt the same as she did and went around in mood of sorrow for some time until he found paperback copies of *Scoop* and *Brideshead Revisited* in Thacker's bookshop at Elphinstone Circle and they absorbed themselves in those with much happier results.

She was slowly learning that love has no logic. All she could do was experience it, suffer it, and hope it would pass but seeing him so frequently only fuelled the fire. She sat and watched him in the enchanted nights and thought him so beautiful, so courtly, so sensitive that more and more he seemed like a god. She ached for him but knew that she would not do anything about it for he was married, she was married and it seemed too irresponsible and scandalous to break up two marriages for a wild infatuation. How ironic it would be, she thought, if one of the hot weather romances that Ben had predicted turned out to be hers!

Shadiv got on almost as well with Guy as he did with Ben, and the Gulmohurs garden became like a man's club, with Dee in her role as the onlooker while the men drank beer, talked about their work – Shadiv was making three films at once now like his wife – laughed, played loud music and discussed whether Jack Teagarden was a better musician than Sidney Bechet. Sometimes Shadiv came over in his new topless jeep – bought with money which hadn't been declared to the tax man – and they went driving through the jungle where there were no roads, leap-frogging from rut to rut, from gulley to gulley, laughing and shouting like children every time he nearly turned the vehicle upside down. It never struck them that what they were doing was horribly dangerous.

As Dee became happier the atmosphere in the bungalow became much less tense and she noticed that Guy was even trying to be nice to her, not making so many cutting remarks and occasionally complimenting her on something she wore. When he said he liked her in the white dress with the spots she was so surprised that she had to go into the bedroom and scrutinise her reflection in the mirror, suspecting him of being sarcastic.

For her part she found that she liked him more and began to understand his confusions. If he loved Ben but couldn't admit that love even to himself, how awful for him. She began to realise his struggle – part of him attracted to men, the other part to women. There were also many things she could learn from Guy because he came from a milieu that was very different to the one that had spawned her. By osmosis she absorbed a knowledge of what food to serve with what, how to make guests feel appreciated – for he was surprisingly good at that – how to arrange the furniture in a room or put on a party. She liked him best of all on the night when he and Ben came prancing together down the verandah steps and executed a dance routine to the music of 'Won't You Come Home, Bill Bailey' for her and Shadiv who sat laughing on the grass.

The release in tension in the Gulmohurs made her much nicer, much less ready to take offence, more sociable and less critical altogether. This eased her way into society and she began making a few friends. She was loosening up.

She was helped in this by the fact that their financial situation was a little less critical. Now that Guy was back he was paying his share of the house and, amazingly, Ben's company had agreed to give him a modest rise. Added to that, contractors who were bidding to do work on his Deolali plant started turning up at the house with presents for him – bribes in fact.

He was very strict about not accepting money or anything valuable – although it was established business practice among some Europeans to line their pockets with bribe money – but he did take baskets of fruit, the odd bottle of whisky, and even a live piglet that turned up one day. A man who owned a welding company began driving out to the bungalow with little gifts for Dee – usually flowers, especially heady-scented tuberoses that she loved, but sometimes boxes of Moti soap, Indian sweetmeats – and, for Mohammed, bundles of yellow dusters which were much appreciated for some obscure reason that Dee could not fathom because she never saw any of them being used in the house. The dusting was done by the second boy, Ali, with what looked like old underpants.

When he saw his wife was happier, Ben was much relieved. "I told you old Guy would settle down," he said to her. "Now all that should happen is for him to find himself a woman and things would be really good." Ben steadfastly refused to believe his wife's theory about Guy's ambivalent sexuality.

Unknown to Dee, her friend Baby was also suffering over love but her problem was different. She telephoned Dennis, who was beside himself with anxiety after asking her to marry him, and said that she wanted time to think about her answer. Would he promise not to talk about it until she was ready to tell him her decision?

He was in his office in the High Commission and could hardly keep the phone receiver to his ear because his palm was so slippery with sweat. "Of course, of course," he gabbled. "I'll do anything you want."

So they kept on going out on dates about twice a week, going for drives and to the cinema, with the question of his proposal sitting between them like a barrier. They rarely kissed or held hands, and they were excessively considerate of each other for he felt that to make advances to her would be taking advantage of her in some way. Baby, instead of being relieved, was slightly irritated by Dennis's meek compliance with what he thought she wanted. If he'd grabbed her and made violent love to her, she would have been far more impressed.

The question of whether or not to marry him was on her mind all the time – when she woke in the morning, when she went to bed at night, when she swam at Breach Candy, even when she sat gossiping in the Gym with Winks and Mags.

The 'gels' were much excited because Mags had finally manoeuvred the banker into offering marriage and the wedding was to take place in September in the little church on top of Malabar Hill where Baby's parents had been married. Their talk now was all of weddings and Baby had the unsettling feeling that Mags thought all her troubles would end the moment she walked back down the aisle as a married woman. She hadn't given a thought to what would happen afterwards, to what life with the precisely spoken banker might actually be like. If Baby had liked the girl more she would have been sorry for her but, listening to Mags prattling on, it struck her that perhaps the one to be sorry for was the groom.

"I'm having a gown flown out from London," said Mags airily, "Daddy's so pleased to be getting rid of me that I can have anything I want. Can't I Winks? Winkie here is the bridesmaid of course. I think she should wear pink, don't you Baby?"

Winks had a florid complexion and pink was definitely not her colour as Mags well knew.

"Wouldn't a pale green be better?" suggested Baby but Mags swept on, not expecting anyone to disagree with her about anything.

"It'll be a big wedding of course, we think about two hundred guests, don't we Winks? Winks is sending out the invitations and she's forever making lists, putting names on and striking them off. I'm leaving it all to her."

Poor Winks, thought Baby, and said playfully, "Don't forget me darling."

"Of course not. How could I forget you – and your parents too, of course," gasped Winks, who never saw a joke unless it stood up and hit her.

"Isn't it such a nuisance that we have to have so many *old* people?" complained Mags, "Mummy wants all her cronies and Daddy says his golfing partners must come as well. They're creaking with age most of them. It's such a bore."

Baby stirred her cup of coffee and asked, "Will anyone be coming from the groom's side? What's his name by the way. I don't think I've ever heard it."

Mags looked surprised. "Really? It's Ronald – Ronald Browne with an 'e'. Only a couple of his friends from the bank will come I think. He's living with them in a chummery but Daddy's going to rent us a nice flat in Malabar Hill as a wedding present. We've looked at that new block, Blue Skies."

"There's not a block called Blue Skies," said Baby, genuinely shocked. The enormous amount of building going on in previously leafy Malabar Hill horrified her. Soon it would be a concrete jungle.

"Oh yes, it's almost finished. The flats are to be quite expensive, at least two thousand a month. And simply awful key money – hundreds of thousands! That means the neighbours'll be our sort. We've looked at one on the second floor: two beds, two baths, sea view and all that sort of thing."

Baby sipped her coffee. "What about Ronald's parents. Are they coming?" she asked.

Mags made a face that was meant to express regret but didn't. "No, poor dears. His mother has some sort of heart condition and can't fly and they don't want to be away from home for the length of time it takes to sail, so they can't come."

"Has he any brothers or sisters?" persisted Baby, exactly why she wasn't sure except that she saw it annoyed Mags.

"He has a brother and a sister, one older and one younger, but they don't get on. They're not coming either. We'll have lots of photos taken though and send them home an album. I've ordered them already, pale-green leather with gold lettering. *Very* expensive."

"It sounds as if it's going to be the wedding of the year," said Baby as she stood up, preparing to go home for lunch.

She found her mother alone, her father being absent because he was lunching with some business associate in the Yacht Club. Lady Barbara looked wan and there was a pale sheen of perspiration over her face but she brightened when she saw her daughter.

"Come and cheer me up darling. I'm finding the heat a bit much this year for some reason. I didn't used to mind but when you get older your thermostat goes on the blink. I remember my father saying the same."

"Perhaps you should go to the hills earlier than you planned," said Baby.

Her mother looked at her with stricken eyes but then she smiled and said, "Perhaps, perhaps. Now tell me what have you been doing all morning?"

"I've been with Mags and Winks. They're up to their necks in planning the wedding. It's going to be huge."

"I know. Elisa's told me. It's costing them lakhs of rupees but Mags is insisting on a big show and they're all too afraid of her to argue. Tony and Elisa are not that rich, you know, and this is biting into their retirement money."

"Mags told me her father's renting her a flat in a new block called something awful like Blue Bird . . . Blue Skies."

"Yes, he is. The bank would give them a flat but it's in Colaba and not grand enough for Mags."

"I think they're stupid going along with her the way they do. They've always indulged her."

Baby's mother sighed, "Well in a way I can understand them. There's something very special about your daughter getting married. You want to send her off in style. If it was *you*, darling, I'd want the wedding to be in the cathedral and a huge reception at the club, and I'd want you to go to Ooty for your honeymoon. I'd be so *happy!*"

Baby felt a sharp pang of anxiety as she heard this. The conversation she'd had with Dr Green had not been reassuring and she knew he expected her to read significances into it, and that she was deliberately avoiding.

"Are you feeling better, Mummy?" she asked.

"Well maybe not one hundred per cent, but I think it's the heat."

"I'll go up to Mahableshwar with you if you'd like that."

"Actually I've changed my mind. I don't think I'll go up this year. Instead I've told your father that I'd like an air conditioner in my bedroom. It's being installed tomorrow."

Baby was astonished. Her mother had always scoffed at air conditioners. If people needed to freeze their air, she used to say, they shouldn't come to India in the first place. The best thing to do in hot weather, according to her, was just lie and sweat till it cooled down.

"I thought you didn't approve of air conditioners," she said.

"I've decided to give one a try," replied her mother.

When they were eating lunch, Baby started to talk about the subject that so occupied her mind.

"Do you think people have to be deeply in love in order to make a happy marriage?" she asked her mother.

"Why do you ask?"

"Well, it's because of Mags really. I don't think she's the least bit in love."

"Some people never fall in love because they're too much involved with themselves, and Mags is one of them, I think. Happy marriages are made when people have mutual interest and respect . . . they've got to like each other. I've seen some very happy marriages between people that grew to love each other after they married. The Indians work on that system and it succeeds for them pretty well."

"You must have fallen in love with Daddy though or you'd never have married him."

Lady Barbara laughed. "We were both poleaxed when we met. I was concussed, I think. There were dozens of reasons why I shouldn't marry him but he amused me and I've always had the greatest respect for him. We're friends. You have to be friends as well as lovers."

Baby nodded, thinking, Charlie and I were friends. I like Dennis and I respect him because he's a very decent man but could we be friends? We haven't talked enough to each other to really know.

Her mother pushed her plate of spaghetti away almost untouched and said, "Don't wait for a great romance, darling. It might never come and you might miss something really good by not noticing it." Then she rang the bell and told the bearer to bring her a glass of gin, which she bore off to her bedroom where she would sleep away the afternoon.

Disturbed, Baby again sought out Parvati, who she found sitting in the shade of the servant's house with a very sad expression on her face.

Baby sank onto the ground beside the old ayah. She never found it difficult to adopt the crouching sitting position of the servants because she'd sat out in the garden with them since she was a baby.

"What's this about an air conditioner, Parvati?" she asked.

"Your mother cannot sleep any more. She sweats much. It will cool her."

"What's wrong with her exactly?"

"The doctor sent up pills for her yesterday. I tested one. It made me *womit*."

"You took one of her pills?"

"I would not let her take something that might hurt her."

"What did you do after the pill made you vomit?"

"I told her not to take them but she said she had to . . . she said there's nothing else."

"That was what she said exactly?"

The ayah nodded, "She said, 'There's nothing else for it, Parvati. They'll see me through.'"

Baby also went to bed but lay sleepless, thinking, debating with herself. She didn't love Dennis but it was unlikely that she'd ever love anyone again the way she'd loved Charlie, and Dennis would never let her down. Most of all, her mother obviously wanted her to be married and settled, as soon as possible too. Her love and pity for her mother overwhelmed her. She could not bear to speculate about why it was so important for her destiny to be settled quickly, but she knew that it should.

At four o'clock she went downstairs to use the telephone and rang the Australian High Commission.

"Dennis," she said, "I've made up my mind. Meet me at the pool in an hour and I'll tell you. No, I can't tell you on the phone. I want to tell you face to face."

They met in the pool but did not swim. Instead she walked up to him and said, "We can't talk here. Let's go over to Bertorelli's cafe. It'll be quiet there now."

They walked, without speaking, out of the pool, over the road and into the cafe where they found a table at the back.

"What would you like?" he asked.

"Iced coffee, please."

When the drinks were brought they sipped them through straws until Dennis's patience broke. "You said you'd something to tell me. You said you'd made up your mind." For the first time he sounded irritable. He'd been in an agony of indecision ever since her call, one minute being sure she was going to send him packing, the next hoping, just hoping that she might accept. Her coolness irritated him beyond endurance.

She looked up at him almost relieved at his show of temper. "Yes, I have. I've come to tell you that yes, I'll marry you if you still think it's a good idea."

He stared at her blank-faced, as if he'd been handed a refusal, then a huge grin split his face, making him look about twelve years old. "D'ye mean it? D'ye really mean it?" he asked.

"Of course I mean it. It's not the sort of thing you joke about, is it?"

"No, no, of course not." He wondered what he should do now. Should he run round the table and kiss her, should he stand up, throw out his arms and give a victory yell? What he did was sit still and stare at her, dumbstruck. She was equally impassive, watching him, deeply disappointed but hiding it. She'd expected a much more enthusiastic response.

"I'm over the moon," he said at last with a quaver in his voice. "I didn't think you would. I'm not nearly good enough for you, you know."

"Oh nonsense. You're much nicer than I am. The next thing we must do is for you to come home with me and talk to my father. Do you feel strong enough for that?"

"Sure," he said, straightening his shoulders.

The green-eyed Pathan guarding the Maling-Smith gate never smiled, not even when one of the family greeted him on their way in or out, but he used body language to express his approval or disapproval of the people for whom he opened the gates.

With a lenient wave of the hand, he gestured to Baby to go through when she tooted the car horn for admittance, but when he saw Dennis sitting beside her, he favoured the stranger with a low-browed stare, a mixture of menace and warning. 'Don't step out of line,' his look said.

Dennis, who had no intention of stepping out of any line and was totally intimidated by the grandeur of Baby's home, couldn't even meet the Pathan's eyes, a failing that was to be held against him that evening when he was well and truly discussed in the servants' quarters, for the household retainers found out almost as soon as Baby's parents the purpose of the stranger's visit.

Sir Robert was with his wife in her now air-conditioned bedroom which had been turned into a boudoir by the addition of a low sofa and two armchairs. Fortunately it was a large room and the extra furniture only made it look more comfortable and not overcrowded. Two throbbing machines encased in shiny wood purred away in the closed windows and the atmosphere was like a pleasant summer day in England, which did not stop Sir Robert complaining about the 'bloody cold'.

"Are you sure this is good for you, Barbara?" he asked, drawing deeply on a fraying cigarette.

"Of course it is, darling," she said. "I'm loving it. I've stopped that horrible sweating. I'm going to simply *live* in here till the rains come."

"For nearly three months! You'll get double pneumonia."

"Nonsense. What I won't get is prickly heat and Bombay belly."

He laughed. She always had a reply for him. A guarded expression came into his eyes, however, as he regarded his wife, stretched out of the sofa with the inevitable glass of gin in her hand. She didn't look well and she was as thin as a rake. She'd never been a fat woman, not even plump, but now she was all bones. It worried him because she was the centre of his life, even more than his work, even more than his immense riches, even more, in fact, than his beloved only daughter for whom he'd have cut off his right arm.

"You don't eat enough, and you drink too much of that bloody gin," he told her.

She raised her glass to him in defiance. "What's that you have in your tumbler? Whisky, isn't it? I don't count how many you take in an evening."

"The ayah said you'd been visiting that doctor down near the Taj," he said. "Why?"

She swilled the liquid in her glass around a bit making the ice cubes clink together. Ice lasts longer in air conditioning, she thought abstractedly, then she said, "He said I should drink more gin."

"Aw rubbish," said Sir Robert, sounding then like the lad who'd left Govan so long ago. She mimicked him and they both laughed again.

Any further discussion of her visits to Dr Green however was prevented by the sound of Baby's feet on the stairs. She burst through the door and cried out excitedly, "Darlings, I've brought someone to meet you but he's a little shy. Can I bring him in?"

Without waiting for an answer she stepped back into the hall, grabbed Dennis by his shirt sleeve and pulled him into the air-conditioned room, the temperature of which made him shiver – or maybe it was just his nerves.

He saw a white-haired woman lying on a sofa with her head propped up by a pile of multi-coloured cushions. Facing her, sitting squarely in a cretonne-covered armchair, was a man who closely resembled photographs Dennis had seen of Winston Churchill. He was smoking a foul smelling cigarette and round his head was a halo of smoke. They both stared at the stranger with totally blank expressions.

"This," said Baby, who suddenly seemed to be filled with enormous energy and enthusiasm, "is Dennis Gillies. He's Australian and he's come to speak to you, Daddy."

Sir Robert's first thought was, 'He wants a job'. Then he remembered Barbara telling him bits of gossip she'd picked up from the servants about Baby being seen round town with a young Australian. This must be him. He was about to snap, 'What about?' when he looked across at his wife and saw on her face an expression of such pure delight that it made him curb his tongue. He stood up, stubbed out the cigarette, and said to Dennis, "In that case, we'd better take a walk in the garden, don't you think?"

The muscles of Dennis's legs felt as if they were made of cotton wool and he had a sudden urge to go to the lavatory but he knew he must keep himself together and appear brave and manly when he asked Baby's father for her hand. Somehow this whole thing had crept up on him, it was running away faster than he'd intended and he felt as if he was on a roller coaster that had got out of control.

He followed Sir Robert's broad back down the stair, across the verandah and into the garden, where his guide strode out across a patch of lawn towards a marble seat positioned beneath an arch of pale mauve bougainvillaeas. There he sat down and pulled a leather cigar case out of his shirt pocket. "I suspect this calls for a cigar.

Want one?" he asked brandishing it in Dennis's direction. Dennis shook his head. The only time he'd smoked a cigar it had made him vomit and he didn't want that to happen now.

"Well?" said Sir Robert settling himself back in the seat. Dennis stood in front of him and cleared his throat.

"It's about your daughter, Roberta," he began.

Sir Robert, who Baby had told Dennis always called her by her given name, said impishly, "You mean Baby." He was always perverse, especially with young men.

"Yes, it's about your daughter – Baby . . ." His throat was dry and his tongue felt as if it was a wad of blotting paper in his mouth. He was very aware of his Australian accent.

"What about her?" said Sir Robert, setting a flaring match to the end of his cigar, "You've not got her pregnant, have you?"

Dennis reeled. "Good God, no. Of course I haven't. I've never . . ."

Sir Robert raised his eyebrows, "I sometimes think people should try each other out before they get married, you know. How does she know you're not impotent?"

This was not the sort of interview Dennis had been expecting. He flushed scarlet. "I'm not impotent," he said.

"Been married before?"

"No, of course not."

"Played the field?"

"Not really but I've had a little experience." He thanked his stars for the girl on the boat and for Carole. My God, he'd completely forgotten about Carole. He'd not told Baby about her.

"How old are you?"

"Twenty-seven."

"And your job?"

"I'm a senior clerk in the passport division of the High Commission here – the Australian High Commission," he added unnecessarily for his accent gave him away anyway.

"Not exactly a career diplomat. Do you intend to pursue that career?"

Dennis sighed, "Not really. I'd like to go home and do something there. I want to run my own business. I miss Australia."

For the first time Sir Robert seemed to unbend slightly. "I like Australia too. If I hadn't come out here when I was a young lad, I'd have probably ended up there. Two of my brothers did."

"Oh," said Dennis, "where did they settle, sir?"

"I've no idea. I haven't heard a word from them since I was seventeen. The Scots are like the Jews, you know – they scatter around the world in a huge diaspora and only think about Scotland when they get drunk. I've got several business interests in Australia though – I might be able to find a place for you in one of them."

Though he wondered what exactly the business interests were, Dennis didn't want it to seem as if he was looking a gift horse in the mouth, so he didn't ask. Instead he said, "That would be great. But would Baby – Roberta, I mean – want to live in Australia?"

"You'd have to ask her that, wouldn't you? But we've already talked about her visiting my businesses there in the coming year and she seemed very enthusiastic."

"So what do you think about me marrying your daughter, sir?" asked Dennis. He wished the old man would ask him to sit down because he was still trembling with nerves, and he wondered if he should have brought his birth certificate to prove who he was and his bank statement to show he was solvent, but Sir Robert didn't seem a bit interested in any of those mundane things. Instead he stood up and shrugged, "If she wants to marry you, I don't see any reason to stop her. She's a girl that's always known her own mind and made her own decisions. Come on, let's go back in and put them out of their misery."

Dennis could see Baby watching them out of the boudoir window as they climbed the wooden staircase up from the verandah again, and she threw open the door before they reached it.

"Is it all right, Daddy?" she asked, throwing her arms round her father's neck.

He grinned. "If it's what you want, it's all right by me," he told her. They're talking about me as if I was some sort of purchase, thought Dennis.

It was Baby's mother who came over to him and took his hand, "Now, my dear boy," she said, "you must come and sit here beside me on the sofa and tell me all about your family. I want to know *everything*. Do you have a dog at home?"

"A dog?" asked Dennis in a dazed voice.

"Yes, a dog. I think people with pets are always nicer and they're always better with their children. I have a dog, a dachshund but it prefers spending its time with the servants. They overfeed it and teach it tricks."

"We had a dog but it died . . . It was called Bluey," Dennis told her.

She patted his hand softly and when she did so he noticed with a sinking heart the glory of her jewellery.

I'll have to buy an engagement ring for Baby, he thought but he'd never be able to afford anything that could hold a candle to her mother's. Perhaps he should write home and borrow some cash from his father. His mind was racing around like a drunk hamster in a cage, idea after idea surging up like numbers on a slot machine.

"Now tell me about your parents. Are they both alive? Both well?" asked Baby's mother.

"Oh yeah. They're fine. They're not that old, you see . . ." He bit back the last words because he felt they might be tactless. Baby's parents looked as old as his grandparents, all four of whom were still hale and hearty.

"Good. What does your father do?"

"He's a mechanic. He mends cars. He's got his own little workshop in a suburb of Sydney." Denzil's workshop was very small and he only employed one other man and a boy but he was good with engines and had a long list of regular customers who relied on him to keep their old bangers running.

Barbara Maling-Smith clasped her hands in ecstasy. "He can mend cars! My word he'd make a fortune out here. All the cars on the road are ancient and they break down *all the time*. Can you mend cars, Dennis?"

"As a matter of fact I can. I used to help my dad during the school holidays."

"How wonderful!" She sounded delighted, as if he'd told her he was the heir to a multi-millionaire. He looked at her gin glass on the table in front of them and wondered if she was drunk. He was rescued by Baby who slipped onto the couch beside them and chided her mother, "Don't give poor Dennis the third degree, Mummy."

"But, darling, I want to know all about him. What's your parents' names, Dennis?"

"Gillies," he said stupidly, "I mean Denzil and Maud Gillies. My mother's maiden name was McNab and she had Scottish ancestry. Her brother Joe's a policeman in Sydney. He's a good bloke, Joe . . ."

They were all staring at him, trying to absorb the idea of in-laws called Denzil and Maud, but he didn't notice because he was still talking. "It was Joe who told me to take the job here in Bombay. He said it would be good for me to get out of Australia, good for me to travel . . ." He almost added, 'and get the government to pay for it', but changed his mind.

"He sounds sensible, your Uncle Joe," said Barbara. "Will he be coming to the wedding, do you think? Have you any brothers or sisters who might want to come too?"

The wedding! He hadn't thought about the wedding. He felt as if he was being kidnapped.

"I'm an only child but I guess Joe might come if he got enough notice."

Barbara looked across at her daughter and said brightly, "I don't think we should wait too long. Why don't we arrange it for the end of May or the beginning of June? Then you could get away somewhere nice for a honeymoon before the rains begin."

Baby shot up in her seat. This suggestion surprised her as much as it did Dennis. "So soon, mummy? People will say I've *had* to get married."

"Don't be silly, darling. When there's no baby, they'll have to eat their words, won't they? June's over two months away. Your father and I got married exactly six weeks after we first met and you've known each other for ages, haven't you?"

They looked at each other, unable to work out exactly how long ago they'd first met. "It must be six weeks," said Baby.

"That's more than long enough. When it's the real thing you just *know*," carolled Lady Barbara, "and just think, darling, you'll steal a march on Mags. Won't she be furious?"

Dennis Gillies left the Maling-Smith bungalow that night an engaged man, scheduled to walk up the aisle in the last week of May. Nothing that was said by Baby in favour of delaying the nuptials could change the bride's mother's mind.

Carole was waiting in the marble-floored upper hall of his block of flats when Dennis reached home that night. The moment he emerged out of the antiquated lift, she ran up to him and threw her arms round his neck. "Denny! I've been waiting for you for ages and that horrible bearer of yours won't let me in!"

He disentangled himself with difficulty. She smelt of that awful patchouli and the pungent talcum powder she always used. Somehow she didn't look pretty any longer, at least she didn't excite him sexually as she used to do.

"It's late, Carole," he said, backing away from her.

"Late?" She consulted the little watch on her wrist. "It's only ten o'clock. That's not late. I haven't seen you for nearly three weeks and now you say it's late!"

"I'm tired," stumbled Dennis, acutely conscious of the way her voice was taking on a screeching note that would make it audible to all the other residents of the block. He got out his latch key and opened his door. She was through before him and off, running up the corridor to his bedroom where she threw herself face down on the bed and sobbed heart-rendingly.

He stood in the bedroom doorway, conscious of Govind hovering behind him, and said, "Get up Carole. It's not necessary to take on like that. I've been very busy . . . Let me get you a taxi."

She lifted a tear-blotched face and said, "You've found another girl. Who is she? What's her name? It's not Florrie, is it?"

He'd never heard of a Florrie and shook his head. "Get up please Carole," he said weakly.

"Then it's a boy. You've got a boy, haven't you? That bearer of yours would find one for you. He used to do it for another sahib he worked for before Bob."

Behind him Govind hissed in outrage. Dennis advanced into the room and shut the door at his back. "You have to get up Carole. You have to go home now. I'll send for a taxi. I'll pay for it. Get up. If you insist on staying here, I'll send for a policeman."

He wouldn't of course but that was the first thing that came into his head. Miraculously it worked. Carole, like all the girls of her profession, preferred to give the police a wide berth for she knew that in any dispute between her and a white man, she'd be the one that came off worst even if she was an innocent victim.

She got up from the bed and regarded her ex-lover with a baleful glare. "You haven't heard the last of this Dennis Gillies. You promised to marry me and take me to Australia."

"I never promised anything of the sort," protested Dennis but she wasn't listening to him. She was too aggrieved at realising such a catch had slipped through her fingers.

When she was finally loaded into a taxi and driven away, Dennis sat on his verandah with a bottle of duty free brandy and the telephone by his side. Should he phone Baby and tell her about his affair with Carole?

He should have told her long ago, of course, but it was over as far as he was concerned and it had never been serious. Carole was always what Bob called 'troops' comforts' like Monica had been.

He swallowed down a slug of brandy and looked at his watch. Eleven thirty. He couldn't phone Baby now. But he'd have to tell her – what exactly? That he'd slept with an eighteen-year-old Anglo-Indian girl because he was randy.

But he had certainly never said he'd marry the girl, had never gone along with all her talk about going to Australia. It was her who dreamed all that up.

But, said his conscience, you let her prattle on about marriage so's you could fuck her. You never paid any attention to a single word she was saying. My God, what would Baby's father say if he ever found out! There wouldn't be any wedding then and suddenly, though he had been nervous about the idea of getting married before, now he wanted nothing more in the whole world than securing Baby as his bride, and as soon as possible.

He'd not tell her about Carole. It wasn't necessary. Carole was only trying to hang on to him by fair means or foul. There wasn't a thing she could do if he decided to drop her.

Twenty

For the next week the Bombay phone lines were burning hot with the voices of gossiping women.

"Guess what! Baby Maling-Smith's getting married!"
   "Who to?"
   "Some new man who's just arrived."
   "When?"
   "I've no idea. About a couple of months ago, I think."
   "Not him, not the man, the wedding, when is it to be?"
   "It's not fixed yet but soon . . . before the monsoon at least."
   "Is she pregnant?"
   "I shouldn't think so. She just wants to get married."

"Baby's getting married."
   "Baby Maling-Smith?"
   "What other Baby do we know?"
   "I don't believe it. Has he come back after all?"
   "Who?"
   "Charlie Grey, of course."
   "No, of course not."
   "Who's Baby marrying then?"
   "Some Australian. Nobody knows anything about him. God knows where she met him."
   "Breach Candy I expect. All the Australians go to Breach Candy. It's their substitute for Bondi Beach."

"My dear, have you heard, that handsome Australian with the flat on Marine Drive is marrying Baby for her money."
   "Poor Baby!"
   "Not poor Baby at all. She's only doing it to cock a snook at Charlie. I'll have to ring Mags and tell her."

"What, what did you say? In *May*? She can't, she just can't. My

155

wedding's going to be the biggest in Bombay this year and it's not till September. The bitch. She's an absolute bitch. She's done this on purpose. She hardly knows anything about him. He's maybe a mass-murderer. I hope he is. She won't drag me to that wedding, not if she pays me. I'll have to go now and tell Winks . . . Winks! . . . Winks! . . . Winks!"

Over the bridge tables, across the low cane tables in the women's end of the strictly segregated Bombay Gymkhana Club where the female sex was only tolerated but not welcomed; between groups of women lying toasting in the sun at Breach Candy swimming pool, the latest item of gossip passed, gaining details every time.

A wedding always caused excitement among the European society because most of the people in it were married already by the time they arrived in Bombay, though many went on to change partners but that was usually done surreptitiously and without ceremony.

This wedding caused more than the usual sensation however because it wasn't every day that the only daughter of a millionaire got married. Baby would certainly be sent off in great style.

Who would be invited, who left off the list? What would the bride wear and, more important, who would be the most fashionable among the guests?

Nobody bothered too much about Dennis. He was only a necessary adjunct, a bit like the bridal bouquet.

Twenty-One

Monica had no trouble tracking down Govind, though he was a canny old fellow who wanted to keep out of her way. She waylaid him on the servants' stairs, in the morning when he was returning from the market with a basket of provisions.

"You've been avoiding me Govind," she said, "I've been to the flat several times and you never answered the door."

He squinted at her and shook his head, "I was not hearing you. I am getting deaf."

"Why did your master change the door locks, Govind?" she asked, deciding there was no point pursuing the question of his loss of hearing.

He shrugged. "My master likes his privacy."

"Has he found another girl? You know he was meant to look after my cousin."

"No other girl has been here."

"Does he have a boy then?"

Govind was angered by Carole's charge that he was a procurer of boys and he shook his head indignantly. "No boys either."

"Then why did he change the lock? It makes my cousin look bad. It makes it seem as if he is afraid she will go into the flat and take things. She is very upset and so is her mother."

Govind looked sceptical. He had seen lots of girls like Carole. "My master has found a white girlfriend. My master is getting married," he said.

Monica was astonished. "Married! So soon? Who to?"

"A girl whose father is a big burra sahib. Very rich."

"What's her name?"

Govind knew but wasn't telling. "I don't know," he lied but Monica was brandishing a thin sheaf of ten rupee notes beneath his nose.

"You do know," she said.

He put out his hand to take the money before he told her and was pleased to see the expression of astonishment that crossed her face when she heard that Dennis was about to marry the daughter of the big burra sahib who owned Britannia Mills. The reflected glory of this alliance was shared by Dennis's domestic staff.

Before she went tip tapping back down the metal stairs, Monica gave him a message for Dennis. "You tell your master he'll be very sorry. He can't treat my poor little cousin like this. She's only a child." She was as disappointed for herself and Aunt Fifi as she was for Carole. There'd be no Australia for them!

Dennis had a bad day in the office. Worried about Carole and his failure to summon up sufficient nerve to tell Baby about her, he was unable to concentrate and was then infuriated by an indigent Australian who'd got off the mail boat in Bombay in order to go to a whore house and missed its sailing later in the evening. Now he was demanding a free air passage either to London or back to Australia – but preferably to London. By the time he'd argued with the man for hours, Dennis's temper snapped and he leaned across the counter to grab the nuisance by the collar of his shirt and hiss, "Get the hell out of my office and don't come back!"

The tourist looked shaken, for Dennis was twice his size, but he wasn't going to yield without a struggle, "Hey, you don't try any bully-boy tactics with me. I'll report you to your boss. I'll report you to my uncle, he's got a pal in Congress. He'll get you fired."

"Report me to Lord God Almighty if you like," yelled Dennis. "I don't give a shit." He'd never in his life let his temper rip like that in public and in a way he almost enjoyed it.

He was still sounding quite grim when he phoned Baby to tell her he was working late and unable to see her that night. He only wanted to go home, lie in a bath and drink brandy while he pondered his situation. When he rang off, she stood with the black receiver in her hand staring into its earpiece and wondering what had got into the normally placid Dennis.

After he made the call, he sprinted out of the office and down the stairs to his car. At the main door of the High Commission he was accosted by a shabby little man in black trousers, a grubby white shirt and a black silk jacket that was frayed round all its hems.

"Mister Gillies," hissed this man sibilantly and tried to put a hand on Dennis's arm but was shoved roughly away. Dennis's fear of being touched by beggars had not left him.

"What do you want?" he asked.

"You are Mister Gillies? Yes?"

"Yes."

"I am Mister Rodriques and I am Miss Carole MacLeod's legal representative. Her mother would like to have a word with you."

Dennis reeled. "When?" he asked.

"Now."

"Where?"

"At her house in Chembur. You know the way."

When they walked to Dennis's car which was parked round the corner, Rodriques casually climbed into the front seat beside him. Dennis's distaste for the little man with the garlicky smell almost overwhelmed him but he drove off into the dense traffic, fighting against his irritation.

It was after six and would soon be dark. As usual at that time, the traffic was nose to tail down Church Gate and along Marine Drive. He drummed his fists on the steering wheel, feeling his anger coming back, but with an effort of will forced himself to remain calm. His passenger seemed determined to be pleasant, making conversation as they drove along – "Do you like our city? Have you seen Elephanta yet? How much are you earning?" This last question was the last straw.

"Just shut up will you," said Dennis turning his head angrily towards Rodriques. "Do me a favour and keep your mouth shut."

Not another word was spoken between them throughout the journey to Chembur which seemed to take three times longer than usual for the road was full of half wits wandering about in the middle of the traffic and coolies hauling loaded barrows who wouldn't pull into the side to let him pass so he was reduced to going at their speed. Eventually he reached the open stretch of road before the golf course and turned into Carole's lane.

Her mother answered the door and stared at them expressionlessly as if she had no idea who they were.

"Is Carole here?" Dennis asked. She shook her head but opened the door wider and gestured that they should enter. In the little sitting room the dog rose from its place in the corner and bared its teeth.

"Down Sheba," she told it.

Gingerly Dennis sat down and wondered how to start the discussion but she did it for him. "I hear you're getting married," she said, "A very rich girl too. You've done well for yourself."

It was genuinely the first time that Dennis had thought about his engagement in this way and he felt slightly unclean. "I'm getting married because I love her," he replied.

"You said you loved my Carole and she's just a child. You promised to marry her. But she is not rich," said Fifi.

"I did not. I never said a word about marriage, so being rich has nothing to do with it."

159

"You did or why would I have allowed her to go to your flat and sleep with you? We're a respectable family and she's just a child, she doesn't know what she's doing and you took advantage of her." She pronounced it 'adwantage' and for a moment he didn't know what she meant.

"I did not," he repeated weakly when he gathered himself together. God, what if Carole's pregnant? he thought, but didn't dare to ask in case it put the idea into her blackmailing mother's head.

"We will take you to court. We will sue you for breach of promise. You promised to marry my little girl and take her to Australia."

Some of his fighting spirit came back into Dennis and he stood up, towering over the woman. "I did not promise to marry her and you damned well know it. She got into my bed. I didn't even ask her. She wasn't a virgin. Even her sister says she's a tart."

Fifi screeched like a barn owl. "A wirgin! Of course she was a wirgin. Her sister's jealous. Carole goes to confession every Sunday. The priest knows she was a wirgin. Who's going to believe you when they see my little girl? She's so young and innocent. I know who you're marrying and I'll go to her father and make things difficult for you, my lad. Her father's a hard man. He'll run you out of India."

Dennis had a sickening mind picture of Carole in her baby-doll pose with her thumb in her mouth. Then she looked about thirteen. Maybe she was. Maybe she wasn't as old as she'd told him. He sat down again with a thud that made the dog spring up.

"Where is she?" he asked.

"She's gone out. She doesn't want to see you. Mr Rodrigues is our adviser and he will sue you for breach of promise."

"That's impossible," gasped Dennis.

"No it isn't. You promised to marry her. She told me about you saying she could go to Australia with you and meet your parents. We'll tell Sir Robert Smith that."

This is a shakedown, thought Dennis, and he was right. Rodriques took over the discussion. "If you pay Miss Carole, she will forget all about your promises."

"How much?"

"When your friend Mr Bob left Monica, he gave her thirty thousand rupees."

That was highly unlikely, Dennis knew. Monica would have been lucky if Bob left her three thousand. "You're kidding," he said sceptically.

"No, we are not kidding. We want thirty thousand rupees."

"Where am I going to get that kind of money?"

"You are marrying much money. You can borrow it from a money lender."

"Huh! I'm not paying. You're trying to blackmail me. I could go to the police."

"Then Sir Robert will certainly find out about your promise to my daughter," said Fifi cannily. "But if you have no money we will let you off with twenty thousand." When she had heard who Dennis was marrying, it was she who hit on the scheme of trying to extract some money from him. After all, most men paid off their mistresses before they married. But Dennis was not proving such an easy prospect as they had hoped.

"I'm not paying that either," he said.

"We'll settle for fifteen," said Rodriques hurriedly. They were very bad blackmailers.

Fifteen thousand rupees is three months' salary for me, thought Dennis, and I've got all the expenses of a wedding, and an engagement ring as well, coming up, but the thought of Sir Robert and Baby being told about his affair with Carole was more than he could face. At that moment he wanted to marry Baby more than anything in the world and he was sure that she would be so shocked if she knew about Carole that the whole thing would be off. His thoughts whirled about in his head like distracted flies.

"Okay, ten thousand," was what he said. It's a pity Bob's left but I can borrow the money from Joe, he told himself, Joe's the only person I know who'll understand about this.

Fifi and the shabby little man looked at each other. Ten thousand was more than they'd hoped for but they pretended to be disappointed. "You are a hard, cruel man who takes adwantage of innocent girls," said Fifi sadly.

"When will you pay?" asked Rodriques.

Dennis put his hand into his back pocket and drew out his wallet. It contained two thousand and twenty five rupees. He counted out two thousand and handed it to Rodrigues. "On account," he said. "Give me a receipt."

"You are not trusting us. No receipt," said Rodriques shocked, "We must have the rest before your wedding or we will tell."

Dennis strode towards the door and flung it open. To his surprise Rodriques trotted behind him and put his hand on the passenger door of the car.

"Where are you going?" he asked.

"Bombay, back with you."

"Are you hell, mate. You can bloody well walk as far as I care."

161

Twenty-Two

O f course it was Ben who'd noticed Carole first. Since he was the sort of man whose eye was always caught by a pretty girl, he'd seen her weeks ago at the Chembur bus stop and marked her down as a likely-looking piece, on the game almost certainly. When he decided to find a woman for Guy, to stop him being so bitchy to Dee as much as anything, she was the first possibility that came into his mind. It was much safer for his friend to get involved with a local girl than enter into some potentially dangerous affair with one of their acquaintances' wives which would be easier to arrange but could turn out messy because he knew Guy certainly couldn't afford getting mixed up in a divorce.

Without saying anything about what he had in mind, he began deliberately scouting for the tall chi-chi girl, driving slowly through Chembur village as he came back from work in the evenings with Guy at his side. Then after about a week, when he was on the verge of giving the whole idea up, he saw her sauntering along the road, swinging a white plastic handbag and holding a paper parasol over her head.

"Take a look at *that!*" he cried, pointing at Carole's long legs. "Legs all the way to her neck."

Guy laughed and leaned forward in his seat. "Impressive," he agreed.

Ben swung the car over to her side of the road and stuck his head out of the window. "Can we give you a lift anywhere?" he asked.

She dimpled at them and her spirits, which had been low because of Dennis's defection, took an immediate upward rise. Two white men together. What luck! The one that was driving was very attractive but the little fat one would do at a pinch. She fluttered her eyelashes at Ben and said, "How kind of you. I've a blister on my heel and it hurts so much. I've been walking for ages."

In fact she'd only walked from the bus stop because she'd been in Bombay, at Monica's, discussing her future which seemed distinctly bleak at that moment.

Carole was not taking an active part in the campaign to extract money from Dennis. It wasn't that she had been in love with him. Her emotions were never engaged in any of her affairs. It was just that she felt discarded yet again for this wasn't the first time it had happened. How Amy was crowing, throwing her failure in her teeth. That was the worst thing to bear. "Dumped again. You're going to end up like Mummy, dressing up and whipping some old lecher like Major Motiwala who wouldn't be seen dead with you socially . . ." jeered her sister. Her mother too was acting as if Carole was a failure for not making a marriage that would transport them all out of India.

It was no use to retaliate with, 'I'm going to marry a white man and go away from here.' To Amy she said, "You're just jealous because no man of *any* colour ever looks at you." Amy only curled her lip.

Carole never stayed down in the dumps for long however; she believed in luck and in astrology and lucky omens. That afternoon at Monica's she'd read her horoscope in *Eve's Weekly*. 'Look out for a new opportunity,' it had said and here it was. She beamed with delight at the men, one of whom might be her saviour. She was an eternal optimist.

Guy reached over and opened the back door of the car. "Jump in and we'll take you home," he said gallantly. He had a wonderful voice, she noticed, so very gentlemanly. Remembering to limp slightly she eased herself into the car and sat back against the grey leather upholstery. "I live down at the side of the golf course," she said. On the way to her house they passed Amy trudging home from work and Carole took the utmost pleasure in waving to her sister from the back window of the car.

When they dropped her off, they told her where they lived and invited her to drop in on them any evening. "Come and meet my wife," said the handsome one carefully, so she knew the score and wouldn't behave indecorously when she met Dee.

She didn't believe in letting a good opportunity go to waste so that very night she hired a taxi and drove to the Gulmohurs. It would have been quite possible for her to walk there but she wanted to arrive in style.

There were four people sitting on cane chairs in the garden when the yellow and black cab stopped at the gate. She hopped out, immaculate in her best white dress and white shoes, paid off the taxi driver, waved and shouted "Yoo hoo!" at the watchers in the garden. None of them waved back but unabashed she tripped over the lawn towards them, smiling brightly.

163

"Oh Christ," said Guy when he saw her.

Ben grasped his wife's hand and whispered, "It's a girl Guy gave a lift to in the village this evening. He said to her to come and see us and she's taken him at his word."

Shadiv, sitting on the other side of Dee, just laughed.

By this time Carole was amongst them, beaming down at Guy who levered himself out of his chair and said out of force of habit, "How nice to see you my dear. Can we offer you a drink?"

"How sweet. But I don't drink alcohol. A cola would be lovely."

Guy gave her a chair and went over to the verandah for another, calling out to Mohammed as he did, "A cola for the lady, Mahmud."

When Mohammed came out with a glass of dark red liquid on his tray and saw Carole sitting in state in the middle of the group, Dee noticed how his eyes suddenly gleamed like the eyes of a tiger in the jungle when it catches first sight of its prey.

They stayed talking and laughing till after midnight when Shadiv left. Then Dee drifted off to bed and soon Ben followed her.

Next morning when she got up, she found Carole at the breakfast table, wrapped in Guy's towelling bathrobe and tucking into a huge plate of sausages, bacon and eggs.

"I love sausages," she said with a beaming smile and Dee sat watching while the girl disposed of her first plateful and then ordered a second. Dee's spirits sank because she and Ben paid for all the Gulmohurs food, while Guy was responsible for the rent. If Carole was going to stay for a while, their budget would be sorely stretched.

She stayed for six days the first time. Her appetite was enormous though she was as thin as a racing whippet, an animal she uncannily resembled when clad in her black shorts and bikini top.

Always in evidence at meal times, she spent most of the morning and afternoon in bed, rising about half past three to take tea with Dee on the verandah. Then she retired to the kitchen where she chattered away in Hindi to Mohammed with whom she was on the most cordial terms. When she wasn't asleep, she never stopped talking, regaling Dee with the story of her life, a very different version to the one she'd told Dennis.

To Dee she made no pretence about the way she was trying to make her way in the world. She was a good girl really, she said, who was in search of a man to marry her and take her away from India. Guy had said he'd do that. He'd promised to marry her and take her to London, she exulted. When she told Dee this her eyes shone. Once again she believed though man after man had let her down apparently. "But Guy's a good man," she said complacently.

Dee did not disabuse her of this idea and found herself entranced by Carole's saga, looking forward to each afternoon's episode in the same way as Scheherazade's listeners must have anticipated her tale-spinning.

"I don't like Americans," said Carole one day. "I used to live in the compound beside the oil refinery over there," – she nodded towards the other side of the island – "with an old American who paid my mother three thousand chips for me when I was twelve."

Dee looked at her in horror. "Twelve?"

"Yes, but I looked older. He kept me till I was sixteen and then he went home. But before he went he got me a job teaching in the nursery school there. The teacher fired me because I was too pretty."

"What happened then?" asked Dee.

"I went home to mummy and she sent me to live with her cousin Monica who had an Australian boyfriend but he went home too and left her behind. I don't like Australians either. One of them said he'd marry me as well and then dropped me, just like that!" She snapped her fingers loudly and grimaced. "But I don't care now that I've met Guy. You know he's written to his mother about me. He says we'll get on very well when he takes me to London."

Dee wouldn't put it past Guy to string the girl along but she knew he was far too cautious to mention marriage, and as for writing to his mother, that was even more unlikely. Guy never wrote home and never received any letters for he did not get on with his mother, a lady who had been married three times and lived in considerable comfort in Chelsea with her third husband, a stockbroker. Guy's father, who had been husband number one, was long since jettisoned.

Though they were not on close terms, Guy was in awe of his mother and the last thing he'd do would be to introduce half-caste Carole to her as his wife. He was far too snobbish for that.

Yet for day after day, Carole sat on the verandah daydreaming aloud about meeting Guy's mother in London. "He says we're very like each other. She'll take me to the theatre and out to meet her friends. I'll have to get a lot of new clothes, won't I? What do you think I'll need?"

Dee felt a pull of pity in her heart for the girl. There was something very appealing about Carole though she was obviously an out and out fantasist. "Perhaps it would be best to wait till things are more definite before you start buying clothes," she suggested but she needn't have worried because Carole hadn't any money and Guy wasn't prepared to subsidise her new wardrobe. It was all just pie-in-the-sky talk that Carole liked to mull over. Taking away her dreams would have been like taking toys from a child.

To do her justice Carole was not only interested in herself. Somehow she winkled out of Dee the admission of how much she longed for a baby.

"I don't think I ever will have one though," said Dee sadly but Carole grabbed her hand and turned it over, "I can read palms," she cried. "I'll tell you if you'll have children."

Then she pored over Dee's hand, oohing and aahing and making the recipient of her interest feel very stupid and awkward for putting up with it. At last she was told, "Don't worry about children. You'll have at least three – maybe more – and you're going to live a long time. Not like me. My hand says I'll only have one child and that I'll die in my forties."

"Surely not!" exclaimed Dee but Carole only shrugged. To an eighteen year old, forty seemed a very long time away.

Dee folded her hand up slowly, as if to hide its secrets. She didn't ask Carole if she saw anything in it about her marriage or about Shadiv. That was her secret and she didn't want to know in advance how it was going to work out.

On the seventh day Carole had disappeared and to her own surprise Dee missed her though, while Guy's mistress had been in hungry residence, she had thought that she resented the perpetual presence which interrupted her happy isolation.

"Where's Carole?" she asked Mohammed for she was sure he would know. When Carole was not with Dee or lying in bed sucking her thumb, she and the bearer talked together for hours. Dee often heard their voices in the distance, something she found disquieting because Mohammed knew more about Guy, Ben and herself than any of them knew about each other. He read all their letters, she suspected, because he was more fluent in English than he liked to pretend, and nothing escaped him. They were the sole objects of his attention and scrutiny, like flies in a bell jar. Dee didn't trust him an inch and if he found a tool or an ally in Carole, what mischief might he not create?

"Her mother sent her a message to go home," he said solemnly, but offered no more.

Two days passed before she came back, once again late at night in a taxi, all dressed in white and crying out cheerfully as she came running across the lawn. This time she brought them each a present

– cigarettes for Ben, a pair of hairbrushes with tortoiseshell backs for Guy, and for Dee a box of Moti soap and a baby's bonnet made of white cotton with frills around the face.

When she unwrapped it, Dee thought for a moment that Carole was playing a cruel joke but the girl leaned across to her in the dim light coming off the verandah and said, "I bought you that because I'm sure you'll be able to use it soon. It's in your hand."

Twenty-Three

D ennis's weekly airmail letter to his parents arrived regularly every Saturday morning and Maud perused it over the breakfast table, reading choice bits out loud to Denzil who received his news of his son second-hand and never actually read the letters himself.

On this particular morning Maud was unusually quiet as her eyes ran along the neatly written lines. Then she gave a funny little gasp and said in a sort of moan, "I don't believe it. I don't believe it."

"What's up Maud?" asked her husband, "Is Denny all right? He's not sick, is he?"

"I think he's gone potty," said Maud. "He says he's getting married at the end of May. That's only about six weeks away!"

"Aw you've got it wrong. Hand it over and let me read it," said Denzil adopting his head-of-the-household attitude.

"I haven't. He's getting married. He must have got some girl up the spout."

Then, leaning back in her chair in an attitude of martyred shock, she passed the two sheets of fragile paper over to her husband who held them close up to his face while he read. Then he cried, "Christ, Maud, you're right. He's getting married. He says he's head over heels in love with some girl called Roberta Maling-Smith. Did you ever hear a name like that?"

Wisely Dennis had decided the shock of a double-barrelled surname would be sufficient for his parents. They wouldn't have been able to cope with a future daughter-in-law called *Baby* Maling-Smith.

"Does he say she's pregnant? She must have caught our Denny that way," said Maud who was now wiping her eyes.

Denzil read the letter again. "He doesn't mention it but he wouldn't, would he? He says she's the most wonderful girl he's ever met and he can't believe his luck."

"He's putting a good face on it," said Maud.

"He wants us to go to the wedding," Denzil told her.

"All the way to India! I've never even been to Perth. How can we go to Bombay just like that? The fares'll be enormous."

Denzil handed the letter back to her, "Denny says he's going to phone tomorrow night and talk about us going. You'd better get your act together for that, Maud."

"How can I pretend to be pleased? What sort of girl marries a man she's only just met? We don't know anything about her. Oh poor Denny, he's just a kid really. He's not ready to get married."

Before Dennis's call came, his parents contacted Uncle Joe, the fount of all knowledge in their family. Unknown to them Joe had already been telephoned by his nephew who asked for the loan of a thousand dollars but had the grace to tell the truth about why he wanted it. Instead of being shocked, Joe had been impressed. Going to India had made a man of Denny, he thought. He wired the money the next day.

"Do you know something about this, Joe?" demanded his sister whose suspicions were aroused by the mild way her brother received the news.

"Yeah, well I do actually. Den phoned me the other day and told me but he said not to tell you because he was writing to you about it."

"Joe! How could you keep it from us. He's our *son*! I hope he's not been caught by one of those chi-chi girls. They're all trying to get into Australia now. When he phones, I'll tell him it's not too late to call it off," cried Maud.

"Don't be too hard on him, old girl," warned Joe. "She's not a chi-chi. She's a lady, a real lady with a father that's a Sir. Den's done well for himself."

"You seem to know a lot about it," said Maud jealously. "But when I speak to him I'll tell him he's far too young to be getting married."

"Christ Maud, he's twenty-seven. You were married at twenty-one and I was married at twenty-four," said Joe.

"And look what happened to you," snapped Maud. Joe had been married three times and each marriage ended in divorce.

The call was booked for eight o'clock on Sunday night and Dennis's parents sat with his uncle Joe staring at the silent telephone receiver for half an hour before it was due to ring. The men had glasses of beer in their hands; Maud smoked half a pack of cigarettes, she was so tense.

At last it rang and they all jumped as if taken by surprise. When they were finally put through to Dennis, they had difficulty making up their minds who should speak first but it was Maud who wrested the receiver out of her husband's hand.

"Oh Denny, I'm so upset. My baby's getting married and I won't be there!" Then she burst into a storm of weeping and had to hand the phone to her husband, who was more matter of fact. "What's all this, Den?" he asked.

"I'm getting married, Dad," came Dennis's voice through the static, "I'm very happy about it. She's a lovely girl. I'm the luckiest man alive."

"Yeah, well, your mother's a bit upset," said Denzil.

"But I want you to come to my wedding. And Uncle Joe as well. Gran and Granpa too, both sets of them if they can come."

Denzil said over his shoulder to the others, "He wants us to go to the wedding – and you as well, Joe. The old folks too. He's gone mad."

"The fares," moaned Maud.

Dennis pre-empted her though. "Don't worry about the fares," he told his father, "Roberta's father is insisting on paying for you. He's very rich, Dad. And he's got a title. He's a Sir."

Denzil held the phone away from his ear. So Joe was right. "A *Sir*?"

"Yeah, he's Sir Robert Maling-Smith. He's a good guy. He says you and Mum and Joe and the others must fly out first class and he's going to book suites for you in the Taj Mahal hotel here. I wanted you to stay with me in my flat but he says you should do the trip in style and, believe me, the Taj is style. Say you'll come, Dad. I really want you to be here with me when I get married."

Denzil looked at his wife. "He wants us to go to the wedding. His father-in-law will pay. Joe's right, the guy's got a title apparently."

Maud looked stunned and said nothing.

"We'll come, and so'll Joe but I don't think we can bring the old folks. Just let us know the details," said Denzil, taking control. He was hanging up the phone, ignoring his wife, who was reaching for it because she had suddenly remembered something she wanted to ask.

"Is she pregnant? You didn't find out if she's pregnant."

But Dennis had rung off.

In Bombay the excitement was also running high in the Maling-Smith residence. Sir Robert spent hours with his lawyers, writing up a marriage contract. It wasn't that he suspected Dennis of coveting Roberta's wealth. As far as he was concerned he would have preferred it if his future son-in-law had been more avaricious and worldly, but Sir Robert didn't believe in leaving anything to chance.

He also spent a great deal of time contacting his Australian business contacts trying to find a suitable vacancy there for Dennis. Three possibilities were put to him, and he decided to get all the details before suggesting them.

While her husband was concerned with business affairs, Lady Barbara involved herself with the arrangements for the wedding – with the dress, which was to be copied from an illustration in *Vogue* by her durzi who sat whirring away on a black and gold handle-operated Singer machine on the verandah floor while chaos reined around him; with the catering; the flowers; the music; the guest list; and the location. Every waking moment was taken up with it and total concentration took her mind off her illness and seemed to restore her to health.

She rushed about from morning till night, more active – and more sober – than she'd been for years. Even Dr Green was astonished by the improvement in her condition and allowed himself to hope that the diagnosis was not as hopeless as he'd first thought.

"You must be careful not to over-tax yourself," he warned when she came to see him wanting a renewal of the prescription for her pain killers.

She beamed at him, positively girlish. "Dear Moses, I've not felt so fit for years. This wedding is keeping me alive. I'm absolutely determined to stay well till it's over. After that – after that it won't matter any more. My Baby will be settled and happy and I'll be able to die in peace."

He'd seen examples of determination like this defying death before and did nothing more to stop her.

Baby came to consult him too. She wanted to know sure ways of conceiving.

"Do you want a baby very soon?" he asked her.

She stared into the wrinkled, simian-looking face above the white coat and knew he was a very wise man. "I don't know, doctor," she said. "I'm not actually very maternal, but my mother would like me to have children. She wants to be a grandmother . . . I just wondered when I should start planning for a baby."

"I think you should follow your own wishes on that matter," he said quietly, knowing that unless a miracle happened Lady Barbara would not live long enough to see any grandchildren.

The girl on the other side of his desk stared at him, remembering

171

their last conversation. He was trying to tell her something, she knew. "One of the reasons I'm getting married, Doctor Green, is to please my mother," she said in a rush.

"Only because of that?" he asked.

She furrowed her brow. "No, not only because of that. I'm very fond of Dennis. He's a splendid man. Also I want to start a new life. I want to start again, to remake myself really. And I couldn't find a better man to do it with ... I want to go far away and start again."

"But are you sure you love him?"

"What's love? People who fall in love only open themselves up to being hurt. I like him. I respect him. Isn't that enough?" She wanted it to be enough but she still could not forget the mad passion she'd felt for Charlie, how her heart thudded when she caught sight of him, how she longed to touch him whenever they were together. It wasn't like that with Dennis and it wouldn't be like that with anyone else ever again, she was sure. Oh Charlie, Charlie, her heart sighed, I wish I'd never met you and I'd be a happy girl now.

The doctor sighed, "Probably. Lots of people make do with that and are perfectly happy. It depends on you."

When Baby reached home, she was looking determinedly happy, but she found her mother bogged down with the mechanics of the wedding which was to take place in Bombay Cathedral, where so many of the Maling relations were commemorated.

"The bishop thinks you should have at least three bridesmaids. He says it takes three girls behind a bride to make a decent show," said Lady Barbara looking up from her voluminous lists.

Baby became mulish, with her father's determination showing in her face. "Nonsense, mummy. I don't want that sort of show and neither does Dennis. One bridesmaid will do."

"But it looks so meagre. I want you to have a magnificent wedding. Please have three."

"I don't want to go down the aisle like a ship in full sail with a retinue behind me," moaned Baby, "but to please you I'll settle for two. Winks and another one."

"In that case, you'll have to ask Mags as well," said her mother.

"Not Mags. I can't stand her. Anyway she wouldn't do it. She says she's not even going to come to my wedding. She thinks I'm only getting married to steal a march on her. We'll have to ask someone else."

There were plenty of possible candidates but Lady Maling-Smith knew that if she asked one, she'd have offended another or her mother. "But who?" she asked.

"Can't we just have one bridesmaid?" asked Baby again.

But her mother shook her head, "No, darling, it looks skimpy and unbalanced. We have to have at least two. But who'll be the second one?"

At that point Dee Carmichael's battered old car drove into the compound. She was returning the books borrowed from Sir Robert's library. With her arms full of leather-bound volumes, she walked in on the wedding conference, and her opinion was immediately sought.

"Do you think only one bridesmaid looks unbalanced, Dee?" asked Baby.

Dee laid down the books carefully and replied, "It depends on the church, I suppose."

"It's the cathedral."

Dee laughed. "In that case I think you should have at least ten."

"When you got married, how many did you have?" asked Baby.

"None," said Dee shortly, "but I'm not a typical case."

"Would you be my second bridesmaid?" asked Baby on a sudden impulse.

"I don't think I can, can I? I'm married."

"You can be matron of honour."

Dee laughed again, "God, that sounds very important. Matron of honour! I'd love to but there must be someone else who'd do it better."

"Believe me, there isn't," said Lady Barbara. "Let the durzi take your measurements and he'll make your dress. Is apple-green all right for you? The other bridesmaid is Winks and not every colour suits her."

At half-past five, while they were all being measured by the durzi, an awkward-looking Dennis turned up and was taken off by the bearer to be served with tea in solitary splendour in the enormous sitting-room on the ground floor.

Baby rushed in, kissed him on the cheek, and said, "Everything's in chaos, darling, and I simply can't stop, the durzi wants to take my measurements again. Would you like a whisky soda? I'll have one sent in to you. Daddy'll be back soon to keep you company."

The company of Sir Robert was not something Dennis craved. He looked woebegone. "Will we be able to go out to dinner tonight?" he asked. Joe's money had arrived and he was feeling rich, though he knew he'd be poor again very soon because Rodriques had been hanging around outside the office waiting for the second instalment of the blackmail money.

Baby frowned, "Not tonight I'm afraid. There's so much to do. Tonight Mummy and I are making up the invitation list – she thinks hundreds of people have to be asked."

"Hundreds?" asked Dennis apprehensively.

"Yes, hundreds but I'm going to make her cut them down. What about dinner tomorrow?"

"We're going to buy the engagement ring tomorrow," he reminded her because the next day was Saturday and it had been arranged that he and Baby should go to Lady Barbara's jeweller and pick out two rings – one for the engagement and the other for the wedding. Dennis was very anxious about this appointment because of the limited funds he had available for ring buying.

Baby smiled at him and went onto tiptoe to kiss him gently on the lips. "You look so worried! Come and pick me up at eleven o'clock and we'll have the whole day to ourselves. Do sit down and have a whisky. You look as if you need it."

So he sat down, drank his whisky and when it was finished, rose again, peered into the verandah which seemed to be full of people and waved a hand at Baby. Instead of coming out of him, she only waved back and blew him a kiss.

He was being sent home, he realised. When he drove back through the gate he thought the Pathan had a sceptical expression on his face as he watched him go.

No wonder, he told himself. Since the wedding was arranged he'd hardly seen Baby. They met in passing as she was rushing here or there, and what worried him was that she didn't seem to mind their separation. It was almost a fortnight since he'd really kissed her and he was beginning to wonder if he ever would again. Paradoxically, now that he had found the woman of his dreams, he was almost as lonely as he had been during his first weeks in Bombay for he did not have the diversion of Breach Candy. He didn't want to go there without Baby and run the gauntlet of her watching friends.

When he left Baby's home, he drove moodily down to the racecourse and then back via the Maidan to Colaba where he stopped the car on Cuffe Parade and walked along the sea wall, watching the sun go down. Then he went to the cinema where Frank Sinatra's *Man with the Golden Arm* was playing. Its mood of degradation and despair was exactly right for Dennis.

He drank too much that night, sitting alone on his balcony while he worked out exactly how much he could spend on Baby's rings. He would have given her every anna he possessed but Rodriques lurked in the background. There was still eight thousand rupees to be paid to him. Dennis decided that it would be prudent to spread payment out, to give it all at once would only encourage the blackmailers to ask for more. Their short-sighted greed would make them settle for what they could get if he kept them dangling. He'd pay out another two thousand at the end of next week and make them worry about the rest later. The last payment would be on his wedding day – after the ceremony preferably – for he shuddered at the thought of Carole standing up and disrupting the ceremony, shouting out in her sing-song English, 'But he promised to marry me and take me to Australia!'

Don't be daft, he told himself, downing another brandy. That won't happen, they're only shaking you down. But he couldn't risk ignoring the threat. "Oh Baby, I wish I could tell you about it," he groaned aloud. He didn't dare however because he did not know enough about her to guess how she would take it. As the night darkened and the roar of traffic quietened, he realised he was marrying a stranger, entering unknown country where he had no guidelines about how to behave or read the signs. Maybe that was one of the reasons he loved her.

He woke with a throbbing headache that was still pulsing away when he drove into Baby's compound at five to eleven. Cool and starched-looking even in the oppressive heat, she was waiting for him on the verandah and when she climbed into his car, her full skirts rustled and crackled in a way that roused his longing.

"Give me a kiss, Baby," he pleaded.

She laughed, "Not in front of the servants darling. They're all watching."

They drove away with Dennis unkissed.

He drove distractedly, thinking about the huge rings, especially the glittering emerald, that always adorned Lady Barbara's hands. How on earth could he afford anything so magnificent? But he wanted Baby to be able to hold her head – or her hands – up alongside her mother.

To his wry amusement the jeweller's shop turned out to be in Grant Road – number 87. When he parked the car he stood on the pavement staring along in the direction of the higher numbers. Some of them seemed to be big, shabby houses with a few straggly trees in the front yards. Which one had been Madame Mae's, he wondered, which one did Joe remember? He'd drive the old boy along this road when he came for the wedding and let him take a trip down Memory Lane.

Baby was waiting for him in the shop doorway which was being held open by a fierce looking doorman with waxed moustaches and an enormous turban. Inside it was air-conditioned and cool. They were invited to sit down on bentwood chairs while the proprietor was summoned.

He proved to be a smooth-looking old Parsi with twinkling eyes who enthused over Baby, before congratulating Dennis on his good fortune in being about to marry such a jewel of a young lady. The compliments poured from him like cream from a jug and as he smiled and smiled, Dennis's headache grew worse.

"Maybe I've got a brain tumour," he wondered distractedly. "It would be just my luck."

If he thought he was merely there to pay the bill while Baby picked out a ring, he was wrong. Velvet pads were laid on the glass-topped counter and precious jewel after precious jewel was brought out and reverently laid out for their admiration. They looked at diamonds as big as finger nails; at sinister looking emeralds; at rubies with fire in their hearts; at amethysts, cats' eyes, aquamarines, alexandrites . . . at a truly dazzling array that made Dennis quail because of their quality and price.

Baby sensed his disquiet. "I want a very small ring," she told the jeweller whose name was Mr Homi. "I have small hands, you see. And because we're just starting out I don't want a very valuable stone. I've really set my heart on an opal."

"Ah, I have a beautiful opal in the safe. I bought it from a maharajah in Sind recently. He had it in a pendant but it would make a superb ring," said the jeweller, who, unknown to the young couple, had been contacted by Lady Barbara and told that though they would be sure to ask for something cheap, he was to make sure they ended up with a good ring, charge them a reasonable figure and send the rest of the bill to her.

The opal was magnificent, egg shaped, as big as a stamp, glowing like silk with a sheen of pink and purple on its surface.

"I will set it in a claw mount in gold and it will look wonderful on your hand," said Mr Homi, laying it reverently in Baby's palm.

She sighed in genuine admiration and glanced sideways at Dennis before she asked, "Is it very expensive?"

"No. Not expensive at all. Only three thousand made up."

"Do you like it darling?" said Dennis. "If you really like it, we'll have it."

"If you buy it," said Mr Homi, "I will give you a golden wedding ring as my present."

The deal was done. The rings would be delivered in three days' time. When he walked out of the shop, Dennis loosened his collar.

"Are you all right?" asked Baby, noticing this.

"Yeah, sure. Just a bit of a headache. It's hot, isn't it?"

"Not as hot as it'll be at the end of the month when we get married. It'll be lovely to go away."

He looked down at her in surprise for he hadn't yet got round to arranging a honeymoon. That had slipped his mind. More expense, was his first thought.

"Going away?" he queried.

She smiled at him. "It's Daddy's surprise for us but Mummy let it slip. She never keeps secrets. Daddy's booked us in at the Ooty Club. It's where he and Mummy went for their honeymoon."

Piqued at being thwarted of picking what looked like being his only opportunity for making a choice in the business of this marriage, Dennis frowned. "Where's Ooty?" he asked.

Baby took his arm, "It's Ootacamund, in the south, in the Blue Mountains. Not far from Mysore. You'll love it, it's always cool. In the winter they need fires! It's one of the most beautiful places in the world. I adore Ooty."

"That's great," said Dennis dolefully. Another decision had been made for him and not for the first time he began to wonder what his life would be like in the future.

Twenty-Four

"Are you sure that's a good idea?" asked Guy that evening when Dee excitedly told him and Ben about Baby's invitation.

"Why not? It's an honour." Dee felt that Guy was back at his old game of putting her down. To be Baby's matron of honour would mark her acceptance into Bombay's European society, where till now she'd been the odd woman out. Though part of her scorned them, another part of her longed to be accepted.

"Oh yes, it's an honour all right. But you and Ben are a bit hard up aren't you? How are you going to be able to afford a suitable present?"

"But we'd have to give a present even if we were only going as guests," said Dee.

Guy nodded. "Yes, but then we'd get away with something small. Something from the three of us – a tablecloth probably. If you're matron of honour you have to give something big."

Dee and Ben looked at each other. "What sort of present?" asked Ben. They used Guy as their guide through the complex social maze which was very unlike anything they'd known at home.

"Silver, I expect."

Dee laughed. "*Silver!*" She and Ben were down to their last ten chips and you didn't get much silver for that.

When she had been bridesmaid to friends in Edinburgh, she'd taken them out to dinner – and then she had more far disposable money than she had now. Not for the first time she bitterly regretted her loss of financial independence. Though Ben's financial situation was slowly improving, and he was showing a new enthusiasm for his work, they had a lot of leeway to make up and many bills still outstanding.

Next morning she went over early to the fruit farm to use the phone. Shadiv and his wife were both away from home, making films in the hills, and there was no hope of seeing him but she stared up at the verandah of his flat hopefully none the less. Her infatuation was as strong as ever and she dreamt about him almost

178

every night. When she woke she was always worried in case she'd been talking in her sleep.

The phone was in a little office guarded by the fruit farm manager, a pleasant young man who always wanted to get into deep conversation about religion which seemed to prey on his mind. He was a Roman Catholic, he told her, but found himself increasingly attracted by Hinduism. Normally she was quite happy to indulge in speculation about this for an hour or so but not today. She had to phone Baby.

Because the farm manager was hanging over her, listening to every word she said, she could only tell Baby that she was anxious to meet her.

"When?" asked Baby.

"Today."

"Where?"

"Breach Candy . . . How about eleven o'clock?"

As she drove into the city, Dee was surprised to realise that she was feeling extremely feeble. "It's this heat," she told herself, wiping her wet brow and pulling out the neck of her dress to let some air into her body.

At Breach Candy she was early, so she put on her swimsuit and plunged into the water, standing there with it lapping around her shoulders while she waited for Baby but even then she still felt rotten.

Baby jumped in beside her soon and laughed, "This is the best place to be right now, isn't it? It's a ninety-five degrees today, you know, and ninety-five per cent humidity as well."

"That must be why I'm feeling so hellish," sighed Dee. Baby looked at her. "You are a bit white. You should go over to the hospital and get a Vitamin B jag. It works every time for me."

"Does it? I might try it. I just don't have any energy recently . . ."

"What did you want to speak to me about?" asked Baby.

"It's about being your matron of honour. I'm terribly flattered to be asked but I don't think I'm quite the right person. We're not in your society really. People will be surprised."

Baby laughed. "I've never worried about what people think. Don't be silly. You'll make a wonderful matron of honour. Mother says you'll look lovely when we get you all dressed up in a pale-green gown. Much better than Mags would."

"But . . ." said Dee.

"But what? What's the problem? Please tell me."

"It's the bloody present. Ben and I are terribly hard up and

Guy says the matron of honour should give the bride and groom a good present – preferably something silver. Baby, we can't afford silver."

Baby looked at the troubled face beside her and laughed. "He's pulling your leg. You don't have to give a present at all if you don't want to. As for silver, forget it. My father's business associates will be loading me up with that sort of thing."

"But I want to give you a really nice present. What would you like?"

"Well, certainly not silver. What about something that will always remind me of India no matter where I go. Something very local, something Indian . . ."

Dee suddenly felt much better. "I'll put my mind to it," she said with a grin.

"And you'll be my matron of honour?"

"Oh yes. I'd still love to."

Shadiv had been away all week filming in the hills on the way to Poona and he looked very glum when he came slouching over their lawn at about ten o'clock that night.

"I finished one film today and start two more on Monday. They're billing me as India's answer to Tony Curtis," he said gloomily. "Offers are rolling in. I can see that I'm going to spend the rest of my life running down mountainsides with my arms spread out, singing about love. I'm never going to be given a part I can get my teeth into."

Ben laughed, "It's better than not working, mate. You'll be raking it in."

"Yes, I'm making money. Leila bought a huge refrigerator yesterday and she's talking about us moving into a flat on Malabar Hill. She's got her eye on a block called Blue Skies. There's a penthouse going there apparently . . . but I'd miss the fruit farm. I'd miss this place. It's not grand enough for a big star though Leila says. We'll soon need security guards according to her . . ."

Heartsick, Dee listened to him. If he stopped coming over in the evenings, she would miss him so much she couldn't bear it. She'd miss listening to his soft, lilting voice, she'd miss watching him, seeing the expressions on his handsome face, thrilling at the way his shoulders blocked out the light when he moved towards her . . . Is this what being hopelessly in love is like, she asked herself? This ache, this longing.

Her confusion was terrible because she loved Ben too and remembered her fury when she saw him kissing that other woman.

Was it possible to love two men at once? How did you decide which one you loved the most? For someone who had doubted the very existence of love not so long ago, she was now living in an emotional maelstrom. In a way she longed for the return of her old scepticism – but not for long; as she watched and listened to Shadiv, she felt her heart melting again and wondered what would happen if she took her courage in both hands and told him how she felt.

Though she gave every outward appearance of being very confident, she was actually riddled with self doubt and terrified of rejection. If she stuck her head above the parapet, the consequences might be terrible. What if he was shocked? What if he turned out to have no feelings for her at all? That would be harder to bear than seeing him go away unaware of how she felt.

But, she told herself, even if he felt the same as she did, what could they do? Would they run away together? Did she have the nerve for it? She imagined her father's reaction if she wrote and told him she'd left her husband – initial relief, she was sure – for an Indian – complete horror. She doubted if her father had ever met an Indian socially. He'd certainly never met one like Shadiv.

The low mood cheered up when they all settled down, drinking bootlegged beer Shadiv had brought with him and listening to Louis Armstrong tracks, with Vilma Middleton singing, on the record player.

"What's been happening here?" asked Shadiv, and Ben told him about Dee going to be matron of honour at a big city wedding.

He grinned at her. "What do you have to do?" he asked.

"Nothing really. Just wear a long dress and walk behind the bride. If she has a train on her dress, the other bridesmaid and I'll have to carry it but I don't think she's having a train . . . I'm looking forward to it. The only problem is finding a present for her. She wants something that will always remind her of Bombay, no matter where she is."

"Which gives you plenty of scope," joked Guy. "Like a bottle full of air from Kurla Creek. Or one of the old sweeper's headcloths . . ." Durga, their sweeper, the man who came to clean their bathrooms twice a day, and whose services they shared with Shadiv, was the filthiest person Dee had ever seen, so dirty that she hated the idea of him swilling out her bath. When she suggested that she could do the job herself, Guy and Ben reacted with horror. "Don't even try, don't even say you could think of trying or every servant in the house will leave," they told her again.

Apparently, cleaning a bath was the job of an untouchable who

181

was to be avoided by every other Indian. If she cleaned her own bath, she'd become untouchable too and none of the servants could possibly work for her any more.

"Ugh," she said at the thought of one of the sweeper's headcloths, "but seriously, I'm really bothered about choosing a suitable present for Baby."

"There's a couple of craft shops in Hornby Road where they sell pottery and Kashmiri lacquer-ware and things like that," suggested Ben, but she shook her head.

"I'd like something a bit more imaginative than that. She'll get a lot of that kind of thing."

Shadiv looked up. "What about giving her a plaster effigy of one of the Hindu gods. You'll have seen them being carried to Walkeshwar Beach when people are doing puja."

At first they thought he was joking because the processions they'd seen carried effigies painted in hideously glaring colours and Guy laughed, "Yeah, she could get one of the elephant god or one of the monkey . . ."

"Well, Ganesh the elephant god is one we invoke at the beginning of any important undertaking," said Shadiv, "and getting married is pretty important, isn't it?"

Dee saw that he was serious and said, "I think that's a good idea. But where could I get an effigy? I've never seen any for sale and I'd like a good one, not a coarse or garish one . . ."

His eyes shone when he looked at her, "There's a street in Parel where the craftsmen who make those figures live. Some of them are genuine artists. You should go there and look at their work. It's not all rough and ready."

"Where's the street? Tell me and I'll go," she said for there was nothing she liked better than poking about in Bombay's dizzying network of back streets.

"It's difficult to find but I could show you. If you're not doing anything tomorrow night we'll go then. It's best to go when it's dark. You get the full effect then."

At eight o'clock the following evening, he turned up in his jeep and Ben and Dee climbed aboard. Guy wouldn't go with them. "Don't buy anything. You're going to be fleeced by a bunch of beggars and rogues. Shadiv's a nice chap but he's an Indian like all the rest of them and though he says he isn't, he's as much in awe of these gods as any temple priest," he privately warned Ben before they left.

Though Dee tried to keep landmarks in her mind in order to

be able to find the place again, she was soon totally lost as they drove into a maze of narrow alleys, sometimes lined by high walls, sometimes by ramshackle, leaning houses. The streets were one-vehicle narrow, lined on each side by deep ditches for carrying away monsoon rainwater and, judging by the smell, sewage from the houses as well.

"God, look, rats," she exclaimed at one point when she saw a scurry of grey bodies running out of the beam of the jeep headlights in one noisome area.

Ben laughed. "At least they're alive. When I came out first I was told not to worry if I saw rats unless they were lying on their backs with their paws in the air."

"Yeah, that's the sign of the plague," agreed Shadiv equably.

At last they found the road they were looking for, a brightly lit tunnel of stalls twisting in front of them. They parked the jeep at the head of the street and climbed out, Shadiv taking care to put on a pair of dark glasses because already he was gathering fans and did not want to be mobbed, though in that area dark glasses at night surely marked him as someone special.

The road was even narrower than the ones they'd driven through already, and was lined by open-fronted booths, lit not by electricity but by hissing Tilley lamps which gave off a pleasant smell that mingled with the strong scent of joss sticks which every stall holder was burning to keep the mosquitoes away. Underlying those smells, of course, was the ever present stench of sewage and urine. It used to turn Dee's stomach but she was used to it now and hardly noticed – in fact she almost liked it, for it was the smell of real India, the India that so few European people – especially women – ever saw. There were people she knew who never ventured beyond a small sanitised and Europeanised section of the city and who knew nothing of the real India though many had lived there for years.

There were few beggars and no touts in this street, and only one or two of the stallholders lifted their heads to look at the strangers. It was obvious you only came here if you knew what you wanted and each stall seemed to concentrate on a single god, for Indian households tended to worship one special god for whom they erected little domestic shrines. This was where they bought their effigies.

Because Ganesh was a god much revered by the people of Bombay, there were many stalls filled with his plaster image, garishly coloured, in various sizes from the tiny that could go into a pocket to the enormous that it would take three men to carry. Dee liked Ganesh, a cheery looking chap with an elephant's head and his trunk slung in various negligent attitudes round his own neck or over his shoulder. Round his neck he often wore garlands of flowers or in delicately poised fingers he held out a lotus blossom.

"I love him," she said. "I think he's the one I'll buy."

"Don't be in any hurry and don't show which one you want," warned Shadiv. "Have a look at others. You might see one you like better. Look, there's Hanuman, the monkey god. He's a cheeky fellow, always playing pranks, but he really represents the ideal of man's devotion to God, and again people make offerings to him when they're about to take any important decisions."

"I like him too, but I like Ganesh better," said Dee, and then her eye was caught by a truly beautiful figure of a dancing god with four elegantly raised arms.

"Which one is that?" she asked and in spite of herself her voice sank to a whisper for the god looked so spiritual and transcendental.

Shadiv's voice was low too. "That's Vishnu. He is a powerful god who steps out the earth and supports the heavens. He set the world in motion and made the days . . . He is very great . . . the greatest."

Shadiv worships Vishnu, Dee thought, but did not ask the question. It would have been too intrusive. And she also knew that she could not buy Vishnu for Baby.

They kept on walking, past stalls selling effigies of a fearsome woman riding on a tiger, who, Shadiv told them, was Durga the mother goddess and obviously another who had to be regarded with great respect. After the stalls full of images of Durga came figures that scared Dee, especially the ones of another woman round whose neck hung a rope of skulls and whose tongue stuck out in a terrifying grimace.

"Oh," she gasped, stepping back a little when she first caught sight of this goddess.

Shadiv took her arm and guided her on, "That's Kali. You don't want her. Nor do you want Siva, the destroyer and lord of the dance. Look, here's the stalls that sell Lakshmi, she's the wife of Vishnu and the bringer of good luck and beauty. That would be a good image to give a bride perhaps . . ."

But Dee was intimidated by the array of greater gods, the significance of which she did not understand. As she walked along that street she realised that there were areas of Indian life, realms of thought, that would forever be closed to her. It would be grossly insensitive to buy a figure of an important god or goddess for Baby's wedding present, much safer to keep to the minor figures. So her choice either had to be Ganesh or Hanuman, as she was sure Shadiv had intended from the beginning.

They retraced their footsteps back to the first stalls and she at last made her decision. "I'll have Ganesh," she said. "Help me choose the nicest one."

They eventually bought a softly coloured figure that stood about two and a half feet tall and had an expression of complete benevolence on his chubby face. Considering that he had been moulded with love by a real artist whose work showed far more finesse than the others around him, the price they paid was derisory – only one hundred and fifty rupees – and Shadiv said that if he hadn't been with white people, he would have been able to bargain the price down to less than half that, but Dee wouldn't let him. She liked the smiling artist who'd made her Ganesh and she didn't want to bargain.

On the drive home, she sat in the back of the jeep with her arms round the elephant god who was wrapped up in newspaper and carefully bound round with string. Ben looked back at her and said with a laugh, "It's a good thing it isn't raining or he'd be a puddle of mud by the time we got him home. They don't last long these things."

Made aware of the fragility of her purchase, she held Ganesh even tighter after that and as they rattled along she saw that Shadiv was watching her in the driving mirror and she looked back at him, holding his eyes. I wonder if you have any idea how much I love you? she thought. But you're as mysterious to me as one of those strange gods. You're like that beautiful dancing Vishnu.

Twenty-Five

D ay after day the heat built up. People moved more slowly, for the moist air seemed to press heavily on their bodies. Clothes were soaked with sweat within an hour of being put on. It was too hot to go out in the middle of the day; it was too hot to sleep at night. A film of dust lay over the leaves of trees, making them all the same colour, a peculiar greyish green. Pye-dogs lay panting in the shade, the birds were silent, and in the jungle nothing moved, everything and everybody waited for the rains, counting off the days like children counting off the days till Christmas.

As Dee tossed fretfully in soaking bedsheets, a terrible scream suddenly broke the silence of the night.

It ripped through her like an assassin's knife, and a few seconds later it was followed by another, and another, and another – then silence – but only for a while.

She lay listening in the stifling darkness, waiting for the screams to start again as she knew they would. They were the cries of the brain fever bird that only called in the hot weather and got its name because its incessant calls, without rhythm or marked sequence, were blamed for driving Europeans mad.

She thought of some East India Company cadet lying in a stinking hot up-country bungalow and listening to those uneven and unending blood-chilling screeches before deciding to get up and put a bullet through his brain.

The trouble with waking in the middle of the night was the way one's thoughts went skittering around without rhyme or reason.

I'm in love with Shadiv. I'm sure of it. I've never felt this way about any other man and I'm sure I never will again, but I'm married to Ben and I promised to stay with him death do us part.

Since their trip to Kandala she and Ben had grown closer and he was far more considerate of her in every way. He was also drinking less and working far harder than he'd ever done before, and so was earning grudging respect from his employers. He was obviously trying to make their marriage work.

186

She turned on her side, and gently stroked his straight shoulder heaving up from the mattress. I love him too, she thought. What the hell's wrong with me? Am I some sort of nymphomaniac? What can I do? If I took life less seriously, I'd just go to bed with Shadiv and get him out of my system. But somehow her passion was too strong and too pure for a hole-and-corner affair. She needed more than that. She needed something spiritual as well as physical.

I'm an emotional mess. I should speak to a psychiatrist, she thought as she fell asleep again. The brain fever bird kept on screaming.

There was another brain fever bird in the Maling-Smiths' bungalow garden and it too was screeching. Lady Barbara woke and lay waiting for the crunching, twisting pain to start but it didn't. Her body felt light, so light that she could almost float out of the window and over the trees like one of those swamis she'd heard about. Her thoughts turned to darling Baby.

She liked Dennis but he was just a child really, so innocent, so naive. Would he grow up soon? Physically he was a magnificent specimen and that was why Baby had chosen him, but Barbara doubted if his brain was very developed.

Her Baby was developing however, more so every day. She watched it happening as day succeeded day. Would she soon outgrow Dennis? Not before the wedding, not before he gave her some beautiful babies, Barbara hoped, and turned over on her side to sleep again as the pills she had swallowed took her over once more.

The bird's cries also woke Baby who groaned aloud when she realised that she was doomed to several hours of unwanted consciousness. She didn't want to think because it always ended up with her remembering Charlie and contrasting him with Dennis.

Dennis is far more handsome, she told herself, but a nasty little voice in the back of her mind said, But Charlie made you laugh. When does Dennis ever make you laugh?

Dennis loves you, and Charlie never did, said the voice of reason again.

But I don't want to be loved with such blind devotion. It should be more equal, he should see my faults the way Charlie did. I was the one who loved Charlie. I loved him enough for both of us, replied the voice she did not want to hear.

It isn't Dennis's fault, she told herself. He comes from a different continent, from a different culture. Charlie and I came from the same background, we spoke each other's language. Maybe that's why Indians insist on people marrying within their own caste. It's so much easier.

"*Eeeeeeeee . . . Awwwwwwwwww . . . Eeeeeeeeee,*" screamed the brain fever bird and Baby closed her eyes. Charlie had gone, she'd lost him. She was lucky, very lucky, to have found Dennis. Hang on to that idea, hang on to it, hang on, hang on, hang on . . .

Twenty-Six

There were no brain fever birds in Marine Drive but Dennis had a sleepless night too, petulantly throwing the pillows onto the floor when he found them too stifling for his head to lie on.

Instead of counting sheep, he was counting off his last days of bachelorhood.

Only thirty-two more and he'd be a married man.

Was that what he really wanted? How the hell had it happened?

He loved Baby, of course. He was mad about her. That was probably why he found it impossible to sleep. He was being driven mad with frustration. Every time he laid eyes on her, he couldn't believe that she'd agreed to marry him. And though he lusted after her, dreaming agonisingly about her every night, he would not have dreamt of inveigling her into his bed before they were married. You didn't do things like that with girls like Baby. They weren't Caroles. Their embraces were passionate but stopped short at petting, and he'd never had his hands below her waist.

They'd done everything properly. But what if he couldn't do anything when he eventually got her into bed? What if he was so overcome that he couldn't manage it? Oh my God, he thought, rolling onto his face in bed and drumming his feet against the footboard. The noise he made caused Govind the bearer, in the servant's room behind the kitchen, to raise his eyebrows and imagine his employer was enjoying an orgy of self-abuse.

Another reason for his frustration was that Baby's friends all seemed to be throwing parties for her – and for him too of course, as her consort-to-be. Every evening recently they'd been invited to yet another flat where people were crowded in, swilling drink, wolfing Europeanised versions of curries that few Indians would have recognised and yelling at each other. They only stopped talking to look at him, ask him a few questions, then dismissed him as unimportant, written off, just like that. For some reason Australians weren't taken seriously in their set.

Sometimes women talked to Baby about him as if he wasn't there.

"Such a handsome fellow," said one raddled, painted harridan. "Even better looking than Charlie, darling. You've done well." As if he was some sort of shopping trophy.

When they left that party, he said angrily, "I hate those affairs. Do we have to go to many more? Those people look at me and talk about me as if I was an animal in a fat stock sale."

She was immediately contrite. "Oh darling, I'm so sorry. I know it must be awful for you. We won't go to another single one. I don't enjoy them either."

His worst ordeal however had been a second interview with Baby's father. They sat facing each other in Sir Robert's library with glasses of whisky and soda in their hands and the smoke from Sir Robert's foul-smelling cigarettes spiralling to the rafters. The old man seemed impervious to the oppressive heat. He didn't even sweat while rivulets of perspiration ran steadily down both sides of Dennis's face and found their way into his wilting collar.

The topic of their conversation was money. "I don't know how much my daughter has told you about our financial position," said Sir Robert rolling his cigarette in his mouth, "but she will be a very rich woman indeed when I am dead. So rich that it would not be necessary for you to work if you didn't want to."

Dennis stared at him aghast. "But I don't want to live on my wife's money, sir. I'll always want to work."

"But when we spoke last time you gave me to understand that you weren't too eager to remain in the service of your High Commission," said Sir Robert.

"I'm not. I'm finding it difficult settling down here in fact. I'd like to go back home and set myself up in business there."

"Doing what exactly?"

"Well, my dad's got this little workshop and I've always liked tinkering with engines. When I said I'd come out here in the first place I thought if I could get some money together by working abroad, I'd be able to go back and help him expand it a bit. With two of us working there, we'd be able to make enough every week to keep two households going."

Sir Robert didn't blink but he registered that it was obvious Dennis hadn't a clue how much Roberta was worth. He certainly couldn't be accused of cupidity.

"My daughter will inherit something like three million pounds when I die," he said carefully.

Dennis visibly reeled. "Jeez-us!" he sighed, "She won't want a mechanic for a husband then, will she?"

"Why not? I was a mechanic myself when I first came out here. I was thinking that perhaps you could set up a machine-repairing company. I've got contacts with a chain of car salerooms in Australia and you could have all their business."

"That's a bit like running before I'm able to walk," said Dennis, "and I don't know how my Dad would cope with something on that scale. I'd rather start small if you don't mind, sir."

Sir Robert grinned. "You're a sensible fellow," he said. "Have another whisky. And by the way, I'm making a will that leaves everything I possess to my daughter and if you and she break up, you'll get none of it. Not even as a pay-off. I'll take care of any children of course."

"I don't want any of it," said Dennis with dignity. He felt more powerless than before now. The memory of that interview chilled his blood even in the stifling heat of the pre-monsoon night.

In spite of their separate misgivings, which they never mentioned to each other, events were crowding in on Baby and Dennis and they were swept along like nut shells on a river.

First of all Winks organised a 'shower party', to which all Baby's female friends brought their wedding gifts. It was held on a steamy morning, in Winks' parents' bungalow and one noticeable absentee was the sulking Mags who watched balefully out of her bedroom window as the guests arrived.

Most of the gifts were predictable: beautifully embroidered tablecloths and napkins, made by the nuns in the convent above Kemp's Corner; bales of soft towels; brass ornaments; lamps; discreet items of silverware. There was a stunned silence however when Dee Carmichael unveiled her Ganesh. He sat in the middle of the floor, smiling beatifically at the women around him, and no one said anything till Baby threw her arms round Dee's neck and said, "I love him. He's just what I want. I'll keep him forever."

The other present-givers contented themselves with saying things like 'original' while they were at the party but as soon as they left, their tongues wagged with less restraint. Dee Carmichael was getting odder than ever was the general consensus. What was Baby thinking of asking a person like that to be her matron of honour!

Then her mother gave another party at which the presents were on view. Ganesh came in for a good deal of critical comment there too, even from Dennis who stared at the figure and said in disbelief, "Who gave us *that*?"

"I love him," said Baby.

"Do you?" he replied in a stunned voice and it was obvious that he

191

didn't believe her. She'd never be able to persuade him that Ganesh was a perfect present as far as she was concerned and she was horrified to realise that not only were their tastes radically different, but she was actually happiest when she and Dennis were apart. As soon as they were together, she found herself getting irritated to a point of wanting to scream and found it very difficult to hide this irritation from him because she knew he would do anything in the world to please her.

One morning, when they were discussing the table layout for the guests at the reception, Baby mentioned her confusion of feelings to her mother, who looked up, pouched old eyes watchful.

"My sweet, most brides get cold feet just before they walk up the aisle. I remember the same feeling the night before I married your father. I drank a whole bottle of gin – and I wasn't a drinker in those days, but when the morning came I knew I wanted to go through with it . . . everything just cleared up in a marvellous way."

"I hope that happens for me," said Baby glumly.

Her mother laid down the table plan, and said quietly, "You're only marrying him because you love him, darling, aren't you?"

"What other reason could there be?"

"I don't know. You might be trying to escape from the present or the past . . . you might be trying to get out of India . . . you might be trying to please someone else . . ."

Her daughter looked at her. "Who?"

"Me, perhaps. You know how keen I am to see you married, but I don't want to see you married to the wrong man."

Baby stood up and started walking around the room. "Mummy, I'm sure he's not the wrong man. He's such a decent person. You can't fault him. He does anything I want and he's so sweet and clean and decent . . . I like him so much."

Lady Barbara listened and nodded but she noticed that her daughter didn't say she loved him. That night she lay on her bed with the ayah Parvati sitting on the floor beside it and talked her thoughts aloud. "Is Baby getting married because of me? Does she know I'm ill, Parvati?"

"I've not told her but she went to the doctor. He might tell."

"No, I don't think he would."

"Then she might guess."

"Is that likely? I've been so much better lately. No, I don't think it's because of me. I hope it isn't anyway."

"It's because of that other man. She thinks if she gets married she'll forget about him."

"Oh, what a mess. What should I do?"

"You do nothing. Miss Baby is a woman now. She makes her own decisions and she is not a fool. This will make her grow up."

Twenty-Seven

C arole came back after an absence of three or four days, but Dee noticed a change in her. She seemed harder and more brittle, as if she'd aged years in her time away.

"What's the matter Carole?" she asked when they were having tea that afternoon and Carole was eating as much as ever, demanding bacon sandwiches and cheese on toast, but her attitude was different, almost as if she was shovelling the food away like a hamster, determined to get something out of being at the Gulmohurs.

"Don't you know?"

"No, why should I?"

"I thought you'd be able to tell. You're always watching people so hard."

"Am I? Sorry. I can't help it. What's wrong?"

"I'm pregnant."

Dee felt as if all the air had been punched out of her body. She leaned back in her chair, took a deep breath, and stared at the girl. "Are you sure?"

"Yes. I've had the test. It's Guy's and he says I've to get rid of it. He says it isn't his, but it is. There hasn't been anybody else since I started coming here."

I want a child and I can't conceive, thought Dee. I bet Carole doesn't want one and she's pregnant.

"Do you want it?" she asked.

"I thought he'd marry me if I had his baby," said Carole bitterly.

"So you didn't take any precautions."

"He wouldn't. He said it's better without."

Typical Guy, thought Dee, have it his way and bugger the consequences.

"What are you going to do?" she asked.

"He's going to pay for me to have it taken away. My mother knows a doctor at Kemp's Corner that'll do it. I'm going tomorrow. He'll drop me off on his way to the office."

"Will you have anyone with you?"

"Monica, my cousin, said she'd be there."

"I'm very sorry," said Dee.

Next day the house was very quiet when Dee got up; everyone had left before half-past seven. At one o'clock a taxi drove up and a bedraggled vision staggered out. It was an almost unrecognisable Carole, walking shakily on skinny legs, yellow-skinned and pouch-eyed. She looked about fifty.

Waving a hand at Dee telling her not to interfere, she went into Guy's bedroom and closed the door.

At four o'clock there was a terrible confusion, with Mohammed running about carrying towels. The sound of wailing came from Guy's room. Dee went to the door but was stopped before she could open it by Mohammed who said firmly, "Do not go in memsahib. She doesn't want you. I have sent for a woman from Raj Kapoor sahib's house. She knows what to do."

Raj's wife had suffered several miscarriages and her ayah knew how to look after a woman in that sort of trouble. She was a tall, grim-looking woman with a masterful manner who bossed the other servants, took over the Gulmohurs kitchen and brewed up horrible smelling herbal liquids which she forced Carole to drink. By seven o'clock she'd staunched the bleeding and washed the weeping girl who then fell asleep in a drugged miasma.

Guy spent that night on the sofa in the sitting room but neither he nor Dee mentioned the reason for Carole's occupation of his room. Next day Carole did not appear, and Dee saw little of Mohammed either for he was always running to and fro with different things for the patient. On the second morning she emerged, miraculously restored. Looking at her, Dee found it difficult to believe she was the wrecked girl who'd come back in the taxi.

Once again she was eating like a horse, once again she was smiling. "Are you all right?" asked Dee sitting down by her at the breakfast table.

"Perfect."

"Was it awful? I was very worried about you."

Carole looked up, brown eyes inscrutable. "I'm all right. The worst thing was that I really wanted that baby."

Then she got up and walked away, back into Guy's room and shut the door. Neither of them mentioned the aborted baby again.

Now it was Dee's turn to feel sick and low in spirits. Shadiv was away again and day after day depression weighed her down. She did not go into the city though she knew the Maling-Smiths would be wondering where she was and probably needing her for rehearsals and dress fittings but she could not motivate herself to go. Eventually, spurred on by guilt, she remembered Baby's advice about the vitamin B injections and took herself off to Breach Candy hospital to consult Ralph.

The waiting room was full of people, mostly women, because this was the late morning surgery and men usually went earlier. There were wan-faced Americans with whining children who lived mostly on vitamin pills because they were terrified of catching some terrible disease from local food but who still insisted on putting ice cubes in their drinks, forgetting that the water the cubes were made from was never boiled; there were a few elegant, chattering Indian women wearing gorgeous saris and carrying expensive looking handbags. It was amazing, thought Dee, how the really rich managed to get all the trappings of luxury although there were technically no imports into India. They smelt of Parisian perfumes, drove around in American cars and wore stiletto-heeled Italian shoes.

In a far corner sat two women whose husbands were in the rugby team. They recognised her and gave her frosty smiles for she was still not forgiven for Ganesh or for her outspoken criticism of the way people behaved at rugby club parties and this pair were enthusiastic singers of dirty songs as well as eager participants in wife-swopping romps.

Dee had brought a book with her – Shadiv's *Brideshead Revisited* which she was reading for the second time – and immediately lost herself in it because she could tell by the crowd that her wait would be a long one. An hour passed without her really noticing and she felt relaxed because she'd found a seat near a fan and with a view of the sea through a low window. Perhaps I shouldn't bother waiting, she wondered, lifting her head a little later and finding that her depression had lifted. Perhaps there's nothing wrong with me after all. But she knew if she went away, she'd be feeling as bad again tomorrow.

On her way out one of the rugby wives paused beside Dee. "Waiting for Ralph?" she asked. "Nothing serious I hope. I heard you're going to be matron of honour for Baby Maling-Smith next Saturday. You don't want to miss that, do you?"

Dee smiled. "I only want a Vitamin B jag," she said.

"We all need that at this time of the year," sighed the other, wandering away, curiosity satisfied.

At last, an unusually solemn, sober-looking Ralph in a long white coat with his stethoscope slung round his neck, beckoned to her from the waiting room door. When they were in his little cubicle of a room, he regarded her over folded fingers and asked, "Well, what's the matter with you, Dee?"

For some unaccountable reason she felt tears at the back of her eyes but fought them back. I like Ralph. If only I could tell him that I've fallen in love with another man and don't know what to do about it, she thought, but what she said was, "I'm just terribly tired all the time and I've lost my appetite. I'm pretty depressed too."

"Nothing else?"

She knew what he meant because she'd already told him about her anxiety at her lack of success in conceiving. She shook her head, "Not really." Her last period had been scanty but it was a period. She was convinced she was barren.

"It's probably the weather," said Ralph. "This heat is killing. This was the time of the year when old timers used to top themselves, you know."

Dee laughed, "Thanks a lot, Ralph. That's just exactly the sort of thing I want to hear right now."

"Thought it would cheer you up," he said, "Now let's have a look at you. Open your mouth."

He looked into her eyes, sounded her chest, shone a light into her ears even and then said, "You're definitely anaemic. I'm going to order a blood test, a urine test and a faeces test in case you've got galloping amoebic dysentery. Then the nurse will give you a Vitamin B injection to perk you up. You can have another one tomorrow and then you'll be fighting fit to play your part in Baby's wedding. That's going to be some thrash. Two hundred guests apparently and old Sir Robert's got every bootlegger in the Gulf running in the booze. He's too important for the prohibition police to do anything to stop him. I'm getting into training for it already. See you there."

After she'd provided samples for her battery of tests, Dee went into a lavatory and stared at herself in the mirror above the wash-basin. She was very tanned, far more brown than she'd imagined, though she ought to have expected it because she spent most of her days in the sun, and the colour of her skin made her eyes look brilliantly blue. Her cropped hair was tied back from her face with one of Ben's large white handkerchiefs and there was a heavy dusting of freckles across the bridge of her nose. Though immaculate grooming was never her style, her farouche appearance was a shock even to her.

I'll have to get tidied up for the wedding, she thought. When I come back into town tomorrow, I'll go and get a proper haircut.

But where to go? The only hairdressing salon she'd noticed was in the Taj and what would that cost? There was a telephone in the main hall of the hospital so she went to it, looked for the Taj number and rang it up. The hairdresser sounded very superior. "A hairdo, madam? . . . Tomorrow? Of course . . . How much will it cost? Fifteen rupees."

Dee could afford fifteen rupees by cutting short Mohammed's cookbook money – after all on the day of the wedding none of them would be eating at home – so she booked herself in for the next morning and then drove slowly back to Chembur, going by roads through the oldest parts of the city where there were lovely, ramshackle houses that dated back to the earliest days when the East India Company held sway over Bombay. She drove with all the windows down and a luscious warm breeze blowing into her face like a lover's breath.

She was weary when she parked the car at the Gulmohurs. Carole was nowhere to be seen and the house was very still, as if it was holding its breath, but as soon as she stepped out of the car, Mohammed emerged from the kitchen, looking ruffled with his normally carefully combed hair standing on end and his eyes bloodshot.

She noticed this with annoyance for she knew that when he had time on his hands, he was in the habit of lying in his room smoking bhang which not only had the effect of making him behave as if he was in a dream, but also made him excessively loquacious.

It seemed she was right. When he served Dee's late lunch, he started on his usual lecture about religion, telling her that his beliefs and hers were really very similar and not like the idolatrous Hindu creed. "Your Jesus is one of our prophets. We believe in the same thing," he said, swaying slightly as he stood hovering over her chair.

She wanted to put a stop to it for good and all by confessing to him that she was not a Christian. She was an atheist, had been since she was fourteen years old, and so they certainly did not believe in the same thing, but mindful of Ben and Guy's prediction of what would happen if she cleaned the bath, she dreaded the outcome if she told Mohammed that she thought religion was load of rubbish. He might burn the house down. So she confined herself to making non-committal noises but when he went on and on till she decided, I'm too tired for a religious lecture now, she stood up and said abruptly, "I don't want any lunch, Mohammed. I'm not hungry. I'm going to bed."

At the door of her bedroom she turned back and asked, "Where is Carole?"

The expression on his face surprised her. He looked absolutely astonished as if he'd never heard of any Carole. Then he said, "She has gone out. She has gone to see her mother." Dee was relieved. She was too tired to make conversation with Carole and she certainly didn't want to be reminded of that aborted baby. Thank God, with any luck she'd be left on her own till evening.

She slept through the return of Ben and Guy; she refused to get up for dinner; but in the morning she woke greatly refreshed, convinced that a Vitamin B injection was the world's best pick-me-up. She hadn't felt so energetic or optimistic for months.

When Dee emerged from her shower, Carole was up, drinking coffee and obviously bursting with a need to talk.

"When's the wedding you're going to?" she asked. "It's that Maling-Smith girl that's getting married, isn't it? The man's an Australian, isn't he? What's his name?"

"It's next weekend. Yes, he's an Australian called Dennis Gillies."

Carole smiled sweetly. "So I heard. What's he like?" she asked.

"He seems all right. I haven't seen a lot of him actually. He's very good-looking at least but doesn't say much."

"Is Guy going to the wedding too?"

"Yes, he is. He's an old friend of the bride. He's known her longer than I have."

Carole seemed unusually interested and persisted, "Are you sure he's going to the ceremony?"

"Yes. Why not?" Dee was surprised at this cross-questioning. Why didn't Carole ask Guy these things if she was so anxious to know?

"Because he's a Catholic like me. He said he wasn't going to the ceremony because he couldn't go into that cathedral. He said that's why he couldn't take me to the wedding."

Suddenly Dee realised she was on shaky ground. "I don't think he could have taken you with him anyway," she said. "There's a limited number of guests. There'll only be a place for him on his own at the wedding."

"But he could ask for a place for me. I've told him that. I want to go to the wedding with him. I'm his girlfriend. He's said he's going to marry me. If he wanted, he could arrange for me to go. Do you think he's ashamed of me? But if he's ashamed of me, why does he talk about writing to his mother about me?"

Dee held her coffee cup between her two hands and stared at

the angry girl who sat with eyes flashing on the other side of the table.

"He's just using me," blazed Carole. "He's treating me like a tart." She was hissing words out like a venomous snake. "I've got a good mind to teach him a lesson. He knew I wanted to go to that wedding. *He promised.* I went into town last week and bought myself a lovely hat. My cousin Monica's lending me a dress. I'd look as good as anybody there – if not better." In her agitation, she slopped coffee over the white cloth and shouted to Mohammed to clean it up. He came running so quickly, cloth in hand, that Dee knew he'd been listening behind the kitchen door.

"I've got to go back to the hospital this morning," said Dee standing up, anxious to be away.

"Are you sick?" asked Carole, suddenly calming down.

"No, I'm just getting a Vitamin B injection, and I'm going to get my hair cut."

"I'd have cut your hair," said Carole.

"I'll remember that next time," said Dee, grabbing her bag and running for the door because she was late and wanted to get away.

But just before she disappeared, Carole shouted something else after her, "That Indian actor was here yesterday afternoon wanting to speak to you but you were asleep so I didn't wake you. He said he'd come back tonight . . ."

Shadiv had wanted to see her. What about? Why did he come during the day when she'd be alone? It was not till she'd driven nearly all the way to Bombay that she realised Carole must have been in the house during the afternoon when Mohammed said she was out. Odd, very odd. Suddenly she felt there was a whole lot more going on in her home than she realised.

When she went to the Taj, the male hairdresser who presided over the old-fashioned salon on the ground floor looked down his nose as he lifted strands of her brown hair between finger and thumb as if he was afraid he'd catch something from them.

"Who did this?" he asked.

She stared at him through the flawed, spotted mirror. He was a middle-aged Goan with a gold crucifix round his neck and a pencil-thin moustache. "I did it myself," she said coldly.

"What a mistake," he sighed. "I'll do what I can with it but I'm guaranteeing nothing. Do you want it washed as well?"

"No." She washed her hair twice a day under the shower. There was no need for it to be shampooed again here. When he'd finished she looked even more like a schoolboy than before and, unable even to smile false thanks, stared ruefully at herself, wishing she'd saved her money and let Carole loose on her head with the scissors.

There was a pleasant surprise for her at the desk however. The girl making out the bills said, "You only had a cut, didn't you? Ten rupees."

Dee was paying at the desk and about to go away when she felt a hand on her arm and turned to find Baby's mother beside her. "Fernando's always like that," she said. "I was watching the way he was with you. You have to stand up to him because he believes in intimidating his customers. But you look lovely my dear, very original, very young . . . so lucky!"

A rush of affection for the woman filled Dee. She wished she had a mother like that. Unaccountably tears rushed into her eyes and she wanted to throw her arms round Barbara and be hugged back. But habitual reticence triumphed and she only smiled. "Thank you," she managed to say, hurriedly adding, "Do you have time to have a cup of coffee with me?" The extra five rupees in her pocket made her feel rich.

Lady Barbara shook her head. "I'd love to my dear, but I've still got to have my hair shampooed and get home before half-past twelve. You're coming to have your final fitting this afternoon, aren't you? See you there." And waving airily, she was ushered away to one of the cubicles by Fernando himself.

Before Dee went to the Gym for a sandwich with Ben, she drove to Crawford Market in search of Jai. As usual he came running when he spotted her car, pushing the other importunate little boys out of the way. "It's my memsahib, it's my memsahib!" he cried. "What you want today, memsahib? Oranges? Flowers?"

She shook her head. "Nothing. But I've brought something for you."

And she gave him her crumpled five rupee note.

He looked at it in disbelief. Five rupees represented two days' wages for one of the coolies labouring on the roads, and more than a week's subsistence money for Jai. The eyes he turned back to Dee were suspicious. "What you want?" he asked.

"Nothing. I want nothing. It's a gift," she said, climbed back into the car and drove away.

The dress fitting took a long time and was both tiring and irritating with Winks fussing about the fit of her gown and the old tailor crawling round their feet with a mouthful of pins, blandly ignoring every suggestion that was made to him. The dresses, though made of beautiful silk, were surprisingly dowdy and old-fashioned with childish puff sleeves and heart-shaped necks.

Lady Barbara never made an appearance and Baby only looked into the room a couple of times, saying on both occasions, "You look lovely darlings!" but she seemed distracted and Dee doubted if she actually looked at her bridesmaids at all.

When, at last, they were taking the dresses off for the last time, Winks said, "I'll feel a frump in that. He should tighten the waists and fill out the skirts a bit."

"And cut off those awful sleeves," agreed Dee.

"But he won't. We're stuck with them. Dear old Lady B stopped looking at fashion magazines around 1932, and so did he," said Winks, "but don't worry, darling, I'll bring some pins with me on the big day and we can pin each other in a bit round the waist, then we'll look better."

Dee laughed, "Good idea. Bring scissors as well and we can cut the sleeves off. I don't think anyone here would even notice."

When Ben picked her up at half-past five, he said, "I arranged to meet Guy in the Ritz bar. We've not been there for ages and Thomas and Raju'll put our drinks on the slate."

Thomas and Raju were the Ritz barmen, one fat and the other lean, but both always smiling and highly intelligent. They'd been at the Ritz for years and never forgot a face. Customers who'd been gone for fifteen or twenty years would always be greeted by name and given their favourite drink unasked if they returned. The pair of barmen also never forget how much anyone had on their slate and when the sum got too large, the customer would find that his beer was warm, no peanuts would be offered and he'd have to wait an unconscionable time to be served.

If Thomas and Raju served them, Dee thought, the bill couldn't be too astronomical but she was nervous when they stepped into the cool, air-conditioned dimness of the bar. She needn't have worried. Thomas raised a hand in greeting, smiled, pushed a dish of salted peanuts across to them and busied himself with Ben's beer and her gin and lime. They were still on the right side.

It was nearly midnight before they drove home, singing lustily as they went. Carole was in bed and the house was deserted, still holding its breath. Dee knew that somewhere in the back premises, their servants were lying, listening and hoping that they would not be summoned. They weren't.

Twenty-Eight

The point of no return was reached four days before the wedding when Maud, Denzil and Uncle Joe got off the Qantas plane at Santa Cruz airport. Fortunately none of the grandparents had any wish to face the ordeal of a long-haul flight. Though it was late afternoon and the temperature had dropped from its midday high, Maud visibly reeled when she stepped out of the fuselage door and a blast of heat from the airport tarmac hit her like a blow in the face.

"Aw gee, Den," she gasped to her husband, "it's like stepping into hell. I'm not going to be able to stand this."

"'Course you can, Maud," snapped her brother. "Just remember your Denny's getting married and you've got to back him up."

Dennis was waiting in the reception area with a pretty, brown-haired girl clinging to his arm. He waved when he saw his parents and Joe walking over the tarmac and they waved back.

"Is that her, do you think?" whispered Maud nodding at the girl.

"I hope so. What other girl would he bring to meet us?" said Joe who was taking over as leader of their party because Denzil was totally overawed by the whole thing.

When they cleared customs, Dennis came running to his mother with his arms outspread and the girl walked more circumspectly behind him, but after Maud let her son go, he turned and said, "This is Roberta, Mum." The girl too threw her arms round Maud and kissed her cheek.

"It's so lovely to meet you at last," she said. "Did you have a good flight?"

She wondered if she should kiss brick-faced Denzil and Uncle Joe as well but decided against it and instead shook their hands. They were trying not to stare at her too hard, she knew, and was glad that she'd worn a plain, green cotton dress and sandals for this encounter.

She showed them her engagement ring, agreed with them that it was lovely. "Very tasteful," said Maud, but her heart sank when she saw that the stone was an opal. Opals were bad luck to Maud's mind and she wished that she could have warned Denny against them.

For her part Baby was hoping that none of them would notice the glory of her mother's jewellery when the parents eventually met. Then she and Dennis ushered them towards an enormous American car that was drawn up in the parking lot. In order to please his parents but not embarrass them, Dennis had asked Baby if she would mind not bringing her driver but allow him to drive her father's Cadillac.

"A Cadillac!" gasped Joe when he saw it, "Den, when did you get a Cadillac?"

"It's not mine. It's Roberta's father's car. He's lent it to us for the day."

They climbed inside and, in spite of the air conditioning, which, it had to be admitted, found it hard to lower the temperature much, complained about the heat all through the drive into the city. Between gasps, they stared out of the window, making comments about what they saw.

Maud was a nervous passenger, "Take care Denny. Go slow. Look at all those cows. Don't they keep them in fields? What a stink! Give me my bottle of lavender water Den, please. What a lot of people! Do they always wander all over the road like that?"

"What do you think of Bombay then?" asked Baby with a smile when they finally drew up outside the main door of the Taj Mahal hotel and a squad of servants in red and white livery came running to attend to them.

Denzil found his voice at last. "It's – eh – different," he suggested. Neither of the others said anything because they thought it was horrific.

When they were shown into their luxurious, air-conditioned rooms, Baby tactfully left Dennis alone with his parents but not before reminding him that everyone was expected at her parents' house the following day for lunch. This was to be the first meeting between the two families and she dreaded it because as far as she could see the Gillies contingent had absolutely no common ground with the Maling-Smiths.

Though, out of family loyalty, they did not discuss their fears, both Baby and Dennis were apprehensive of what would happen when their respective sets of parents met for the first time.

The Gillies family, exhausted by the long flight, spent the first twenty-four hours of their time in Bombay asleep in the air-conditioned haven of the Taj Mahal hotel but on the second day they were invited to lunch with the Maling-Smiths.

After a good deal of private deliberation, Baby said to her mother, "I wonder if you'd mind calling me Roberta in front of Dennis's people? He hasn't told them I'm known as Baby in the family. They might think it odd apparently."

Lady Barbara looked slightly put out and agreed at once. "Of course my sweet. It's just that I always think of you as my baby . . . I'll have to stop though, won't I, now that you're old enough to be married?!"

Having won that concession, Baby decided not to put her second request and ask her mother to take off her rings so as not to dazzle the visitors, and also not to put her own engagement ring in the shade.

"They'll all have to accept us the way we are," she thought. "Why should Mummy change or pretend to be different?" In the 'all' she unconsciously included Dennis.

Dennis was even more worried. How would his family go down with Lady Barbara and Sir Robert, he wondered? After having been away from them for almost six months, on seeing them again they struck him as being aggressively 'Aussie', products of a different culture to the rarified Europeans he knew in Bombay.

He tried to see his surroundings through his parents' eyes and once again was staggered by the squalour, the din, the anarchic chaos of the city; and he visualised the way they'd look at the Maling-Smith residence.

"What a dump!" would be the first reaction but they'd be intimidated by it, he knew, and also, with the possible exception of Joe, they'd be overpowered and perhaps terrified by the effusiveness of Lady Barbara and the grumpiness of her husband.

Because he'd made no close male friends since Bob left, he asked Joe to be his best man at the wedding and his uncle accepted without protest or demur.

"I'll do you proud, Den," he said. "I know the score with weddings. Been round the course three times myself after all. Though I say it myself, the boys in the force think I'm one of the best speakers they ever have when we give our police dinners."

Oh God! thought Dennis. I forgot about the speech.

To Joe he said, "You'll keep it clean, Joe, won't you?"

Joe looked shocked. "'Course I will. There'll be no smut, but a good speech always has a couple of jokes in it. People expect it." Dennis was not reassured. He'd heard some of Joe's speeches and they'd made his toes curl.

But, like Baby, he told himself, Joe and the folks are my family. If Baby's people don't like them that's their hard luck.

All three Maling-Smiths were waiting on the verandah when the Cadillac, with driver this time, drew up in the drive and Dennis ushered his mother into the house with his father and uncle bringing up the rear. Maud was terrified and looked it, staring around wide-eyed. The house – Dennis had called it a bungalow but it looked more like a mansion to her – was full of peculiar, ill-matched furniture and enormous pictures. And the host and hostess! What a pair!

Sir Robert was short, tub-shaped and so red-faced that he looked as if he might burst into flames at any moment. He didn't say much, just watched in such a piercing way that even the brash Joe became uneasy under his stare.

His wife, Lady Barbara, towered over him and had the most peculiar voice that any of the Australians had ever heard. She sounded to them as if she was speaking in some foreign language, drawling her words out and interspersing everything with strange giggles, because, though she did not show it, she was nervous too and had recourse to the gin before the guests arrived.

She advanced on Maud and took the newcomer's plump little hand in her big, bony ones. "Do come in, darling, would you care for a pinkers?" she asked.

Maud rolled her eyes, having no idea what a pinkers might be. Should she say yes or no? Baby rescued her. "Perhaps Dennis's mother would prefer a gin and lime," she suggested and Maud nodded. That she understood.

Baby was in a quandary about what to call the visitors – not Mother and Father yet, surely, nor Uncle Joe, as Dennis did, so she settled for 'Dennis's mother' and 'Dennis's father'. Uncle Joe she addressed as 'Mr McNab' and he did not correct her.

The lunch was purgatory for everyone involved. The guests gaped in surprise when Sir Robert was served with his usual sausages and mash on silver – and the rest of them ate lobster salad. In the dim light of the shuttered dining room – because the glare from outside was blinding – Lady Barbara's rings, especially the huge emerald, shone with a venomous cold fire, catching every glimmer that came through the louvres of the shutters and the conversation limped from topic to topic with Lady Barbara throwing in non sequiturs whenever she thought they were running out of things to say.

"It's so sweet of your High Commissioner to come to the wedding, Dennis darling, while there's so much trouble going on," she said after they'd been discussing the Dalai Lama's escape to India from Tibet.

The exalted High Commissioner for Australia had only accepted the invitation because he was staggered at the exalted alliance one of his passport clerks was about to embark upon, and also because he hoped to corner the elusive Sir Robert at the reception and have a word in his ear about opening some new businesses in Australia.

"The bishop's marrying them of course," she announced to Maud during the sweet course – a trifle. "He was so pleased we're holding the ceremony in the cathedral but where else would we go? All my people are in there."

Maud looked surprised. "Do you have family out here, your ladyship?" she asked.

"Oh, do call me Barbara. Lots of family, poor things, all dead as mutton though. It's their gravestones and memorial plaques that are in the cathedral."

Joe intervened, "Army men were they, Babs?"

She shot him a hard glance but immediately relented. "Yes, Joe, they were. As far back as 1750."

"It must have been a hard life in those days," said Maud.

"Not any worse than today, I don't expect," said Barbara. "I'm sure they'd recognise the place if they came back. But, as I said, you'll love the bishop. He's a scream! So terribly effete . . . loves wearing skirts. That's why he joined the church."

Joe practically choked on a glacé cherry at that for there was nothing he hated more than 'poofters', but his hostess was sailing on, "He's offered to give you a tour of the cathedral this evening and point out all Baby's ancestors' memorials. Would you like to see the poor old things?"

The Gillies family stared at each other for they'd never heard the bride referred to as Baby before.

"Baby?" asked Maud.

"My baby, I mean, Roberta," said Lady Barbara, remembering too late that she'd been asked to refer to her daughter by her given name.

But her husband jumped into the conversation then. "We call her Baby. Always have done. It's the name everyone calls her," said her father who didn't use that name and never had, except during that first conversation with Dennis – and then only to provoke.

The meal ended with what the hostess said was Scotch woodcock but tasted to the guests like anchovy paste on toast. It was obvious by this time to Baby that her mother's strength was draining away so she stood up and invited Maud to go upstairs for a viewing of the wedding dress while the men sat round the dining table with coffee. Sir Robert, who had decided to go back to his office as soon possible, did not offer them any more alcohol.

In one of the cavernous bedrooms of the first floor, the wedding dress was spread out in its shining glory on the bed. Though he hadn't taken much trouble with the bridesmaids' gowns, the durzi had surpassed himself with the bride's. It was made of the finest slipper satin, a long, slim tube of a dress copied from a photograph in a recent *Vogue*. The sleeves were long and tight, tapering to little points on the backs of the hands; the neck was a seductive slit framed by stand-up points. The skirt, which hugged the hips, was swept back into a swirling train. The effect was delightfully Edwardian and when she saw her daughter in it for the first time, Lady Barbara remembered photographs she'd seen in her youth of the beautiful Lily Langtry.

How lovely dear Baby will look walking down the long aisle of the cathedral on her father's arm! Please God I'll see her. I've only two more days to live through, thought the gaunt woman gently stroking the material of the skirt with a loving hand.

Maud had no such morbid thoughts. She looked at the dress and tried to imagine how much it had cost. A keen home dressmaker, she could tell that the satin was of superb quality. "It's beautiful," she sighed.

There was a wizened old Indian woman sitting on the floor beside the bed, sewing little rosettes of rosebuds onto the bodice of a long silk slip and Lady Barbara bent down to examine what she was doing. "That's lovely, Parvati," she said, and turned to Maud to explain. "The rosebuds are something old. You know – something old, something new, something borrowed and something blue. I had them on my wedding underslip and now Baby – Roberta'll wear them too. Parvati remembered about them. She's kept them all those years." The mother and daughter stared at the servant with brimming eyes while Maud, embarrassed, looked away.

All of a sudden the strength left Baby's mother. She felt her legs go wobbly and the pain in her gut came back with such a rush that she almost cried out.

"Oh darlings, I can't stay up any longer. I'm going to bed," she managed to say and Parvati immediately jumped to her feet to lead her away.

Baby took her future mother-in-law by the arm and said, "You must be tired too. It takes days to get over such a long flight and everyone here sleeps the afternoon away at this time of the year anyway. I know Dennis is having a family dinner with you tonight in his flat but I'll see you tomorrow morning. We'll go for a drive and I hope you can come to the wedding rehearsal in the evening. The bishop would like to show you round the cathedral and he's not as bad as Mummy made him sound."

That was it. The dreaded introductory meeting was over. On the way back to the hotel in the car Maud wept while Denzil and Joe sat grimly silent, not daring to talk in case the driver overheard.

"That woman was pissed as a newt," said Joe eventually when they stepped into the hotel lobby.

"And why didn't you tell us she's called Baby?" his father asked Dennis. "What kind of a name is *Baby* for God's sake?"

Angrily he told them, "It doesn't matter what her name is, surely? I love her. I want to marry her. We won't have to live with her mother and father and we won't have to stay here in India. We can go anywhere we want. Back to Australia, anywhere. Her father's told me that. He's a decent old stick in spite of the way he appears. He's been very fair with me . . ." So his parents stopped criticising the Maling-Smiths and decided to make the best of it.

If Dennis was happy, that was all that mattered to them. They hugged their son, they wept in private and, later that night, got mildly tipsy in Dennis's flat sitting on the verandah staring out over the magical expanse of sea that gradually relaxed their dislike of Bombay. It was probably quite a nice place after all, they thought, and the girl was pretty, well brought up and very polite to them.

"And she's bloody rich too," added Uncle Joe after his fifth beer. "Good on ya, Den."

"I wish she wasn't so rich," said Maud softly. "That could make things difficult for you, Dennis."

But her son took her hand and reassured her, "I'm going to have my own job. I'm not going to take a cent of her money. She knows that and so does her father. It's simply not important if we really love each other, is it?"

"Oh that's lovely, Denny," sighed Maud, who was a romantic. She read love stories in magazines and believed in the happy endings. So far nothing, not even Joe's three divorces for they weren't altogether surprising she had to admit, had spoiled her fairy tale vision of life.

"I'm so happy for you," she said leaning over to kiss her son's cheek.

While Maud was viewing Baby's wedding dress, Dee was perched on the flat rock in the nullah waiting for Shadiv.

It was very hot and the river bed was rust-red, hard as concrete and criss-crossed with enormous cracks; the jungle was crackling dry and sere, starved of water and not as luscious or as encroaching as it had been three months ago. There was a deadly stillness in the air, a smothering silence that was deeply sinister, as if the hidden jungle was full of listening ears and eyes watching the woman on the rock.

She hugged her knees and waited. She was sure he would come.

It was well after four when he came crashing through the undergrowth. There were traces of make-up around his eyes and in the folds of flesh by his mouth. He'd been made up to a peculiar shade of yellow, as if he'd been jaundiced.

Without speaking he sat down beside her. Their arms were touching and Dee was acutely conscious of every microscopic part of his skin that brushed hers.

"Have you been here long? I was filming down the road. I've to go back in an hour. Your bearer said you had gone for a walk and I reckoned you'd be here."

"Not long," she said.

"I came to see you the day before I went off filming and that girl said you couldn't be disturbed."

"I know. That's why I came up the nullah today. I thought you'd be here."

"I wanted to tell you something. We're leaving our house on the farm. We'll be gone next week."

She nodded and used the walking stick she held in her hands to trace an invisible mark on the hard soil. "I thought it might be something like that."

"Leila thinks we should have a better place. She's been talking about it for ages. And she doesn't like me spending so much time across the nullah."

"With us?"

"Yes. She doesn't like that."

"Does she think we're a bad influence?"

"Yes. She doesn't like me drinking, or eating your food, that sort of thing. She's very strict in her observances. And she doesn't like the books."

Dee lifted her head and stared at him. "The books?"

"The books we read. The ones we share."

"I see."

The sat in silence for a little while until he spoke again. "I don't really want to go. I'm very happy here. It's been like another world for me – Guy and Ben and you, the music and the books. The jokes, the talking, driving in the jungle at night. Things I've never done before. Nowadays when I go out in Bombay I'm an object of curiosity – a film star. People make a fuss of me, flatter me, say what they think I want to hear, offer me things, ask for my autograph, try to touch me . . ." He pulled a face.

"That's because you're a success now. I told you so. You've got to make the best of it."

"I know. It's what I thought I wanted. But it's nice just to be an ordinary fellow. In the city I won't be that ever again. I'll have to leave my ordinary fellow out here in the jungle."

"I'm sorry about that," said Dee.

"Do you think I ought to go?" he asked.

She was looking at him still. What a wonderful, poetic face he has, like Byron, she thought, and his eyes really are green, as green as Baby's mother's wonderful ring.

"I don't want you to go but I see that you must," she said. "Your wife wants it and your career demands it. You must live in style, because there'll be articles about your wonderful penthouse in film magazines. An article about living out here on the fruit farm wouldn't make your fans go 'oooh' and 'aaah'. You're going to be famous, really famous. You'd have to go away eventually."

"I'll miss you," he said softly.

Don't, don't, don't say it! cried her heart.

What she said was, "I expect we'll be going soon ourselves. I don't think we can afford to live here much longer and I'm getting very fed up with Guy. Ben and I have to be on our own if we're going to make a go of our marriage. This idyll's over for us too, I'm afraid."

"I'll miss you," he said again.

She whispered, "And don't you know I'll miss you? I'll never forget you."

"I can't understand what's happened," he said. "It was like a thunderclap. I came up here and saw you sitting on this rock. You looked as if you'd dropped from the sky."

"It was like that for me too. When you came out of the jungle I thought you were a god. A god with a gun."

"It's not logical, is it? I'm married, you're married. I'm not unhappy with my wife and you are obviously not unhappy with Ben. Why did this have to happen to us? What can we do?"

"Nothing, we can't do anything. I wouldn't break up your marriage and I can't walk out on Ben. He went through a lot of trouble when we were getting married. He put up with awful treatment by my people. He could have bolted and left me to it. I'm sure he thought about it, but he didn't go. He stayed by me and we got married. We're only getting to know each other now really."

He nodded. "I know. So what's happened?"

211

She threw the stick violently into the undergrowth. "I know what's happened. I've fallen in love. That's what's bloody well happened. It's awful. It's agony."

He turned on the stone and put his arms round her. They'd never touched each other like that before, they'd never kissed. "I know, it's agony. What are we going to do?"

"I don't know. I don't know if I've got the nerve to do anything. I know that there are times in your life when you've just got to take a chance but I'm not a good gambler. When I back horses, they lose. I'm scared. Oh God, I wish I wasn't Scottish. We're all such Puritans. It's Calvinism to blame. We think that it's dangerous and wicked to enjoy ourselves. We've got to suffer."

He laughed. "Indians don't believe that," he said.

"Then you're lucky. You've no idea what it's like to have this terrible sense of morality. It's crippling."

"I'm sure it could be cured."

She put her head on his chest and listened to his heart beating. The silence came down again and overpowered them. His hands were stroking her cropped head and the back of her neck. "It's that way with me too," he said at last.

When they kissed it was as if the world stopped turning around them. Though the kiss lasted quite a long time, there was only one. The silence and their solitude was soon broken by the sounds of someone coming down the nullah bank and Shadiv's servant appeared from his side of the river bed. "The car has come for you, sahib," he said with his head down examining his bare feet as he spoke.

"I have to go. They'll be waiting for me to start. Think about what we're going to do and don't be scared – or Scottish. I'm filming away tomorrow but I'll see you on Saturday."

"No, not Saturday. Saturday's the wedding. Come here on Sunday."

"Oh yes, the wedding. The bride who got Ganesh."

"Yes. She liked him. She knew what he meant."

He was standing up looking down at her and she saw he looked tired and strained.

"Don't work too hard," she whispered.

He grinned, stroked the top of her head and walked away.

Twenty-Nine

N ext day Baby made a tremendous effort, driving Dennis's
parents and uncle around Bombay while he was working at
his office.

She showed them Colaba, she took them to the Jain temple on
Malabar Hill and the Towers of Silence where Maud turned faint
and had to be helped back to the car. She drove them to Worli, Pali
Hill and the beach at Juhu before ending up with late lunch in the
Ambassador Hotel, though by that time they were all too exhausted
to do more than pick at the food.

When it was then suggested that they might want to attend the last
wedding rehearsal at five o'clock on Friday, Maud took the initiative.
"My dear, I hope you don't mind but Denzil and I'd rather not. It's
so hot here and I'm terribly tired. Anyway it'll be a bigger thrill for
us seeing the cathedral and everything for the first time tomorrow.
I don't want to spoil it . . . Joe'll be at the rehearsal of course,"
she said. Behind her, Joe nodded glumly in agreement. He'd much
rather be able to spend the rest of the afternoon in bed.

Baby quite understood. She kissed them all before she said
goodbye and told Denzil and Maud, "I hope you have a good
rest this evening. I won't see you again until the wedding but I'll
look out for you specially when I walk down the aisle."

It was dim and surprisingly cool in the cavernous cathedral where
every footstep rang and echoed with an eerie resonance and even
irreligious people spoke in hushed voices in spite of themselves.

There was nobody else about when Dee and Ben arrived and
walked down the side aisles reading the inscriptions on the monu-
ments. Lots of them *were* in memory of members of Baby's family,
who lay on carved biers, brandished swords, or posed with laurel
wreaths around their epitaphs. How strange, thought Dee, for Baby
to be getting married under the cold, carved marble eyes of her
progenitors. She shivered at the thought and felt Ben's hand suddenly
reach out for hers and grasp it.

Elisabeth McNeill

"OK?" he asked in a concerned voice because, although he didn't
show it, he'd been worried about her recently. She seemed to be
slipping away from him somehow, retreating into a different world.
She'd always been a bit remote, living as she did in the world of
books as much as in the world of real people, and sometimes he
wondered how much contact he was really making with her apart
from the physical, but for the last few days she'd seemed more
distant than usual, lost in her own world.

She'd been under the weather of course. The hot season didn't
suit her though he thrived on it. Perhaps that was the trouble.

"Have those jags you got from Ralph helped?" he asked as they
walked slowly down the stone-flagged aisle.

She looked up at him and nodded, "Yes, I think they have. I'm
not so tired. Ralph said I'm anaemic and he took tests. I should get
the results next week."

Ben nodded. "He's a piss-artist, old Ralph, but he's a good
doctor."

"Yes, I like him a lot."

"You're looking better anyway," he said encouragingly. "In fact
you look great. You'll be the best-looking bird at the wedding, just
wait and see. The sexiest by a long way."

She stared at him, surprised. "Do you really think so?" she
asked.

He slipped an arm round her waist and hugged her to him. "You
can bet on it. You're streets ahead of anyone else as far as I'm
concerned. I get randy just thinking about you – even here, in the
cathedral."

She didn't laugh and her eyes looked enormous and troubled. I
wonder if he knows, she was thinking. I wonder if he knows what
a quandary I'm in. I wonder if he knows that whatever decision
I make, I'll always worry in case I took the wrong one. Am I a
prude? Am I repressed? she asked herself. Or am I just a coward?

One thing was certain: she was hopelessly, painfully, agonisingly
in love and she knew that when Shadiv went away from Chembur,
she'd probably never see him again because he was giving her the
chance to develop the situation between them or allow it to stop
before it really started. A crossroads indeed.

She and Ben sat down in a pew, waiting for the others to arrive,
and she wondered what would happen if she tried to tell him about
her problem when there was a scurry of footsteps and voices at
the massive doorway. Winks, Baby, Dennis, his Uncle Joe and the
bishop all arrived together.

214

"Dear hearts," carolled the pink-faced bishop, "are we all here? Are any of the parents coming today? No? Then let's get started. I'll just give you a quick run-through so's you all know where to stand and what to say and then we can all go home to our sundowners. This heat's sweltering, isn't it? I swear it gets worse every year. I've nothing on underneath this cassock but a jock strap!"

Joe visibly blanched at this sally.

They were easily marshalled and instructed though both Baby and Dennis looked anxious and stumbled awkwardly when being ushered into their positions. When they confessed to nerves, the bishop laughed, "I'd be worried about you if you weren't nervous now. But it's like going on stage, darlings, you'll perform magnificently when it's the real thing. Don't worry. I'll see you through."

After two rehearsals of the responses, the bride and groom progressed back up the aisle, Winks, Dee and an uncharacteristically abashed-looking Joe bringing up the rear. Dennis and Baby walked stiffly, shoulders tense as if they were afraid of touching each other, and both were greatly relieved when the bishop declared himself satisfied.

"See you tomorrow. Don't forget, ha ha ha!" he joked as he swept off with a flurry of his soutane.

On the open space beside the cathedral main door, they stood awkwardly looking at each other as if they were complete strangers. While the girls began discussing the arrangements for the next day, the men stood side by side and Ben asked Dennis and Joe, "Fancy a beer? We could go to the Ritz. Dee's still got some points left on her permit and Thomas and Raju, the barmen there, always let us have a bit extra."

But before Joe could accept, Dennis shook his head. "I promised the parents we'd have supper with them in the Taj tonight. We'd better go there now." In fact he had more on his mind than dinner at the Taj. He had to make another payment to Rodriques.

"No stag night?" asked Ben in amazement. The idea of a Bombay bachelor taking the plunge without a stag night was unheard of in his acquaintance.

"I don't know enough people. I've only been here a few months," said Dennis. Joe said nothing. In fact he'd said nothing during the whole rehearsal. Ben wondered how he was going to articulate a speech.

"God, if I'd known that I'd have organised one for you . . ." Ben dropped his voice and nudged Dennis in the ribs. "I'd've got some girls in from Colaba."

215

Dennis visibly reeled, reminded again of Carole, almost looking over his shoulder to see if she'd turned up as he was terrified she might. Did Ben know about his liaison with her? he wondered, but Ben's face was pleasant and guileless. He wasn't being snide.

"No, I'd better go off to the Taj now," he said and walked across to Baby to kiss her on the cheek and tell her how much he was looking forward to the next day.

"I'm counting the hours," he whispered in her ear. She flushed crimson, which made the others laugh.

"What on earth did he say to you, darling?" asked Winks, but Baby only shook her head.

"Anybody for a beer at the Ritz?" asked Ben almost desperately. This occasion couldn't be allowed to collapse like a damp squib, he thought. Winks said she had to go home and so did Baby.

Seeing his disappointment, his wife took his arm, "All right, I'll go to the Ritz with you," she said, "but only for one drink," though she knew they'd be there till closing time once they stepped into the bar's womb-like interior.

Baby did not go straight home however. Instead she set off walking towards the Gateway of India for she wanted to see the sun setting over the ocean, a sight that always filled her with awe. She stood watching the play of light on the water, straining her eyes for the green flash that was meant to come just as the sun sank below the horizon. She'd only seen the flash twice in her life but she always watched for it, and especially tonight she wished she could see it again, but she didn't.

Then she turned, and sticking her hands into the pockets of her loose skirt, she headed for Dr Green's consulting rooms. There were lights shining in his windows when she looked up at them, so she rang the bell and was admitted by the little boy who guarded the door.

"Doctor finished," he said but Baby swept past him.

Mrs Gomez was shuffling together a pile of papers on her desk and putting a plastic cover over the enormous old typewriter that stood there. "Miss Maling-Smith! The doctor isn't expecting you, is he?"

"No, but I must see him. I must. I'm getting married tomorrow, you see . . ." Baby's voice was cracking and she looked distraught. Without argument, Mrs Gomez opened the door into the doctor's office and showed the girl in.

He'd taken off his white coat and was sitting in his revolving chair smoking a hand rolled cigarette. He looked very tired.

216

Baby ran up to the desk and leaned her fists on it as if ready for a fight, staring over the papers at him. "If I ask you a question, Dr Green, will you tell me the absolute truth?" she demanded.

He stubbed out the cigarette in a metal ashtray and said slowly, "I don't think I'd deliberately lie to you, my dear."

"You know I'm getting married tomorrow?"

"Yes, I've been invited to the wedding."

"You know one of the reasons that I'm getting married is so that my mother can see me settled . . ."

"Is it?"

"Yes, it is. I know how anxious she is for me to settle down. I know she feels that she has very little time left. I love her and I want her to die happy."

"I hope that is not the only reason you are getting married tomorrow. Please sit down Roberta, you're upsetting me standing there like that."

She flopped into the chair behind her, legs at the same awkward angle as her mother adopted, like a new-born foal. "I don't know. I'm trying to work it all out but I've come here to ask you to tell me the absolute truth about my mother's health. Please, please, Dr Green. I won't tell another soul what you say, not my mother, not my father, not anyone, but I want to know. It's very important."

He scrabbled in his desk drawer for the little metal machine he used for making his cigarettes but then didn't use it.

"Your mother is dying," he said eventually. "By most standards she should be dead already but the excitement of this wedding has extended her life. She has an inoperable cancer and nothing can be done for her. She's known about it for some time."

Baby sank her head into her hands. "I thought as much. So me getting married has given her extra time," she said.

"Yes, it has. That sort of thing happens occasionally. People keep themselves alive – then when they achieve their object, that's it. They usually die within weeks or even days."

"My mother won't keep on going till I have a baby?" asked the girl.

"That's impossible. I saw your mother last week and I'll be astonished if she is still alive when the rains come. I doubt if she has more than two or three weeks life left to her."

"But she's surprised you before, why can't she do the same again?"

"If you have come here seeking hope for your mother, I'm sorry, but that is impossible. She doesn't eat any more. Haven't

217

you noticed? She can hardly walk. The ayah practically carries her around. She's so thin you can almost see through her."

Baby gave a convulsive sob. All those things were true and she'd turned her eyes away from them, not wanting to see.

"Don't cry," said the doctor almost roughly. "I wouldn't have told you this if I'd thought you were going to break down. You've got to face it as bravely as your mother's facing it."

The girl suddenly straightened in her chair and though she in no way physically resembled her mother, a new, unexpected similarity between them took him by surprise. She stood up, looking taller, and held out a hand to him which he took. "Thank you," she said and left his office.

Conversation was strained during the dinner with Dennis and his family at the Taj; Denzil and Maud didn't talk much because they were exhausted, run into the ground by Baby's city tour.

Dennis found it difficult to chat because he was worried and confused – very worried, with thoughts jumbling up in his head like a kaleidoscope. Every time he concentrated, the pattern shifted. The uppermost thought however was that he had to get out to Chembur and pay off Fifi and Carole. There was still two thousand outstanding, for the other instalments had been collected by Rodriques who came to the office for them, but Dennis had insisted on holding back the last payment till the wedding. Now, in a sudden panic, he changed his mind. He must complete the transaction tonight and get a promise that there would be no attempt to disrupt his wedding. He dismissed the possibility that even though he paid, they might make trouble anyway. That was too much to worry about. Why should they wait quietly for their money? The moment he was married, he was off the hook and not vulnerable to their demands any more.

He could see Joe looking hopefully at him over the stiff white tablecloth. Joe wasn't tired. Joe was champing to go out into the night-time city.

"That guy at the rehearsal thought you should have a stag night, Den. Can't you round up some cobbers and hit the town?" said Joe when Maud announced that she and Denzil were going to bed.

"I don't know enough people for a stag night," said Dennis.

"That's a pity. Every young chap should have one last blow out before he gets married," Joe said.

"I don't really want a blow out," his nephew told him. Joe regarded him with pity. Denny hasn't learned much since he left home after all, he thought. He's still a bit of a mummy's boy. I wonder where

the little bint is that he's paying off? Maybe he's going there instead
of to a stag night. I hope he is.

"I'll go out with you if you like," Joe offered, thinking about
Grant Road and Dennis's mysterious girlfriend. Dennis could read
his mind and mentally cringed.

"Thanks Uncle Joe but I'm really tired. I want to go home
and sleep."

Chagrined, Joe laughed, "Build up your strength for tomorrow,
eh?"

"*Joe!*" said Maud in a shocked voice.

They went to bed at last and Dennis literally ran out of the Taj's
pillared back entrance – it had been built back to front by accident,
according to local stories – jumping into his car and revving up the
engine loudly while still in the forecourt.

He roared his way to Chembur. The last two thousand chips were
in his pocket and he couldn't wait to get rid of them. Poor Joe, he'd
so wanted to go out on the town, and not only had Dennis let him
down but he was using Joe's money to pay off the blackmailers.

I feel like a split personality, he thought as he drove along, the
little car throbbing beneath his feet. I'm in a mess. One half of me
is saying one thing and the other half says another.

One half said, 'Pay Fifi and keep everything quiet.'

But the other said, 'To hell with her. Let her try to disrupt the
wedding. She hasn't a leg to stand on even if she does. She's only
trying to frighten you. Keep your money.'

The cowardly first half said, 'But I am scared! I'm scared of Baby
and even more scared of her father.'

'Are you always going to be scared of them? Is that any way to
go into a marriage?'

'When we're on our own we'll get onto a better footing. I won't
be scared then.'

'Who says?' scoffed the bolder voice.

He felt as if he was in a trap that was about to close. In his mind's
eye he saw the gate falling in front of him, falling, falling like the
portcullis in a castle. Did he want to be trapped inside? Was it still
possible to duck under the descending gate? Did he want to?

Of course not! He was the luckiest man in Bombay, the luckiest man in India. Baby was a wonderful girl who'd transformed
his life. When he looked back on the way he was before he
met her, he thanked his lucky stars he'd ever gone swimming at
Breach Candy.

It was just they didn't really know each other yet, they were both nervous. Though they had kissed and embraced since the engagement, all passion seemed to have left them recently. The urgency had gone. But surely that would come back when the strain of the wedding was over, when they were on their own in that place that sounded so peculiar – Ooty. He wished he had some friends he could ask about this. But there was no one except Joe.

Though it was after midnight when he reached Chembur, there were lights showing in the downstairs windows. He drove up to the door very slowly, not wanting to excite the dog, but all was silence. Because he was so tall he could see over the lintel into the open front window. Fifi was playing some sort of card game on her own. No one else was there and the dog was lying asleep, stretched out at her feet.

Dennis knocked on the door and she shouted, "Come in."

There was no surprise in her face at the sight of him and she went on turning over cards, occasionally covering one lying face up before her.

"You want something?" she asked eventually. Waking, the dog growled but it didn't get up.

"I've brought you the last of the money."

She raised her semicircles of eyebrows. "I thought you were keeping it till tomorrow."

"I hope I can trust you."

She said nothing to that but after laying down some more cards, she spoke again. "Carole's not here."

"It doesn't matter," he said, laying the envelope containing the last two thousand rupees on the edge of the table. It was a relief to get rid of it, almost as if he'd cleared his conscience about Carole though he knew that paying money was a bad way to do it.

"Goodbye," said Fifi, and he was turning to go when there was a commotion at the beaded kitchen door and Amy came bursting through. Her feet were bare and she was wearing a thin cotton wrapper which she was clutching around herself. It looked as if she'd just got out of bed.

"Why's he giving you money?" she asked her mother. "It wasn't his baby."

"Shut up," snapped Fifi. Suddenly galvanised into action, she grabbed the money and shoved it into her deep cleavage.

Amy stared hostilely at Dennis. "It wasn't your baby," she said. "It was that man's she's been living with up the hill. He paid for it already anyway."

Dennis stared at her in blank astonishment.

"Oh don't look so *stupid*," shouted the girl. "You're being cheated. How much are you giving her?"

"Two thousand, but I've already given eight."

Amy turned to her mother. "How could you? How could you? You are shaming me." And to Dennis, she said, "Did she say it was your baby?"

"I don't know anything about a baby," he told her. "I was afraid they'd break up my wedding. They said they'd sue me for breach of promise."

There were two bright red spots in the middle of Amy's cheeks and she threw back her head to laugh. "Some chance. My sister's a tart. I told you that already. She's been living up the hill with another man. You've been taken for a ride. Take your money and get the hell out of here."

Fifi was on her feet, shouting too. "Stay out of this. You're jealous."

The girl took a lunge at her mother, "Give him back his money. What you've done is shameful. What if he went to the police? You'd go to jail. Give it back to him. If you don't give it back, I'll take it."

The dog was on its feet snarling, but to Dennis's surprise it was snarling at Fifi. It was obviously Amy's dog. Fifi backed away, hands spread, trying to placate her furious daughter but to no avail. Amy was virago-wild, talons out, eyes blazing. As he backed away Dennis guessed that there was a lot more behind her rage than this money business.

"Give him the money," shouted Amy through clenched teeth.

Fifi fished into her breast and brought out the crushed envelope which she threw onto the table top among the scattered cards.

"I don't want it back," he said.

Then Amy turned on him and he backed away. "Take it! Take it! We're not all criminals. You were cheated. Take it back."

Reluctantly he lifted it up and pushed it into his trouser pocket. He really didn't want it. It was tainted money.

"Now, get out, get out, get out!" cried Amy pushing him towards the door with both hands. She was weeping, with tears coursing down her cheeks.

He went. As he drove back to the city, he kept shaking his head as if to sort out his ideas. It seemed like some sort of nightmare; his whole world was out of joint, everything had gone wrong. What a way to spend the night before your wedding, he said to himself as he finally parked the car before his block of flats.

Thirty

The Wedding Day

On Saturday, the thirtieth of May, 1959, the sleeping city of Bombay came to noisy life as soon as the first creamy streaks of light marked the sky.

Jai and the other little boys sleeping on the pavement outside Crawford Market sat up rubbing their eyes and wondered where they could find something to eat. Jai felt like king of the pack because he still had one rupee six annas of Dee's money left. It didn't matter if he earned nothing today. Tomorrow could look after itself.

Pye-dogs and their scab-covered pups snarled and fought over the corpses of dead rats in Hornby Road.

Unlit bullock carts driven by exhausted men, who had been working all night, disappeared from the main road out of the city to be replaced by ramshackle buses, paint-scraped, wing-dented taxis and hundreds of hooting motor cars.

A dark-green police wagon toured the streets of the Fort and a uniformed constable jumped out whenever he saw a body lying still asleep under the trees. He poked it with his foot. Sometimes it shouted in protest and stood up, but more often it lay unprotesting because it was dead – the soul of the person who'd inhabited the body had drifted away during the night. Then the policeman called two coolies out of the van and they manhandled the corpse into the back where it lay tumbled with dozens of others to be driven away to be burned on a funeral pyre that was already lit on the burning ghat by the sea. The smoke from it spiralled upwards into the still air.

Wing-flapping vultures swooped down from the palm trees where they'd spent the hours of darkness onto the high stone-built Towers of Silence at the top of Malabar Hill. The corpse of a prominent Parsi had been put on the tallest tower during the previous day for his bones to be picked clean by the birds.

Down in the business section, hooters started to blare and the streets round Sir Robert Maling-Smith's cotton mills were filled with hurrying men. The exhausted, staggering night shift was coming off

222

and the day shift just starting. The machinery behind the high walls did not pause for a moment.

The air felt heavy, like an invisible weight pressing down on people's bodies. On the distant horizon over mainland India, dark purple storm clouds that presaged the monsoon were gathering. Now and again a jagged bolt of lightning could be seen ripping through the clouds, tearing them apart like celestial scissors. Soon, everyone hoped, that lightning would be raging over Bombay island and when it came, the blessed rain might come with it. Young and old, rich and poor were longing for the rain and when it came they would run into the streets or gardens to let it pour over their heads like a libation.

It was Roberta Maling-Smith's wedding day.

Nobody in her house – except the servants – got up early for it was too hot to go outside, too hot to leave their air-conditioned or fan-cooled rooms where bamboo chicks shrouded the windows to keep out the intrusive sun. The humidity was so high that it hurt to breathe.

Ben and Dee, Guy and Carole slept late in the Gulmohurs as well. The wedding was not due to start till five o'clock when it would be cooler, and Ben, Dee and Guy had decided to leave home at lunchtime to spend the afternoon in the Ritz bar, which was air-conditioned. After that the men would dress in the Gym before going to the cathedral from there. Dee intended to go straight from the Ritz to Baby's bungalow in Nepean Sea Road.

"What a bloody day to get married," grumbled a sweating Guy as he pulled on his cream-coloured trousers. Mohammed was in the room carefully putting his master's best lightweight suit into a suitcase. "Don't forget my Haileybury tie, M'mud, though God knows why I bother. We'll all look like damp dishcloths before this is over," he said fretfully.

Carole lay in bed, watching narrowly, her long, sensual body clad in a flimsy baby-doll nightdress. Her caramel-coloured eyes were cold as ice.

"I want to go to the wedding with you," she said when Mohammed took the suitcase next door to pack Ben's clothes.

"You can't. I'm not turning up with some chi-chi girl on my arm," said Guy cruelly.

"You said you'd take me. You promised. Other men take their girlfriends out. You never take me anywhere."

"If I promised to take you, I was telling lies. Or I was drunk."

"I might not be here when you get back," she threatened. Her strategy was to ignore his insults.

"Quite frankly I don't give a toss," was his reply.

Mohammed did not pack for Dee. It was beneath him to do that for a woman but she did not have to carry anything more than her underwear and make-up which she put into one of Ben's rugby holdalls. Her dress was still at Baby's and she would change into it there.

As Mohammed put down the lid of the suitcase, he asked her, "Will you be home tonight for dinner, memsahib?"

"I don't think so. No. Certainly not. The reception'll go on for hours. There's going to be a dinner and a dance afterwards as well . . ." It'll be well into Sunday before we get home, she thought. Sunday, when I've to meet Shadiv again. It was all she could think about.

"Then I'll give the cook the night off," said Mohammed grandly.

Baby spent a sleepless and tearful night, only falling into a fitful doze an hour before dawn. Both her parents had been in bed when she reached home the previous evening, for she'd driven out to Juhu beach on her own after seeing Dr Green, and parked by the beach to stare out over a black heaving sea while she wept. Then she'd taken her grief to bed unconsoled.

Parvati woke her at eleven o'clock. "Sssssss," she hissed softly, laying a glass of freshly pressed orange juice at the side of the bed. Baby opened swollen eyes and groaned.

"How's my mother?" she muttered.

"Sleeping."

"You know she's dying. She's only got a few days left. You know that, don't you?"

The ayah nodded and agitatedly wound the end of her cotton sari around her hands. Her little face was screwed up in a grimace that showed she was fighting back tears.

"How will she get through the wedding? How can she stand such a strain?"

"She will manage."

"I want to see her. I'm getting up now." Baby stuck her legs out of bed and grabbed a cotton wrap from the chair.

"Wait. Don't go yet. She has taken a pill and will sleep for an hour or two more. You must let her sleep. Then you can go in."

Baby lay back against the piled pillows and put her hands over her eyes. "Oh, I don't know what to do . . . I don't know . . ."

Parvati had no suggestions to make. She only shrugged and slipped out of the room. Her main concern was for Lady Barbara and Baby would have to fend for herself.

I should be happy. I should be excited. I should be getting up and rushing around, but I'm miserable. I'm so miserable that I could pull the sheet over my head and stay here all day. I'm too sad to get married, thought Baby rolling over in bed.

She knew her unhappiness was mainly about her mother, but there was something else. Something terrible. As she walked up the aisle on Dennis's arm the previous evening she had finally accepted that she did not love him. Even the mild affection she had previously felt for him was rapidly draining away. It was as if a blindfold had been snatched from her eyes and she saw everything in the cold light of reality. She was marrying on the rebound and Dennis was her chosen victim.

"It's all my fault," she said aloud. "I started this. I led him on and forced him into it. And now I don't want to go through with it but it's too late. It's too far gone to stop. Tonight I'm going to marry a man I don't love. Tonight I'll have to sleep with a man that I don't want to touch me. Oh God, what a mess! The rest of my life is going to be a huge pretence. And it's all my own fault."

She lay agonising, tossing and turning, sunk in paralysing misery until half-past one when Parvati came back to tell her, "My lady is wakened. She is asking for you."

Lady Barbara's room was a haven with mechanically cooled air, providing a welcome relief from the furnace outside. She was lying in the middle of her high, four-poster bed and she looked so old and tired that Baby immediately forgot her own troubles in concern for her mother.

She climbed into the bed as she used to do when she was a child, lay down and took her mother's hand. "I went to see Dr Green last night, darling. He told me about you."

Lady Barbara sighed, "He shouldn't have done that. I didn't want you to know."

"I'm glad he did. You should have told me yourself. Have you told Daddy?"

"I'll tell him tomorrow. I didn't want to worry either of you yet. I want you to be happy, very, very happy today."

"That's not possible now."

"Damn Moses Green!" said Lady Barbara irritably.

"It's not only because of that. There's something else too. I'm broken-hearted about you of course but I wouldn't be happy even

225

if I didn't know because, you see, I've only just accepted that I'm marrying a man I don't love."

Her mother turned her head and her tired eyes scanned her daughter's face. What she saw there worried her. "Not at all?" she whispered.

Baby shook her head. "Not at all. Dennis is a very nice, decent man. He's kind, he's gentle, he's considerate, he'd never let me down but I have absolutely no romantic feelings for him. I've been deceiving myself because I was so hurt about Charlie. I couldn't understand how he could prefer another girl to me, after everything that happened between us. I slept with him you see. When he left me I was so raw. Every time I went to a party people crowded round and told me about Charlie. They wanted to see how I'd react. I suppose I wanted him to hear I'd married a handsome Australian and perhaps be jealous too, but now that the wedding's so near, I've got to face the truth and it's terrible."

"Are you only marrying Dennis because you're on the rebound from Charlie or was it also because I want so badly to see you settled?" her mother asked.

"Partly both I suppose. I want to please you so much. I want to make you happy. Even before Dr Green told me how bad your illness is I think I knew. I wanted to do something wonderful for you and this is such a major thing."

"You want me to die happy?" Lady Barbara gave a little smile as she asked the question. They were driving away the taboos between them.

"I did, I do," agreed her daughter.

"So what are you going to do?" asked Lady Barbara.

"What can I do? I'm going to get married this evening."

"But that won't make me happy if what you've just said is true. Are you absolutely sure you don't love him? This isn't just an attack of nerves, is it?"

"I don't love him. I like him. He's very good-looking and everything but he doesn't make my blood run faster if you know what I mean. He's boring. He doesn't argue with me, he does exactly what I want even if he doesn't want to do it . . . We don't really understand each other, I suppose. When we're out together I'm always glad when I'm on my own again because talking to him is such a strain. We don't talk the same language."

"You don't laugh together?"

"No. Not really. Some of the things I think astonish him, like the way I am about India. He just thinks it's dirty and it smells. And my Ganesh. He really hates it!"

"Then you mustn't marry him. It'll only get worse between you. Marriage isn't easy at the best of times but if you can't talk and laugh at each other's jokes, it's doomed. I know Indians say that love grows but it only does that if there's good growing conditions and Indian parents take care to match people. Perhaps I should have listened to Parvati and consulted an astrologer about this marriage."

"She wanted you to do that?"

"Yes, she thought there was trouble there, she said you weren't right together, but I didn't listen to her. I was so keen to see you married. This isn't just your fault, it's mine as well."

Baby hugged the thin body beside her. "Don't talk rubbish. It's not your fault. I just wanted to please you. I don't think I've ever done very much for you and Daddy. Not as much as you've done for me."

Her mother raised herself on one elbow and exclaimed, "What rubbish. You've enhanced our lives. You've been our delight ever since the minute you came into the world. We adore you and that's why I can't sit back and watch you doing the wrong thing now. What are we going to do about this wedding?"

"What do you mean?"

"Do we call it off?"

"We can't. It's gone too far. We can't call it off now. It's nearly two o'clock."

"I admit it would have been easier if you'd decided this a few days ago but we can still call it off." Lady Barbara's fighting ancestors had bequeathed her a lot of grit and the ability to face up to the impossible.

"Oh Mummy, I can't. How awful. All those guests, Maud and Denzil and Uncle Joe, the bishop . . . and Dennis. God, what about Dennis? He'll be shattered. I can't do this to him."

"He'd be more shattered if he found out you'd married him and didn't love him. Let's talk to your father about it. He's always good in a crisis," said Lady Barbara, ringing the bell at the side of her bed to summon Parvati who was sent to find the head of the household.

When he arrived Sir Robert took charge of the situation with remarkable sang froid and complete decision. "First of all I want you to be absolutely sure you don't want to marry him," he told his daughter. "Lots of brides get cold feet at the last moment. Maybe you'll change your mind back again."

"She's not your daughter for nothing," said Lady Barbara. "She won't change her mind again. As far as I can see she's not loved the poor fellow from the very beginning."

"It's a good job he's not a fortune hunter," mused Sir Robert, "but I told him from the beginning that he wouldn't get any of our money and he accepted that. He can't sue on those grounds. I'd better ring the lawyer first though."

This was something that hadn't occurred to Baby and she quailed. The thought of being dragged through the courts appalled her.

"He won't sue. I'm sure of that," she said.

"You've no idea what he'll do when he hears what you've got to say, have you? This is going to be a terrible slap in the face for him," said her father, who seemed to have accepted that the wedding could be called off.

"Oh Daddy, can we call it off now?" asked Baby.

"Why not?" replied her father whose business career was built on an absolute refusal to accept the idea that there was anything he couldn't do.

"Tell us what to do," said his wife from her bed.

He made it sound very simple.

"You'll have to go and tell him yourself, that's only fair," he said to Baby. "I'll come with you and we'd best go now."

"No Daddy, I'll do it on my own. It's my responsibility and he'd hate it if there was someone else there to hear everything."

"Then take big Saleem with you just in case."

"In case of what?"

"In case he gets difficult. Saleem looks terrifying and I'll have a word with him so he knows what to do. Now what else?" He was counting off ideas on his fingers. "There's his people. They'll have to be told. I'll go to the Taj to see them. That's not going to be easy, but they have to be stopped before they set out for the cathedral." He consulted his watch and saw with disquiet that it was a quarter to three.

"What can I do?" asked Lady Barbara. Her husband and daughter looked at her with sympathy. "Just stay here, my dear," said Sir Robert.

"But what about the guests? The only way to tell them all at once is to get them into the cathedral and do it there. I'll take care of that because you might not get away from the parents in time. You can't just rush in, break this kind of news and rush out again."

"You can't tell the guests," said her husband sharply.

228

"I will. I want to. Don't argue with me." There was no point arguing when they saw the expression on her face.

It was half-past three when Baby arrived at Dennis's flat. Refusing Saleem's offer to accompany her, she ran up the stairs and rang the doorbell. The driver followed her anyway. Sir Robert had impressed on him the consequences if any harm came to Missy Baby.

When Govind answered, she brushed past him into the sitting room where Dennis was sitting, already dressed in a white shirt and pinstripe grey pants. A grey tail coat, copied from a 1930s style magazine by a tailor near the docks in peculiarly shiny lightweight material, was hanging over a chair waiting for him to slip it on. A buttonhole of roses stood on the table in a glass of water but already they were wilting in the heat.

He stood up in amazement at the sight of his bride suddenly materialising before him in crumpled pink slacks and blouse.

"What's wrong Baby?" he asked. "What's happened?"

She stopped dead in the middle of the floor and wrung her hands. "Oh Dennis, I'm so sorry. I'm so terribly sorry . . . I don't know how to tell you."

He thought she was going to say that one of their parents had died but when he took a step towards her with the intention of giving comfort, she held up both hands palms outwards to fend him off and said in a rush, "Stop. Listen, listen. I can't marry you. It's all been a terrible mistake."

He didn't take it in or feel anything at first. It was as if she'd shot him. "What do you mean?" he asked shaking his head in confusion.

"I'm calling it off."

"*Now?*" He looked at his watch. It was twenty-five minutes to four. They were going to be married at five o'clock. She'd gone mad. That was it, she'd gone mad. But she was still talking, babbling on like a child.

"My father's gone to the Taj to tell your people. We had to stop them before they leave for the cathedral. He'll be there now."

Dennis shook his head again for he had trouble taking all this in. "Your father's gone to the Taj . . ." he repeated and sat down in the chair on which the tailcoat hung. She was still standing in the middle of the floor staring at him.

"Say all that again," he told her. This is a nightmare, I'm dreaming it, said another part of his brain.

"I'M CALLING OFF THE WEDDING. WE'RE NOT GETTING

229

MARRIED THIS AFTERNOON." She spoke slowly as if every word was in capital letters.

A deep furrow appeared between his eyes. He'd heard that people could get cold feet before they were married. That's what has happened, he thought, she's panicking.

"Sit down and have a drink," he said.

A touch of asperity came into her voice. She hadn't expected him to be so obtuse. "Are you listening to me, Dennis? The wedding's off. I've made up my mind. What are you going to do now? Do you want my driver to take you to the Taj?"

She'd made up her mind.

"Why?" he asked. "Why have you called it off?"

"Because I don't love you."

"Why have you decided that now? Why didn't you think of it before?" Anger was rising in him like a red tide and he fought to control himself for he knew if he gave into rage, he might attack her.

"I know I should have, but it only really struck me today."

Suddenly he jumped to his feet with such force that she took a step back and held out her hands again. In fact she was not so much terrified in case he hit her, in a way she thought she deserved to be slapped, but her real dread was that he might plead with her, tell her how much he loved her, debase himself at her feet, she couldn't bear that. But he took another tack.

"You're a spoiled brat," he yelled, giving way to fury. "You've been given everything you want all your life by those stupid parents of yours. How can you do this to me now? How can you?"

His anger was so overpowering, so all engulfing and transforming, that she was almost admiring as she watched him raging like a Titan round the room. With a sweep of his arm he made the wooden standard lamp crash to the ground, its bulb shattering on impact. Then he lifted the tumbler in which his buttonhole sat and threw it at the wall where it shattered into a thousand pieces, spraying them with shards of glass. Govind, looking scared, appeared in the doorway and Baby heard her driver's feet come thundering along the passageway from the front door where he'd been waiting.

Bravely she stood her ground while she wrestled the opal ring off her finger. "I'm very, very sorry, Dennis," she said holding it out to him.

"Get out," he roared at his servant, who disappeared. Saleem's face showed at the door as Dennis slammed it closed.

"Sorry's very good," he shouted at her, "Sorry's great. Have you any idea what you've done to me and to my mother and father? You've made us look like fools. Why do it *now*?" He was walking towards her with his fists clenched and she backed away to the door, knowing that Saleem was behind it. She still held the ring out in his direction.

"I'm sorry I waited, I should have done it before but I wasn't sure till now," she said sadly.

"Has this all been a sham, have you been acting all the way through?"

"No, of course not . . ."

"But you say you don't love me and people don't stop loving other people overnight." He was quietening down a bit.

She said nothing and he groaned, "I'm a fool. What a fool. You never said you loved me. I should have known that a girl like you couldn't love a man like me. Christ, why did you agree to it in the first place? Why did you go so far?"

"You're a very good person. You're too good for me," she said.

"That makes me feel great. That solves my problem," he said sarcastically and turned his back on her, walking away with his hands thrust deep into his trouser pockets as he kicked broken glass about the floor. She could see the tension bunching his shoulders and knew he was having the greatest difficulty in restraining himself from taking a swing at her. Again she almost wished he would because it would put him more in the wrong.

"Please take back your ring, Dennis. It's beautiful but I can't keep it now," she said and laid it on the table.

He was on the verandah now, staring down into the roadway, gripping the rail tightly with both hands. For a moment she was afraid that he was going to vault over it and plunge to his death below but after a few seconds she heard him say in a tight and furious voice, "Get out of my flat. Get out and don't ever come back. I never want to see you again."

He watched blank-faced from the verandah as the driver helped her into the car. Then he ran back into the room, took the ring off the table and chucked it down into the roadway. It bounced off the roof of the Cadillac and rolled into the gutter where it was found later that night by a beggar woman hunting for cigarette ends.

At four o'clock Maud had just completed her toilette and was smelling most sweetly of apple blossom talc when there was a tap at the door of their sitting room and Sir Robert was shown in.

He didn't beat about the bush but said his piece straight away.

"The wedding's off. My daughter has decided she doesn't want to get married. She's gone to tell your son herself. I expect he'll be along to see you any minute . . ."

The three Australians stared at him as if he was talking Mandarin Chinese. "There's no wedding?" asked Joe in disbelief.

"That's right. It's called off."

"Jesus Christ!" exclaimed Joe but at that point Maud fainted and had to be revived with brandy. When she was herself again, Denzil sat utterly silent, stunned, but Joe became belligerent, stood up and faced the older man. "You've a bloody nerve telling us this. You've made a fool of us just because you think you're better than us, don't you? Bloody pommy snob."

Sir Robert glared him down. "Don't be an idiot. I'm no snob. I'm a working-class man like yourself. Dennis is a good young man and I like him but I don't want my daughter to contract a marriage that isn't right for her. She doesn't love him and there's nothing we can do to change that. It might have been better if she'd thought about it before but she didn't and now we must get them both out of it with as little damage as possible. Would you prefer them to have a miserable marriage and a messy divorce?"

Divorce was a touchy subject with Joe and he recoiled. "You've made our Den look a fool," he shouted.

"Who knows about it? Not many people in Australia, I bet. Only people we know here in Bombay. Dennis can leave and go home any time he wants and nobody'll know anything about it except his own family. It's not going to be so easy for us. All Bombay'll be gossiping about it tomorrow. I'll see Dennis doesn't suffer financially and I'll arrange for you all to fly out of here on the first available plane. You won't have to worry about a thing."

"You're paying us off," sneered Joe.

"If that's the way you want to look at it," said Sir Robert. "When do you want to leave? I can book seats on the first plane for you now." He hadn't made his fortune by hanging about indecisively.

Dennis's family stared at him helplessly as he picked up the telephone from the bedside table.

The Maling-Smith bungalow had a hushed, waiting air when Dee arrived from the Ritz and found Winks sitting on the verandah with a glass of lime soda in her hand.

"Isn't this odd?" said the blonde girl anxiously, "I arrived ten minutes ago and there's not a soul about and the servants are acting so strangely. Baby's out apparently – where to, for God's sake? Parvati's going about with her sari up to her eyes, moaning and groaning as if someone's died, and I can't get a word of sense out of her. I've asked to see Lady Babs but they said she's busy."

"Maybe they're all getting dressed and want to be left alone to get on with it," suggested Dee sitting down beside her. "We should be doing the same. It'll soon be four o'clock."

"That's true. I'm going to have a shower before I get dressed. This heat's terrific," said Winks, ringing the brass bell that stood on the table beside her.

They were shown to separate rooms, where huge bath towels and their dresses were already laid out for them. When they were clean and powdered, they zipped themselves into the gowns and met again on the verandah. By this time it was fifteen minutes past four.

"This is so odd. Where on earth is everybody? Where's Baby? I haven't heard her come back. Have you?" said Winks when they met again in the drawing room.

At that point the bearer came padding in to say that Lady Barbara wanted the girls to meet her in her bedroom.

She was sitting in a high-backed chair by the closed window, wearing a very plain grey silk dress. A wide-brimmed white hat and a corsage of pale pink roses lay on the bed beside her. Her voice was perfectly calm and she even managed to smile when she told them, "Darlings, I've got some rather upsetting news for you. There's not going to be any wedding. Baby's called it off. She's gone to break the news to Dennis now. I'm so sorry. Especially since you're both looking beautiful. That colour's so good for you, Winks. But I want you both to come with me to the cathedral. We've got to tell the guests and I really need your support."

Winks looked at Dee, gasped, and found her voice, "No wedding! What's happened?"

"Baby has decided she doesn't love him. She's gone to tell him herself and my Bobbie's gone to tell his people in the Taj. Neither of them have come back yet. We'll tell the others. Will you help me please?" Lady Barbara seemed distracted and suddenly feeble as if she was having difficulty coping with what was happening. The girls helped her to her feet and, one on each side of her, walked out to the car, where they sat like the three wise monkeys in a silent row behind the driver, who had hurriedly ripped white ribbons off the bonnet before they came out.

It was a quarter to five when their car nosed up to the cathedral and they could see crowds of smartly dressed people making their way inside. Lady Barbara suddenly came to life, leaned forward and directed the driver to go round the back to the bishop's residence that stood behind a high wall in the cathedral's shadow.

"Come on girls, this is it," she said like a general directing her troops into battle when the car stopped.

When Lady Barbara explained why she and the bridesmaids had turned up and there was to be no bride, the bishop was remarkably calm though this was the first time that such a thing had happened in his forty-year career.

"Do come in and sit down, dear Lady Maling-Smith. Have a gin and I'll have one with you. I think we both need it. What about you girls?" he said. As if shell-shocked, Winks and Dee shook their heads.

"Well now," went on the bishop, "We've got to work this out. Let's give all the guests time to be in their seats before you break the news to them. That'll save you having to repeat yourself, what? I'll tell the organist to play something solemn – a nice little bit of Bach perhaps. Or Beethoven? Certainly not Mendelssohn."

"Something solemn, Bach I think," said Baby's mother.

At seven minutes past five, the bishop, in his glorious cope but without his mitre, stepped up in front of packed pews of restive people and held up both hands in an attitude of supplication.

Immediately the music stopped and the chattering ceased. All eyes were fixed on him.

"Dear friends," he said, "I have an announcement to make. The wedding has had to be cancelled. But the bride's mother would like to say something to you. Please listen to what Lady Maling-Smith has to say."

She looked taller than usual, spectral in fact, as she walked in behind him with her attendants Winks and Dee in their girlish green gowns standing in the vestry doorway at her rear.

Her eyes ran along rows of the expectant faces staring at her, most of them people she'd known for years. Dear Moses was sitting on the aisle near the back so she looked directly at him as she spoke with apparent total aplomb, her beringed hands folded in front of her.

"Darlings, I'm so sorry to disappoint you but there isn't going to be a wedding here today. In fact there's not going to be a wedding at all. My daughter has changed her mind about getting married and her father and I back her up completely. We want you to go to the Gym however, drink lots of champagne and eat up all that food . . . at least you won't be cheated out of a party."

Then she turned and with magnificent dignity walked back to the shadowy vestry where the bridesmaids were waiting. Behind her, the

234

surging music of the organ started to play again and the guests were standing up, exclaiming to each other. "Amazing! Who'd believe it? Poor Lady Maling-Smith. Poor bugger what's-his-name-again. He must be feeling pretty sick."

Spotting her husband and Guy, Dee ran down the aisle towards them. "Go to the Gym with the others, Ben. Winks and I'll meet you there later but we have to stay with Lady Barbara just now," she said.

When she got back to the vestry, Baby's mother was sitting in a high wooden chair and looking ghastly with the bishop fussing round her. "Let me drive you home, your ladyship," he said, but she shook her head. "Sir Robert will come for me when he's finished with the poor Gillieses. I'll wait for him," she whispered.

He arrived from his unpleasant job at the Taj a few minutes later and folded his weeping wife in her arms, bending down and hugging her to him.

"I'm sorry I'm late, darling," he said. "But I've heard what you did. You're a wonderful woman, wonderful. I've never met anybody like you." They drove away together, leaving the second car for Winks and Dee.

With tears running down her face, Winks sobbed, "What should we do now? I want to see Baby. She must be in a terrible state."

What about Dennis? thought Dee, but she said, "We can't go to see her now. They won't want us there."

"I think we ought to go. She must have been overcome by nerves. By this time she'll probably be wishing she hadn't called it off. Her mother and father are far too soft with her, you know. She's awfully spoiled. Besides we should pick up our ordinary clothes from their house. Even if we just look in and have a word with Baby it might help."

"Help to do what?"

Winks didn't really know. "Change her mind?" she suggested.

"I don't think that would be a good idea now, would it?"

"You never know. Dennis is such a sweet man. He'll forgive her if she's really sorry, I'm sure."

Winks has about as much intelligence as a pussy cat, thought Dee, but she said, "You go on your own. You've known her far longer than me. I'll go to the Gym."

But Winks grasped her arm. "Darling, you can't leave me. You must come too. She'll listen to you. She thinks you're clever."

"I don't think we'll do any good but all right, I'll come with you – but only for a few minutes. Just long enough to pick up our clothes.

If Baby doesn't want to see us, I want you to promise you won't argue or make a scene."

Winks blinked her red-rimmed eyes. "Of course I won't make a scene!"

On the drive to Nepean Sea Road, Winks kept up a running monologue about how long she'd known Baby and how much she hoped this whole business would just 'blow over'.

"It's Charlie Grey's fault of course," she said. "If he hadn't jilted Baby she wouldn't have rushed into marrying somebody so soon."

"It's pretty hard luck on Dennis," said Dee.

"I'm sure it'll all work out in the end. She'll probably marry him eventually."

"I do hope not," was Dee's reply. In fact, as she thought about what had happened, she realised that, though she felt pity for Dennis, it had also put Baby Maling-Smith greatly up in her estimation.

Till now she had privately thought Baby too rich and too spoiled, as well as being painfully unenterprising. If I had as much money at my disposal as she has, I wouldn't shuffle to and from from England to Bombay year after year looking for somebody to marry, she'd often told herself. I'd travel to distant and wonderful places. I'd go to live in New York or someplace exciting and get a job.

But all Baby had done was go back and forward to the UK in a first class P&O suite bemoaning the fact that Charlie loved somebody else.

In her place, I'd say 'sod Charlie' and go trekking in the Himalayas or exploring in the Andes, thought Dee.

But now stick-in-the-mud Baby had suddenly shown some real enterprise and done this astonishing, out of character thing. What courage it must have taken. Well done, Baby, thought Dee, I certainly won't try to persuade you to change your mind. This is your chance to be a really self-determining woman.

Baby's astonishing decision to call off the marriage also made Dee resolve to be bold herself.

I'm going to throw my hat in the ring too. I'm going to take a chance with my life. I'm going to leave Ben and run away with Shadiv, she decided as they drove away from the cathedral.

At the bungalow however Baby wouldn't see them.

"I'm going to leave her a note," said Winks. 'Darling do reconsider. It's not too late – Winks xxxxx' she wrote.

"I'll leave one too," said Dee but hers ran, 'Dear Baby, What you've done is incredibly brave and I admire you for it. Dee.'

When the car dropped them at the Gym the wedding party was

in full swing. In a huge marquee erected on the maidan in front of the club buildings, Goody Servai's band was playing and the dance floor was already full. The noise was deafening, for people with full glasses in their hands were going over and over the events of the afternoon. Some expressed shock at Baby's callous behaviour, though none had been close to Dennis and were not particularly worked up on his behalf.

Others were only enjoying the scandal. Mags, who had finally relented and come to the wedding because she couldn't bear to miss out on a big party, was particularly delighted.

"It serves Baby right," she told her cronies, "She only arranged to get married to spite me. Now my wedding will be the best in Bombay this year by a long way."

The best but not the most talked about certainly.

A hush fell over the people near the doorway of the marquee when Winks and Dee appeared, still in their bridesmaids' dresses. Women rushed towards them avid for the latest news and Winks was borne away in the middle of a squawking crowd of females.

Ben came towards his wife with two glasses of champagne in his hand. "I grabbed one for you. It's all getting drunk up and there won't be any left soon."

Dee thrust the champagne away and started to weep, composure broken at last. Ben hugged her awkwardly, hampered by the glasses full of drink in his hands, "Don't take on, sweet. This must have been terrible for you. Are you all right?"

"No, no, I'm not all right . . ." She wanted to tell him about Shadiv. She wanted to follow Baby's example and be really brave, defy convention, break the mould.

'I've fallen in love with somebody else. I want to leave you,' she wanted to say but suddenly the world swam around her and she slumped forward, about to faint. Anne materialised beside them then.

Putting an arm around Dee's shoulders, she said to Ben, "I'll take her to the ladies' changing room in the main building. This has been a terrible shock for her and in this heat too. She's awfully white. Find Ralph and ask him to come to take a look at her."

There was a cretonne-covered chaise longue in the ladies' changing room that had stood there since 1929 and given repose to many weeping memsahibs. When she came to, Dee was stretched out on it; she started to cry again, unable to stop, though she was bitterly ashamed of herself for giving way to weakness.

237

Anne soaked a cotton hand towel and wrung it out before laying it on her brow. "It's heat exhaustion, I think. That cathedral was sweltering. Don't talk. Close your eyes. Ralph's coming," she said soothingly.

He had obviously had his fair share of champagne but, as usual, the moment his professional skills were needed, he sobered up. She felt his cool hands on her wrist taking her pulse, and opened her eyes to find herself staring directly into his face.

"Hi, Dee," he said, "feeling faint?"

"Yes."

He grinned. He was a very handsome man who looked like a younger version of Rex Harrison and she smiled back, immediately reassured by him.

"Don't worry. It's hardly surprising. You've been through a trying time and that's not easy when you're pregnant."

She struggled to sit up but he put a hand on her shoulder to keep her down. "Lie still. You'll be OK. I'm going out to fetch Ben."

"Pregnant? But I can't be pregnant, Ralph." She was crying again much to her chagrin.

He laughed again. "You are. It's definite. I was going to tell you when you came back for the results of your tests next week but I reckon you deserve a bit of good news now. You've cracked it, girl. You're pregnant. I thought you might be when I saw you last week but I wanted to make sure before I suggested it to you. The frog test proved it though." He knew how much she had longed for a baby and was delighted to be the bearer of what he thought was good news.

Dee's face crumpled up however and she groaned as if he'd dealt her a death blow. "Pregnant. Oh no. Not now. Not pregnant."

Funny way to take it after she'd been so anxious before but there was no accounting for people, thought Ralph as he got up to fetch Ben who was waiting at the ladies' cloakroom door.

"Is she all right?" he asked anxiously when the doctor appeared.

"Tip top. Excellent health. And the baby should arrive about Christmas," said Ralph clapping him on the back.

Ben stared, then a grin split his face and he let out a war whoop that startled everyone in the Gym and the revellers in the marquee as well. "A baby! We're having a baby! Great, wonderful, marvellous," he cried and ran into the ladies' sanctum, not caring whether he was breaking protocol or not.

Ralph, following him, said, "You'd better take her home though. She's not in a fit state for this bun fight."

They had driven to town in Guy's car so he was summoned to take them back to Chembur, which he did with ill grace, grumbling all the way about missing the party.

"You can go back after you've dropped us," Ben told him. "It'll go on for hours yet."

"But the drink'll have run dry," said Guy, eyeing Dee balefully through the driver's mirror as if she'd deliberately sabotaged his evening.

She lay stretched along the back seat, her skin almost the same colour of pale green as her dress. She didn't have the strength to protest – all she could do was silently weep, tears running warm down the sides of her cheeks and wetting the upholstery beneath her head.

Ben looked over at her in concern from time to time, "OK, Dee?" he asked. Ralph had warned him she might act a bit temperamentally. Pregnant women did apparently, but he wished she would cheer up a little. After all she'd been wanting a baby for months and even he was beginning to wonder if there was something wrong with one or the other of them. Now that fear was removed and she was weeping! He never understood the way her mind worked.

"Great about the baby, isn't it?" he tried, "Ralph says Christmas. Won't that be wonderful?"

"Yes." A baby at Christmas meant an end to her love for Shadiv. She couldn't leave Ben now. She couldn't take another man's baby into a new alliance. It was over. It had only been a romantic dream. She'd meet him in the nullah tomorrow and say she was staying with Ben . . . It would be easier for them all really. He'd have had to break up with Leila and that wouldn't have been easy either. He might not have done it in the end. Her stopping the course of events at this stage would probably be a relief to him. She was aborting their love affair.

She wept again because her heart was literally aching in her breast. She'd read about heartache but, like love, thought it was only a literary expression. Now she knew it was real.

The car swerved jolting into the lane. Guy was not taking any care about avoiding the ruts. A few minutes later they pulled up at their own front door.

"I'll change my shirt and then go back to the city. This one's soaking," snapped Guy and was out of the car first. His haste to get back to the party was urgent but he hated to be unkempt and sweaty. Sometimes in the hot weather he changed his shirt four times a day.

Dee was only on the doorstep when Ali, the second bearer, appeared from the kitchen looking agitated and tried to stop Guy going into his bedroom. "You are wanting tea sahib," he gabbled standing in front of the bedroom door.

Guy pushed him aside. "Tea? Why should I want bloody tea? Get out of my way. Where's Mohammed?"

Ali tried to stand his ground but was unsuccessful and Guy swung open the door. Inside his room the air conditioner was purring away in the window above the bed head for the room was so arranged that the big double bed faced directly towards the door. On it, looking like Adam and Eve, lay Carole and Mohammed, their sleek brown limbs entwined. They were breathtakingly beautiful, sleekly silken in their nakedness, like figures in a painting by Michaelangelo.

Guy's howl of fury woke them up.

"Aaw, my God! Get up you buggers. I'll kill you. I'll bloody well kill you," he yelled.

They jumped up like jacks in the box, both unsuccessfully grabbing for the sheet with which to cover themselves.

Guy was in the doorway, face purple and eyes popping. "Get out this minute. You're fired Mohammed. Get out of this house and never let me set eyes on you again."

Ben was behind his friend, putting a placating hand on his back. "Calm down. You'll give yourself a stroke. They're going."

The naked pair ran past into the sitting room. Though they pretended to be abashed there was a jaunty air about them that further infuriated Guy. "I'll bloody well murder him," he shouted at Ben. "The bugger was in *my bed*. In my own bed. The bearer was fucking in my bed!"

Though she was still weak Dee felt laughter bubbling up inside her but she knew she must hide it. She sat down on the sofa and shut her eyes till Mohammed and Carole were well out of the way. It wasn't that she was prudish but she knew that if she looked at them she might burst out laughing.

Without changing his shirt Guy slammed out of the house and drove off with a scream of tyres. Dee and Ben went into their bedroom and lay down side by side on their bed without speaking. After a bit she felt him shaking and turned her head to see that he was laughing too. That started her off and they rolled together laughing and laughing till they fell asleep.

Next morning the house was in chaos because Mohammed had decamped in the night, taking with him all the cook's book money and much of the contents of their store cupboard, at least everything that was fairly portable – soap; light bulbs; matches; tubes of Veganin tablets to which he was addicted, eating them like sweets; a few tins of button mushrooms that fetched a high price in the bazaar and all that remained of Guy's Fortnum and Mason pâté.

Ali was running about distractedly trying to do the dusting and setting the breakfast table at the same time. In the kitchen Pasco, the cook, was slamming pots about, infuriated at Mohammed for making off with his cook book money. Durga, the sweeper, peered through the kitchen door to see how the white people were taking it. Only Birbal, the silent gardener, went on as usual dragging his long green hose from one part of the garden to another, directing the jet at the roots of the tall orange, pink and yellow canna lilies that always made Dee think of monster gladioli.

There was no sign of Guy and his car was not in the garage.

When Dee wakened it was nearly noon and her legs shook in a peculiar way when she tried to walk. She knew she'd never make it up the nullah, for all of a sudden it seemed very important to cherish the tiny baby that was growing inside her. She lay back in bed and closed her eyes again and when she woke a second time Guy had returned and she could hear him haranguing Ben on the verandah next door. "In my bloody bed. I can't believe it!"

Their voices droned on and then she heard Ben say, "We're thinking of going too. I'll find a flat in the city. It'll be better for Dee to be nearer the hospital when the baby comes."

She got up, pulled on her dressing gown and walked through to sit with them. Ben looked up and said, "Guy's leaving the Gulmohurs, Dee. He's taken a room in Robin Grahame's flat. I think we should go too, don't you?"

She smiled sadly, "Yes, I'm afraid we should. It's a pity but we can't afford this place on our own, can we?"

"No, we can't, but Ratanlal's promised me a rise and we can rent a place now. We'll take a six month rent from somebody that's going on leave. There's always plenty of those."

She sighed as she looked around their idyllic garden. Paradise Lost, she thought, I'll always remember it like this with the sun beaming down and Birbal watering the plants, with the vultures brooding in the palm trees and the huge creeper clambering up the end wall.

"I think I'll go back to bed for a bit," she said.

Ben's face expressed concern. "You OK? Guy and I'll just work things out and arrange it. Go and have a sleep. It's stinking hot today."

In the bedroom she wrote her letter to Shadiv. She could always

241

express herself better on paper than speaking. She told him that she loved him and always would but that she was having Ben's baby and couldn't leave him.

'I can't go away now,' she wrote. 'I can't take his baby to another man. And I want this baby, you see, I want it so badly that I can hardly think of anything else.' She took care that her letter did not leave any impression that she might change her mind.

When the letter was finished she went looking for Ali. On the verandah Ben and Guy were drinking beer and laughing. Guy had obviously cheered up. She gave Ali the note and said, "Take this to Shadiv sahib in the nullah. He'll be there now. Say I couldn't come and that I'm sorry." She knew without a shadow of doubt that she'd never see Shadiv again. What had happened between them would only be a shared memory of sweetness, of might have been.

Ali, who was little more than a boy, pocketed the note and nodded without surprise. The servants know all about my meetings with Shadiv in the nullah, she realised. You can't keep secrets in India.

Thirty-One

S ir Robert pulled strings, made phone calls, called in favours and succeeded in reserving three first class seats on the Qantas flight leaving Bombay for Sydney on Sunday morning.

A grim-faced Dennis drove his family to Santa Cruz airport, where he unloaded their luggage and then them onto the baking hot tarmac.

His mother wrapped her arms round him sobbing against his chest. "I hate that girl. I hate her. I wish you'd never met her," she gulped.

Dennis said nothing. In fact he'd said very little since picking up his family at nine o'clock.

Joe slapped a hand on his shoulder. "What're you going to do now, Den?" he asked.

"I've been to see the High Commissioner and resigned my job but he's asked me to stay until a new passport officer arrives – in about two or three weeks. He's sent a cable about it. I'll be back with you by the end of June with any luck."

"And what'll you do then?" asked Joe.

"Start working with Dad. It's what I want, it's what I'm good at." Dennis didn't tell his people that Sir Robert had offered him a considerable sum of money to start a new life and he'd angrily refused.

'I don't want your money,' he'd said through gritted teeth.

"Pity you ever came here in the first place," said Denzil.

Dennis looked around the airport. Dad's right, this place is a dump, he thought. I should never have got off that ship when I saw how awful it was. I'll not have a glimmer of regret for the stinking hole.

As for Baby, he was deliberately closing his mind to any memory of her. If he tried very hard he'd forget all about her in a very short time. The prospect of him and his father repairing cars together seemed very attractive. He'd wear greasy overalls and lie on his back under engines, tinkering happily away. On Sundays he'd go

243

to the beach, swim, ride a surf board and drink a few tinnies with his friends. It was a world that could never have embraced Baby Maling-Smith. How could he ever have imagined it could?

He stood waving on the square of grass by the airport building as the plane lifted itself into the air. He knew his mother would be looking at him out of the window and she would still be weeping.

When the sky above his head was empty, he turned and walked back to his car. Heat hit him like a blow in the face when he opened the door. God, how many more days of this! he thought as he drove away. The monsoon was said to break on June fifth and tomorrow was the first.

The Marine Drive flat was silent but Govind appeared looking very solemn when he walked into the sitting room.

"Beer, sahib?" he asked.

"Yeah. Beer."

He drank two big bottles and then, slightly tipsy, retired to bed where he slept till half-past four. When he woke he had a raging thirst and was burning with a desire for violent action. He wanted to run, walk, swim, do something very vigorous in order to work off the rage and sense of frustration that filled him.

But Breach Candy was out of bounds. How could he show himself there? It would be full of people who knew about him and Baby.

He remembered Juhu beach with its furling waves but he couldn't go there either and face the old French woman.

The race course was not far away. He'd seen people running round its perimeter but when he walked into the main room he realised that running in such terrible heat would probably kill him – which might not be a bad thing, but an awful shock for his mother.

In a corner by the front door he saw the golf bag he'd brought out from Australia and never used. Back home he'd been a good and enthusiastic golfer. That's what I need, a game of golf, he thought. Walking down the fairway, smacking golf balls into the air, would help to work off the fury that was burning within him.

But the only golf course he knew was at Chembur, beside Carole's house. To hell with Carole, with Baby, Fifi, Lady Barbara, with all women. They couldn't do anything more to hurt him. He'd go and play a few holes of golf and to hell with them all.

There was a rage inside him that could only be assuaged by blasting a ball over the golf course. Today he knew he'd play better golf than he'd ever played in his life. He didn't care if it was stinking hot; he didn't care if he died of heat exhaustion out there in the middle of the course – he had to be doing something active or he'd go mad.

His once careful driving had gone to pieces in Bombay and he tore along the road to Chembur like a maniac, scattering in his wake cars full of families out for a peaceful outing, and making pye-dogs and their puppies, which he usually slowed down to avoid, run for their lives.

It was late afternoon and slightly cooler but still uncomfortably hot when he arrived at the course and because there were few people wanting to play in such weather, he had no trouble in booking a round.

Major Motiwala, who took his money, stood on the club verandah and watched him drive off. The tall young man seemed rather peculiar and distant, he thought, but he could certainly play golf.

"Magnificent," he sighed in admiration as Dennis's ball soared into the sky, over a tall clump of mango trees and onto the distant green. There hadn't been such a good drive off that first tee for years.

Dennis went on smashing his way round, breaking the course record if he but knew it, though he wasn't bothering to mark a card. All he wanted to do was hit and hit and hit, slamming ball after ball into the abyss, not bothering to even go and look for them when they went into the rough.

By the time he reached the eighth tee, he was almost opposite the front windows of Carole's home and unknown to him a girl was standing at one of the bedroom windows staring out. She wasn't looking for anything or anyone in particular, only looking to see the sun sink behind the tops of the trees. Then she saw the solitary golfer, swinging with such ease and skill that her attention was immediately caught. When he hit the ball and went walking after it towards her, she gasped, "My God, it's Dennis," and ran swiftly downstairs.

He was on the eighth green, squatting down to get a good line on the ball, when he heard someone calling his name, and asking, "Dennis, Dennis, can I walk round with you?"

He swung round, looked in the direction from which the voice came and found himself staring into a bush on which red hibiscus flowers were blooming in seductive luxuriance. "No," he said.

Amy, Carole's bolshie sister, walked out of from behind the bush with a flower between her fingers. She was smiling at him and he straightened up like a man expecting a knife to be jabbed into his chest.

"Please let me walk with you," she said very sweetly.

"No. I walk fast," said Dennis.

"So do I. I'll not get in your way. I'll just walk with you. I've been watching you and I know you're very angry. I heard what happened about the wedding. It must have been awful . . ."

A jubilant Carole had brought the news when she returned home alone the night before. Their mother was delighted and asked for the details over and over again.

Dennis paused and leaned on his putter. The possibility that Carole or Fifi had sabotaged his wedding suddenly occurred to him.

"They didn't have anything to do with it? They didn't talk to Baby, did they?" he asked.

"Of course not. They were only bluffing when they said they would. They were out for money. You shouldn't have paid them anything."

"What the hell. It doesn't matter now," said Dennis, squatting by the ball again.

"Don't you mind?" asked Amy.

He looked up and said, "Of course I mind. Wouldn't you mind if someone who said they'd marry you suddenly backed out at the last minute? I'm pretty angry, furious in fact . . ."

She listened in silence, watching him with her face inscrutable. Then she asked, "Do you love her?"

He was suspicious of her, waiting for the barbed tongue he knew her to possess to suddenly savage him, but she actually seemed quite sympathetic, so he gave the question serious consideration. "Do I love her? Not any more. I thought I did but now I see that I was only kidding myself. I never want to see or hear anything about her again."

To his surprise, as he spoke, he realised that one of his underlying feelings was relief. As well as being angry at being jilted so publicly, he was secretly glad not to have been married to Roberta Maling-Smith yesterday.

"But to call off the wedding was a brave thing to do, don't you think?" asked Amy, unaware of his conflicting emotions.

"Brave? What she did?" he stared at her in surprise. "It was selfish. She was only thinking about herself."

"I think she was brave. It would have been much easier for her to go through with it but she called it off at the last moment. That was brave. Don't you realise people will be talking about it for months – and they won't be on her side, they'll be on yours. You'll be the martyr, she'll be the villainess. You'll be well out of it but she'll still be here. She'll never live it down."

Dennis hit his golf ball and had the satisfaction of seeing it roll straight into the hole. Walking to fish it out, he frowned, thinking about what Amy had said. "I'm going home so I guess there's something in that," he agreed.

"If she didn't love you, you've had a lucky escape," said the girl. "It would be terrible to marry someone who doesn't love you. They can't go on pretending for ever. At least I couldn't."

"I thought you didn't believe in love," he said. "I thought you were a cynic."

"I am but sometimes I do believe in love. It's in books, isn't it? There must be something in it. It does happen to people though it's never happened to me."

Dennis fished a driver out of his bag and leaned on it, staring at her. She stared back, her bright eyes shining. "I'm very sorry about what's happened to you. I really am. You don't deserve it," she said simply and he knew that she was speaking the truth. Suddenly his engulfing fury had softened and he didn't want to play any more golf.

"Would you like a cup of coffee or something?" he asked.

When she smiled her little face seemed to light up from behind and she looked like a mischievous child. She was really pretty, he noticed with surprise, far sweeter-looking than Carole.

"How's your sister?" he asked as they walked to the club house.

"She's back at home – resting like an out-of-work actress," she said, "but she'll be back in action soon I'm sure, like Monica who's just picked up another man too – an American this time. Do you want to see Carole?"

This time it was his turn to laugh and when the muscles of his face relaxed, he felt more carefree and optimistic. Once more the world seemed full of possibilities, but different ones now.

"No. I'd sooner talk to you. I need someone to listen to me. Come on and I'll buy you a coffee in the clubhouse," he said.

"I'm very fond of coffee and I'm quite a good listener," she said and threaded her arm through his. He hefted his golf bag on his shoulder and thought, She's a nice girl after all. Life goes on. I'm going to be all right . . .

Thirty-Two

W hile Dennis was slamming balls all over Chembur golf course and the people in the Gulmohurs were finalising their plans to move, Sir Robert Maling-Smith, his wife, his daughter, his wife's doctor, and her ayah Parvati were driving to Mahableshwar, a hill station high in the Western ghats above Bombay.

They had made the decision to leave the city on the previous evening after Dr Green arrived and was shown into Lady Barbara's boudoir.

She was very tired, waxen white and having difficulty breathing but she managed to smile when she saw him bending over her.

"Dear Moses," she whispered, "Didn't you go to the reception? There's some very good champagne there."

He lifted her hand. "I don't care about champagne. How are you? That's more important."

"I'm tired and the pain's back. I just want to go to sleep I think."

"You were magnificent in the cathedral. I was proud to know you. Just relax your arm and I'll give you a little injection." Very gently he slipped the needle into one of her fragile blue veins and within seconds she was asleep.

Sir Robert and Baby, who were watching, stood up and led the doctor downstairs to the drawing room. "Have a whisky soda, doctor," said Robert, "and tell us what we should do about Barbara."

"I'm afraid this is going to come as a shock to you, Sir Robert, but your wife has cancer – and she's dying. It's only a few days off I'm afraid," said the doctor.

"My God, I had no idea . . . is there anything we can do for her?" asked Sir Robert.

"She wants to go to the hills. She's booked rooms in the club for the whole of next month," said Baby. "She told me that this evening. She says she wants to die in Mahableshwar. It's so lovely. She wants to be buried in the little church there."

"She can't go to the hills in her state," protested Sir Robert hoarsely. He was finding it hard to accept that his beloved wife was really dying.

"Why not?" said the doctor, "You can take her there in eight or nine hours, can't you? You've got huge cars and one of them's air conditioned, isn't it?"

"Will you come with us?" asked Baby.

"If you want me to."

Early next morning their cavalcade set off. There were four cars – one containing Sir Robert and his wife who was stretched along the back seat; another with Baby and Dr Green; a third with servants, the bearer and Parvati, and a fourth loaded up with their bags, boxes and an odd assortment of paraphernalia collected by Parvati. Travelling slowly so as not to upset the patient, for the roads were very rough, they reached the hill station at five o'clock that night.

Mahableshwar was a beautiful place, a tiny village crouching on a hill top, embowered in closely growing trees. Long ago it had been the place where the government of Bombay spent the hot weather, and old bungalows, many of them decrepit now, were still there as was the Club, a series of long narrow barrack-like buildings which had been erected to house sick Army officers who needed a spell in a cool climate. The little church with its lines of carved epitaphs paid testimony to the many times when the cure failed.

As well as the Club there was a boating lake – with no boats left; a shopping centre where the little shops were illuminated at night by the soft light of paraffin lamps and where goods which had long disappeared from shops elsewhere still adorned the shelves; a native bazaar where hawkers sold vegetables, strawberries, honey and native medicines guaranteed to cure almost every disease, even cancer.

They were received with great civility at the Club where Lady Barbara had been a regular guest since she was a child. They took over one entire block of rooms and settled down to wait.

The morning after the journey found Lady Barbara so improved that she was able to rise from her bed when the sun came out and walk shakily to the verandah rail, where she stared out into the Club garden at an old woman who was sweeping ineffectually in the dust beneath the pine trees. There was a beautiful fresh smell in the air and every bird in the world seemed to be singing.

"I love this place. I'm so glad you brought me here. It's the nearest place to heaven," she said without turning round when Sir Robert stepped up behind her and put his hand on her shoulder.

By lunchtime her last burst of energy was exhausted and she was back in bed. Parvati spread her favourite lace bed cover over her knees and bent to wind up the portable gramophone which she'd brought up from the plains.

She'd brought some records too, thick black vinyl ones with fading labels. Baby came in and looked at them. "Where on earth did you find those, Parvati?" she asked.

"They are my lady's favourites. She likes them and there's no electricity here so I brought this machine."

The ayah set the record spinning and gently brought down the arm with the needle. It scraped a little and then the tune began. 'There's a small hotel, beside a wishing well . . .'

"Oh, I love that tune," said the woman in the bed. "I used to dance to that."

"I have the other one too, my lady. The one about tea for two," said Parvati.

"You're so clever," sighed Lady Barbara.

She never got up again. Slowly, quietly and, thanks to Dr Green, without pain, she slipped into unconsciousness. On the fourth day of their stay, she died as dawn was breaking, and the first rain of the monsoon was falling, with one of her hands gripped by her daughter and the other by her husband.

When it was all over, Baby found her father standing at the end of the verandah, staring out towards the trees that marked the edge of the ghats. Suddenly the hill station seemed very bleak. She put an arm round his shoulders and said, "If you want to go back to Helensburgh, I'll come with you. It sounds like a nice place."

Grief had aged him and taken all his bombast away. "I don't want you to do that," he said but she knew he was lying.

"But I want to go. I can't stay here, can I? I'll always be remembered as the girl who called her wedding off at the last minute here."

She looked out at the trees clustered round the sun-baked earth of the yard; she watched the leaves sway as if a giant hand had ruffled them from above; she smelt wood smoke from the bonfire at the back of their rooms where water for the baths was being heated.

I love this country but now I must leave it, she said to herself as she turned her head to kiss her father's creased cheek.

"Let's make a new start, Daddy," she said. "Let's find another paradise."